Michael Brooks is the physics consultant to *New Scientist* magazine in London. Before joining the magazine as a features editor five years ago, he wrote freelance for many publications, including the UK's *Guardian*, *Observer*, and *Independent* newspapers, and edited a book on quantum computing.

MICHAEL BROOKS
ENTANGLEMENT

BANTAM
SYDNEY • AUCKLAND • TORONTO • NEW YORK • LONDON

ENTANGLEMENT
A BANTAM BOOK

First published in Australia and New Zealand in 2007
by Bantam

Copyright © Michael Brooks, 2007

The moral right of the author has been asserted.

All rights reserved. No part of this book may be reproduced or transmitted by any person or entity, including internet search engines or retailers, in any form or by any means, electronic or mechanical, including photocopying (except under the statutory exceptions provisions of the Australian Copyright Act 1968), recording, scanning or by any information storage and retrieval system without the prior written permission of Random House Australia.

National Library of Australia
Cataloguing-in-Publication Entry

Brooks, Michael, 1970–.
Entanglement.

ISBN 978 1 86325 656 8 (pbk.).

I. Title.

A823.4

Transworld Publishers,
a division of Random House Australia Pty Ltd
Level 3, 100 Pacific Highway
North Sydney, NSW 2060
www.randomhouse.com.au

Random House New Zealand Limited
18 Poland Road, Glenfield, Auckland

Transworld Publishers,
a division of The Random House Group Ltd
61–63 Uxbridge Road, Ealing, London W5 5SA

Random House Inc
1745 Broadway, New York, New York 10036

Typeset by Post Pre-press Group, Australia
Printed and bound by Griffin Press, South Australia

10 9 8 7 6 5 4 3 2 1

*To Kevin Conroy Scott for his sixth sense,
Phillippa Brooks for her uncommon good
sense, and Deborah George, whose sudden
passing made no sense.*

CHAPTER 1

LASZLO GIEREK WAS TO be left alone.
But Paul Radcliffe was expendable. In fact, making a bloody little mess of Radcliffe would be a good thing. It would remind Gierek that he wasn't off the leash just because his machine was working now. Gierek was still part of the team.

They had a lot to do in the next few days, and they were all on edge. So it was best that Gierek didn't engage in whispered conversations. He could keep his job at the university, he could teach, he could continue to publish a stream of stuff that was nicely behind the times. But whispered conversations in hotel bars were definitely out.

Alex Genovsky swiped the card-key through the lock. The security here was shocking; getting the key from reception was hardly a test of anyone's skills. Hotel staff were too easily charmed by a smile and an apologetic excuse.

The room was dark. Radcliffe hadn't opened the drapes. Genovsky walked to the window, pushed them aside and looked out at the view. Sixteen floors down, three ships bobbed gently in Baltimore's inner harbour. In the fading light of the late November afternoon their masts were lit up with coloured bulbs, like Christmas come early.

Radcliffe had packed already. Genovsky stepped towards the case, put the knife's blade against the lock, then backed off again. Better to get it from the horse's mouth, so to speak. Better to wait and see what spilled out with the blood.

Getting what you wanted was always about patience. About waiting. There was no point searching for something when you didn't know what you were looking for, or where it might be. Best just wait.

Genovsky sat in the plush armchair by the bedside, invisible from the door, and waited. In the half-dark, the vertical stripe in the wallpaper was mesmerising. Something about the spacing made the stripes merge into a green haze if you stared at them long enough. It was like transcendence: time passed unnoticed.

Then the lock clunked, and Radcliffe wandered in, oblivious. It was easy, effortless, to strike the blow that rendered him senseless for a few minutes. Long enough to strip him, tie him up, prepare him.

He came round easily, his eyes suddenly bursting wide in terror. He was right to be terrified; he was going to die in that room. The smell of his shit and piss made the bound man retch and heave against the cords, but the stench was hardly his fault. It was only human to lose control over your body in a situation like this. It happened every time.

The left thumb came off first. Only then did Genovsky ask a question.

'What did Gierek tell you?'

The other thumb. For a moment, the smell of blood and meat hung rich and fresh in the room's warm air.

It was impossible to tell how any particular body would cope with the trauma; some were more resilient than others. This one was on the weak side, already wheezing like someone was trampling over his chest. He could barely stammer out an answer. Still, at least he was no hero: Genovsky didn't have to ask twice.

'He said he wanted me to look after a disk.'

The last word came out as a falling hiss. Radcliffe was losing consciousness already.

'Where is the disk?'

A careful incision in the face, from the eye to the mouth. A trademark, if you will.

'I haven't got it.'

Then came the resistance. The realisation of imminent death produced a senseless bravado in some – it could even arise in the weak ones sometimes. It just appeared out of nowhere. Then you had to push. Trouble was, some of them – especially in this diseased, desperate, god-forsaken country – had hearts that were already one tick from the exit. It's not like you could take a medical history. *Tell me, before I slice into your hamstrings, any history of heart disease in the family?* It was true that you could go too far too fast. But there was no way of knowing, no rhyme or reason to it. And if you wanted to get the job done, you had to take the chance.

The blade had hardly marked the cartilage of Radcliffe's right ear when he began to fade out. He fought the disappearance of consciousness for a moment, and then he simply let go.

But not before he whispered a name. It was barely audible; his mouth hardly moved as he spoke. Something Virgo.

It was enough to go on. It would have to be enough. Paul Radcliffe was dead.

CHAPTER 2

TWELVE FLOORS BELOW, NATHANIEL Virgo looked up from his laptop for a moment and surveyed the dark wood panelling and glowing brass fixtures that dominated the hotel lobby. His eyes fell on the pegboard sign at the entrance to the conference suite, and he smiled to himself.

The Renaissance Baltimore Harborplace Hotel welcomes the first American Quantum Information Conference.

Maybe it was a journalist's cynicism, but Virgo found it hard to see why anyone would welcome a collection of bearded nerds into their midst. Maybe the conference fee and the booked-out rooms had something to do with it.

A tall figure hesitated in front of the sign. He was heading across the edge of the lobby, towards the conference room. Quickly, Virgo stuffed his laptop into his bag and stepped across the floor. He would look at that disk again later. For the moment, he had to block this guy's path.

'Excuse me, Dr Hillborough?'

The final hour of the conference was in session, but Virgo wasn't going to let this opportunity pass. Hillborough, the head of the quantum technology group at the government's Los Alamos labs, had just made a provocative announcement. Virgo would be on a plane in a couple of hours, and it would be good to arrive back at the paper with another story on the go.

'Your statement – this morning? You're taking this stuff seriously?' he asked.

Richard Hillborough glanced at Virgo's press badge. 'We have to,' he said. 'It's my job to make sure all government codes remain unbreakable for the next twenty years. We don't know if the quantum computer will be built in that time frame, but we know it's possible. And that means we can't be confident about the safety of our codes.'

'But the quantum computer's a dream. It's a powerful idea, but no one knows how to build one. Anyway, it's been possible since Daniel Born published his blueprint fourteen years ago. What's changed now?'

Hillborough smiled slyly. 'Nothing's changed,' he said. 'We're government. We take time to make decisions.'

He was glancing around, looking for an out. He wasn't going to get one just yet. But he was going to get an easy question before the next real one. A softener. Virgo shifted his stance, lowered his notebook. Made himself a little more submissive, a little more friendly.

'You know, I interviewed Born for a magazine feature back then,' he said. 'He told me he came up with the blueprint so people could build a machine to investigate the laws of physics. He said he was disappointed it had become something that spies wanted to use. Do you think he was being naive?'

Hillborough hesitated, then glanced down at Virgo's badge again. 'You're from the *Herald*? In London?'

Virgo nodded.

'Your paper broke that story on the leaked Homeland Security report last year. The one about future security technologies – teleportation, remote viewing, all that sci-fi stuff. Did you write that piece?'

Virgo shook his head. 'It was a colleague of mine; I've only just come onto the science beat.'

5

'So how did your colleague get hold of the report? That was quite a scoop. Embarrassed a lot of people.'

Virgo acted out a shrug. 'She got lucky, I guess.' He knew much better than that. Embarrassment caused to the US government was entirely deliberate. Always.

Hillborough raised an eyebrow. He didn't buy it either.

'But that's why I'm over here,' Virgo continued. 'My editor wants me to separate science truth from science fiction.'

It was Hillborough's turn to shrug. 'Yeah,' he said. 'That's hard. Especially where Homeland Security is concerned.'

Virgo lifted his notebook. 'Can I quote you?'

A flicker of a smile crossed Hillsborough's face. 'I'll deny it.'

Virgo returned the smile. Fair enough. Back to the real question.

'So – was it all science fiction?' he asked. 'The report also mentioned quantum computers and quantum encryption, as I recall. The kind of stuff you say you're looking into. Was there more truth than fiction?'

Hillborough pursed his lips. Then he smiled again. 'Maybe we could talk some more later,' he said. He neatly sidestepped Virgo and headed towards the hall.

Interesting. Frustrating, too, but interesting, nonetheless. There was something there. Virgo followed Hillborough into the hall, and reclaimed his seat.

He struggled to listen. He was still trying to make sense of Hillborough's announcement. The US government was starting to step up its security in the light of the threat posed by the quantum computer. A machine to break every government code on the planet – if you believed what Hillborough said. But these things were decades from being useful. It was like the difference between knowing you could split an atom, and being able to build an atomic bomb. What did that take? Forty years? Anyway, if you were worried, why tell anyone? Hillborough's announcement made no sense. Unless he was trying to get a message out. Unless . . . no, it made no sense.

He couldn't think. These quick hops across the Atlantic were a nightmare. The jet lag killed him every time. He consoled himself with thoughts of the flight ahead: he could sleep on the plane. The *planes*. They'd be away on holiday – some quality time with his family, at last – almost as soon as he got back. He would take the Tylenol he'd bought yesterday, and sleep all the way to Cuba.

Just one more hour to get through.

He looked up at the screen above the stage. It was covered in an array of numbers:

```
2519590847565789349402718324004839857142928
2126204032027777137836043662020707595556264
0185258807844069182906412495150821892985591
4917618450280848912007284499268739280728777
6735971418347270261896375014971824691165077
6133798590957000973304597488084284017974291
0064245869181719511874612151517265463228221
6869987549182422433637259085141865462043576
7984233871847744479207399342365848238242811
9816381501067481045166037730605620161967625
6133844143603833904414952634432190114657544
4541784240209246165157233507787077498171257
7246796292638635637328991215483143816789988
5040445364023527381951378636564391212010397
122822120720357
```

'So, this is the Rivest, Shamir, Adleman protocol: RSA – an unbreakable code.'

The presenter stood with one hand in his jacket pocket while the other ran repeatedly through his thick grey hair. Virgo glanced down at the program next to him to find the speaker's name. Laszlo Gierek. Boston University.

'Actually, it might be the industry standard, but it's not unbreakable,' Gierek continued. Maybe it was just the trace of Eastern Europe in his accent, but to Virgo's ears he seemed distracted, like he wasn't here to talk about the details. 'It's just tiring. Factoring, the technique behind RSA, is really only child's play made difficult. I could give a ten-year-old child a two-digit number, and they could find the factors: the two numbers that multiply together to make it. I say 'fifteen', they could tell me 'five and three'. They're in a position to break a very simple RSA-type code. The British government, the White House, the Bank of England, the CIA – they're all relying on the fact that no one, and no computer, can search hard and fast enough to do the same with big numbers.' He pointed up at the screen. 'Like this one.'

Gierek walked to the far end of the stage, and stood at the top of the steps. His clothes were simple but smart: a plain, leaf-green sweater and grey, baggy moleskin trousers. His hair was grown long and skimmed his shoulders. A thick moustache drooped over the corners of his mouth. The corners of his eyes drooped too; Gierek must have been around fifty, but the years hung heavy. He had stopped stroking his hair now, but even from his position at the back of the auditorium Virgo could see both of Gierek's hands were shaking. His eyes kept darting over his audience, like he was looking for someone.

'Enter the quantum computer,' Gierek said, walking quickly back to the lectern. 'Super-fast computing using the weird rules of the quantum world. Even though it doesn't yet exist, any of you computer scientists in the audience should look on the potential of this machine with envy. With all the Intel chips in China, you can never have anything like it. We use single atoms instead of silicon chips. We can use superposition, where the atoms exist in several different states at once – our atoms can encode more data than standard processors can dream of. And with entanglement between the atoms we can do a million calculations at once.'

Gierek stood still and stared out from the podium. 'Einstein hated the idea of entanglement, called it "spooky action at a distance", but it is no curiosity,' he said. 'It is all around us. Every process in the universe, at its most fundamental level, is creating entanglements. When you look at a star, the photon of light hitting your eye is still entangled with the atom, deep in that distant star, that fired it out.' He paused, then looked up at the ceiling. For a moment, he seemed enraptured, and he raised his right arm heavenwards. The shakes had gone. 'I could change the quantum state in a star, light years away, just by changing the state of its entanglement twin rocketing towards my eye. In theory, that is.'

He brought his hand back down, and tapped his laptop. The screen showed a huge black question mark.

'There's only one problem.' His lips parted in a faint smile that reminded Virgo of a snake about to bite. 'None of us knows how to do it yet. No one knows how to get such a grip on entanglement, how to keep it under control when every bit of energy that hits the atoms can kick their delicate link out of kilter. So no one knows what the quantum computer might look like. We know how it might work, but it's too difficult to control the entanglement: we're simply not there yet.'

Gierek was standing behind the lectern, leaning heavily on it with both hands. He looked out at his audience for a few moments. The pause was too long, and Virgo felt a tension creep into the room.

'But that doesn't matter. You should know something. You are being watched. It's inevitable: if you are the people that can make this technology work, then you are the people that the authorities will be interested in. Everybody wants this. The Americans want it for information: they love to know everybody's business. The European governments are so keen to beat the Americans to it that they're willing to work together on it. And the criminal underworld, if I may use such a dramatic phrase – the drug runners, for instance – they want it more than anyone. Just one application – opening up FBI and coastguard communications – would make it worth any investment.'

Gierek's face was deadly serious, his eyes narrowed. His

voice had dropped to a low murmur, conspiratorial and urgent. 'The spoils for the winner of this race are fantastic. Whoever has this first wins. And if they can keep their victory quiet, nothing will ever be hidden from them again.'

The room was silent. Gierek drew breath.

'This quantum computer,' he said, pointing at the question mark on the screen, 'is gold bullion.' He strung out the last two words, turning to face his audience. 'Unfortunately – for you, anyway – you are the cashiers with the keys to the vault. The bank robbers are on their way, so you'd better decide what you're planning to do when they arrive.'

Gierek stretched out a hand. It was shaking again. He made a final scan of the audience, pulled the lid of his laptop closed, and mumbled thanks to his audience for listening.

There were two seconds of silence, a faint applause, and then a loud buzz of conversation. The session chair stood up to invite questions. Nothing came to Virgo's mind. Except 'why?' Gierek's talk seemed to lock together with Hillborough's announcement. But what could either of them gain by scaremongering about the potential of a quantum computer?

Virgo looked at his watch. He had a plane to catch. But he noticed with relief that he had watched Gierek with his heartbeat a little pumped up. With characters like this around – with the weird intensity of Gierek and the strange behaviour of Paul Radcliffe earlier – maybe the science beat wouldn't be a complete washout.

CHAPTER 3

'M SORRY, SIR.'

The girl at the airport check-in was yielding to none of Virgo's charms. 'I'll make a note that you would be interested in an upgrade on your next flight with us.'

She said it with that sweet service smile. The one that meant nothing. He thought about offering her the chocolate-covered cranberries he had bought for his wife, but quickly thought again. Rachel always got so excited whenever he brought her a present home from one of his trips; she never showed even a glimmer of disappointment when it was obvious that it had been bought in the departure lounge.

He had to call Rachel, let her know what time he'd be landing. Virgo strolled away from the check-in desk and sank onto a blue plastic chair. He smiled at the woman in the next chair, but she scowled back, her face contorted with suspicion. Virgo looked away again. Air travel knows no camaraderie these days, he thought. All that's left is the fear of every stranger. He pulled out his mobile phone and speed-dialled home.

Rachel picked up almost immediately.

'Rach? Hi, it's me. I'm at the airport.' He looked at his watch. 'You OK?'

'I'm in bed, thanks.'

'Did I wake you?'

'Not quite. I'd just turned out the light.'

'What about Katie? Is she in bed?'

'She's at a party.'

His daughter was fifteen years old, and still out with her friends at 11.25 at night. What were you supposed to do? It wasn't like the other parents seemed to care. He sighed. Four thousand miles away, Rachel sighed too. They did that a lot these days. It's what you did when your baby morphed into a teenager overnight.

'When will she be back?'

'She's on a midnight curfew. She'll be back in half an hour or so.'

'But you'll stay awake until she's in?'

'You know I can't sleep while she's out. She knows it too. You're worrying again, Nat. She's my concern at the moment, remember. You just get yourself back over here. This bed feels too empty.'

Virgo swallowed all his concern. 'OK,' he said. 'I'm getting on the plane now.'

'And I'll pick you up in the morning, even though you abandoned me for three whole days just to cover some stupid science conference.'

It made him smile; she knew it would.

'I love you,' he said.

'I love you too. Get back here, will you?' Rachel's voice softened. 'Have a safe flight, sweetheart.'

She hung up. Virgo held his phone and savoured the connection, just for a moment, before he flipped it shut.

The short notice on this trip hadn't done him any favours at home, but his editor had at least promised it would be an exception; he wasn't planning to send his new science reporter across the globe at a moment's notice every week. That was good news – Virgo had promised Rachel that everything was going to change now he was taking more of a back seat. He was going to be with his family a lot more from now on. That's why he'd booked the Cuba trip – so they could start afresh.

The guard beyond the departures gate asked him to remove his shoes for inspection but didn't even glance at the laptop bag in his hand. What kind of security was this? Putting his shoes back on, Virgo wondered how to pass the time until he could board and take the Tylenol. He wasn't going to risk his weakness for in-flight movies; he didn't like the idea of sleeping pills, but he'd take some anyway. Which meant he needed food.

He headed for the food hall, sat down and ordered pizza. He could almost hear the pepperoni laughing at the Diet Coke. Instinctively, he pulled in his gut, then looked down. He wasn't paunchy yet, but his early forties were getting later every day. How long before his abs gave up the fight?

Virgo pulled his laptop from its case, opened it up and checked Radcliffe's disk again. It was blank – unformatted, it seemed. Same as it was an hour ago when he'd checked it in the cab on the way to the airport. Same as it was two hours before that, when he'd checked it at the hotel. What did he expect?

That thing with Radcliffe bothered him. Virgo had asked a question from the floor towards the end of the last session, introducing himself as a reporter from the *London Herald*. A moment after he'd sat down, some guy was tapping him on the shoulder, asking him to step outside. He had 'something a good reporter would be interested in,' he said.

It was an envelope containing a CD. An optical disk and a business card – Paul Radcliffe, Department of Physics, University of Maryland, a couple of phone numbers and an email address. That was it. By the time Virgo looked up again, Radcliffe had walked off towards the elevators and disappeared. All he had said was to call him on his mobile phone in a couple of days.

And the disk was blank. Was it just a mistake? A North American format? As far as he knew, there was no such thing.

Virgo sighed, and looked up at the airport screens. How come these places were so much less crowded, so much less frenetic, here in the US? Heathrow would have been heaving with people, each one of them making a second tick past faster than the one before. People were his lifeblood: watching them, talking to them, interpreting them – that was what had made his reputation as a journalist. That was what had persuaded the *Herald* to give him the investigative reporter's job. Understanding the strangeness, the vagaries of people – knowing the lengths they will go to given the right provocations – had put him onto award-winning stories. And now here was another enigma in human form: Paul Radcliffe. Was this a story? Was the disk a message? Or did he just want to make Virgo curious enough to call him later? Maybe there was a better time and place for them to talk.

Well, it would have to wait now. Virgo knew himself too well: make that call from London tomorrow morning and it could be a disaster. If he smelled a story it would either stop him getting on the plane to Cuba or taunt him through the holiday. Every grain of white sand would scream out for answers. This time, for the first time in years, he was going to walk away from work without looking back. Rachel and Katie had put up with a lot, and pretty much without complaint. Now, he was going to put them first.

CHAPTER 4

'HELLO, STRANGER.'
Rachel threw her arms around him. They kissed – their airport reunion kiss: passion with just a little bit of propriety. A suitcase barged into them, and they stumbled apart.

Somehow, each time he went away, Rachel always managed to look more beautiful when he came back. She would have got up at 6.00 to make sure she was there when he emerged at the Heathrow arrivals gate. And still she took his breath away.

'Hello, gorgeous.'

'I'm so glad you're back,' Rachel said. 'I missed you. Come on.'

They headed towards the parking, his wheelie case in tow. Heathrow was already bustling. In the five-minute walk from the plane, he'd passed hundreds of people heading in the other direction, and he'd been shuffling along with hundreds of people. The whole world had itchy feet: a habit it couldn't kick. What would happen if everyone just stood still for a while? What would the world be like if everyone agreed to stay home for twenty-four hours and deal with what they found there: would civilisation stumble and fall?

He had to lighten up a bit: the airline coffee, an attempt to come up from the Tylenol, had him wired.

'How's Katie?'

'Her tops are too tight.' Rachel turned towards him and did the cute shrug she'd done since they first met at university. 'She's the same teenager she was three days ago.'

'Well, that's a relief.'

He waved towards the crowds passing by. 'Where do all these people come from? Where are they going at this time of day?'

Rachel grinned at him. 'Wrong question. Why are so many of them wearing bermuda shorts? Am I missing something, or is it still November?'

He laughed. It was good to be back.

'So, Mr Science Reporter, was it as bad as you feared? The conference, I mean.'

'It wasn't exactly rock'n'roll. But it was OK.'

'Any big stories?'

He hesitated. Was Radcliffe going to be a big story?

'What?' Rachel looked at him, curious. 'Someone's pen leak into their white coat?'

He laughed again. 'No,' he said. 'No big stories.'

The house seemed to close in around him as he walked in from the early quiet of their street of Victorian terraces; it squeezed him and hugged him and surrounded him with the scents of family and home.

'I've got to get ready for work,' Rachel said. She paused at the bottom of the stairs and turned to smile at him. 'One day to go,' she said. 'It's going to be so *fantastic*.'

Katie appeared at the top of the stairs. Her long brown hair was dishevelled and her pyjamas were crumpled, but she was as perfect as he remembered.

'Yeah,' she said. 'At last, this family takes a holiday worth taking. Hello, Dad.'

'Hello, sweetheart. Come and give me a kiss.'

She wasn't wearing her prosthetic, and she hopped down the stairs on her right foot. The left leg of her pyjama trousers, empty below the knee, flapped at each jump. Watching her come towards him, Virgo told himself, as he had done every day for two years now, that he would get used to it. Just give it time, like Rachel always said.

He closed his arms around her. She smelled like she always did. No matter what state she was in, even when she'd come home half-drunk and reeking of cigarettes from her friend Sarah's house party last month, she smelled like his baby, the baby they'd brought home from the hospital fifteen years ago. Would she still smell like that when she grew up and moved out of home, out of his reach?

Katie wriggled, already trying to get free. With a wrench of his heart, he opened his arms and let her go.

'Do you want a cup of tea, Dad?'

'That's very kind, thank you.'

She grinned at him. 'Make me one too, would you?' The grin broadened. 'And then bring it upstairs? I'm going back to bed.'

He watched Katie work her way back up towards her room. Making a cup of tea was the very least he would do for her.

It was late morning by the time he got to the office. The atrium was awash with light, despite the threat of rain. Hundreds of feet above him, the roof glass framed the pigeon-grey clouds as they dragged their burden over central London. As he waited for the lift that would take him up to the *Herald*'s fifth-floor offices, Virgo gazed out at the street.

The lunchtime queue was already spilling out from Angelo's: a line of spiked haircuts and designer jeans; low and baggy on the men, figure-hugging sculptures on the women. These were the worker bees of London's media: runners from TV production companies, junior editors on the glossy magazines, copywriters at the trendiest ad agencies.

MICHAEL BROOKS

Most of them stared at nothing as they waited, pretending they were alone in the universe. The motorcycle couriers, ready to run pictures and pages around the city, were ranged along the parking bay outside the glass, watching them without interest. The couriers were used to waiting outside; they were dressed for it, paid to wait, eat and mumble to each other under the sky, whatever it might loose on them. The precious office space of the capital was not for their shelter.

A squat brown cardboard crate sat waiting on his desk. Someone had piled all his awards into it and dumped the box here. There was a reason he'd left them over in the news room – he didn't want his reputation to fade, just because he was taking a break from the heat. But that was journalism: awards tarnish, and you were only ever as good as your last story. He just hoped he could make the science desk work.

Virgo slumped into his chair. Of course he could, he told himself: he'd done plenty of science stories when they needed someone to fill in. Though he had always tried to escape his past – a first degree and a PhD in physics – by going into journalism, every editor he had ever worked for dragged it up again. Everyone was always impressed at his qualifications – much more impressed than they should be, Virgo always thought – and assumed he'd willingly turn his hand to the science beat at any opportunity.

Nothing could be further from the truth. He had become addicted to the heart-thumping moment when a hint is dropped and a hunt is about to begin. He craved the excitement of chasing down a story that doesn't want to be found, and science rarely gave him that. The slow pace of scientific research had led him out of the lab, and the same slow pace had led him away from writing about it. Corporate scandal, ruthless political manoeuvring: that was his passion. Science couldn't come close.

And his email inbox proved it. It was flooded with news releases and other hand-out story tips. Their banality took his breath away. He would have to develop a whole new swathe of contacts if he was to do science reporting he could be proud of. His mind switched back, just for a moment, to Paul Radcliffe. He had one interesting contact now, at least.

A shadow looming over his desk distracted his thoughts.

'Did you miss me?'

Imogen Hennessey leaned her elbows on the grey partition that screened Virgo's desk from the walkway.

Virgo smiled up at her. 'I thought about you every day. Every hour. Every minute I spent in that conference, I cursed your name.'

'Oh, that's not nice.'

He watched as Imogen folded her arms over the partition, then placed her chin on top of them. Her skin was milky caramel, her eyes deep and opaque. Her lips parted in an irresistible smile.

'I didn't meet your guy,' Virgo said. 'David, is it? The NSA man. Does he go to things at that level?'

'Maybe. We don't talk about stuff like that. He gives me great story leads, and I write them up.' She paused, then grinned again. 'I'm like the unofficial spokeswoman for the US National Security Agency. And then you're sent to pick up the crumbs. Have you been in to see Charles yet?'

'Not yet.'

'He's looking forward to your work. This is the first phase, he says. The new, intelligent tabloid is in the throes of birth.' She paused. 'I quote, obviously.'

'So you get to write about ridiculous science fiction, and I have to follow up and make it sound plausible?'

'It *is* plausible. Didn't you get that from the conference?'

He shrugged.

'Hey, you're the one who asked for the science beat when the job came up.' She grinned again. Her smile was dangerous, could move mountains. No wonder she got such great stories. He watched her walk back to her desk. As she sat down, she turned and flashed a smile at him, then picked up her phone's receiver. Almost immediately, his phone buzzed.

He picked up, and glanced across at her again.

'I still blame you for three days lost from my life, you know,' he said into the mouthpiece.

'Is that any way to talk to your editor?' The gruff response made Virgo ricochet upright in his chair.

'Charles? I didn't –'

Charles Mercer cut in before Virgo could finish the apology. 'You'd better come over, Nat. There are some people here looking for you.'

CHAPTER 5

VIRGO WAS STILL FIFTY steps from his editor's office when he saw them. Two men, standing in front of the double doors leading out to the lift lobby. They seemed to be assessing the layout, glancing in all directions. Charles Mercer hurried out of his office.

'Nat, come in here.'

The two men saw Virgo, and stepped into his path.

They were both tall and heavily built, wearing charcoal suits and grim-set faces. One of them had shocking ginger hair, neatly combed into a side parting. The other was dark, with a thick moustache. It didn't take Virgo's degree in physics to work out that their interest in him was not going to be a good thing. They flashed warrant cards in his face as he got near. The ginger man spoke first, his words nailed onto a harsh Glaswegian accent.

'Nathaniel Virgo, would you come with us, please?'

The voice was calm and business-like, but it was clearly not a request. The dark man reached a hand out and placed it lightly on Virgo's upper arm.

Virgo shook the hand off. 'Why? What's this about?' Against his will, his gaze moved momentarily past the two men. Every one of his colleagues was watching.

'Don't make a scene, Mr Virgo.' This time it was the other man who spoke. He stepped closer. His breath smelled of coffee, and there was a sliver of white pastry on his moustache. They had stopped for refreshments on the way. This was all in a day's work.

Mercer had reached them now. 'What's this about? Let's step into my office,' he said. The men ignored him.

'We have some questions concerning a Paul Radcliffe,' the Scot said to Virgo.

Virgo's brain wheeled, but he could think of no response. The dark man gently gripped his arm, and Virgo allowed himself to melt into submission. They led him into the lobby. Mercer's face, normally on the edge of a wry smile, showed both anger and concern, but even he was doing nothing now. The office was as silent as Virgo had ever known it. Everything around him had halted – either that, or he had simply stopped hearing anything but the rapid, insistent thudding of his own heartbeat. He sensed his field of vision narrow and his cheeks started to burn, as if the stares were focusing all the light in the office on his face. What had these people said at reception to just be allowed to come up and take him like he was theirs?

Both men now kept a hand resting lightly on Virgo's upper arms. He moved forward as if propelled by their touch. As the lift doors closed, he found his voice.

'Are you police?'

The reply was curt. 'Not exactly.'

The lift doors opened again at the ground floor, and the three men moved silently through the glass and steel atrium. Above them, the glowering London sky pressed down on the building. They hesitated at the polished revolving doors, then the Scotsman thrust himself into the cycle while his partner held Virgo back until the next opening came round. Outside, they marched to the edge of the pavement. The parade of motorcycle couriers eyed Virgo with what looked like contempt. The Scotsman spoke into his sleeve. 'We're out.'

ENTANGLEMENT

A black Jaguar swung round the corner and glided in towards the kerb. The dark man pulled the door open and got in. The Scotsman pushed Virgo in beside him, then crouched, squashed himself in and slammed the door. The windows were blacked out, and Virgo felt nausea rise in his abdomen. He had had a few brushes with the police, but this felt different. Very different. The Jaguar pulled away smoothly, without a sound.

The journey might have taken a few minutes, it might have been half an hour. In the dark cocoon of the car, Virgo simply couldn't tell. Every one of his questions hit a wall of silence; any attempt to move was quietly resisted. Eventually, he was led from the vehicle into the enclosed courtyard of what appeared to be some kind of mansion. The Scot pressed him through a narrow oak doorway into a cramped corridor with a low, damp-spotted ceiling.

He was sure that no one knew where he was. Had anyone at the office even asked who the two men were? Why had Charles given in so easily? This was the whole problem with the new international obsession with security. There were unchecked powers at work these days, and they were accountable to no one. Even newspaper editors were flinching. Virgo could feel the panic trying to establish its grip on him as they marched quickly forward. His breathing was becoming more laboured – the damp, the anxiety and the pace of the march made his head spin. He stumbled over a small hump in the floor and fell forward onto the stone. It was cold, and covered with a thin layer of greasy dirt.

Strong hands pulled him up again and propelled him forward, but only for twenty more paces. The march stopped in front of a metal door that looked just like all the others. The dark, moustached man pushed it open, and they went in.

The contrast with the dingy corridors shot a searing pain into his eyes. Harsh striplights, suspended from the concave ceiling, lit up a technological paradise. One wall was covered, floor to ceiling, by what appeared to be a bank of computers covered in a vast array of tiny, flashing LEDs. Their intermittent light created random, dancing patterns of red and green across the wall. A row of slim dehumidifiers sat against the wall to Virgo's right, emitting a low hum as they sucked and processed the atmosphere.

Straight in front of him stood racks of electronic equipment. He recognised many of the boxes: signal generators, oscilloscopes, parametric amplifiers – the same kind of stuff that had competed for space on the shelves in the lab where he'd done his PhD. Huge strings of cables and connectors hung from hooks beside the shelving. He had enjoyed the company of these boxes then; looking them over, knowing what they could do, gave him a sense that anything was possible, given the right kinds of connections. Now, they just looked threatening.

The wall to his left was almost entirely filled by a plate of blackened glass. In the centre of the room were three gunmetal chairs and a large oak table. Though its plain legs were dark and angular, the table's top had been sanded into smooth, gentle slopes. It looked unnervingly like a butcher's counter.

'Sit down, please, Dr Virgo,' said a voice. An American voice. Virgo turned. A powerfully built man in his fifties came into the room behind him. He looked like he might burst out of his navy blue jacket at any moment.

Virgo remained standing.

'Just sit down, Virgo.' The voice was rich and deep. 'We need to ask you some questions.'

Virgo risked his voice. 'Who are you?' It came out thin and reedy, weak. No matter: he knew his rights. He remained standing and looked around the room. 'This isn't a police station. You can't question me without proper recording equipment.'

A slight lift at the corner of the man's mouth betrayed amusement. 'I think you'll find we can pretty much do what we like.' He motioned again to one of the chairs. 'My name is Frank Delaney. I work for the FBI. Virgo, I need to find out what you know about certain things. Sit down.'

FBI? OK. That was a start. Virgo walked over to one of the chairs, and sat. The seat was cold. He got up again and removed his phone from the back pocket of his jeans. The display told him he had no signal.

'I'm afraid you'll find that rather useless here. The science guys tell me it's a Faraday cage down here. You studied science at college, Virgo – you ever heard of a Faraday cage?' Delaney looked amused. 'The walls are lined with steel. No signals in, no signals out.'

Virgo leaned back in his chair. Delaney had been through his résumé. That was thorough. Too thorough. What was this about? What had Radcliffe done? The steel pressed into his vertebrae and chilled his skin through the thin cotton of his shirt. The Scotsman shut the door. Virgo was alarmed by the sound: no metal clang, but the soft hiss of a tight seal. Glancing around the room, he could no longer see the other man, the one with the moustache. Then his focus changed, and he saw him in the reflection of the blackened glass. He stood inches behind Virgo's left shoulder.

With the door closed, there was a new quiet to the room; the hum of the dehumidifiers seemed to have faded into silence.

'Now,' Delaney said, squeezing his bulk into a seat opposite Virgo. 'What do you know about the quantum computer?'

Virgo felt himself relax. 'A bit,' he said, trying to inject confidence into his voice. 'Where do you want me to start?'

Delaney fixed him in a cold gaze. 'Why don't you start by telling us about progress in the field? You've just been to a conference on this machine: what did you find out?'

'It's meant to be the ultimate code-breaker. When it's ready, that is.'

Delaney stared at him, not moving. 'Go on.' What had happened to Paul Radcliffe, that Virgo was here giving an FBI agent a lesson in quantum technology? They could find this stuff out for themselves. Where was this leading? Virgo took a breath.

'Quantum computers encode numbers in single atoms rather than on bits of silicon like ordinary computers, and that enables them to do enormous numbers of computations in parallel.' He paused. 'But that's just the theory. No one has managed to build one yet. At least, not one that's worth anything.'

Delaney raised an eyebrow. 'What do you mean?'

Virgo shrugged. 'Code-breaking is just a big maths problem: you have a huge number, hundreds of digits long, and you need to find the factors, the numbers that multiply together to give the number. It's designed to be hard. And the best attempt at building a quantum computer so far can only do maths about as well as a ten-year-old child. It can find the factors of . . .' – Virgo stumbled around for a suitable figure – '. . . I don't know, fifteen? It can work out that five and three multiply together to make fifteen.' He allowed himself a smile. 'Impressive, huh?'

'And where is this computer?'

'At the US government's standards lab in Colorado.'

'Have you seen it?'

'No.'

Delaney seemed not to be listening. He was simply observing, his eyes shifting back and forth, looking for the smallest crack. Somehow, this wasn't going well. Cut to the quick.

'So what's this about?' he said. 'What's happened to Paul Radcliffe?'

Delaney stared at him for a moment, his eyes fixed and unreadable. He leaned forward.

'He's dead.'

Virgo tried to contain his shock. Delaney watched him in silence for a full five seconds.

When he could breathe again, Virgo asked the obvious question.

'And you think this has something to do with me?'

The grimmest of smiles cracked over Delaney's broad face. 'He died a very horrible death, Virgo. For some reason I don't yet understand, he was tortured.'

For the first time since he left the office, Virgo realised he hadn't even stopped to pick up his jacket. He shivered, then leaned forward and spread his fingers out on the table, letting them stroke the rough grain of the wood. He could handle this kind of attention. He'd done nothing wrong. And there was obviously a story here with Paul Radcliffe. Just keep to the truth.

'You think I did it?'

'Did you?'

'Of course not.'

Delaney smiled coldly again. 'But we have witnesses saying you had a – what did they say? – a very intense conversation with Paul Radcliffe in Baltimore just yesterday. What was it about? Did he give you anything? Anything to look after?'

Virgo maintained the direction of his gaze, but shifted his focus to stare beyond the leathered face across the table. Keep to the truth, he told himself.

'He hardly said anything. He gave me a disk,' he said. 'It was blank.'

Delaney's face didn't flicker. 'Where is it?'

Virgo hesitated, a fleeting moment that escaped his clutches. 'I Fed-Exed it back to him.'

'Already?'

Virgo nodded, and concentrated on holding Delaney's gaze. He didn't know why he'd lied but there was no point in trying to take it back now.

CHAPTER 6

GABRIEL MACINTYRE SWUNG HIS car into the back lot, grabbed a Red Sox cap from the glovebox and pulled it down hard over his brow. He liked to call this – his building in Newton, Massachusetts – his 'satellite office', but no one at the company knew about it. It wasn't registered to Red Spot Industries, but to a holdings company in the Caymans. It was untraceable.

He felt the breast pocket of his jacket. The disk was there. He picked up the yellow legal pad from the passenger seat, then jumped out and scurried down the covered walkway that led to the office door. A passer-by would mistake him for a lonely, two-bit accountant who crunched numbers for a low-grade clientele. But no one would be passing by down here: he was in the nether regions of an anonymous Boston suburb. The set-up was perfect.

In all the time he'd been using it, nothing had gone wrong. No interference from neighbouring offices, no break-ins, no incident at all. Not that anyone breaking in would consider it worth the effort. Gierek's machine looked like a crappy old computer, abandoned on the bottom shelf of an unlocked cupboard.

He shut the door behind him. The shabbiness of the place

always made him smile; compare it with his downtown offices and you'd think he was out of his mind. How could Red Spot's Vice-President of Energy even *be* here? How could anyone wearing a Gucci suit sit on this plastic swivel chair? MacIntyre remembered spending long, sweaty summers sitting in a chair just like it. He had been grateful to do the filing at Delgado and Preece, Arkansas' least prestigious law firm – he really had worked his way up from the bottom. Which made it all the sweeter. Now he was sitting on this cheap upholstery out of choice, making millions with a half-hour manoeuvre.

>Load activator

MacIntyre always hesitated before he put the disk into the machine. He liked to savour the moment, contemplate the extraordinary nature of what he was able to do. Then, with a soft touch, he slid the activator disk into its slot.

>Location:

MacIntyre tapped at the keyboard.

>Facility:

A few more keystrokes.

Another prompt asked him about prices. MacIntyre referred to the legal pad, and typed in the numbers. Jakarta Power and Light was about to get its control systems tweaked. He pressed *Send*. Let the magic begin.

MacIntyre wasn't foolish enough to think he understood the entanglement. No one understood it. Even Einstein had said it made no sense that two atoms could have an invisible, untraceable link across space and time. But it was written into the equations of quantum theory. It was real, it was *true*, even if it made no sense.

And it wasn't like he had gone into this blind. He had checked it out in the science section at Barnes & Noble after the first approach, read enough to assure himself it wasn't voodoo. It made his head spin – give him economic theory, any day. He knew enough, though. The details of the experiments eluded him, but at least they were all written down in black and white, with names and places – he had even heard of some of them. Schrödinger, the guy with the cat, was one. And there was Einstein, of course. Things happened in Copenhagen and Vienna, Brussels and Geneva. There were even quantum things going on at IBM and the government labs in Los Alamos these days. He had got so caught up he sat down to sip a cappuccino while flicking through the pages. It was wild, wild stuff. Who would have placed him, an Arkansas farm boy, at the forefront of quantum technology?

The machine had worked perfectly from the get-go. Gierek and his business partner had chosen this place, far from prying eyes, scoped it out and installed the stuff before MacIntyre had even seen it. They chose him some targets and brought him over on a Sunday afternoon to see how easy it was. He still remembered the thrill of discovering that Global Energy was using Red Spot's firewall and systems protection software. Such irony that a competitor's caution had opened it up so wide. Its automatic software update had pulled in the hidden entanglement codes that Gierek had created; within just ten minutes, MacIntyre was getting a tutorial in how to reset his competitor's pricing structures.

Of course it came at a price: dealing with Vasil Marinov. They had met in the car park outside. That was where MacIntyre first saw those glacier grey eyes – he looked into them as he shook Marinov's hand and something inside him told him to walk away. But he had long ceased listening to that voice. Following your gut instinct is for when it leads you into something, not out. That was the path to success. And to an ulcer, of course.

Marinov had a long streak of grey ponytail running down his back. Put that together with their odd accents, Gierek's drooping moustache, and their affinity with electronics, and it would have been easy to dismiss them as a pair of Eastern European nerds with a new toy to show off. Until you saw Marinov's eyes. If Marinov had made the first approach, maybe MacIntyre would have run a mile. But Laszlo Gierek was a professor at Boston University: it couldn't hurt to see what he said he had invented. And when he mentioned a novel form of access to the Asian markets – well, how could MacIntyre turn him down?

They didn't say a word to each other until they got inside. Then Gierek flicked a switch and blew MacIntyre's mind.

'It's that simple?'

'It's that simple.'

They were gathered round the screen, but Marinov's head was turned and he was staring directly into MacIntyre's eyes. 'However you store information or instructions on a computer, it's physical. A hard disk, a floppy disk – whatever – the information is encoded in something physical.' He tapped the machine. The information here is in the magnetisation of the atoms on the hard disk. And that's a quantum thing.'

'Tell me what you do again,' MacIntyre had said.

Marinov's eyes narrowed slightly, and he'd almost smiled. 'I'm a businessman,' he said. 'But I trained as a software engineer in Bulgaria. And then NASA brought me over here to work for them in Houston.'

MacIntyre broke eye contact to look back at the screen. Marinov had been headhunted by NASA. He must know what he's talking about.

'So this entanglement can manipulate the atoms on a hard disk halfway across the world, and no one would ever know how it happened?'

'From halfway across the universe if necessary. And no, no one can tell. It looks like magic.'

Gierek broke in. 'You have to set it up right,' he said. 'You have to put the atoms into the right quantum state to begin with. But, ironically, that's getting easier every day. We'll soon be getting a gigabyte on every square millimeter. That means every piece of binary data – every 0 and every 1 – is pretty much on the atomic scale.'

'So how do you control the atoms?'

'That's a software issue,' Marinov said. 'It's about creating instructions that set up the right kind of magnetisation on the atoms in the hard disk.'

Gierek interrupted again. 'Think of it like a silver dollar spinning on its edge. All the data in computers – all the magnetisation – it just comes down to heads and tails. If it's heads, the computer sees a 1. If it's tails, it sees a zero. And our software keeps that silver dollar spinning on its edge until you decide whether you want heads or tails.'

MacIntyre's head was spinning too. He was ready to cut to the chase. 'And all this translates into control of remote computers?'

Gierek nodded. 'Exactly.'

'Control of your competitors' computers to be precise,' Marinov said. 'Maybe we should show you?'

MacIntyre's mouth was dry. If this worked like they said, he could guarantee the shareholders their share of Asia.

'OK,' he croaked. 'Show me.'

Gierek punched a few keys. 'We set it up to interact with Global Energy's servers in Tokyo. For the demo we had to slip a Trojan into their system to activate the entanglement. But with your help we can do much better.'

'If we kept using the Trojan, it would be found eventually,' Marinov said. 'But bear with us – it's just a demo. With Red Spot's software subsidiary dominating the e-security industry, you'll be able to do this untraceably. It will be in your product as it is shipped.'

MacIntyre's eyes were drawn up from the screen towards Marinov's. It was like being hypnotised, he thought. He pulled his gaze downwards again, and stared at the numbers. Here, at last, was something that made sense: the power utilities pricing charts for Tokyo. He knew this screen well. Energy was all about supply and demand – and cost. Utilities bought power from the cheapest source; the supply companies used sophisticated programs to keep their prices down yet still make a profit from their power stations' outputs.

'So we're now ready to hike Global's prices,' Marinov said. 'We've got the dollars spinning on their edges. Will it be heads or tails?'

MacIntyre could see Marinov's face reflected in the screen. There was no hint of a smile. Just those eyes.

'What would you like to set their price to?' Marinov said.

MacIntyre looked at the figures. 'One-eight-one,' he said.

Gierek tapped at the keyboard. The screen refreshed. Global Energy were selling at 181 – not much higher than Red Spot's price, but high enough to price them out of the market.

The next week had been terrifying; he was convinced they would somehow trace it back to him. Marinov's repeated assurances that the entanglement was untraceable did no good – he hardly slept for four nights. But Global's share of the Japanese market had dropped like a stone. That rush, the phone calls, the boardroom gloating; that was how it started. It was like the first rush of cocaine. Only better: the high lasted.

Leaning back against the vinyl, MacIntyre stared at the grey plastic box on the desk. Somewhere inside it, the entanglement link had atoms shaking down other atoms inside grey boxes in Indonesia, resetting data buffers, altering chip functions. Jakarta Power and Light had bought the hardware configuration routines from Red Spot's software division. Thanks to MacIntyre's access, Marinov had been able to insert Gierek's entanglement protocols into the software. What a team they made.

And their influence was untraceable; it lay in the setup for the magnetic fields that flipped the 0s and 1s in the data storage. Who could ever find the atom that had flipped a bit from halfway across the world? No one ever looked at anything at that level. Marinov was a genius.

Somehow, MacIntyre didn't see Gierek in the same way. He knew the quantum stuff, but it was Marinov who seemed to be leading the work.

And now they had finally cracked the quantum computer too. Frankly, that terrified him. The same atom clusters could sit, entangled together, in their weird superposition state: a 256-bit register holding the key to every code on the planet. Government protocols, nuclear test data, military communications – terrorist networks, of course – all accessible in seconds.

MacIntyre shuddered. He didn't really want a part of it, especially the thing they were planning with the planes. But they needed him to get the entanglement software into the flight-control systems of all those aircraft. And, let's face it, he was involved, like it or not. Still, Red Spot would come out of this development with government contracts, that was assured. The shareholders could never be told about the means, but what did they care? They paid him to take risks like this. He was paid to put himself on the line in a gamble that could reasonably be expected to push the share price higher in the long term. Once the opportunity presented itself, it was pretty much his duty. He was no lawyer, but he knew what was expected of him.

He glanced at his watch. Three more configurations to set before heading into the downtown office. He'd be a little late today, but no one would care. The share price; that was what they cared about. And that had skyrocketed since they started outperforming their competitors at every turn. Gabriel MacIntyre was a master strategist, everybody said so.

Damn right.

CHAPTER 7

THE REVOLVING DOOR WAS still turning as the Jaguar pulled away. Across the street, Angelo was closing up his deli for the day. He waved, and smiled. Nathaniel Virgo waved back and surveyed the scene, breathed it in like smelling salts. The clouds had cleared, and the muddle of architecture that ranged along Wardour Street was lit by the cold sunshine of approaching winter.

The couriers were still there, chatting amiably, a couple of them studying maps and arguing about routes and congestion charges and football grounds. Up the street, outside the George and Dragon, men in suits and sunglasses stood drinking golden lager, wiping away raindrops from the elevated tables before leaning unsteady elbows onto the damp wood. Soho seemed defiant like the sun; the cafes even had clients sitting outside now, polished chrome tables displaying speckled cappuccinos. A man in a production house T-shirt and jeans falling from his hips brushed past, two film reels in huge silver canisters under his arm.

Virgo's lie had spun out of control for a couple of minutes. Delaney wanted to know why mailing a blank disk back to its owner was so important that he'd done it first thing that morning. He had shrugged. Said Radcliffe seemed like a bit of a crackpot, a waste of time, and he just thought he should send it back. There had been another long pause, and then Delaney's face seemed to lighten. He'd instructed the two agents to take Virgo back to his place of work; they led him out of the room, across the corridor and up some steps. Through another door they emerged into the courtyard where the Jag was still parked. Virgo shook his head. That whole fast march through the damp, echoing corridors – probably his public removal from the *Herald* office, too – had been designed to soften him up.

First thing to do when he got back was to Fed-Ex the disk back to Radcliffe: Delaney would surely check for it. But the timing would be wrong. He'd have to spin out the lie a bit – get someone to say they forgot to send it straight away like he'd asked.

Not that he had to send *the* disk. After all, if Radcliffe's death had anything to do with this disk, what kind of story was he sitting on here?

The adrenaline creep was beginning. It always started like this: the sly chemical suggestion of right place, right time; the sudden exhilarating sniff of a lead. Virgo pushed the feeling back. He didn't want this story. He wasn't doing dangerous any more. And he was going away with his family tomorrow, come hell or high water. Radcliffe would still be dead when Virgo got back from Cuba; if the trail was cold by then, so be it. He had made promises to Rachel and Katie, and this time he meant to keep them.

But he could send a blank disk back to Radcliffe and get someone to look at the real one in his absence. Just in case.

He pulled his phone from his pocket, and dialled. Old friends could come in useful sometimes. Especially old friends who worked in the Metropolitan Police's digital forensics labs.

He stopped mid-stride in front of the lift. 'Andy? Hi, it's Nat. I need a favour.'

*

All eyes fell on Virgo as he stepped into the office. Virgo raised a hand.

'The show's over, citizens – go back to your lives.'

There were a few smirks, and the eyes dropped back to their screens. Deadlines were imminent, and he was suddenly a non-story.

He'd put the disk in the courier bag he used for hand luggage, inside the front flap pocket. He checked it was still there. It was. Why wouldn't it be?

Andy would be here in fifteen minutes; he'd agreed to take the disk and have a look. As always, Virgo felt slightly guilty at the request – he inevitably couched it as 'one last favour, I promise'. It was a breach of regulations, and Andy would probably lose his job if anyone found out. But he'd looked at tapes, hard drives, all kinds of stuff, over the years for Virgo's investigations, and never once had there been a problem. Andy insisted he liked the break from the drudgery of standard police work.

Virgo walked over to the stationery cupboard and pulled out a blank CD, a plain brown envelope and a plastic Fed-Ex bag. Back at his desk he slipped the disk into the brown envelope. He scribbled the address from Radcliffe's card onto the paperwork, then onto the plastic bag. In a few minutes, the disk would be gone. All he had to do now was tell his editor what was going on.

'Paul Radcliffe?'

Mercer's voice sent Virgo's pen skidding down the plastic, leaving an ugly blue scar on the label.

'Isn't that the guy they wanted to talk to you about?' Mercer was looking over Virgo's shoulder. 'What are you sending him? We need to talk, Nat – come into my office.'

Virgo grabbed Radcliffe's disk and followed Mercer through the newsroom. Mercer shut the door of his partitioned office behind them.

'Have a seat,' he said. Virgo laid the disk gently on the table between them.

'Tell me what that was all about this morning,' Mercer said. 'I've not had a reporter pulled out of here by the security services before – not even you. What's going on?'

'It was about a guy I met in Baltimore. He's been killed.'

Mercer put a hand on the disk. 'And he gave you this?'

Virgo shrugged. 'It's blank. As far as I can tell.'

'But you were about to send it back to him?'

'I told them I'd already done that.' Virgo looked up. 'But I'm giving it to a contact at the digital forensics lab. I thought there might be more to it.'

Mercer held silent for a few seconds, then leaned in towards the table. 'They'll check whether you sent it, you know.'

'I know. The lie was a reflex. A good one. I think there might be something going on with a quantum computer.'

Mercer fell silent again, then looked up and grinned. 'You just can't keep out of the action, can you? I told you there was something in Imogen's story. You said it was all rubbish. Were you wrong for once, Nathaniel Virgo?'

Virgo laughed, then glanced at his watch again. 'My contact will be here in a moment. I have to go and meet him downstairs, on the street.'

'And then what?'

'And then I'm going on holiday, remember?' He looked up. Mercer's features radiated disappointment. 'Oh come on, haven't I earned a holiday?'

Mercer steepled his hands together and gave Virgo a measuring look.

'Can't you put it off? The timing's terrible.'

'The timing's always terrible. That's why I've hardly taken a day off in two years. I had a month off after Katie's accident, and pretty much nothing since.'

Her name hung in the air between them. He and Mercer never talked about their shared guilt over Katie's injury, but they both felt it, suffered it, like a presence.

Mercer leaned back in his chair. 'You're right,' he said.

'The man's dead. Tell your guy to get the disk back to me when he's done with it. I'll cover your back if they come calling.'

'Thanks, Charles.' He got up. 'I have to go. He – the forensics guy – he's called Andy Davenport. I'll give him your direct line and your mobile. Don't get him into any trouble – he's an old friend, and a bloody useful one.'

Virgo headed back across the office, finished packaging up the blank disk, and dropped it in the courier mail tray. Picking up Radcliffe's disk, he went through to the lift lobby. He would meet Andy Davenport, do some shopping for beachwear, and then head home. Everything else would wait until he got back.

CHAPTER 8

THE SALES ASSISTANT SMILED. 'Good choice,' she said.

Virgo wondered if she was flirting with him. She was – what? – nineteen? Very pretty. Her big brown eyes looked up at him as she tucked the beach shorts into the brown bag.

'My boyfriend has a pair of these.'

Oh. She was just trying to make him feel better about being old enough to be her father.

Still, he needed new shorts: his old ones had fallen apart when he hit the stones and gravel too hard coming off his bodyboard last summer. A weekend in Brighton: that was all the holiday they had managed. Katie passed the time sulking about the lack of sand – the pebbles hurt to lie on, she said. She had a point: it wasn't exactly Cuba. But by sundown tomorrow, they'd be striding over miles of golden sand, sipping mojitos as the sun fell into the sea.

He took back his credit card, then walked out onto Oxford Street. He called Rachel. Her phone was switched off, as he knew it would be. She worked for a decent firm, but the senior architects were all men and the clients were demanding; with some of them, she had to give the impression that she had no life outside of work. She could always tell, she said, when the client was disappointed that a woman was handling their project. No one ever said it out loud. It was in the eyes. In the things they didn't say.

He went straight through to her voicemail.

'Hi Rach. It's been a very James Bond afternoon. Call me if you get a chance.'

He headed towards the tube. Oxford Street was preparing for Christmas – had been for weeks now. By Christmas, after all, retail was gearing up for the January sales. It was like climate change: all the seasons were blurring into one. The population seemed to be happy with it, though: there was no longer any noticeable lull between the January crowds, the summer sales and the Christmas shopping rush.

Oxford Circus station was closed, the steel gate pulled across to bar the entrance. Waiting crowds spilled out onto the pavement, threatening and engulfing the shoppers, hindering their urgent passage into Regent Street. It was always the same when it rained. People panicked and ignored the emerging sun; instead they ducked underground, clogging up London's arteries.

He stood in the throng, absent-mindedly looking back along the street to see whether a bus would come to save him. It was never worth the risk; there was no telling when the gate would slide open again and permit him a descent into the stifling tunnels.

Slowly, gradually, frustrated faces peeled hesitantly away from the crowd. They left singly or in pairs, with a huffy sigh, and other faces shuffled into the gaps and wondered whether they too should give up. Virgo looked behind him again down Oxford Street. There were no buses. He glanced up and around. There must have been a time when Oxford Circus didn't exist, when Regent Street was a narrow carriageway. And before that it must have been fields or forest. It was hard to imagine.

The gates opened, and he shuffled in with the rest of London: down the stairs, through the rattling gates, and down again, through the escalator chutes and turning, on autopilot, towards the trails of sky-blue paint that announced the Victoria Line.

The platform was airless. New oxygen only arrived with each train, pushed into the tunnel to stifle the adrenaline of those who stood wondering if this would be the day someone – some psycho on day release – pushed them onto the tracks. Three minutes till the next train. Two stops to Victoria, change trains, then a billion more stops to Richmond. He hadn't missed the commute while he was away. When the train came, and he relaxed into the seat, the jet lag caught up and took over.

'Hi, Dad.'

Virgo put his head round the door of the sitting room. Katie was watching TV with two friends.

'Hi, sweetheart.'

He kept out of their way – he'd only embarrass her if he tried to interact with them. The curse of the teenage daughter: damned if you do, damned if you don't. He went through to the kitchen and pulled a beer from the refrigerator. When Rachel got home, they'd all go out for some food. As far as he was concerned, the holidays had started.

CHAPTER 9

'CAN'T YOU FIND HIM?'

Gabriel MacIntyre sat back in the booth. A burger joint, for Christ's sake. The coffee was barely drinkable, and the menu – look at this stuff. America's obesity problem, neatly encapsulated on laminated card.

He shifted his body to take a look around. Sure enough, there were a lot of fat people in there. He avoided these kinds of places as a rule, ate sushi – macrobiotic even – most of the time. Jennie had wanted her birthday party at a Burger King, and he had given in to that – what daddy wouldn't? But he hadn't eaten anything. He wasn't going to put that crap into his mouth. He worked hard to maintain his looks, his trim physique. If only something could be done about his hair. It was definitely thinning – and much faster lately. That would be the stress of the job. The shareholders were always hungry, and winning out in the global energy markets was becoming more demanding every day. But then, his troubles went far beyond the job. Working with Marinov, being in his debt, had become more stressful than he thought.

And now Laszlo Gierek had disappeared.

MacIntyre turned back round. Across the table, Marinov exuded an unnatural calm. Here was the source of his success, come back to bite him in the ass. The most successful vice-president in Red Spot's history, a rising star in the *Fortune* lists, a career built on the jello foundation of a Bulgarian programmer-turned-gangster and a reliance on under-the-counter technology. This morning, everything had been beautiful. And now he was swimming in crap.

'What do you know about Gierek?'

Marinov smiled. 'I know a lot about him. More than anyone. He's been working for me for years. And it is all about to pay off.'

MacIntyre's stomach tightened. 'Is that what it's all about in the end? The money? I've already given you hundreds of thousands for his skills. For the entanglement software. Do you really need more?'

He sounded like he was pleading. Calm down. Stop drinking the shitty coffee. Get a grip. He looked up at Marinov's blank face.

'Can you find him?'

'I've got someone on it now,' Marinov said. Cool as you like.

'Who?'

'Alex.'

MacIntyre winced. Alex – Dr Death, by all accounts. Gierek was in trouble.

'There's nothing for you to worry about,' Marinov said. 'Nothing has got out. The FBI are off the case – it's been handed back to the Baltimore Police Department.' He smiled a sickly grin. 'Your brother-in-law is a powerful man. What have you got to worry about?'

'The disk?'

MacIntyre wished he could control the tone of his voice, keep it level, unhuman. Like Marinov. God, his eyes were bleak. Empty.

'We don't know there's anything on it,' Marinov said.

Did anything ever get to this man?

'When we have it back, we'll have a look. We have all the

quantum computer's plans. We have the machine. We've not lost anything.'

MacIntyre lifted an arm and rubbed the back of his head. Yep, he was definitely thinning.

'If there's any hint . . . anything at all, I could lose everything.' He pushed manicured fingernails into his scalp. He thought for a moment about threatening Marinov, saying they'd all go down together. Like in the movies.

Don't be ridiculous. *Get a grip*. Marinov had those eyes fixed on him. He seemed fascinated. MacIntyre suppressed a shudder. There was nothing to worry about. Marinov wouldn't tolerate a loose end. He was far too meticulous for that.

'What did you do to him?' MacIntyre said. 'To this Radcliffe guy?'

Almost imperceptibly, Marinov lifted his eyebrows, then leaned his body slightly forward. There was a smile on his lips.

'It wasn't me. It was Alex.'

MacIntyre opened his mouth, then paused and shook his head. Marinov's smile broadened.

'Alex will do the same to Laszlo. If there's anything more to know, anything that Radcliffe held back, we'll soon have it. My hunch is, Laszlo will lead us to this Virgo character.'

'How soon?'

Marinov shrugged, and sipped at his coffee. 'Laszlo's on a flight to London, apparently. I'd give it twenty-four hours at the most. He is well practised at hiding. He knew a lot about that even before he got in with us. But Alex is more –' He searched for the right word. 'More determined.'

The waitress appeared at their table. MacIntyre waved her away before she had a chance to speak. Her smile faltered, but only for a moment. Service with a smile, the American dream. Did she recognise him? He was surely imagining it: she was a waitress; she was hardly going to have read *Forbes* recently. He breathed deeply, then assumed his hardest stare. For no reason that he could think of, his daughter's face flashed into his mind. Jennie. Five years old. Her daddy in prison.

'You know how important this is.'

Marinov returned the stare. 'You've told me enough times. How long have you been using the software now? Has anyone ever caught so much as a sniff of it?'

MacIntyre shook his head. Like a scolded schoolboy. Marinov leaned back into the bench seat.

'I keep my business under very tight control, MacIntyre. No one else in your company knows about it: you should have learned to trust me by now. I have nothing to gain by this coming out – and everything to lose. Just like you.'

Had this all been worthwhile? Jennie flashed into his mind again. Five years old, and her daddy going to prison. MacIntyre concentrated on breathing.

He looked up. Marinov was smiling. A cold, empty smile, like Death on vacation.

Enough.

'I have to go.'

Marinov opened his arms. 'Call me later. I'll bring you up to date. Alex is landing at Heathrow in a couple of hours.'

'And then?'

'Finishing up, then coming back. We all have to be there for the spectacle; Wheelan insisted on it.' Marinov almost smiled. 'Relax. This will all be over in a couple of days.'

MacIntyre didn't want to know. The *spectacle*? Is that how he saw what they were about to do? What if it all went wrong? Connections made you in this world. And connections could break you.

He looked at his watch. 'I have to go,' he said again.

Marinov didn't say anything more. Just raised his hand, and stared his empty stare.

MacIntyre could feel Marinov's eyes on his back as he walked out into the parking lot.

CHAPTER 10

THE DOOR SLAMMED.
'I'm back,' Rachel called. 'Present your hard-working wife with a drink, sweetheart. I'll be on the sofa.'

Two minutes later, Virgo was standing before her, holding out a gin and tonic. Rachel smiled as she reached for it.

'Thanks.'

'Good day?'

She nodded. 'These clients are not like the other apes: they like my work and they like me.'

'Someone out there likes you?' Virgo took a sip from his gin. 'No wonder you need a drink.' Despite himself, he let out a sigh. Rachel sat up slightly and looked at him out of the corner of one eye.

'I got your message, international man of mystery. What was that about?'

Some of their friends would be enthralled by a tale of covert interrogation. But Rachel would just be furious with him for lying about the disk.

'I'll tell you about it later,' he said.

He left the room and headed up the stairs.

'Nat,' she called after him, half-irritated.

'Can't hear you. What?'

She appeared at the bottom of the stairs, leaning against the banister in a mock-seductive pose. 'Did you say something about James Bond?' She pouted. 'Tell me more, Mr Virgo, I'm intrigued . . .'

He couldn't help but smile. 'I'll tell you over dinner,' he said. 'I thought we could eat out, then come back and pack. Katie's upstairs in her room with some friends – they can come too.'

'Katie's got a race tonight.' Rachel followed him up. 'We told her we'd go and watch. Don't say you'd forgotten?'

'No, of course not.'

A lie – and a lame one, too. He couldn't hold the blank look from his face. How come he could spin a convincing line to an FBI interrogator but not to his own wife? And there it was again: work making him forget his daughter had a life too.

'You know she wants to take her running prosthetic away with us?' Rachel said. 'She's worried about missing a whole week's training with the Leicester meet coming up.'

The British championships. His daughter, competing for the 100-metre paralympic sprint title. The thought made him glow and choke up in equal measure. He had cried the first time he watched her bound down the straight. It wasn't in pity; it wasn't even in guilt. It was the fact that she had got up after the accident and gone straight back to the track. It was the broad grin on her face as she crossed the line, the defiance in her eyes. Nothing could stop Katie Virgo from running wherever, whenever she liked.

Rachel was watching him, reading his thoughts.

'She is amazing, isn't she?' she said, and took his hand. 'I don't understand where she gets that sheer bloody-minded determination.' Rachel squeezed her palm against his. 'You, maybe?'

It was 9.30 by the time they got back home. Katie slumped on the sofa in her track pants, nonchalant about her victory.

She flicked on the TV, and began the ritual of phoning round her friends. She'd waved goodbye to them three hours ago; it was time to check in, see what everyone was doing, make sure no one missed out on any of the gossip. Virgo sat down next to his daughter, put his arm round her shoulder and pulled her towards him. He kissed her hair, and she turned and smiled at him. Then her friend picked up, and Katie shifted away from him.

'Gem – hey – it's me. Where are you? Are you out? Is that Darren I can hear? What are you doing?'

Their moment was over. It was always over too soon these days.

'Come round,' she said. 'I've got to pack, but come round and I'll tell you all about this boy at the track.' She laughed down the phone, a sound like joy unleashed. 'He totally checked me out, gave me *that* look, you know? And then he saw my leg.' She laughed again. 'He didn't know what to do.'

She was away; Virgo knew he wouldn't get onto her radar screen again tonight. It seemed cruel that he could love her that much, need to be around her, watching her, and yet seem so peripheral to her world. But that was a father's burden. Still, they'd all have a week away together now. It would be paradise. He got up from the sofa, and went upstairs.

Rachel was already packed. She was never happier than when throwing stuff into a battered case. The dilapidated state of their luggage reminded him of the times they'd travelled together as students, meandering through the vibrant tones of Morocco, the shock of West Africa, the slow luxury of camping below Arizona's towering landscapes. This time it would be a lazy week of sunbathing, late breakfasts in a hotel room, and long, slow dinners over rich wines.

He nearly wrenched his shoulder out heaving Rachel's case off the bed.

'God, Rach, what've you got in here?' he said.

She grinned defiantly at him. 'All my shoes.'

'All?'

'Almost all. You still don't understand about a girl and her shoes? Katie will do the same, you know.'

'Only because you've taught her your evil ways.' He dragged the case across the floor and leaned it against the wall. The handle creaked.

'This case was built before women's shoes took over the world,' he said. 'I hope it can handle the weight.'

'Of course it can.'

'Well you can carry it. It weighs a bloody ton.'

'Weakling,' she said, laughing, and walked into the bathroom. He breathed a relaxed sigh. In twelve hours they'd be among the clouds.

'Did you get the passports out?' he called.

'I put them on the dining table with the tickets and stuff.' She wandered through to the bedroom, dripping foam from her toothbrush. 'And I left a note for Maria with the hotel details and your phone number in case something happens. I'm not taking my work phone. Jeremy's bound to call it as soon as he loses my drawings.'

'Maria's still coming, even when we're away?'

'The house is dirty whether you're here to see it or not, Nat.' She wiped toothpaste from the corner of her mouth with one finger. 'Come on, let's get to bed. We'll finish up in the morning.'

CHAPTER 11

WHEN VIRGO WOKE, THE first hints of cold sunlight were filtering through the blinds. He looked at his clock: 7.25. He got up, pulled on a T-shirt and knocked loudly on Katie's door.

'Time to wake up, sweetheart. Rise and shine.' Not that it would do any good.

He went downstairs to make some coffee.

Through the kitchen window, he could see birds hopping on the lawn that ran down to the alleyway at the back. Their garden was big – too big, really – but Rachel said she couldn't live with less. She called it her therapy area: some corner always needed attention, which meant she always had somewhere to lose herself. Sometimes she talked about having someone come in to do the weeding, but she never followed up on it.

The kettle was just beginning to throb with the pressure of boiling water when something snagged in his mind. He replayed his walk past the dining room; how he'd glanced towards the table. Rubbing a sleep-crusted eye, he went back through. He was right: the plane tickets were topped by two passports. Not three. He lifted them up, and opened the burgundy covers.

Rachel's and Katie's. He leaned down to look on the floor, under the table. Nothing there. Had he put his passport back in the desk? He didn't remember doing anything with it. He went upstairs again, to the spare bedroom, and pulled open the desk drawer. The jolt sent his wireless internet router tumbling off the desk. He picked it up, and pushed the power lead and phone connection back into place. His passport wasn't in the drawer.

Frowning, he made a pot of coffee and put it, with two mugs, onto a tray. He carried it upstairs and slid it silently onto Rachel's bedside table.

'Rach.' She always slept so deeply, so peacefully; he envied her easy contentment. He leaned gently on her shoulder and kissed her cheek. She stirred and smiled, but didn't open her eyes. He kissed her again.

'Rachel, time to wake up.'

She screwed up her eyes, then flashed them open and reached out to pick up her polished chrome alarm clock.

'What time is it?' she asked, squinting at the clock face. 'We're not late, are we?'

He pursed his lips. 'No.' He hesitated. 'Do you know where my passport is?'

'I put it on the table, with mine and Katie's.'

'It's not there.' He tried to keep his voice calm, but he could feel a disquiet rising.

She pulled herself upright. 'It must be. I put them all there last night, before we went out.'

'Mine isn't there,' he repeated.

Rachel fumbled on the bedside table for her glasses. 'Where have you looked?'

'On the table. On the floor under the table. In the desk drawer.'

'I remember putting it on the table, I'm sure. Is it under the other stuff?'

She got up, looked again at the clock, and swore. 'We've only got an hour to get out of the house. Is Katie up?'

She swung her legs from under the duvet and planted her feet on the carpet. 'I remember getting it out of the drawer. It *is* there.'

He shrugged, and went downstairs to start a search.

They went through the house, emptying every drawer, checking every pocket of his clothes in the wardrobe, every file in the spare room. After twenty minutes, Rachel began to give up. He knew she was right to; it wasn't going to turn up. He felt sick. This couldn't be happening. He closed his eyes for a moment, then opened them again. Everything was the same.

'You hear about these things,' he said. 'Pickpocketed last time you came through the airport and you never even notice it's gone. It's probably being used by some drug mule.'

Rachel still looked bemused. 'But I –' she began. She didn't bother to finish the sentence.

He reached into a cupboard in the lounge, pulled out the Yellow Pages and flicked through to the general enquiries number for Heathrow. He picked up the telephone and dialled.

The girl who answered his call listened patiently while he explained his problem. She couldn't help, but put him through to the airline's ticket desk. He listened to the low buzzing of the hold tone for an excruciating three minutes. Why were these places always deserted when you needed them? What kind of shifts did these people work? Eventually, someone picked up.

'Hi, I hope you can help me.' He tried not to sound desperate. 'I'm meant to be flying with you to Cuba today and I seem to have mislaid my passport. Is there any way I can travel without one?'

'If your flight is this afternoon, you might be able to get a replacement in time.'

The woman sounded weary.

'It's this morning.'

'Then I'm afraid you won't be flying with us today, sir.'

Virgo slammed the phone down. Of course he couldn't travel without a passport. He didn't know why he'd even made the call.

Rachel slumped into an armchair at the other end of the room, staring into space. Katie appeared at the doorway, wrapped in a dressing gown.

'Your dad's lost his passport,' Rachel said, trying hard to retain some calm in her voice. She looked up at him. 'So, what's the plan?'

'I'll drive you to the airport, you two go, and then I'll go and get a new passport. There must be another flight they can put me on.'

Rachel raised her eyebrows and sighed heavily. Katie shrugged and turned to go back up the stairs. 'OK,' she said. 'I'll get showered.'

Virgo watched Rachel trudge off behind her daughter, then followed them. He pulled on some clothes, struggled back down with Rachel's case, set it by the front door, and went into the kitchen to make a piece of toast. Just as he was finishing the last bite, Katie appeared, her hair still damp.

'I put my case next to Mum's,' she said. 'Are we really going without you?'

'I'll be out on the next flight,' he said. He resisted the impulse to ruffle her hair. He was learning. Slowly.

Rachel stuck her head round the door. 'Come on,' she said, her tone flat and defeated. 'Let's go.'

Driving out through west London took nearly forty minutes of awkward silence. The drop-off area at the departures terminal was bristling with taxis and traffic wardens. Whining jet engines punctuated the grating noise of dragging cases and rattling luggage trolleys, while a dozen nervous, halting goodbyes were taking place beyond the parking bay. Virgo pulled the car to a halt, opened his door, and went to get the cases out from the boot. He set them down next to where Katie and Rachel were standing. Rachel wrapped her arms around him.

'Don't be long,' she said, her voice softer now that they were here and really parting.

They kissed, then settled their foreheads together.

'I won't. I'll be out as soon as I can get a flight. Maybe even later today.' He turned to Katie, who offered only a perfunctory objection as he hugged and kissed her.

'Look after your mother,' he said. 'Don't let her talk to strangers. You know what she's like.'

Katie smiled. 'Well, just make sure you hurry out, Dad. Mum will be much harder to live with while you're not there.'

So she did appreciate him after all.

Virgo watched them disappear into the terminal. You could hardly tell Katie was walking on a prosthetic leg, her gait was so smooth these days. He got into the car and headed back into the traffic.

The house seemed strangely empty. He threw his jacket onto the kitchen table, and looked at his watch. The passport office next to Victoria station had already opened, but he needed to organise photographs, the legal stuff, and someone to countersign his application. One of the neighbours would do it. He ran upstairs and opened the door of the spare room.

The shock at the sight was physical, visceral. The pain in Virgo's chest might have come from the sharp expansion of his lungs as he took in breath. Or it might have been because his heart tried to bounce through his rib cage. A man was sitting on the sofabed, holding Virgo's passport in the air.

'Hello, Nathaniel. Were you looking for this?'

'What the . . . ?' Virgo said. He lost the power of speech for a moment. Then it returned. 'Who are you? And what the hell are you doing in my house?'

Immediately, Virgo realised he knew the answers to both questions.

CHAPTER 12

THE MAN HELD OUT a hand. 'Laszlo Gierek,' he said. Like they were meeting at a conference. Virgo recognised the gaunt look, the drooping moustache, even the agitation in the set of his mouth. But he didn't remember seeing a hunted look in Gierek's eyes before.

'I couldn't find the disk last night.' Gierek's gaze shifted back and forth, like he was scared to make eye contact. 'I'm sorry that Paul involved you in this, but I need the disk back.' He hesitated. 'You should lock your doors at night, by the way. I thought I'd at least have to pick a lock, break a window or something.'

Virgo stared at the hand still extended towards him. 'Last night?' he said. He wasn't thinking fast enough. He was dazed. 'You took my passport last night?'

Gierek handed it back. 'Only because I couldn't find the disk. I'm sorry to postpone your vacation, but I need the activator disk back.'

Virgo slid the passport into the back pocket of his jeans. 'Activator? For what?'

'For a little machine I built.'

Whoa. Slow down.

'What's going on, Gierek? Who killed Paul Radcliffe?'

'My guess would be Alex Genovsky,' Gierek said. 'But I'm sure that name means nothing to you.' He raised an eyebrow, and the motion lifted the left side of his moustache. 'At least I hope it does.'

A bursting anger rose in Virgo's chest, but he held it back. If Gierek had travelled across the Atlantic for this, there really was a story here. Fine. This was an opportunity: a shortcut. They could go and get the disk from Andy, and on the way, Gierek could tell him exactly what was going on. He owed him that much. And it would save Andy's forensics work getting him into any trouble.

'I don't have the disk on me. I gave it to someone to look at.'

Gierek's eyes widened. 'And what did they find?'

'You tell me – what's the machine it activates?' Virgo took a leap. 'Have you built a quantum computer?'

Gierek looked away. 'I don't know what Paul told you, but he made a bad mistake bringing you into this. It was unnecessary – I think he wanted to punish me; I told him I'd been working on something without him.' Gierek looked back at Virgo. 'Paul and I have shared many projects, but I had to keep this thing from him. I was working with . . . with someone else, someone I wanted to keep away from Paul. For his own sake, you understand?' Gierek's eyes were pleading for a moment, like he was seeking absolution. 'And then it all got out of hand, and I didn't know who else to turn to.'

Gierek moved across to the window and craned his neck to look up and down the street. 'I just wanted him to help me expose . . .'

'Expose what?' Virgo asked.

Gierek turned, but ignored the question. 'I saw him speak to you: I followed you both outside the hall in Baltimore. I saw him give you the envelope. I knew straight away what was in it. What did he say to you?'

Two could play at not answering questions. 'You don't know?'

Gierek stared at him. 'You want a story? Is that it?' He shook his head. 'You don't want this story.'

Virgo held his stare. Gierek seemed nervous enough to keep talking as long as there was silence to fill.

'No, the disk doesn't activate the quantum computer,' Gierek said. His gaze had dropped away now; he was looking at the floor. 'It activates another machine. For what it's worth, I call it the entanglement generator. It looks like junk – it's wrapped up in a blanket in a cupboard in my lab – but it has its own peculiar power. I gave the disk to Paul so he could go and have a look at it; I thought he could help me decide what to do about it.'

Gierek really was giving nothing away here. What was going on?

'And now you want the disk back?'

'It's the only one I have. It's vital evidence if I'm to stop . . .' He broke off. 'Yes, I want it back.'

Virgo was furiously calculating in his head. Where was the story here? The disk? Or the quantum computer?

'Is there a quantum computer?' he asked.

Gierek suddenly looked grim. 'Why don't you call your friend? We can talk in the car.'

It was something. Virgo stood up. 'OK,' he said. 'Let's talk in the car.'

Gierek pulled the door open and headed downstairs.

Virgo followed. By the time he reached the bottom of the stairs, Gierek had wandered into the sitting room. He was staring at the pictures on the mantelpiece.

'I'll just get my jacket,' Virgo said, heading for the kitchen.

'Is this your daughter?' Gierek called. 'She's very beautiful. How old is she?'

Virgo picked up his jacket from the kitchen table. He realised that he hadn't locked the back door last night – he'd unlocked it to put the rubbish out after they came back from Katie's race, and hadn't locked it again. He wondered how many other nights the door had been open access for burglars.

'Fifteen,' he called absent-mindedly. Where was the key? He'd lock it now. The key was on the top of the microwave. Where it always was. He could almost hear Rachel say it. The thought made him smile.

A crashing sound came through from the sitting room, the shrill ring and tinkle of breaking glass. Virgo ran through to the front of the house, key in one hand, jacket in the other, to see what Gierek had broken.

He froze at the doorway. One small window pane was shattered. Gierek was sprawled over the coffee table, blood pouring from a dark hole in the middle of his forehead.

In the back of Virgo's mind, the part that was still working, he heard a mild scratching at the lock on the front door.

His mental processes were grinding slowly, on rusted neurons. Eventually, it clicked. Someone had shot Gierek through the window. And now they were trying to get in through the door.

He ran. By the time he reached the back door, he heard a sound that he had only ever heard in the movies. Three gunshots, fired through a silencer. They would have destroyed the lock on the front door. As Virgo yanked the back door open, he heard the front door crash against the wall in the hallway. It crossed his mind that this must be a mistake, that somehow everybody had converged on the wrong house. He heard the front door slam shut.

Virgo careered out of the back door and ran across the block paving of the patio. In a couple of seconds, whoever had killed Gierek would be coming after him. The dead man's voice rang through his head.

My guess would be Alex Genovsky.

CHAPTER 13

VIRGO SCRAMBLED DOWN THE garden towards the back gate. Halfway across the lawn, he slipped on the wet grass; it was only as he fell to the ground that he realised he was still holding his jacket. Good: his car keys were in the pocket.

He got up again and made for the gate. Pulling it open, he leapt into the narrow alley between the rows of houses. Pushing past the overgrown thorn bushes that reached up from the cracked base of the alley walls, he ran parallel to the street and then turned sharply down a gap between two houses. He stopped. There was no sound except birdsong and the thud of his heart.

He looked back. Was anybody chasing him?

Not that he could see. They would still be frisking Gierek, looking for the disk.

This could only be about the disk.

If he came up out of the alley, onto the street here, maybe he could get to his car. Whoever it was wouldn't know him. If he looked nonchalant enough, maybe he could just be a passer-by, getting into a car and driving away. Then what? It didn't matter, not yet.

Virgo slipped his jacket on, then pulled the car keys from

the pocket. He held the remote lock between finger and thumb, finger on the button, and began to walk.

He came out into the street forty metres up from the house. The car was twenty metres away. He would have to walk towards the house. Without looking up. Without his eyes lifting to the front door.

He only managed ten paces before he risked a glance.

The day's light was cold and harsh; the street looked unwelcoming. It was empty too; that time of day when everyone had gone to work or was immersed in their morning routine at some anonymous shopping centre. No one else was there to see the black-coated figure standing on his doorstep, just behind the bay tree in his front garden. He saw a mesmerising rainbow flash of dispersed sunlight as the figure slipped something into a pocket. He knew that refraction: it was some kind of CD. Gierek had been carrying a disk. Another disk.

Virgo felt an overwhelming urge to stop everything, to think. But not here. He hit the button on the car's remote lock.

He'd forgotten about the beep. The jolly electronic chirp sang out from his silver Ford and told him the doors had been successfully unlocked. Virgo was only five paces away from the car, but he saw the dark figure turn and move out from behind the bay tree.

He knew he wouldn't make it. Time to decide. He turned on his heels, the most suspicious of moves. Now, he really had to run.

Virgo heard the accelerating steps behind him. Gierek's killer would have seen him turn back into the alley. But if he got to the wall fast enough he'd be able to scale it and disappear into the allotments behind the trees.

He hit the wall at full pace, leaping at the last second. The jump took him halfway up, and he scrambled the rest, oblivious to the scraping of flesh on brick. He could hear no noise now, just the insistent willing in his head to get over the wall.

He dropped to the ground, and pumped his legs on past the trees, into the allotments, then leapt the fence. He risked a glance behind. His pursuer was coming over the wall now. If he kept going, he would be in among the row of cottages in thirty seconds. There was a cut-through. He'd be able to double back, go round the back and head along Beaufort Road, then back down to the car. It was facing the right way; he could make the getaway. Then what? Past the cottages now. He couldn't hear anything behind him. He would make it. He'd be OK. Keep running. The car was open; all he had to do was jump in and start the engine.

There it was. And he could hear running feet behind him, a light tread, an athlete's stride. He kept going. He had the car door open. The key went in. The engine started. Don't stall. Rev hard. Bring up the clutch. The engine screamed, and he pulled out into the road.

He had made it.

The car roared beneath his feet, but not loud enough to cover the sound of three more distinct pops. He was being shot at. *He was bloody well being shot at.*

He threw the car sharp left into Kingston Road, turning to look over his shoulder. A silver Mercedes pulled forward, advancing effortlessly up the road. He rolled back in his seat and took another sharp turn, then another, and another. With each manoeuvre there was a two-second respite, then the Mercedes appeared again, unshaken.

Fifty metres ahead, a green light beckoned him over a crossroads. He could hear the deep burn of the engine as he floored the accelerator, plunging the car towards the mess of traffic ahead. A line waiting to turn right, across his lane. The light before him was amber.

Then red.

The engine roared higher, now whining, and Virgo shivered with adrenaline. The clenched muscles in his jaw pulled his face taut. He didn't have time to draw the seatbelt across his chest, and now he couldn't move his arms. He tried to imagine what it would be like when he hit the windscreen, whether he'd feel the lacerations or just the dense thud of impact and then the vacuous relief of unconsciousness. He remembered the look of disbelief on Katie's face as the car knocked her off her feet. He remembered his own initial shock – that someone would run a red light, careen into a thirteen-year-old girl, and then make the decision to keep going. Just drive away, leaving a body and a life in tatters.

One of the waiting cars skimmed across the road in front of them. Would the next one wait? Virgo wondered what it felt like to have metal rip the flesh off bone. Katie knew. He remembered running to Katie's still body as it lay bleeding onto the asphalt, the sense that it was his fault, that he had done it. He hit the horn, and kept his palm pressed down on the centre of the steering wheel. The sound filled the road. People on the pavement were turning to watch. He could sense the Mercedes behind him, gaining ground with each second that ticked past.

He glanced at the dash. Eighty miles per hour. Time slowed and he saw the wrinkled face of the driver waiting to turn right ahead, the man who held power over his life. He was wearing a brown tweed hat. The look of pure terror on his face told Virgo it would be OK. He was frozen to his spot on the other side of the road. He wasn't going to make the turn. The Ford flew on down the hill, and Virgo took his hand off the horn. Turning to look behind again, he saw the traffic kick back into life, and then halt in chaos again. Three cars were piled up at the crossroads, and a silver Mercedes ploughed into the fray.

As he rounded the bend at the bottom of the hill, he breathed again.

He had got away.

CHAPTER 14

O N THE OTHER SIDE of the world, Gabriel MacIntyre wrenched at the wheel of his Escalade. *Jesus*. How could he drive around in a vehicle this size and still have people not let him into the traffic? Maybe because he couldn't steer the fucking thing. It was like a tank. When he bought it, he told himself that Jennie would be safe inside, that nothing would get to her through this amount of metal. He hadn't considered the fact that it would drive like a leather-upholstered cargo container. It was a battering ram on wheels. He'd kill somebody else's kid one day, for sure.

It was all getting fucked up. Marinov didn't seem to give a flying crap about Red Spot's vulnerability. He knew nothing about this journalist, but he wasn't 'overly concerned'. Why the hell not?

If Gierek had passed on something about the quantum computer – maybe even the blueprints – they needed to nail this journalist to the ground.

He never used to be like this. Ellie had fallen in love with a gentle, sweet-tempered Arkansas boy, so gentle he couldn't bear to brand the cattle on his daddy's farm. He believed in love at first sight. It had happened there in his first semester at college. From the first moment, he would have moved heaven and earth to give her everything she ever needed.

It was still true. But look at what the world had done to him. Now, he was only the simple, lovelorn farmhand when he was at home. The rest of the time, he was doing everything he could to stay afloat. Like the rest of the rats in this stinking ocean. *Christ*, what was with this traffic? He punched at the radio's buttons, willed it to find a station that would tell him why every soul in Massachussetts was sitting inside stationary vehicles on the Interstate. What kind of monster had they created here? People spent hundreds of dollars every month for the privilege of encasement in their own metal box. How fucked up was that?

Gierek was a liability. They had a working quantum computer: what did they need Gierek for now? And if he was going to start going weak at the knees, talking to his colleagues after all this time, they couldn't waste a moment. Every minute he was out of their sight was a catastrophe.

Come on. *Come on*. At college, before all this shit happened, he used to drive a Corvette that moved like a cat.

Jesus. They had a quantum computer. They were going to listen in on White House communications while a trick that baffled Einstein brought a fleet of airplanes under their control. He was so far out of his depth, he could hear his father laughing till the whisky snorted through his nose.

He could understand the entanglement, the idea of his box in Newton connecting with atoms across the world, flipping bits and erasing data. But the way entanglement tied billions of calculations into one inside the quantum computer, then performed them all simultaneously: that blew his mind.

Marinov had assured him it was the same thing as his own little box, really. But his box just messed with people's computers. It was a white-collar crime – hardly even a crime. *Caveat emptor*. These companies had compromised their own computers by using a competitor's software. But the quantum computer was something else – that was a violent, unprovoked assault; that was a street mugging, a hit and run.

It beat passwords to a bloodied pulp: found them, crushed them, walked away with the key. It seemed wrong that something as elegant as quantum entanglement could be used for something so mindlessly brutal.

They had to get this under control. They had to nail Gierek. And the journalist. Of course, he was being selfish – who the hell wouldn't be in this situation? Gierek had created the entanglement software, and Marinov had delivered it. But he would be better off if they were both dead. At least he knew what made Marinov tick: it was green and it had George Washington's face on it. But Gierek? What if he was turning over a new leaf after all this time?

And where did the journalist fit into this? Maybe Marinov was right to be glad they would get them both. Alex would pop them both out of the picture, he'd said. And get the disk.

What was on this disk, anyway? It was hard to believe there was anything on it. He'd imagined Radcliffe's muffled screams in his sleep last night. There was no way the scientist would have lied to protect anyone. Not when that kind of agony – the kind that these people knew how to inflict – was running through his system.

The traffic queue evaporated as quickly as it had materialised. How did that happen? Ten more minutes and he'd be at the office. Ten more hours and he'd be home again, home in time to kiss Jennie goodnight. He'd just creep into her room and stare – like he did almost every other night. The desire, the drive to see her dark, melting eyes was taking him over, though: it was all he'd seen in his mind yesterday. He'd go in and kiss Jennie while Ellie fixed him a drink. She never let the maid do that; it meant there was at least one thing she could do for him every day, she always said.

He didn't deserve her.

It damn near stopped his heart to think about Ellie and Jennie. And to think about the damage if this stunt with the planes all went wrong – well, that gripped his lungs and squeezed them empty.

Marinov said it would all be taken care of in just a few hours. And he would just have to trust him.

He shook his head. Marinov gave him the fucking creeps.

CHAPTER 15

VIRGO KEPT ON DRIVING. His mind was racing as fast as his pulse; both refused to slow down, refused to settle. He should go to the police. What did he know? That there was a body in his front room. One to match the body in Baltimore. He put himself in the police's shoes. Would they suspect Virgo was involved? Would he be in the frame? Of course he would. But would being taken into custody at the moment be such a bad thing?

He had his passport now, at least. He could go to Heathrow, get on the next plane to Cuba. His heart ached at the thought of Rachel and Katie alone there. He couldn't even call them yet; they'd still be on the plane. He had no luggage, but he could buy everything he needed.

And if he was stopped while trying to leave the country with a dead scientist in his front room?

He would go to the paper. He would talk to Mercer, get him to call the police, explain that his reporter had got caught up in something no one had seen coming. It would be OK that way. But he had to get the disk back first: he couldn't get Andy caught up in all of this.

He pulled over in a layby and flicked open his phone. Andy took forever to answer.

'It's me, Nat. I need to get that disk back.'

'Nat, I was going to call you.' Andy was talking in a low voice: someone could overhear him. 'I've had a look. It's pretty strange – no wonder it just threw out a formatting error. It's like a normal disk – a normal CD – but the pit size is ridiculously small.'

'Pit size?'

'The zeroes and ones embedded in the plastic. The laser scans them to read the data off the disk. But these are about an eighth of the normal size. The laser just can't cope. These things are down at the quantum level.'

Whatever that meant, it fitted. But it was too much information. He didn't have time to take it in now. And he didn't have time to talk.

'Andy, I need it back. How soon can you meet me? Can you be in Wardour Street in fifteen minutes?'

'No can do, Nat. I'm just about to run a section briefing. I can be there in an hour at the earliest.'

It would have to do. 'OK. An hour. Outside, as usual.'

As Andy hung up, Virgo looked at his phone. The battery was running low. Best turn it off for a while.

This was going to be a long sixty minutes.

As he rolled the car through Soho, Virgo sank in his seat, his breathing shallow. Every other car seemed to be a silver Mercedes. He found a parking space a hundred metres from his office, and fed the meter. No point risking a wheel clamp just now. His hands were shaking and the coins rattled against the metal as he pushed them in.

Wardour Street was bustling, as usual. Now, suddenly, there wasn't a Mercedes in sight. The observation made his heart beat faster. He ran across the road. The quicker, the better.

Charles Mercer was in his office; Virgo could see him way over there across the ocean of desks. Thank God. He kept his head down as he walked. He couldn't afford to get into conversation with anyone but Mercer. Maybe he'd go and find Imogen afterwards. Maybe she knew something. He had to fight to keep his legs moving; talking without betraying his anxiety was going to be even harder.

A tentative knock on the door was enough to lift Mercer's head.

'Nat, what the hell are you doing here? I thought you were jetting off to the sun, leaving us all behind?' Mercer's eyes gleamed with a rising hope. 'Anything from your friend about that disk?'

'Charles, I need you to call the police.'

Mercer's face went blank. 'What?'

'Someone just tried to kill me for it.' The words tumbled from his lips. 'A researcher called Laszlo Gierek is dead in my front room. Andy – the digital forensics guy – is going to meet me here in forty-five minutes, and when I have the disk, I need you to call the police. I'm going to stay here until they come. I'll explain about still having the disk – you can back me up that it was just a mistake – and they can take me away. But I don't know where this assassin is. I'm not going home without police protection.'

Mercer stood up and eyed Virgo with growing concern. 'What about Rachel and Katie? Where are they?'

'On a plane. They're safe.'

Mercer pursed his lips, the way he always did when he was thinking. 'Sit down, Nat. We'll get you a cup of tea. And I'll call the police whenever you give me the nod. But tell me what's going on.' He walked to the door of his office and politely asked his assistant Anita to make some tea. Then he shut the door.

'Did you say the disk was blank?' Mercer sat down.

'No. It's just unreadable. Andy said something about quantum stuff.' The adrenaline was still kicking at him, twitching his muscle fibres.

Mercer's eyes started to shine. 'Really?' He let out a low whistle. 'So, has there been some breakthrough, do you think? Are we sitting on the high-tech story of the century?'

'A quantum computer, you mean?'

'A quantum computer. Your man Daniel Born's machine, brought to life.'

Mercer stood up, then stared at the wall. He was thinking, calculating.

'I'll tell you what, Nat,' Mercer said, eventually. 'I want one of the lawyers here.' He headed for his office door. 'Don't go anywhere. I'll be back in two minutes.'

Mercer nearly knocked the tea out of Anita's hand as he hurried out. She set the cup down on the table and went out again. Virgo picked up the pages on Mercer's table: mock-ups for the weekend magazine. The spreads were lavish and colourful: *The Perfect Garden for the Perfect Life*. Some chance. He threw them down again, then looked at his watch. How long would Mercer be?

Anita poked her head round the door again. 'By the way, Nat, there was a call for you from Kathy at reception downstairs,' she said. 'Someone you're expecting – they're on their way up.'

Andy? Already?

Virgo's heart kicked against his ribs. Andy wouldn't come into the building.

'How long ago did Kathy call?' He tried to keep his voice calm. He failed.

'Oh, just a minute ago. While I was waiting for the kettle to boil.' She looked at him, and raised her eyebrows. 'Everything all right?'

It better have been just a minute ago. If it was two minutes, he had no time. The back stairs were in the far corner of the office, over behind his desk. He'd have to pass the doors to the lift lobby. If his timing was out, he was dead.

Everything was a blur, a pounding of blood. Everything except the sound of the lift's bell. As he passed the lobby, he saw someone in black emerging from the lift's metal cage. That's all he saw. That was all he had time to see before he began to run.

The door to the back stairs always stuck a little. They had called building maintenance out a dozen times, and they sprayed some silicone on the catch each time. And now it was stuck again. Virgo tugged at it. He could hear something begin to happen behind him.

The door opened.

He clattered down the stairs, three at a time. It occurred to him that this was risky, that he might misjudge a step and end up flat on his face, a bullet in the back of his head. That was a risk he'd have to take. He heard the pop again, then a ring as a bullet ricocheted off the handrail. He was still alive; he ran harder. He started to feel dizzy, going round and round inside the staircase. He would go the extra floor, down to the basement, and cut through the alley at the back.

There were no footsteps behind him now. That meant he had to think. Had Gierek's killer turned around and taken the lift back down? He hesitated on the ground floor. And then, through the glass of the fire door, he saw the shape again. It hurtled towards him, and he flung himself down another flight of stairs, and out into Berwick Street.

This time he could hear frantic footsteps behind him, running hard. There were too many people in his way to look back: if he lost concentration for a moment, he would crash into some gaggle of media girls gossiping loudly through their cigarette break. As long as he could hear the steps and the shouts of elbowed pedestrians behind him, he would have to keep running.

He was in the market now, sprinting past the lines of fruit and vegetable stalls, past the fishmonger listening to the cricket on his battered radio. If he made it past the video shops, turned right into Peter Street and cut down the narrow passage past the strip clubs, he could get lost in the crowds around Piccadilly Circus. He could hear the running getting louder behind him. Against his better judgement, he turned. The dark shape was coming round the corner. He had lost a split second by looking, but he could gain it again. He clipped one of the trader's tables as he passed, turned it over with a deft touch that sent fake designer handbags and umbrellas careering through the air.

'Oi, mate, what the fuck do you think you're . . . oi! Come back!'

Virgo ignored the chant of abuse and ran on. It might just give him the distance he needed to make the two turns that would lose his pursuer. His chest was pounding, his lungs burning. People stared as he went past, then looked around for the cameras. That was the trouble with this part of town – everything that went on was a bloody film, everything was some kind of entertainment. The streets here, when he ventured out at lunchtime to get a sandwich, were filled with dressed-up freaks, or actors playing a role in front of some TV crew or other. Some of the pedestrians grinned and waved as he raced past, proud to be part of his program – maybe they would feature on the show, fill the background of the shot with their fake smiles. They were right: it felt like a TV show. But he was running for his life.

The glitzed-up, blitzed-out women in the doors of the gentlemen's clubs watched him sprint past without interest. He saw it in their vacant eyes: tempting willing men in through the doors was their only concern, catching the eye of the wary, the shy, the desperate was what paid their wages. A man on the run wouldn't earn them anything. He halted, just for a moment.

He should go in. It was perfect: a dark sanctuary where he could waste some time. He couldn't hear anything behind him now. Maybe the rasping in his lungs was drowning out all other sound.

Virgo reached into his pocket and pulled out a ten-pound note. He hurried across the threshold, slapped his money on the counter, and passed through the black door.

CHAPTER 16

IT TOOK A MOMENT for his eyes to adjust. The girls on stage were a dusky red under the lights, their features exaggerated by thick layers of make-up. He searched for a dark corner. How long should he stay here? Should he take the table by the door? It wasn't in the shadows, but anywhere else in this room he'd be easily trapped.

The music throbbed in his ears. He felt a revulsion at the sights, the grinding, the cheapness of the thrills on offer. Buttocks waxed and waned under the spotlights, moving in and out of the dark like fleshy moons. The pouts were grotesque, threatening, like the faces in a carnival nightmare.

His heart was still pounding, and he jumped at every figure that crossed the threshold. He should have tipped the girl on the street, told her to say the running man had passed on by, down to Piccadilly Circus. It was too late for that now. He sat, breathing monstrous, barely controlled lungfuls of the sweaty air.

'You wanna drink, love?'

The waitress was barely seventeen. Barely older than Katie, and dressed – if you could call it that – in a gold sequinned thong. A matching necklace hung between her breasts as she stooped, waiting for his answer. She jiggled her chest, ever so slightly, reluctantly, in the ritual she had been trained to give each customer. Her eyes told him she wasn't really there; this was just her body he was seeing, not her soul.

He could find no words; instead, he stared at her breasts. They were blocking his view of the door.

'Whisky,' he said, eventually. 'No ice.'

She left the table, re-opening his view. A couple of men rolled in, already the worse for drink. He turned his eyes back to the stage. The show went on, no matter who or what came in the door. A dancer resting at the side of the stage flashed her eyes at him from across the room. She started towards him: he was her new chosen target. He shifted in his chair, struggling to rip his eyes away from her languid, hip-rolling walk. How long would he have to stay in here?

And then he saw the coat. Long, sleek, black. He couldn't see the face, but from the way the back of the head slowly moved from side to side, he could tell Gierek's killer was scanning the room.

His heart bounced again, raged against his rib cage. But he stood up carefully, not knocking the table. Two women were converging on him now: the dancer and the waitress. They'd cover his exit. He let them come, let them form the blockade: human shields. He slid out from behind the table, and walked quickly towards the door.

'Hey, Mister. Hey!'

It was the waitress. He should have left money on the table.

'You gonna pay for this?' she whined.

Virgo looked back, and saw the figure begin to turn, caught up by the call. Time to run. Again.

He was on the street in less than two seconds, and heading towards Piccadilly. The killer might have been behind him – he couldn't tell. These streets were too narrow, too empty to stop and think: only vagrants and seekers of seedy pleasure ventured into these alleyways. Two more turns, two more quick scuttles to left and right, though, and the crowds would hide him. Piccadilly Circus was always crawling with police, too, watching the tourists with disdainful, sour faces. He should have come straight down here before, not gone into the club.

As the statue of Eros came into view he had to make a decision. Down into the tube station? That would mean crossing the murderous traffic. No, he needed to keep moving. The crowds were thick, viscous, and he couldn't run through them. He'd have to turn left, and just walk up Shaftesbury Avenue past the theatres. Maybe he could fade into the scene. He'd stand out more now if he ran. He risked a look behind. A shadow? No. He had eluded his killer. For now.

It was only a few hundred metres before he hit Wardour Street again. He crossed it and kept going. He would walk parallel to it, up Dean Street, then cut through opposite where he'd parked the car. He would be able to see Andy waiting for him from across the road. Then he would be away.

And if he got away? Would he call the police? Would Mercer have done it already?

No. He knew what Mercer would be thinking – he was thinking it too.

This story was too big, and he hadn't explored all the options yet. He had one more contact to try before he called the police in to rob him of the story. Besides, Mercer was right: he should have a lawyer around when it came to that. He had been stupid. It wouldn't have been hard for Gierek's killer to trace him to the *Herald*'s offices – God knows he left enough business cards lying around the house. But there was no way they could tell where he would head next.

Virgo risked a look behind. Still nothing. He glanced at his watch. Five more minutes, and Andy would be waiting. He walked faster. His shirt was soaked with sweat. He prayed for rain, something to cool his burning brow. He wasn't used

ENTANGLEMENT

to this kind of exertion these days. He should be lying on a beach.

The only risk was his car. Would the killer have seen it and returned there to wait for him? He stood in the lee of a tall Westminster City Council dustbin and scanned the scene. He wasn't even sure who he was looking for; all he'd ever seen was the long coat. There was nothing suspicious, no one was even standing within fifty metres of the car. But that walk across the road would be like the walk of death. If the killer was waiting, hidden, no one would even notice the shot until he fell to the ground.

Except, maybe, Andy. He was there, leaning against the newsagent's window, hands in pockets, just as he always did. He had the brown envelope under his arm. Virgo felt like a shit: he was about to embroil his friend in this. If the wrong eyes were on him, he, too, would be dead once the pick-up was made.

Now or never.

He crossed the road, shoulders tensed, ready to hit the ground, roll, then run again. But the moment passed, and the shot didn't come. Andy saw him and came out of his slouch, grinning.

'Nat, what *is* this thing? I've never seen anything like it.' Virgo looked up and down the street, scanning the pedestrians. He took the envelope, shook his head, then looked away.

'Not now, Andy. Thanks for this. I'll call you.'

Andy looked puzzled for a moment, then nodded. 'OK,' he said. 'Take care.' He turned and walked south towards Charing Cross.

It was over. Andy was safe.

Virgo had twenty steps to take, then he'd be safe too. For now.

He pulled his car away slowly, unremarkably. He could hardly turn the steering wheel; his arms were locked rigid. But he was driving now, he knew where he needed to go, and nothing was going to stop him. Central London to Oxford.

MICHAEL BROOKS

An hour? A bit more? It didn't matter. At least he knew Daniel Born would be at home. That was the thing about eccentric recluses. They were always home.

CHAPTER 17

SPECIAL AGENT FRANK DELANEY liked the idea of quantum entanglement. He thought about it as he set his brush into the water jar and scanned over his paint tray for the perfect base colour for the reed stems. He liked the idea that there were hidden connections in the world; that things – maybe even people – could be tied together by bonds they knew nothing about. It confirmed how he felt about Nancy, even now, years after her death.

He spent almost every daylight hour he could out with his watercolours nowadays. Either here at Quantico Creek, or further out in the tidal marshes of the Nanticoke River. He knew his colleagues sometimes sniggered at the sight: big Frank picking up his easel and heading off like he was some touchy-feely artist, not the coarse cynical old has-been they all knew. But he loved the smell here, the faint ring of the sea that reminded him of a boyhood spent playing guns with his schoolyard friends on the beaches of North Carolina. He'd lost touch with all of them now. A couple had stayed in contact until they had finished college and started earning a living, but the lapses between letters and phone calls gradually drifted into years. In the end, they all just got on with their lives: Johnny had taken up accounting, Chuck was an engineer in some margarine factory, Lowell joined Wal-Mart and became something in store management.

Delaney had been absorbed into teaching literature to ninth-graders, coaxing them into forming stumbling poetry, making honest attempts to introduce them to Shakespeare's subtleties, to Whitman's rhythms, to Harper Lee's cool prose. Something in the job sucked the life out of him and, six years down the line, out of nowhere, he applied to join the Bureau. A couple of decades later, he was starting to wonder if the Bureau hadn't sucked the life out of him too, now.

The reed heads came up well framed in a burnt umber. As the water evaporated away, leaving the powder embedded in the fibres of the heavy paper, Delaney felt the deep satisfaction of a match cleverly made. He used to get that same feeling from stringing facts together in an investigation, but satisfaction eluded him in his work now. He had felt a glimmer of it when he called Fed-Ex and got them to divert the package Virgo sent to Radcliffe. It was a blank disk, but that particular model wasn't available in the US. It wasn't the one Radcliffe had given him, Delaney was sure of that. But then he was called off the case, told it had been handed back to the Baltimore Police Department, instructed to drop it and head home. The message came from way too high up to ignore, a clear and unambiguous order: the Bureau had more urgent matters to look into than the murder of one science geek. It was probably some drug-crazed Baltimore junkie, the letter from Homeland Security said.

Homeland Security could kiss his ass; he had no time for government stupidity. Things were bad enough already, and then the whole fucking thing got turned upside down after 9/11. How could something as uniquely crafted as the Bureau be squeezed into some rabbit's ass of a government department? The proof of the fuck-up was there in that call from on high. Radcliffe's murder was nothing to do with drugs. Or at least with any junkie. Maybe the cartels would inflict those kinds of injury if someone had snitched, but it was certainly no junkie looking for cash.

But Delaney complied, and dropped it. He had lost the will to disobey direct orders; he lost it just about the same time he found the Creek, and its birdlife, and understood why Nancy had spent all her spare time out here. She'd taken the bullet running on a hunch, flouting an order, and the investigation had exonerated the Bureau. Maybe the order had been right. Delaney had even said so at the inquiry and earned himself a sense of betrayal: when it came down to it, he'd betrayed Nancy's memory. Despite the fuck-up of the situation she was trying to deal with, despite the mess she had been thrown into, they had all sold her out because she acted on instinct. Well, that taught him something. In the FBI, instinct was yesterday's game.

Still, at least he had got entanglement from the whole charade. At the airport, on the way out to interview Virgo, he had bought an idiot's guide to quantum theory, just to get a handle on Paul Radcliffe's brain. Old-fashioned sleuthing, just like Philip Marlowe. And he felt like it had changed his world. Just one chapter, twenty-six pages, had made sense of everything he felt about Nancy. They were still connected. He didn't have to explain why or how; if the physics geeks didn't know how or why, there was no sense him agonising over it. He just took comfort in it. All those people who thought it was a sordid little workplace affair, all the self-righteous fucks who told him he shouldn't have been sleeping with another man's wife; none of them knew what he and Nancy had found in each other.

Not that they'd had it for long. Almost before it had really begun – maybe it was some fucked-up karma thing he'd brought on her – she was dead. But death hadn't parted them. Here he was now in the Creek; he had become her eyes, taken on the quest to watch her world. He captured the sway of the beech and the yellow poplar, set them down on the stretched paper. When he glimpsed the wood thrushes she had monitored, saw how her conservation project had worked, he felt like he saw them for her. Through him, she was assured of their survival.

Delaney put down his brushes and looked out across the Creek. The dawn was blossoming into full day now and he had to go teach a class of wannabe agents at the Academy in a couple of hours. It had happened again; despite everything, the world had turned once more.

CHAPTER 18

VIRGO DROVE FOR AN hour and a half before the serenity of Oxford's stone towers and spires came into view, rising above the jumble of the city's grey slate roofs.

Dreaming spires? Fuck Oxford! That's what Born said: one quote that Virgo would never forget. For someone who was supposed to be an otherworldly genius, Daniel Born had an unbelievably earthy mouth.

Virgo had been astonished when Born agreed to the profile; he'd done a few science stories before then, but nothing big, nothing to make Born take any notice of his request. Born didn't go to conferences – he didn't need to. He lived off the proceeds of two popular science books about the quantum world, and only communicated with the outside world through email. His motives for accepting the interview had only started to become apparent about halfway through their meeting, when Born started ranting about the university's exploitation of his work.

Born had demonstrated the quantum computer's true potential. He worked out what each component of the machine would need to do, and how the atoms could work together to achieve the impossible. No one else had managed this in the two decades since Richard Feynman first made the suggestion about computing with the quantum world. Born had done it in one night.

Or that's what he said. Virgo was a junior back then, doing a bit of everything – science, arts, health – for any section of the paper that wanted his time. He was too thrilled to have got the interview to be properly sceptical about anything Born told him. Until the venom started to flow. The second half of the interview was almost entirely unprintable: a string of conspiracy theorising. Born had quit his professorship in a storm when the university insisted that it would act on his insight even if he wouldn't. He came across as paranoid. Maybe he was. Maybe he had reason to be.

A light rain was falling. Virgo turned off the ring road and scanned the roundabout for the signs that would lead him to the city centre. If he was going to find Born's house, he needed to go from the middle, the way he went before. The house was out to the north, in a tiny village. The taxi from the railway station had cost a bloody fortune, he remembered.

He tried not to think about Rachel and Katie. He failed. At least they would soon be thousands of miles away, beyond reach. This was just a blip. Born would tell him what was going on. He was a genius – he'd know what to do with the disk. He'd know whether the story was worth it.

He was almost in the city centre now. A bridge took him over the Cherwell. Two figures were huddled together in a punt tied to the bank, smiling up at the sky. Virgo craned his neck to see what they saw, but his view was blocked by the majestic rise of Magdalen Tower, its rooftop turrets like fairy castles. As he drove up St Aldate's, he watched laughing students, wrapped in hooded sweatshirts, throwing frisbees around on Christ Church Meadow. Ahead of them the poised angles of the cathedral tower rose tall into the sky, speaking loftily with the surrounding spires.

He was at the station. Where now? He scanned the road signs. That was it: Banbury A4165.

*

Twenty minutes later, Virgo was heading down a narrow lane flanked by two low hawthorn hedges. The rain had stopped now. The air coming in through the car's vents was loaded with the scent of damp vegetation.

'There,' he said to himself.

He drew the car to a halt outside a whitewashed cottage. The window frames were painted black, and the grey slates of the roof were speckled with a green-brown moss. Roses and ivy competed for space on its walls. Rachel would love this place – however much she gloried in modern architecture, she was always seduced by the secluded, the romantic. Virgo got out of the car, opened the wooden gate into the garden, and walked slowly up the path. All the curtains were drawn. He pulled back the black iron knocker, and drove it against the oak of the front door.

No response. After three minutes of waiting, he knocked again. Another two minutes of silence followed before he took a few steps back down the path and looked up at the windows. No sign of life.

'He doesn't go out,' he muttered.

When did he start talking to himself?

Virgo wandered back out into the lane, and leaned against the car. Was he wasting his time? He looked at his watch. Rachel and Katie wouldn't be landing for a good few hours yet. He could leave a message for them at the hotel. He had programmed the number into his phone when they made the booking. It couldn't hurt to let Rachel know he might not be out for a day or two.

He pulled his phone out of the back pocket of his jeans, and turned it on.

It beeped: there were two voicemail messages. The *Missed Calls* screen told him they were from Charles and Imogen. Charles would be wondering why the hell he'd disappeared from the office. He'd listen to that later, once he had some answers. Imogen would no doubt have heard something was up; she would be checking up on him, making sure he was OK. They could both wait, for now. He scrolled through the directory. He punched the 'dial' button when the hotel's name appeared, and put the phone to his ear.

His Spanish was terrible, and quickly forced the reception staff into halting English. He left a message and his number. Rachel wouldn't remember it: it was programmed into her phone, the one she'd left behind. No one remembered phone numbers any more.

Glancing back up at the cottage, he almost didn't see it. The shiver in the curtain was so subtle it took a half-second to register in his mind. Born was there.

Virgo ran up the path to pound the knocker again. Thirty seconds later, a voice called out from behind the door.

'Who are you?'

He pressed himself against the door.

'Professor Born, my name is Nathaniel Virgo. We met a long time ago: I interviewed you for the *Herald*. For the magazine. Could I please talk to you about something? It's very urgent.'

There was a long pause.

'I'm not doing any more interviews.'

'This has nothing to do with the paper. It's a personal matter. Please, I'm in a lot of trouble.'

A slow minute passed. Then another.

'Professor Born, please. I really need to talk to you.'

The seconds ticked past too slowly. What more could he do? He was wasting his time.

Then, with a medieval clunk, the lock turned and the oak door swung open a few inches. The eyes that looked out from the semi-darkness shone a fierce emerald green. A few long, greying strands of lank hair fell across his face.

'Professor Born, can I come in?'

Born remained behind the door.

Virgo ransacked his mind for an approach that might break the deadlock. Surely Born would at least know Gierek's name? Surely he'd have to react to that?

'Laszlo Gierek was killed this morning. In my house. Something's going on with the quantum computer.'

Bingo.

The door swung slowly back. Daniel Born was wrapped in a threadbare towelling dressing gown. It was a dirty white, with a Hilton hotel logo on the breast pocket. His belly pushed at the gown's belt. His eyes, set in a pale and slightly bloated unshaven face, retained their suspicion as he moved aside.

Virgo hurriedly stepped inside. 'Thank you,' he said.

Born rubbed at his stubble. 'Let me get some clothes on.' He disappeared upstairs.

Despite the light from the windows, the living room seemed unnaturally dark. Its air smelled of warm dust – same as it did when he came here last. The walls were covered with a dark hessian, and almost every surface, and most of the mottled carpet – an orange-red shag pile – was stacked with piles of papers, books, and bits of machinery. As Virgo moved into the room, he saw they were mostly pieces of hard disk drives and other computer parts. Through an open door on the other side of the room, he could see into the kitchen, where a row of chocolate-brown melamine units was lined up against the far wall. Decades had been swallowed up inside these walls.

He turned back into the lounge. It wasn't entirely chaotic: an oak table by the window was clear of clutter. On it sat a laptop and a paperback-sized wireless internet router. Despite his surroundings, Born wasn't living completely in the past. Weird people, scientists. They could live without sanitation, but deny them fast internet access and they crumbled to dust.

Born reappeared in just two minutes, still buttoning up a red and black checked shirt. His baggy beige chinos were too long for his short legs, and rucked up at the ankles. He didn't offer Virgo a seat, but eyed him from the middle of the room, afloat on the detritus.

Virgo pulled the disk from his pocket. 'Gierek's death had something to do with this.' He swallowed. 'I think.'

'You think?'

'He was coming to get it from me.'

Born still hadn't moved. 'Laszlo . . .' he said.

It sounded like a reprimand, a sigh of frustration. He stepped across the room and took the disk from Virgo's hand.

'What's on it?' He inspected it front and back, but didn't remove it from the case.

'Nothing – at least, nothing readable. There's something strange about the data on it. It's . . .' What had Andy said? 'It's quantum-sized.'

Born looked up sharply, then handed the disk back and turned away. 'So? What's it got to do with me?'

'I think the disk has something to do with a quantum computer. Gierek called it an activator.'

That was meant to sound impressive, striding. It came out lame.

'Gierek had a disk too,' Virgo added. 'But whoever killed him took it.'

There was a long, uncomfortable silence before Born sighed and spoke again.

'Let me have another look at this disk,' he said, holding out his hand.

Virgo offered it again; Born took the disk and walked over to the laptop. He put the disk into the optical drive and pushed it shut.

'The quantum computer is a millstone around my neck,' Born muttered as the disk drive whirred into action. 'It took about two minutes to become an end in itself.'

He looked up and locked eyes with Virgo. 'A machine that can probe the strangest features of the universe. And someone turned it into a spy's tool. Do you have any idea how much money people have offered me to make the quantum computer work?'

Virgo shook his head.

'Have you ever paid for sex, Nathaniel?'

It took Virgo a moment to recover from the question. He shook his head again.

'Don't. That's my advice. Some things are too important to be about money.' Born grabbed a pencil from his desk and pressed its point into the tip of his index finger. 'Not once did I get an offer from someone interested in physics. Someone who wanted to find out what it means to exist.'

The laptop screen changed colour, and lit his face in the gloom. The rancour was gone.

'I only wish Laszlo . . .' Born paused. 'Sometimes people have their choices made for them. It can happen to any of us.' He looked up. 'Laszlo was brilliant, you know.'

'You knew him?'

'We worked on a couple of things together. It was years ago.'

Suddenly, Born snapped out of his reverie.

'Your disk is unreadable. I have no idea why Laszlo wanted it.'

That was it? Virgo slumped in disappointment. 'Could it be something to do with a quantum computer?'

Born didn't answer. He was looking down at the blank screen. He jabbed at a couple of keys, and then, without looking up, ejected the disk and handed it to Virgo.

Virgo took it, but stood still. How could this be? All the way here he'd convinced himelf: Born would figure the whole situation out. Without an answer, there was no story.

A minute later, Born looked up again; he seemed surprised to see Virgo still standing there.

'You should go: I can't help you. The other disk might be important, of course. But you don't have that, do you?' He stood up. 'Really. You should go. Now. I'm sorry, but this is your problem, not mine.'

He ushered Virgo out. Virgo offered no resistance.

'Don't come back,' Born said.

Suddenly, he was on the doorstep.

'Just one more thing,' Virgo said, holding a hand against the closing door. 'Does the name Alex Genovsky mean anything to you?'

The pressure on Virgo's hand eased, and Born looked him in the eye. He hesitated before he spoke. Virgo heard a hint of regret, maybe even pity, in his voice.

'It means you're in some very deep shit,' he said quietly.

The door slammed shut.

CHAPTER 19

VASIL MARINOV PUT THE receiver carefully down on its cradle. His mouth was set tight, his clear eyes burning into the wood-panelled wall opposite. He walked over to the window and stared out at the rain-strewn boats moored to the wharf. He had yet to get used to the grey of a Boston winter. Houston had suited him much better; working for NASA had its own difficulties, but at least, after a hard day at the keyboard, you could always have a drink in the sun.

Somewhere across that grey ocean, Laszlo Gierek was dead. Marinov felt nothing at the news: they'd had all they needed from Gierek now. Setting him up at Boston University had been easy; no one asked difficult questions back then. And the cachet Gierek had built up in the past couple of decades had swung numerous deals, brought in some serious money. It was a shame how things had ended, but Marinov had no regrets: Gierek had been a good investment, and now he had been cashed in.

Alex had reported in exactly on schedule, and would be heading back later today. There was still this one loose end to tie up, but that would be quick. It was only a matter of time. They had found Virgo, now that he'd switched his phone on. His cellphone number was just sitting there, on a business card lying on the dining table, Alex said. Tapping into these networks, locating the responding base stations and triangulating a position wasn't a challenge to Marinov's hacking skills. He had hacked into bigger, more secure systems than this.

The location put Virgo in Oxford. Why Oxford?

Daniel Born.

That was not good. Alex had mentioned Born yesterday, as a means of tracking down Gierek. Years before, Gierek and Born had worked together on a couple of projects; Gierek might well have tried getting in touch again. Or told Virgo to contact him.

Marinov drummed his fingers on the window glass. Daniel Born. Alex had tried to recruit Born for their network, but it hadn't worked out; they had nothing on him. Trafficking in minds rather than bodies was a great idea, but building up their portfolio of researchers always relied on having some kind of leverage.

Gierek had been easy: he had pleaded for the gangs to smuggle him out of Poland. He had even cried when he first told them about the price on his head. Two years of collaboration with the communists turned out to be too high a price to pay for bread to feed his family. He betrayed his colleagues, reporting those who tried to continue their work. Some of them had never made it out of prison.

Then Karol Wojtyla, the old Pope, came on the scene, and Jaruzelski started opening up the universities again, and emptying the prisons. Everything came out in the end, and Gierek's family disowned him. But Gierek hardened over the years: he never cried again. He told them he was fleeing Poland in shame, not fear. They didn't believe him, then or now, but he was a good business opportunity. They had taken everything Gierek owned, set him up in the US, and watched to see what might happen. Intellectual property was underrated in America back then.

Intellectual property – quite literally. They were about to

make the final killing from running Gierek. This was the big one; Marinov really had done it now. Back in Bulgaria, he'd been little more than a technician. He went out with the traffickers occasionally – he was there the night that priest had cut the scar into Alex's face – but mostly he did the planning, the logistics, getting the papers together for the shipments. Fifty women to Sofia. Thirty-five to Berlin. Fifteen across Europe into the UK. He was always going to be bigger than that, though. His little trafficking jobs on the side meant he had enough well-chosen people put by to set up on his own. And the day job, programming at the Pravets factory, didn't pay much, but it taught him what he needed to get onto NASA's books. When they came to Sofia looking for programmers, he was first in line. He was shipping out, with a viable business plan.

And leaving things in order. The records on his hard drive – his parting gift to the Bulgarian authorities as he flew out from Sofia – were enough to break the trafficking rings into tiny pieces. It meant they couldn't track him down, of course, but that wasn't the real reason he'd done it. The gangs had provided a living, but he never liked the way the leaders treated the women. They were so small-minded; they thought sex was the only valuable commodity. Really, he was a hero, and no one ever knew it.

Least of all Gierek. In some ways, Marinov was stunned at Gierek's ingratitude. The Pole was on borrowed time after the stunt with Radcliffe. It bothered him that he couldn't figure out what had gone on. What was it – one last attempt at redemption? Or was Gierek simply trying to pull Radcliffe in to give himself a plea bargain tool in case everything went wrong tomorrow?

Gierek to Radcliffe to Virgo. Then back to Gierek – Alex said the disk was in Gierek's pocket. But now Virgo was with Born. Why? What had Gierek told him? Still, they had time to sort this out. He could always lie to MacIntyre, tell him everything was taken care of. He'd been lying to MacIntyre

MICHAEL BROOKS

so long he had to check himself before he told him the truth these days. But Alex still had to be back for tomorrow night. It had to be perfect. There could be no loose ends when they were hooked into the White House and the planes started coming in.

Marinov sighed and walked back to his desk. There was something crass about the plan, something entirely lacking in imagination – as the pinnacle of his career, it was almost embarrassing. At least it wasn't his idea. And innovation was hardly necessary, he had to admit. They had been hired to push buttons at the White House; using the familiar threat, picking at the still-open wound of America's day of terror, was probably the easiest way to do that.

He picked up his phone, and stared at the picture filling the screen. She looked happy, this woman.

The Bluetooth connection had already sent the image to his computer. He opened up the fax software, punched in the number, then yawned as he added the Cuban hotel details to the cover page. Alex was right: it would be no trouble. It was a wise precaution. Just in case the husband caused a problem.

Gierek was dead. A couple more wouldn't make much difference.

CHAPTER 20

BORN DIDN'T ANSWER THE door again, despite the repeated drumming. Eventually, Virgo gave up and moved slowly down the path and through the gate. He leaned against the car in defeat, staring down at the disk in his hand.

'What have we got here?' He spoke at the plastic, as if the answer might be written into the case. He tried to think himself to an answer, but got nowhere. He was stuck with the disk, and a killer on his trail.

Maybe he should check his voicemail, find out if Charles had got the police involved or something. No, he wouldn't have. Not until he'd spoken to him. Maybe he should return his call now. Maybe he should go to the police now. Maybe . . .

Virgo looked up as he heard the cottage door open again. Born bundled out, and ran in a rapid, untidy shuffle down the path.

'Show me your phone,' he shouted, his eyes wide and intense. He flicked strands of hair from his face. 'You made a call from here, didn't you? Show it to me.'

Virgo pulled the phone from his pocket, and Born snatched it from his hand. He gave it a cursory inspection.

'It doesn't have location masking, does it?'

Virgo stared at him, blank. There were beads of sweat on Born's forehead.

'You made a phone call from right outside my house. You might as well have placed a *"We are here"* sign for Genovsky at the front gate.' He waved a hand wildly through the air.

'Get in the car. I've got to pack some things – I'll be two minutes.'

Born scurried back into the cottage, leaving the front door half-open. After a few seconds, Virgo could see his shadow flitting around one of the upstairs rooms.

What the hell had got into Born now?

Virgo headed up the path again, and pushed the front door wide open. He couldn't hear any sound.

'Hello?' he called. 'Born?' Cautiously, he climbed the stairs.

The front bedroom was a shock. It was tidy, neatly arranged. There was a dressing table, with make-up and a hairbrush sitting, waiting to be used. The double bed was faultlessly dressed with pink floral cushions and a white waffle bedspread. On the far side of the bed, a woman's dressing gown was draped over a rattan chair. And everything in the room was covered in a layer of fine dust. There had been a woman in Born's life. But not for a while.

Virgo was about to move across the landing to the room opposite when he heard the harsh crunch of tyres skidding to a halt on gravel.

He ran to the window.

A silver Mercedes, one of its front wings dented and scratched, had pulled up in front of his Ford. A tall rose bush obscured his view of the driver, but he didn't need to see. Virgo drew himself back behind the curtain, his heart drumming against his chest.

He heard a car door open, and leaned forward again. Through a gap in the leaves and thorns and flowers, he could just make out a hand on the garden gate. The air burned his lungs. His legs would not shift. It was all he could do to remain standing. He tried to imagine the scene downstairs, straining to remember the layout of the ground floor. He had left the front door wide open. If Gierek's killer came far enough into the house, he could slip out.

Where was Born?

Ten, maybe twenty seconds passed in silence.

There was a clatter of metal, the tumult of saucepans kicked across a floor.

The kitchen. Virgo's strength returned. He might be able to make it to the car. He checked for the miniature penknife he carried on his keyring. It was a cliché left over from his climbing days at university: always carry a blade – one day you'll have to cut the line.

That day was here. A slash to the Mercedes' tyres and he would be away. He didn't need to plan beyond that.

He edged towards the landing. He could see through the balustrade, down the stairs to the living room.

All clear. He was coiled, adrenaline keeping him on the edge.

He tested each step for a treacherous creak.

Almost there.

The door was still wide open. He could hear a quiet whimper now, punctuated by the occasional whispered threat. From the bottom of the stairs, craning his neck, Virgo could see into the kitchen. The killer was stooped over a hunched form. Born was kneeling on the linoleum floor, crying quietly. The pair were surrounded by cast iron kitchen pans; some had even spilled out into the living room.

A pistol barrel hovered over Born's head. The killer was whispering something, but Virgo couldn't make out the words. He crouched behind the balustrade and turned his head to the front door. He'd be able to get away unnoticed.

Born was shrewd; he had probably struck a deal already. He turned to look at the door, then towards the kitchen. That was when he saw it. There it was, lying on the floor between him and Gierek's murderer. It called to him.

He calculated the number of steps, the number of heartbeats between breaking cover and crashing that heavy pan against the killer's head. Three steps, a quiet pick-up and all the strength he could pull together.

He could do it.

Or he could run.

Virgo looked back at the sunlight creeping through the opening of the front door. The same three steps and he'd be on the path, heading for the gate.

He was hardly breathing, and his heart marked every half-second with a painful thump. Born was crying still. The whispers grew more intense. He heard the click of a safety catch. A glimpse of Laszlo Gierek, crashed out in his front room, flashed across his mind. What could he do?

Virgo tensed his jaw, and took fast, silent steps, crouching low.

Almost there.

He should have fled.

With a dull clink, his wedding ring clipped against the iron of the pan. He swung anyway.

The face was half-turned by the time the pan made contact. As he saw it, Virgo's brain screamed at him to pull back on the blow. But too late: he heard a loud crack as it registered in his consciousness that he was smashing a piece of heavy iron against a woman's skull. What was the sound? The splintering of her cheekbone? Or a shattered earring? She crumpled onto Born's upturned face, and Virgo followed her down, his momentum throwing him into the confusion of limbs and startled faces.

CHAPTER 21

ONLY TWO OF THE bodies got up. Virgo was first, eyes still wide with adrenaline. Then, two seconds later, the woman's body stirred. Born pushed it off from on top of him, and slowly, stiffly, rose to his feet. He wiped his tear-streaked face with a sleeve and pushed back his hair.

'Thank you, Nathaniel,' Born muttered. He looked down at the prone body. 'Is she dead?'

Virgo knelt down and felt for a pulse. His fingers were still trembling, but there was no missing the faint beat at her neck. 'No. Got any rope?'

Born moved through the kitchen and into the lean-to at the back of the house. He returned with a ball of thin cord.

'All I've got is garden twine.'

Virgo shrugged in response, took the twine and set about tying up the body. He felt a twist of awkwardness, a vague notion that he was violating her as they worked. She wore black, head to toe: a cashmere sweater, trousers and polished boots. He kept his eyes away from the violent bruise already flowering on her cheek. A long black leather coat trailed as they laid her out flat on her front. The label said *Armani*. He bound her hands behind her back and tied her feet together. The twine would be strong enough: he knew how to tie a knot. Born stood immobile above him, still snivelling every now and then.

'Help me move her,' Virgo said, standing up.

Together, they dragged her into the centre of the living room.

Virgo picked up the silver handgun from where it had fallen in the kitchen. He held it out to Born.

'Hold this. Carefully.'

Hurriedly, Virgo crouched down and searched her pockets while Born stood over them, the gun shaking in his hands. In the coat, Virgo found two ammunition clips, a phone with a built-in camera, a brown leather purse and a Mercedes key ring. The trousers contained some change and another key.

'What are you looking for?' Born said.

'The other disk.' Virgo sat back, away from the body. 'It's not here.'

They jumped as her phone began to ring. Transfixed by the low buzz, neither of them breathed. After three rings, the buzzing stopped.

'Look in the purse,' Born whispered, the gun still raised towards the prone body. 'See if there's any ID.'

It contained a thick wad of fifty- and twenty-pound notes. But nothing else.

They jumped again as the phone emitted a double tone. Whoever had called had left a message. Virgo grabbed it, inspected the screen, and hit a couple of buttons. He held it in front of his face so that Born could hear.

A robotic female voice announced that there was one new message. After a beep and a slight pause, it began. Virgo felt his heart stop.

'It's Vasil. I'm back in the office. Hope you're busy – Wheelan just asked me how things were going. I told him it's all being taken care of. I forwarded the photo and the details. That shouldn't be a problem. Gupta is being dealt with.'

There was another beep. Virgo hung up.

What the hell did all that mean?

He opened the phone again, hoping to find more information somewhere, anywhere. Numbers, directories. Nothing in the sent messages. Stored photos, calendar . . . he fumbled; he'd accidentally accessed the photos.

He nearly dropped the phone.

On the screen, slightly blurred, Rachel smiled out at him. It was the photo on her chest of drawers in the bedroom. In the original, he was kissing her cheek, but he had been cut out: Rachel was dead centre and filled the screen.

'Who's that?' Born was looking over his shoulder.

'Rachel,' Virgo said. 'My wife.' His voice was flat, disconnected from his racing mind.

Born handed Virgo the gun, picked up the Mercedes keys and moved across the living room towards the front door.

Virgo snapped back into the room. 'Where are you going?'

'To check the car,' Born said. 'We need that second disk.'

He stood over the motionless body and waited. It seemed like Born was outside for hours. He half-expected to hear a car start up, and Born never to return.

Why would this woman want a photograph of Rachel?

It wasn't hard to figure out. Vasil – whoever he was – had forwarded a photo to someone. They weren't just chasing him now. They were looking for Rachel too.

'It's not there.' Born was framed by the doorway, backlit so that Virgo couldn't see his face. Virgo felt nothing at the news.

'Maybe she got rid of it already,' Born said.

They stood in silence. He didn't care about the disk. The photo filled his thoughts. Everything was at stake now. If Rachel was a target, if Katie . . . everything had changed. There was a part of him that didn't mind being shot at for chasing a story. But Rachel and Katie – that was different. He couldn't let anything hurt them.

He pointed to the motionless body on the floor in front of him.

101

MICHAEL BROOKS

'So,' he said. 'What have we got here? Who is this?' He threw the question into the air, let it hover. Maybe it would come down, help him make the next move. Maybe it wouldn't.

Born shrugged. 'I'm not sure,' he said, clearing some papers from a chair by the fireplace. He sat down.

'But I'd say that it's Alexandra Genovsky.'

CHAPTER 22

BORN EYED THE PRONE body on his kitchen floor. 'I got a call a few years ago, from someone calling herself Alex Genovsky,' he said. 'She asked if I'd be interested in a private venture. Two days later, before I'd made up my mind, Laszlo called me and told me to turn it down. He wouldn't say why, but he seemed to know something. I trust – I trusted – Laszlo. I never got back to her.'

Virgo stared down at Alexandra Genovsky, trying to put the pieces together.

'Gupta?' he said eventually.

'Akshay Gupta. I've never met him, but he's a professor at Cambridge.'

'What about Wheelan?'

'Never heard of him.'

Virgo handed Born the gun. 'I'm going to Cambridge,' he said. 'I don't know what that message meant, but I need to find out what Gupta knows about all this. Maybe he can help. I'll be back in a couple of hours.'

He stepped towards the front door.

'I'd be amazed if Gupta knows anything about this,' Born said.

Virgo turned himself around slowly. 'What do you mean?'

'The entanglement. Between the disks.'

What the hell was he talking about?

'You said the data was quantum-sized. Think about it, Nathaniel. Gierek hands his friend what he calls an activator disk. It's unreadable. And then he's so desperate to get it back he gets himself killed in the process. And it turns out he's got another disk in his pocket all along. My guess is that neither disk works without the other. Maybe it's a way of hiding data.'

'But how could the disks activate each other?'

'If it's really quantum computing we're talking about, the disks activate each other by entanglement. Fragile connections between quantum particles. Surely you've heard of entanglement? Jesus, I thought you were a science reporter?'

Virgo ignored the insult. 'Einstein hated the idea, said it was impossible.'

'But it's not: it's written into the equations of quantum theory.' Born hesitated. 'Maybe the data on the activator disk is entangled with the data on the other disk. Maybe it allows you to read it. If we had them both, we might be able to tell.'

'There are easier ways of hiding data, surely?'

'Maybe. But what's your explanation for this whole situation?'

Born seemed fidgety, suddenly alive: 'Does Alex know there are two disks?' he said.

Virgo shrugged. Was Born taking too many leaps? He certainly seemed to have thought this through. But there were lots of maybes in there.

'It all just seems too far-fetched to me. You just said yourself that entanglement is fragile. If it's so fragile, how come Gierek got it to work between these disks?' Virgo hesitated before pronouncing the next thought. He didn't want to say it. But it had to be said.

'So you think Gierek's built a working quantum computer?'

Born raised his eyebrows. 'Possibly. I'm not sure it's quite that simple. But you tell me why else Akshay Gupta is – what was it? *Being dealt with.*'

Virgo frowned. 'What does Gupta do?'

'Quantum cryptography.'

'What's that?'

Born stared like he couldn't believe Virgo had to ask. 'It's a means of hiding information in the quantum states of light. You entangle the photons holding the data, and fire them out through a standard optical fibre, or whatever. Because the entanglement link is so fragile, any eavesdropper leaves a clear trail in the data, like a fox tramping through virgin snow. Even a quantum computer can't break in.'

Virgo absorbed the information without reaction. Gupta's being *dealt with*? What did that mean?

Born answered his unspoken question. 'I've always said it's the quantum cryptography guys who should be the most scared. People – good people and bad people – don't like unbreakable encryption. It puts everything off kilter, destroys the natural balance.' He held up his hands in surrender. 'All I'm saying is that, if I had a quantum computer, I'd want Gupta dealt with too.'

That was it. He had to go. He took the wad of banknotes – just in case. In case of what? To bribe Gupta? It didn't matter. He wrote down his mobile phone number for Born, then turned as he stood at the front door, and motioned towards the unconscious woman.

'If she wakes up, you'll just have to slug her again,' he said. 'I'll be back in a couple of hours. Three at the most.' He paused. 'I have to find out what Gupta knows.'

'Want me to have a look at the other disk again while you're gone?'

Virgo shook his head. He was already at the door. 'I might need to show it to Gupta.'

As he closed the car door, Virgo reached for his phone and called directory enquiries.

'University of Cambridge, Cavendish Laboratory.'

The wait was excruciating.

'Akshay Gupta, please.'

Another wait.

Voicemail.

Who else could he call? Andy would know nothing about this stuff. Should he call Charles? The photo of Rachel came back into his mind. Not yet. There was too much at stake. Best keep it small, keep it manageable. He wasn't out of his depth. Not yet.

He had to go and find Gupta, whatever it took. He flipped the phone shut. Should he turn it off? No, Genovsky was under control, and Born might need to reach him. Virgo set his right foot to the floor and pulled the car away.

CHAPTER 23

HE DROVE WITH THE fastest of the traffic, anxiously scanning ahead for police patrol cars. A check on the licence plates would be the last thing he needed. There was a dead body in his front room, in plain view. Genovsky had sent a picture of his wife to someone. He hoped Mercer had never made that call to the police. He needed some time.

It was raining again: grey November drizzle. He hated winter. That was one of the very many good reasons for spending a week in Cuba about now. Thank God, Rachel and Katie would still be safely airborne, and they'd be thousands of miles away from this mess by the time they landed. That was something, at least.

How had this happened? How the hell had he got involved with the kind of people who would build a quantum computer and then kill anyone who found out about it? Could Born be right about the disks?

No, it was still too ridiculous. There was a perfectly obvious, simple explanation: there had to be. One that explained why Radcliffe was now lying in a Baltimore morgue. And why Gierek was lying dead in a front room in Richmond. Quite a trail. And leading right to his front door. He really did not want to get stopped by the police just now. He turned on the radio, just in case there was any news he should be aware of. A man shot dead in a Richmond living room, perhaps.

Entanglement between the disks could work in theory, he could see that. It was just the practice that seemed ludicrously difficult. You would have to get the molecules of plastic in the data layer of the disk to interact somehow during their formation. Maybe Gierek could do that. Who knew?

Alexandra Genovsky, that's who. He had to find out what he could from Gupta, and then get back.

Gupta is being dealt with. What the hell did that mean?

The radio announcer was running through the headlines of the three o'clock news as Virgo approached the west side of Cambridge. He wasn't in the headlines, at least. Just ahead of him, beyond the cranes towering above the steel frames of two half-finished research blocks and the sleek shell of Microsoft's new outpost, lay the low, stepping rise of the Cavendish Laboratory. A strange sense of fond remembrance flooded over him. In another life, he could still be working here. Everything would be different, if only he had made different choices, nurtured his academic side. The sand-cement blockwork looked ancient and dependable, part of the landscape. He had enjoyed studying here; why had he given up the opportunities it brought?

Because he was born for journalism, not academia. He had no regrets. Even now, with all hell rolling around his life, he wouldn't change anything about his past.

Virgo swung the car into the closest parking space to the entrance. A large blue plaque declared the space reserved for the director of research, but he had no time for protocols now.

He paused in the lobby, and studied the building plan. Gupta's office was only a short run over a raised walkway, past the library, and down a corridor on the right. His labs were deeper in the building. Virgo went for the office.

There was no answer to his insistent rapping on the door.

After two minutes, he gave up. Gupta could be in his lab. Again, he ran. As he turned the first corner, he knocked into two students and sent a flurry of books into the air. He shouted an apology, but kept running.

He crashed into the lab door, pushed it open, and stood in the doorway panting. Four faces looked up at him. Two were bent over a mess of wires and circuit boards; the other two were sat in front of a whiteboard littered with equations. None of them said anything.

'I'm looking for Akshay,' he said, drawing breath. They looked at each other. Eventually, one of the people, an Indian man sitting at the electronics bench, spoke. 'Is something wrong?'

'I just need to talk to him,' Virgo said. 'I'm Nathaniel Virgo. I'm a journalist.' He extended a hand to the man.

'Kumar Changani.'

The tension in the faces eased. 'We haven't seen him,' Changani said. 'He said he'd be in today. You're the second person to come here looking for him. Has he forgotten an appointment?'

Virgo's stomach dropped.

'Who was the other one?' he said, trying to keep his voice level. 'The other person, I mean.'

'I didn't catch his name. He was from a company interested in licensing our crypto system. Said he had an appointment with Akshay. There was nothing in the diary, though. I called Akshay's home but got no answer.'

'Do you have any idea where Akshay might be?' Virgo looked around. All the faces were blank.

'If he comes back, or you hear from him, can you get him to call me?' He dug into a pocket and handed over a business card. 'On my mobile. I won't be in the office.'

He turned, then turned back. Might as well ask.

'Is it possible someone could have built a quantum computer?'

Changani smiled, then shook his head.

'Then how come someone wants to license your cryptography system? I mean, there's only one reason to go that far, isn't there?'

Changani hesitated for a moment. 'Well, I suppose you would want to use quantum crypto if you were paranoid. Then, if someone did develop a quantum computer, you'd still be safe. But if I wanted to find out your secrets that badly, I wouldn't wait for a quantum computer. There are much easier ways. You find someone who will give you the passwords. Or you hack in; someone's always left some part of the system on its factory settings, even in high-security networks.'

'So what's the point of quantum cryptography? You're not a great salesman, Kumar.'

'The point?' Changani shrugged, then smiled again. 'It's fun to work on. And it makes people feel better. It's always good to know you've done everything you can.'

That was it? *That* was the cutting edge of crypto-reasoning: the feelgood factor?

'Thanks.'

'No problem.' Changani raised a hand in farewell. 'I'll call you if I hear from Akshay.'

Virgo backed out of the lab and shut the door. Where now? Back to Born's? Or wait for Gupta to show up? He couldn't afford the wait if it was going to be fruitless. If Genovsky's people had got to Gupta already, there was no point hanging around. And Rachel? He had to get back and face his worst fears.

Virgo was just getting into the car as his phone rang. He looked at the screen. It was an Oxford number.

'Hello? Born?'

'No, Mr Virgo. He's not here any more.' The voice was rich, the accent strange and luxurious. 'This is Alexandra Genovsky. Where are you, exactly?'

CHAPTER 24

THE VOICE IN HIS ear hollowed him, scooped out his guts. What had happened? Where was Born? He was on his own. Again.

Time to step up. He could do this. He could handle Alexandra Genovsky.

'I'm in Cambridge, Ms Genovsky. Learning some very useful things about this disk that Paul Radcliffe gave me. You know – the *other* one?'

There was the slightest hesitation before she spoke again. She was having to think. Virgo's guts started to make their way back into his belly.

'I need you to come to Heathrow airport. I have a plane to catch, and I need that disk,' she said.

'Where's Born?'

'Maybe we could talk about that when you meet me at Heathrow. Terminal Four, at the departures gate. I've no doubt you'll recognise me. And I'll certainly recognise you from that lovely photo of you and your wife – Rachel, isn't it? She's very beautiful.' Genovsky paused. 'But Cuba is a very dangerous place, you know. Anything could happen to her there.'

She waited for a reply, but Virgo couldn't find his voice.

'I'll give you an hour and a half to get there,' she said.
The line went dead.

Virgo started the engine and pulled out of the car park. It was just starting to get dark. He focused on keeping himself moving along the road. The clarity would come back to his mind eventually. He needed a plan: he had to have a guarantee that Rachel and Katie were safe. Did Genovsky know about Katie? She hadn't mentioned her. What difference did it make? They would be together: if anything happened to Rachel, it would happen to Katie too. He felt sick.

He had to assume Born was dead. Maybe the twine couldn't hold her, and Genovsky overpowered him. If so, she wouldn't hesitate to kill him. That would be three bodies. He should go to the authorities now. They could meet Rachel and Katie off the plane, take them into safe custody.

And what if they didn't believe him? He had already lied to the security services, or whoever it was that Frank Delaney was working with. And two, probably three, people were dead now, and he had been at the scene each time. Was there any reason for them to believe he hadn't done it?

He had to meet Genovsky, at least – make sure Rachel and Katie were left out of this mess. Maybe then there'd be a way for him to walk away too.

He shook his head. Who was he kidding? Genovsky was bound to want everything clean – no survivors. If there was a quantum computer, he already knew far too much for Genovsky to allow him to live.

He closed his eyes, just for a second, to expunge the thought from his chattering mind.

He'd worry about that when Rachel and Katie were safe.

CHAPTER 25

GABRIEL MACINTYRE HISSED INTO the phone. He knew he couldn't be overheard; the Red Spot corporation had rewarded him with a corner office, a spectacular view over Boston, and the soundproofing was, of course, excellent – it was designed to keep the vice-president's business safe from prying ears. Their competitors could buy off junior staff too easily; no one could be trusted.

But he kept his voice down anyway: it helped him stay calm. If he couldn't control himself, what hope did he have of controlling anyone else?

'I don't care. I want him dead. Now.'

It wouldn't happen. Marinov seemed intent on finding out what Virgo knew first.

MacIntyre felt bile rise into his throat. What was there to be gained? Nathaniel Virgo might already know about the entanglement software. He wanted Virgo dead. One hole was all it would take.

The power, the potential that this quantum computer possessed – it was so much more than the sum of its parts. He liked the entanglement, it felt like a friend these days, safe and reliable and the source of good things. But it was bringing bad company. The quantum computer, the cipher-smashing power it created, was too much. It was all spinning out of control.

MacIntyre turned his burning gaze out of the window. Here, from the fifteenth floor, the city looked so small. Even the roadworks ranged along the ribbon of road before the sea looked insignificant. Only the Old State House stood out. The city's corporations had tried to get it demolished; they needed to fill the space with another tower. But they had failed; this was where the city first heard the Declaration of Independence. So they tried to bury it, lose it among the rise of the surrounding skyscrapers. But it was still there, speaking, goading. It was crowded by the skyscrapers, but its gold tower still managed to throw light over the surrounding streets. It was beautiful, anachronistic here among all this steel and glass. Somehow it caught the sun, drawing the eye, pulling at passers-by like a nagging conscience. The site of the Boston massacre. How times had changed; five people dead hardly constituted a massacre these days.

Jennie smiled out at him from the photo on his desk. He had her image on his computer's desktop too. He flicked the mouse, and the Red Spot screensaver disappeared, revealing her dark eyes and toothy grin. He tried to carry her with him into work – inside his head, on cheesy snapshots, even on his key ring. But she seemed somehow unreal once he sat behind this vast slab of mahogany. Here, his purpose was to push up profits, shave the bottom line. Business 101, second lesson: you served at the shareholders' pleasure. You couldn't serve both your daughter and the shareholders.

So you compartmentalised. He couldn't even summon up any guilt, sitting here. There was no guilt in the office, just a pathological compulsion to complete the next task. The stuff he should feel guilty about – the stuff that hounded him around the house, in the presence of Barbie, and Jennie's dressing-up clothes – had no power over him here. Sometimes he felt like a corporate Clark Kent. Red Spot's rising star and – when he allowed it to surface –

human being. Husband and father, neighbour and friend.

But Marinov didn't give a shit about his worries. The disconnection tone droned in MacIntyre's ear, and he put the receiver down. He wasn't being entirely selfish. He had done some checks, and he suspected that this Virgo guy had never meant to become involved in their project. But now that he was, he'd be better off dead.

CHAPTER 26

DRIVING BACK INTO HEATHROW, Virgo felt a daze descend over him like mist. The earlier trip seemed unreal: in another life he had waved Rachel and Katie off, thinking he would see them again within hours, maybe a day or two at most. Now – now, in this life – he might not see them again at all. It was unthinkable; the cliché was true. This was what happened to other people.

He put his Ford in the long-term parking but knew he wasn't coming back for it. He had a passport, a fistful of cash and the disk. Everything else was surplus to requirements. He felt a raindrop on the back of his neck as he got out of the car. Overhead, the sky was dark.

The shuttle bus to the terminal building took twenty minutes to arrive, and Virgo huddled in the dark shelter with four other travellers, watching the rain drip down on the grey-green ash trees that bordered the vast car park.

Alexandra Genovsky was waiting for him at departures, just as she said. Her mouth was formed into the thin, distant smile that emerges from a face familiar with pain. The bruise he had inflicted was darkening. Even though the thick layer of newly applied blusher concealed the full extent of its fury, it was obvious that the discoloration would continue for days yet.

'How are you, Virgo?' she said. The smile stayed, forced, on her lips.

'I'm all right,' he said. 'You?'

'I have to say, my face hurts.'

She broadened her smile, her eyes dull and cold. They were a rich hazel, with flecks of forest green. But when he looked into them, he noticed that the pupils were perfectly black: black holes, pulling in the light.

'Thank you for leaving the number for your wife's hotel in your home,' she said. 'It certainly made things easier.'

Virgo didn't return the smile. He was thinking too hard. He needed information. He needed her guard down.

'I have the disk. But how do I know you'll leave my wife alone if I give it to you?' He wasn't going to mention Katie until Genovsky did. 'What's on the disks? Something you can't live without? Do you really need both of them?'

Her face set hard. The movement pulled her cheek taut, and Virgo noticed a line of scar tissue behind the blusher and the bruising. It was a long curve running from one eye, down her cheek to the corner of her mouth. She watched his eyes follow the contour, and ignored his question.

'Are you wondering what damage you did to me?' she said. The anger passed, and she looked amused again. 'You held back, didn't you? Just at the last minute. When you saw I was a woman.'

She was dancing round him, like a featherweight boxer. Virgo looked up at the screens showing departures information. 'Where are you going?'

'It's not Cuba, if that's what you're thinking. I have people there to take care of business.'

'You have people? Or Vasil has people?'

Her eyes flashed at him. He had landed a punch there. He was doing OK.

'Who is Vasil? What exactly is going on? How do I get my wife out of this?'

117

The scar on Genovsky's cheek shivered. 'And your daughter, of course?'

Right back at him. The gloves were off.

She leaned in towards him. 'Nathaniel Virgo, you don't understand what you are into here.'

There it was. That was what he had been waiting for. Despite her better judgement, she wanted to destroy him right now, drain the fight out of him by allowing him to see the magnitude of what was going on. But he was stronger than she knew. She would simply be laying herself bare by giving him the information he wanted.

If he played it right.

'Try me.' Would she bite? She bit.

Genovsky lowered her voice. 'There's going to be a hijack. We have been asked to demonstrate just how vulnerable the United States still is.'

'Who's we?' He hesitated for a moment. What was the name on the phone message? 'Is Wheelan involved?'

Genovsky furrowed her brow, ever so slightly. And he couldn't tell why. Because she didn't know how he knew the name?

She said nothing. He had to move this along.

'This hijack – how does that work, exactly? Have you hired a bunch of terrorists? You don't seem the type.'

Genovsky raised her eyebrows and forced out a laugh. 'Now, come on, Virgo, I have to keep something to myself.' She focused in on him. 'So, what's it to be? Are you going to give me that disk?'

'Are you going to tell me what it's for? Do you even know? Or are you just your boss's courier service?'

She didn't flinch.

'Look, Virgo, you didn't mean to get into this, and there's no reason for your family to die. Do the right thing and save those close to you. A bunch of strangers on a plane don't matter to you. Give me the disk, and I will set your wife and your daughter free.'

It was his turn to force a laugh. 'Oh, come on. Why would you set them free when you have the disk? You'll kill me, then them, and everything will be tidy.' He paused. 'I might as well go to the authorities now.'

She smiled again. They were still dancing, circling. 'Yes, you could go to the authorities now,' she said. 'You could go with what I've told you, and be safe in the knowledge that your family died in a worthy cause. Maybe. Of course, it's not clear that anyone would believe your story in time to stop things. Not with all the bodies piling up in your wake. And it's not clear the UK authorities would be able to do anything to stop our action anyway. Our command comes from very high up, you know. We really do consider this worth doing.'

'Who's we?'

She ignored the question and focused her stare on him. 'Do you want me to give you a sliding scale? Let you know how many people we are going to kill? Would you sacrifice your wife and your daughter to save the lives of a dozen strangers? A hundred? A few hundred? How many would it take? How many people's lives are your family worth? Shall we see if we can reach an agreement?'

Bitch. This was going nowhere.

'There's no way you'll get away with this,' he said. 'They'll know about this without me. The authorities, the intelligence services, they'll be all over you. They will never let you get away with something like this.'

That smile again. 'You really haven't been listening. In this game, we *are* the authorities.' She paused. 'So what are you going to do?'

'I'm not bargaining with you.'

'Then give me the disk,' she muttered. Her eyes flicked to a pair of armed policemen thirty metres across the hall. 'You're making us look suspicious. It's time to move on, Nathaniel.'

Why had she suddenly used his first name? What had changed?

'I don't think so, Alexandra,' he said. He looked over his shoulder at the policemen, then grabbed her hand and squeezed it hard. 'We're just lovers failing to settle our differences before we part. You *are* worried about the authorities, aren't you? On this side of the Atlantic, at least. It would be a shame if they got the disk *and* you and me, wouldn't it? Where are you going, Alex? Maybe I could bring you the disk when I know my family is safe.'

Virgo turned. The policemen were looking directly at him. He pulled out the disk, and motioned towards them.

'Or I could . . .'

She grabbed him before he finished the sentence, his cheeks between her palms. The force of her kiss took him by surprise, and Virgo found himself returning its intensity before it occurred to him to pull away. Genovsky stole a glance at the policemen again, then set her empty eyes back on Virgo.

'I'm going to Boston,' she said. '1629 Atlantic Avenue, Suite 31, on the harbourfront. I will keep them alive until tomorrow at midday. Get the disk to me by then, and I'll make sure they stay alive a little longer.'

She waved, smiled, turned and disappeared through the departures gate.

Virgo forced himself not to look at the police again. Had he won that round?

No.

But he'd bought himself a few more hours.

The woman at the United counter didn't even glance up at his request for a seat on their next flight to Boston. If he could get through security fast enough, he would make it onto Genovsky's plane. But first he had to buy some clothes and luggage. He couldn't afford to raise anyone's suspicion.

Genovsky's cash was more than enough to buy what he needed: an economy-class ticket, a travel bag, a few odds and ends – a phone charger, a toothbrush, a couple of magazines to avoid looking like he was travelling suspiciously light – and two complete changes of clothing. He chose plain clothes: beige and grey and no labels. Maybe he would even wear them. At the moment, that was what his half-formed plan demanded. Tomorrow morning, when he had to fit in with the students at Boston University campus and find a way into Laszlo Gierek's laboratory, he would look just like the real thing.

CHAPTER 27

RACHEL VIRGO LIFTED HER sunglasses and looked around. All the clichés were there: flawless sky, shimmering turquoise ocean, swaying palm trees, white sand. It was just starting to get dark, and salsa music blasted out from a streetside bar behind them.

'Well, what do you think?' she asked her daughter.

Katie looked up at her. 'It's pretty nice,' she said. 'Better than Brighton.'

Rachel laughed and lifted a hand to shield her eyes from the last glare of sunset. A passing Chevrolet honked at them, and the driver waved, holding up his hands.

'You need a ride, my ladies?'

They shook their heads and he pulled off into a dusty side road. Rachel's eyes followed the car. The engine was misfiring from time to time, and the tailpipe belched an acrid smoke. Seconds later, however, the air smelled of sea and spices again. Plenty of Europeans were shuffling along the strip, but they didn't spoil the place. The locals were obviously accustomed to their perpetual presence, and hardly anyone had tried to sell them anything. Rachel looked at her watch. 'Shall we go back and unpack? Or do you want to get something to drink first?'

Katie jumped up from the sand. 'Let's go and have a drink. Can I try a mojito?'

Rachel laughed. 'No chance. You can have some wine with dinner, but you're not drinking in any bars. Anyway, I thought you were in training?'

Katie sunk her hands into the pockets of her long skirt and headed towards the market square. Rachel followed, watching her daughter's walk. Nat was right; you could hardly tell most of the time.

Nat was so desperate for Katie to be normal. When he'd called Rachel from the hospital, he kept telling her it was his fault. She was going to lose her leg, and it was his fault. His editor had him chasing a story; he had texted Katie, told her he'd be late meeting her. But he'd been late for a thousand meetings before that one. It wasn't like Nat needed encouragement to chase down a story; Katie knew better than that. She would have shrugged, carried on chatting to her friends, meandering around at the mall. That she crossed the road at the exact time the lunatic flew through the lights – that wasn't Nat's fault. That was how life worked. Or didn't.

The chaos of bodies forced them to amble, hardly moving, through the main shopping street. The guidebooks said street crime was almost non-existent, but Rachel had the Londoner's habit and occasionally put a hand to her shoulder to pull on the straps of her daypack. How long did it take to get out of that state of vigilance and unease? she wondered. A few hours? A few days? When did you finally consider yourself relaxed?

'What d'you think, Mum?' Katie held a brown leather purse in front of Rachel's face. 'Shall I buy it? It's really cheap.'

Rachel glanced over the stall. There were all kinds of goods: bags, wallets, bracelets and purses, all beautifully crafted. The leather filled the air with a rich scent. 'We're here for a week, sweetheart. You don't have to decide today.'

Katie hesitated, then put the purse back. 'You're right.'

God, that was easy. Katie was obviously in a good mood.

The stallholder came out from behind his table and smiled. '*Americana? Inglesa?* I'll give you good price, beautiful lady.' He nodded at Rachel. 'You too. You two beautiful ladies. You are sisters, yes? I can do good price for beautiful sisters. What you want to pay?'

Katie laughed. 'Tomorrow,' she said. 'We'll come back tomorrow.'

'Come. One hundred pesos. Good price.'

They walked away, and the price dropped to fifty. Two steps later, it was thirty. They both laughed as they heard it drop to twenty-five.

They wandered up the Avenida Primera. The bars they passed all looked the same, and Rachel peered hesitantly into each one before moving on to the next. Eventually, Katie dragged her into a dimly lit room with *El Galéon* written above the door. They sat at an empty table facing the street.

'Mojitos?' The waiter, dressed in a red cotton shirt, startling white chinos, and flip-flop sandals, was tall and attractive. His glance shifted between them.

'Bit early for me,' Rachel said. '*Agua mineral con gas, por favor.* Katie?'

Katie looked up and beamed at the waiter.

'Mojito,' she said.

'No.' Rachel pointed at her daughter, then looked up at the waiter. 'Coca-Cola.'

The waiter paused for a second, smiled slyly at Katie, then walked slowly towards the bar.

'It was worth a try,' Katie said with a smile. 'Anyway, I think he fancied you.'

Rachel didn't bother to reply. When would Nat get here?

A couple of minutes later, the waiter returned with their drinks. He smiled at Katie again. It was obvious to Rachel that she was going to have to keep her daughter on a tight leash. At least until her father got here to take his share of the responsibilities.

She swilled her water, rattling the ice round the glass. Her feet were tapping to the rhythms pounding from the speakers above the door. Across the street, two children dressed in faded T-shirts and over-long shorts were dancing, shuffling their feet around the dusty pavement and clutching at imaginary partners. Their timing and footwork were impeccable, though passing chickens occasionally got caught up in their swirling rumba, and a well judged kick would interrupt the flow of intricate steps.

Twilight was closing in on them. The air was still and hot, but Rachel felt a shiver pass down her back. 'Come on,' she said, eventually. 'Let's go back and get unpacked. Maybe your dad's left a message at the hotel.'

Katie drained her glass, and they both got to their feet. Rachel walked out behind Katie as her daughter turned in the doorway. It took her a moment to realise that Katie's coy wave and even coyer smile was directed towards their waiter.

Rachel hoped to God that Nat was already on his way.

CHAPTER 28

'WELL, LOOK WHO'S HERE.'

Genovsky was in business class, staring at the map on her LCD screen. The white silhouette of the plane was flashing over the coast of Greenland. She seemed lost in thought, and it took a moment before Virgo's words registered and she lifted her face up towards his.

'Don't look so surprised,' he said. Confidence, he told himself again, as he had when walking up the aisle towards her. Confidence would be the key. 'There's not so many planes to Boston, and I didn't want to be late.' Virgo motioned to the empty seat next to her. 'Mind if I sit down?'

Genovsky said nothing, and he sat. A flight attendant in a pencil skirt eyed him with suspicion. He smiled at her, then at Genovsky.

'Do we have anything more to talk about?' Genovsky said. She flashed a glance at him. Something in her eyes looked nervous now, like he was too close, and had pierced her defences. Her features, the contours of her cheekbones, were sharp, but there was a sadness there too.

'Genovsky – what is that? Czech?'

'Bulgarian,' she said. 'But I'm an American citizen now.'

'Congratulations.'

She smiled, but the smile was only on her lips. Her eyes had gone back to just sucking in the light.

'Are you a terrorist?'

'The less you know about me, the more chance there is that I will let you walk away.'

'You're going to let me walk away, then?'

'That's not what I said, Nathaniel.' She took a breath. 'Do you know what's on the disk you have?'

'No. But tell me about the entanglement. It sounds fascinating.'

She looked at him, eyes narrowed.

'I've told you enough already. Give me the disk now, Nathaniel. Ignorance can be bliss.'

'Is bliss,' he said. 'Ignorance *is* bliss. But good use of idiom.' He needed more. 'OK. Just tell me this,' he said. 'Did Laszlo Gierek ever tell anyone else he had created entanglements on a disk? I mean, it's a hell of an achievement. How did he keep it to himself?'

Genovsky scowled. 'He didn't. He told Paul Radcliffe. And you know what happened to him.' Her gaze was fixed on him. 'Wheelan gave the order for that himse–' She pulled up, and her voice dropped. 'There's no protection for you, Nathaniel. The best you can do is save your family.'

Wheelan – that name again. He turned his head to look at her. There was no trace of deception on her face. That would have to do. It wasn't bad, considering. She knew about the entanglement, and she seemed convinced it was real. Now all he needed was some time. And to know who the hell Wheelan was.

Genovsky sat forward in the seat. 'Why don't we bring this to a close now? Give me the disk and it will all go away.'

It was his turn to smile. 'Oh, come on, Alexandra. We both know the disk I have is the only thing stopping you from murdering my wife and daughter.' The words hissed out slowly, like overpressure gradually released. 'Like you murdered Laszlo Gierek.'

'Was Gierek a friend of yours?'

The question deflated his hostility as he glanced out of the window. 'No,' he said, 'I didn't know him at all.'

'Well, I considered him a friend.'

Virgo turned his head back towards her in surprise. 'But you killed him anyway?'

Her gaze pierced him, reaching through him to the window behind. She hesitated before she spoke.

'I had my orders. I had no choice. Laszlo gave me no choice.'

'There's always a choice.'

He felt her gaze move off him, like a searchlight swinging away into darkness.

'That's what I used to think, too,' she said. Her voice was suddenly melancholy. 'But it's not true.'

She was staring out through the window again. This conversation was over now, he could tell. He stood up.

'I've learned a thing or two today, Alexandra,' he said. 'But let's talk some more tomorrow.'

She didn't bother to reply. She didn't even turn her head. Virgo moved back up the aisle towards his seat. Tomorrow was going to be a hell of a day. But he could still pull this off.

CHAPTER 29

THE CLICK AND HISS of sprinklers calmed the simmering air. The lawns of the Hotel Los Delfines were perfectly manicured, dotted with tall, lush palms and threaded with white gravel paths. It felt exotic and decadent to Rachel, who nodded at the gate concierges in their red and white uniforms and then ambled through the gates towards the front entrance. She'd been uneasy about coming to Cuba. In the end she had agreed to come here, hand over her tourist dollars, because she'd heard about the suffering the US trade embargo had caused. She read the newspapers, she knew how screwed up the American attitude to Cuba was. But she had reservations about visiting a revolutionary communist state for a beach holiday. No one was starving but plenty of people were hungry. Not that it was Castro's fault, exactly. But somehow, the two didn't seem to fit together.

Their suite was on the second floor, with a balcony overlooking the beach. Katie headed for the stairs, but Rachel veered towards the reception desk. 'I'm just going to see whether your father has left a message,' she said. 'You've got a key, haven't you?'

Katie pulled a white plastic card-key from her pocket, waved it at her mother, then disappeared up the stairs.

Typical. She wouldn't even take the lift. To Katie, everything was a challenge to be overcome.

There was no message from Nat. Rachel thought about taking the lift herself, but decided it wasn't worth the wait, not for two flights of stairs.

As she approached the door to the suite, she slid the daypack from her back and opened the zip pocket where she had stowed the key. The plastic slid in and out of its slot with a soft click, and she pushed down on the handle and opened the door.

'Nothing,' she called, walking down the hallway towards the living room. 'You would have thought he'd try to call, at least.'

Through the balcony windows she could see the dark twinkling of night falling on a moonlit ocean. The silhouette of a sailboat sat on the fading horizon.

There was no reply, and the living room was empty. Katie must be in her room, unpacking – or daydreaming about that waiter. Rachel paused, unsure whether to knock on the door, or leave her to it. Best to leave her, just for a moment. She stepped onto the balcony, and looked down at the white sand beyond the palm trees. The evening smelled of flowers and wood smoke; someone had lit a fire on the beach.

Where was Nathaniel? Was he somewhere in that perfect sky? She took a deep draught of the cooling air.

She heard a door open. 'Are you hungry, sweetheart?' she said, still staring at the ocean. 'We could go downstairs to the restaurant if you like.' She turned around. 'Or . . .'

Rachel's voice trailed off. She was staring into the blackened muzzle of a handgun. She couldn't pull her gaze to focus on the man holding it. She was aware only of the smell of tobacco and the blur, far behind the barrel of the gun, of a dark face topped by wavy black hair.

'Rachel?' he said. His voice was thin, reedy. She managed to look at him. He was holding a mobile phone, open, and flicking his eyes back and forth from her face to its screen. He snapped the phone shut and smiled. 'Rachel Virgo,' he said. 'It *is* you. Welcome to Cuba.'

They stood, warily watching each other for maybe thirty seconds. Rachel examined his face. It was thin and long, like his tall, wiry body. His clothes were smart but not distinctive: a white shirt and beige slacks. The tasselled tan leather moccasins on his feet looked expensive. He was around forty-five years old. It was hard to tell.

Usually Rachel could read people, see their motivations, tell what they were like. But he confused her. He was pointing a gun at her, and his eyes were calm – peaceful, even. She had seen London traffic wardens more cut up about giving out parking tickets.

'Sit down, yes?' He flicked the gun barrel towards the sofa. Slowly, eyes fixed on his face, she shuffled across the room and sat.

'Where is my daughter?' Rachel's stomach was falling towards the centre of the earth, but she kept control of her voice. Getting hysterical was not going to help.

He nodded towards the bedrooms. 'In there. With my colleague.'

So there were two of them. Her panic deepened, but she controlled it, taking a breath. Somehow Rachel knew, maybe from one of those ridiculous survival programs Nat occasionally watched on TV, that she had to engage him if she was to survive this. They had to be two human beings in conversation. She couldn't just be his victim.

'What's your name?' she asked.

'You don't need to know my name.'

But you know mine, she thought. How? And why did he have her photo on his phone?

'You have my name,' she said. 'Tell me yours. It will help us to talk.'

The gun never wavered, but the man rubbed his thumb down over his moustache.

131

'Vicente,' he said.

She was winning. She could handle this.

'And what do you want, Vicente? Money?'

He laughed. 'Money? No. I do not want money. Not from you.'

'Then what?'

'I want you to do what I tell you. That will be best for everybody. We are going to stay here for a little while. Then . . . then we will see.'

'My daughter. Katie. Is she OK?'

'She is fine. She is tied up, and she have . . . ah . . .' – he wiped a hand across his mouth – '. . . She does not talk.'

'Tape? You put tape on her mouth?'

'Tape. Yes.'

'Are you going to put tape on my mouth?'

'Are you going to scream?'

'I'm not going to scream.'

'Then I'm not going to put tape on you.'

She couldn't think. What next? Keep talking. Be a human being. He is a human being. We're all human beings.

'Are you going to sit down too?'

No reaction.

'Can I see Katie? She's only young. She'll be very frightened. Can she come and sit with us out here? She won't scream. We'll do whatever you say.'

He was thinking about it. His eyes were scanning hers, looking for something. Treachery. She smiled, as sweetly as she knew how.

With an abruptness that made her jump, he whistled, then shouted something in Spanish. The door to Katie's room opened.

Katie was pushed out, or kicked, judging by the way her back arched as she came through the opening. Her hands were tied behind her back and her mouth sealed by a metallic grey slash of duct tape. Her eyes were wide, terrified. Vicente's colleague was younger, fatter, more dishevelled. He, too, wore a shirt and slacks, but he looked altogether more unkempt, and his slacks fell untidily onto his scuffed black lace-ups. He had the same dark wavy hair, but it was set lower on his forehead, giving him a meaner look. There was nothing confusing about his face as he pushed Katie into the room with the muzzle of his pistol. He was enjoying himself.

Katie collapsed onto the sofa opposite Rachel.

'It's OK, sweetheart,' Rachel said, trying to hold back her rage. Everything in her wanted to go wild, leap up at the two men, tear at them, destroy them in any way she could manage. She forced herself to look at the guns. Be rational. Think. She lifted her eyes back to Vicente.

'Please take the tape off her mouth. You can tie me up, if you like.' She held out her hands. 'But please take the tape off.'

Vicente eyed Rachel with curiosity. 'If she makes a noise, I will shoot her.' He nodded across the room. 'Ramón.'

His colleague looked disappointed at first, then a smile played on his lips as he pinched a corner of the tape across Katie's mouth. She suppressed a scream as it yanked free; the tape tore at her skin, and her top lip dribbled blood. Katie licked it as she fixed her gaze on her mother. They locked eyes. We will survive this, said the look that passed between them.

Vicente reached into his trouser pocket and pulled out a length of electrical flex. Ramón nervously flicked his gun between them as Vicente tied Rachel's wrists behind her back.

'Now,' Vicente said. 'We wait.'

CHAPTER 30

GENOVSKY WAS LONG GONE. Virgo had seen her, far in the distance, as he came into the immigration hall, but she was in the fast-moving line for US citizens, and he was joining the back of the non-US line, a nervous, shuffling column of souls under suspicion.

He passed the time watching the silent news pictures that played out on the TVs arrayed along the wall. Some cruel scheduling had littered the headlines with Homeland Security stories. Or maybe that's how it always was on TV over here now. Or maybe that's why they chose this channel: intimidation tactics. The Secretary for Homeland Security cropped up on screen from time to time, a huge, dark-skinned, grey-haired head miming indignation and concern as he silently railed against something or other in front of flashing cameras. The rolling strap declared that Secretary Thomas Wheelan was vowing to secure US borders against the cocaine trade.

Wheelan.

A chill crept into Virgo's guts. He looked up at the screen again, then dismissed the thought. But it wouldn't go away.

We are the authorities. That was what Genovsky had said at Heathrow. Was he up against the Secretary for Homeland

Security? Had the head of the FBI kidnapped his wife and daughter?

He was getting paranoid.

But what if it was true?

If it was true, he – everyone – was in deep. With no prospect of rescue. He was alone. And on enemy territory.

He knew it was true.

It took a full hour before Virgo came to the front of the line. The officer took fingerprints, took his picture, asked him how long he was staying, and why he had come. After a couple of minutes of interrogation, the United States reluctantly let Nathaniel Virgo into its territories.

He advanced through to the baggage hall and picked up his luggage, then headed for the exit. Just customs to clear. He waited in line again, progressing slowly. A Japanese couple ahead of him were sidelined, and their bags searched. Then the beagles came. His heart raced, even though his mind told him there was nothing to fear. He hadn't even tried getting a teabag into the country, let alone something really dangerous like a piece of fruit. Unlike the young woman in front of him. The beagles sniffed at her pockets, then sat down next to her. Her face went white, like a prisoner facing execution. Hurriedly, she surrendered two apples into a gloved hand. They would be incinerated, and the country would be safe. The beagles moved on.

A customs officer took his declaration and waved him straight through into the United States of America: he was in.

Getting out might be harder.

He dismissed the thought and scanned the airport's signposting for directions to the taxi ranks.

CHAPTER 31

THEY WOULD ASK WHERE he was, of course. When the planes started going down, Thomas Wheelan fully expected to hear the President asking for him.

He put down the briefing papers and stared at the mahogany panelling across from his desk. It was beautiful, rich, exquisitely crafted, exactly the kind of workmanship such an important office deserved. When it was no longer his office, when he had the Oval Office, he would come in here and point out the beauty of the wood to his successor, and how it reflected the delicate craftsmanship required to oversee the most important department in the United States government.

There would be questions about his absence during the attack, about the fact that he didn't inform the Pentagon, or the Oval Office, of his whereabouts. Bob Holmes, as Chief of Staff, would be the one to make the biggest fuss. But the tapes would show that an insider had been involved. It would be clear that he did the right thing; that telling no one about the plot he had discovered was the best course of action – until they knew the identity of the insider he could risk nothing. If he had to, he would stand up in court and swear that handpicking a team to break in on the terrorists was the best course of action. The only course. It was regrettable that it took a while to pin down their location. Even more regrettable that so many citizens died at the hands of those who perpetrated these evil acts. But he had acted as swiftly and decisively as was possible; who knew how many more people might have died if he had taken a different course of action?

And when it became public, his personal involvement would be welcomed by the American people. His record was already exemplary. He had served in the army, knew what it was like to face bullets in the defence of his country. None of that National Guard bullshit. The Secretary for Homeland Security would be known as someone who had taken his appointment to public office just as seriously as his postings in the military. Here was a man with no regard for personal or political safety. He would make a hands-on, hands-dirty kind of president. The kind of president that America deserved.

And then his mission would roll on. *Let justice roll on like rivers, and righteousness like a mighty stream.* He had sat up straight in church last week when Reverend Lowden quoted that; it was like he'd been waiting to hear those words all his life. Amos chapter 5, verse 24; he had committed it to memory. Let justice roll on like rivers. That was his mission statement now.

The journalist flashed across his mind. If only they knew what was on the disk this Virgo character said he had. Perhaps it was nothing. Alex had taken a disk from Gierek's body; that one was blank, she said. So what could this second disk be? What kind of stunt had Gierek been trying to pull? It made sense to find out before they killed Virgo. And they had the leverage they needed out there in Cuba. Wheelan made a mental note to call Marinov when he left the office, to make sure this Virgo got the message about just how high the stakes were.

He picked up the papers again. They made interesting reading. Tomorrow, they would take a few planes down.

People would die: maybe a few hundred, maybe a thousand. But look what he'd already achieved since getting behind this desk: the Arizona border-control experiment had shown what could be done if there was the will. They had already seized 200,000 pounds of marijuana more than they did last year. Cocaine seizures were up from 86 pounds to 4777. Heroin from 17 pounds to 1525. That was surely more than a thousand lives saved on the streets of America's biggest cities already. And deaths from exposure were down too: the migrants were getting picked up well before their dehydrated bodies fell limp onto the desert sand. Rescues were up fifty-seven per cent. His was a humanitarian mission, in every sense.

And Arizona's border, what was that – a few hundred miles? The United States had 7000 miles of border, and drugs were leaking through everywhere. He needed more resources, more political will to stem the evil tide. And, after tomorrow, he'd be well on the way to getting everything he needed.

The words and figures started dancing a little jig before his eyes. Wheelan put the papers down again, and rubbed his brow; he could feel the blur coming on.

'Marjorie?'

His assistant put her head round the door, and Wheelan smiled gracefully. He suddenly felt like shit, but he didn't have to make that anyone else's problem.

'Marjorie, could you get me some more water, please?'

'Of course, Mr Secretary,' she said. 'Can I get you anything else? A sandwich, perhaps?'

'Just some water, thank you.' He smiled again.

Wheelan unlocked the desk drawer and pulled out a brown plastic bottle. He stared at it a moment. His last two pills. For a moment, he felt a little pinprick, a dart of panic. But it didn't last. Tonight, he was heading up to Boston and having a late dinner at Gabe and Ellie's place. And Ellie would have a full bottle ready for collection.

Everything was under control.

CHAPTER 32

As VIRGO'S CAB CROSSED the bay, downtown Boston loomed ahead: a confusion of towers in steel and glass and concrete. He leaned forward.

'What's that huge arch on the harbourfront?'

'The Harbor Hotel. Got a few hundred dollars a night?' The driver turned and looked him up and down. It was obvious what he thought. 'The Buckminster's nice enough. You'll do OK there.'

The cab driver had chosen the Buckminster for him. It was close to the Boston University campus – just like he asked – but Fenway Park was just round the corner too. Even if it was off-season, the cabbie reasoned, he at least had to go and have a look on his first time in town. He would divert the ride, free of charge, so he could show Virgo the Green Monster. Thirty-seven feet of left-field wall.

Virgo had no idea what that meant, but nodded in appreciation. Close to BU was good enough.

It felt like any American city: big, bustling, impressive. But oppressive too, with its huge expressways and vehicles to match. By the time they got close to Fenway Park, though, it was becoming friendlier, somehow more intimate. The streets closed in a little, and people seemed to be strolling rather than hurrying down the sidewalks.

'There it is.' The driver pulled to the side of the road. 'The Green Monster.' Virgo looked up. A sheer cliff of green steel rose up from a brown brick foundation.

'Highest in professional baseball,' the driver said. 'Fly balls don't get you a home run so easy when you're taking on the Red Sox.' He turned and grinned at Virgo. The grin faded when he registered Virgo's blank face. 'Anyway, best get you to the hotel.' He swung the cab back into the traffic.

As they approached the Buckminster, the streets gradually became populated by young people, released from classes and milling aimlessly between brightly lit shops and bars.

They drove into a huge open square. The driver slammed a hand onto the horn as a couple of students threatened to step out into the road. 'Kenmore Square,' he said. 'Unbelievable pain in the ass. Here we are. The Buckminster. Want me to wait, make sure they got a room?'

Virgo shook his head and paid the fare. He looked up at the hotel as the cab pulled away. It seemed OK, nothing special. They had rooms. He paid with Genovsky's cash. He was surprised how driven he felt, how lacking in nerves as he spun out another identity. He would eat, sleep, and get into the university first thing. He had to meet Genovsky at noon tomorrow, and he would make sure he had something to bargain with. Something to keep him in the game.

In this game, we are the authorities.

Thomas Wheelan? The name banged against the inside of his skull.

Virgo shook his head. It didn't matter. Whatever this grand scheme, he could only do what he could do. He just had to make sure he kept himself in the game.

CHAPTER 33

THE SECRETARY FOR HOMELAND Security had gone to the bathroom. And Gabriel MacIntyre knew that when Tom came back he'd be a different man. It was a little routine they went through pretty much every time Tom came to the house.

Ellie was her brother's supplier. MacIntyre smiled at his wife; she hadn't worked out that he knew, because she didn't believe people could be intrinsically suspicious or conniving. It wouldn't occur to her that her husband would even watch her moves. But the knowing look she shared with her brother, the way she slipped out of the room for a moment, Tom's shifting, anxious stare that dissipated on her return – the handover was obvious.

There was no need for him to say anything.

It wasn't like he particularly minded the drugs being in the house. Ellie would keep them well out of Jennie's reach, he knew that. He did wonder if Ellie had to lie to her physician to get them, or whether the maid got them for her. Where she lived, Beatrice would certainly know the right kind of people. But he wasn't going to ask. He liked the leverage he retained by keeping the matter undiscussed.

It wasn't like he had a lot of leverage over Thomas

Wheelan. But to have the Homeland Security chief use his house to pick up the pills he needed – that surely had to be worth something. Being married to his supplier wasn't a bad position to be in, either.

MacIntyre stared at the Chagall print mounted on the wall. There was another reason he never mentioned anything to Ellie: he knew it tore her apart. She was ripped in two by the need to care for Tom, to do what she could for him, and the need to always do the right thing for her husband, and for little Jennie. She would do anything she could to do the right thing. But her brother's need for the pills was greater than her own need for an easy conscience. And Tom's addiction was an anomaly, a cruel twist of fate. She needn't feel guilty about keeping its consequences under control.

There was certainly an irony in it: Tom was hooked on sleeping pills and he hadn't had a decent night in eight years. Not since the police found his son lying in a dirty room downtown, track marks peppering his arms, lost to a chemical haze. The papers had gone to town on it: the son of Atlanta's mayor thrown out of home, dead in a rat-infested warehouse.

What a waste. That's all Tom had said. It wasn't like he hadn't tried. He'd locked Joshua away, sent him to rehab – what else was he supposed to do? Every time the boy came back out, he went in search of a score again, stuck himself with needles in the dirty streets. In the end, Thomas Wheelan, Mayor of Atlanta, recipient of a Distinguished Service Medal, admitted he was out of his depth. Joshua was beyond help. They forced him out of the house and changed the locks while his mother wept in the hallway. Kill or cure.

It killed him.

And then Sheila filed for divorce. Tom had slipped into free fall for a while, and Ellie had fallen with him.

MacIntyre had been too busy at work to do anything but watch. The tragedy of the events had almost destroyed their marriage, just like it destroyed Tom's. But they were stronger than that, he and Ellie. They'd already survived the hate of two fathers-in-law; nothing but death was going to drive them apart after that.

Tom came back into the room, and Ellie's gaze sought out his mood, met his eyes. Her brother looked at peace again. He smiled; Ellie relaxed.

MacIntyre saw again how beautiful his wife was. Breathtaking. He was the luckiest guy alive.

'You ready to eat, Tom?' Ellie smiled at her brother.

Tom looked up at her, then at him. 'I am. You ready, Gabe?'

MacIntyre forced a smile onto his lips. 'All set,' he said. 'Let's eat.'

CHAPTER 34

'ANYBODY SEE ANYTHING YET?'
Frank Delaney lifted his head and squinted through the gloom at his trainees. Their faces were lit by the soft glow of the LCD screens in front of them. It was ridiculous: evening class in the dark.

The FBI's new data-management system cost $170 million, came in two years late, and was still appallingly unreliable. But the really appalling thing was that someone had lit this room like it was meant to re-enact the nuclear flash over Nagasaki. No dimmers: the settings were off or blinding-light on. All they could do, if they wanted to see the screens, was operate in the dark. The more resourceful of the students brought flashlights to class so they could read their assignments by something more helpful than the screen's dull glow.

Delaney gazed out the window at the Quantico lights. Beyond, a mile or so away, the Creek called to him. He could be night-fishing. Why was he here?

An age ago, he had been one of these kids in training. But that was when you got issued a notepad and pencil, and you knew who the enemy was. These days, you got a password and a list of enemies as long as you wanted. Every colour, every creed, white collar and blue. Everyone was the enemy. These kids were facing the very definition of mission impossible when they got out of here. Computers weren't enough.

Why was he here? Because he didn't have the guts to go back out in the field. He didn't have the fire any more. That was the truth. He could dress it up as being pissed at the Bureau, at the new idiot culture that presided over everything in government, but was that it? Did he really have the stomach, the balls, to see an investigation through?

He had volunteered to go to London, to talk to Nathaniel Virgo. The Baltimore field office was backed up with an agent-intensive drugs sting, and needed someone to go. The guy at the embassy was on some godawful exercise with the Metropolitan Police. And he had stepped up. Surely that was something? Or was it just a plane trip?

It had been just a plane trip in the end. He'd hardly filed a report before the instruction came through that the investigation was to be closed. The ticket must have cost a thousand dollars, and then someone at Homeland Security – *why Homeland Security?* – shut the whole thing down.

At least the network was up and running for once. And his students, if not particularly gifted, were at least hard-working. Trawling through entries to the US in the last twenty-four hours, looking for possibles, didn't require gifting, it required graft.

What was he teaching them? That everyone is a suspect. That to get an agent's job done involves searching through thousands of names, hoping the computer will put two and two together when it finds the right data. Most of the time, the computer totalled two and two at five.

'No one got anything yet?' He looked at the clock. In another half-hour he could go home. He would get up early again, and go and finish that painting by the Creek.

A hand went up in the corner of the room.

'Sir?'

'What you got, Schlessinger?'

'Arab name, can't pronounce it. *Mush* something. On CIA watch-list. Entered US via JFK this afternoon.'

Can't pronounce it? Jesus. Annabel Schlessinger, rich kid seeking a little danger. A liability-in-waiting. How had she got this far?

Delaney kept his mouth closed, and told himself to calm down. The public education system had failed these kids like it had failed him. Don't judge them, Delaney. At least they're here, not out somewhere trying to become celebrities. At least they'd made a decision to do something with their lives.

'OK,' he said. 'Log it, and send the info to New York.'

'Sir?'

'Is that too tough for you, Schlessinger?' Sometimes he just couldn't help himself.

'No, it's not that, sir. I got another one.'

'Wow, Schlessinger, you're on fire tonight. Go on.'

'Nathaniel Virgo. A Brit. Recently questioned over a murder in Baltimore, entered via Boston Logan earlier this evening.'

No shit.

'Show me.' Delaney walked to Schlessinger's terminal. He leaned in, took over the mouse, and scrolled through the entry.

Well, well. Virgo had made up a hotel name on his immigration card. Delaney knew the entire length of Lincoln Avenue like he knew his own hallway. There was no Marriott on Lincoln. He lifted his head.

'Everyone, come here. Gather round. Schlessinger's kicked all your asses.'

He handed her back the mouse and stood upright again.

'Go to the British police files, and see if anything's come up.'

Schlessinger made a few clicks. 'Report filed an hour or so ago. Some guy found dead in Virgo's house. The Brits are looking for him.'

'And we found him.'

Glory be: these computers weren't entirely useless. Delaney felt a fire kindle in his lungs.

'OK, nice work, Schlessinger. Leave it with me. Back to your terminals, everybody, and carry on. I'm going to make a couple of calls. When I get back, I expect a report from every one of you. This world is full of dangerous people, and I want to know their names.'

Delaney walked to the door, then turned down the corridor towards his office. The fire in his lungs was still burning as he picked up the phone. Virgo was back in the United States, and Delaney knew exactly what he was going to do about it. He would show the idiots at Homeland Security just what it took to get to the bottom of an unsolved crime.

CHAPTER 35

THEY HAD BEEN SITTING an hour or two, maybe. Rachel didn't have a watch on, and Vicente had ignored her every plea for attention. He seemed reluctant to talk at all. Across from her, pale and red-eyed, Katie was staring at the far wall of the room.

Vicente watched them from the balcony. He still had the gun in his hand, but he looked relaxed, and the night breeze played in his hair.

'Vicente,' Rachel called. 'We need something to eat. And some water. Please.'

They had been given nothing so far. They'd hardly even moved.

Vicente didn't react.

'You can take money from my purse,' Rachel said. 'Please, get us something. I promise we won't try anything while one of you is gone. And get something for yourselves, too – you must be hungry.'

Vicente stared at her for a while, then slowly walked back into the room. 'OK,' he said. 'But I don't need your money.'

He pulled some dollar bills from his pocket and handed them to Ramón, muttering something in Spanish. Ramón left the apartment, and Vicente stood over them, gun in hand.

After a couple of minutes, Ramón returned carrying chocolate bars. It was something.

Vicente filled a glass from the kitchen tap. He held it to their lips in turn, first Katie, then Rachel. The water was cool and refreshing, and the throbbing in Rachel's head abated almost immediately. Then he fed them each some chocolate.

Ramón slumped on a chair, playing with his gun, but Vicente did not sit down for more than a few minutes at a time now. Every time he got up he would pull the phone from his pocket, stare impatiently at the screen, then stroll to the balcony and look out to sea. When he came back into the room he seemed calmer, less anxious. But it didn't last.

Whose call was he expecting?

Everyone in the room jumped when Vicente's phone finally broke the silence. He slipped the gun into his waistband, and answered the call. After a couple of seconds, he caught Ramón's eye and nodded urgently towards the captives. Ramón sat upright and pointed his pistol at each face in turn. Rachel forced herself upright on the sofa cushions to listen, but Vicente's conversation was in muttered Spanish, and he had walked away up the hallway. All she gleaned was his agitation.

Think.

This was to do with Nathaniel. Somehow, she knew it. They weren't after money. Cuba didn't have terrorist groups – or even political factions. It was a paradise island, but not a free society, not in the sense that some other places were free. And it was her they were after: they had her picture, they knew her name. What had Nat got himself into?

And who was Vicente? Ramón was a sidekick, that was clear. He looked bored, sitting toying with his gun. She had caught his eye a few times, sparked his interest with a well-timed eye flash, a tiny smile or a studied stare accompanied by a bite of her lip and a flash of her tongue. Katie had noticed, and given her an inquisitive look. Maybe she didn't get it. It didn't matter what Katie thought. For now, it was the only way out that Rachel could see.

The phone call only lasted thirty seconds. Vicente studiously pressed a couple of buttons after he had finished speaking, then looked up at her for a moment in silence.

'We are going,' he said.

Rachel's stomach plummeted. 'Where to?'

She wanted to sound calm, but her voice had cracked, even in those two words. There was something in his face that wasn't there before the phone call.

'That's not your concern.'

'What is this about?' she pleaded. She had to know – was this a random thing, or was there some sense behind it? She knew the answer really, but she still had to ask. 'Is it something to do with my hus . . . with Nathaniel Virgo?'

Vicente crossed the room, and crouched down so that his eyes were looking directly into hers. He turned his head and flicked his eyes to Katie to make sure he had her attention, too. Something in his eyes made Rachel's heart beat faster. There was a new intensity, a new purpose.

'Understand something,' he said. 'We are going out to the car now. I don't even have to unbind your hands. My people own this hotel – if you make a noise, we will simply tell interested passers-by that we are police and you are under arrest for smuggling drugs. There will be no fuss, I can assure you. If you give me any trouble, if you try to run, I will kill you once we get to the car.' He paused. 'Do you understand?'

Rachel nodded. She wasn't sure she could walk, let alone run.

'Stand up,' Vicente said. 'Ramón, come behind us.'

Rachel looked at Katie. Could she still stand and walk? She usually wanted a break from her prosthetic after a couple of hours. She had been wearing it all evening now. It would be sore and heavy. Katie's face betrayed nothing as she stood. Nothing more than defiance.

They filed to the door. Vicente poked his head out of the

room, then pulled Rachel out into the corridor. They went briskly along the stairs, Vicente by her side. She could hear a band playing bright salsa somewhere in the distance. No doubt people were dancing to the rhythms, swaying their hips, having a good time. Maybe getting a little drunk, a little flirty. Just like she and Nat used to do. Rachel felt a hot tear well in the corner of one eye and run down her face. She caught her breath. Yes, she wanted to cry. But she couldn't. Not yet.

She steeled herself as she walked. She didn't have to follow her instincts. She would use her brain to get them out of this. And her body. She turned her head: Katie was following a few steps behind, with Ramón bringing up the rear. She caught his eye again and forced herself to stare a little, just for a moment. It felt dangerous, but what choice did she have?

As they stepped off the stairs, Rachel had to scurry to keep up with Vicente's stride. She looked to left and right, but no one was even watching. The urge to scream, run, do something was overwhelming, but she forced herself to ignore it. Vicente paused at the desk, and one of the clerks handed him some scraps of paper. He slipped them into his shirt pocket, and they headed outside.

The hotel's gardens were drowned in the heavy scent of flowers. She had loved the fragrant air when they arrived, but now it just seemed cloying and oppressive. The air was alive with sound: insects chattering, drums beating in samba rhythms, a trumpet sounding out from the hotel club. A typical Cuban night: scent and salsa. And kidnapping.

Vicente was still walking too fast. Rachel turned to look at Ramón again; this time, he responded. He put his tongue between his lips and waggled it up and down. His face broke into a lewd grin. She turned back quickly. It would be worth it in the end. She would find her moment.

They were in the car park, walking towards a black, high-finned monster of a vehicle. Vicente pulled the rear door open.

'You two get in the back.' He pushed Rachel in first. Then Katie.

The contact with her daughter's flesh was bliss. Rachel looked into Katie's eyes. If their arms were free, they would have thrown them round each other. Katie dropped her head onto her mother's shoulder, and the soft fragrance of her daughter's camomile conditioner took her back home, back into safety for a moment. Hot tears squeezed their way into Rachel's eyes again, but she blinked them away. They would get through this. She and her baby would get through this.

'We're going to be OK,' she whispered.

She leaned back again, into the door. Subtly, slowly, she pulled at the handle, waiting for the catch to respond.

'It only opens from the outside.'

Vicente was watching her in the driver's mirror. 'It's the one useful feature of this broken wreck,' he said. He didn't smile.

The engine clunked slowly into life on its third attempt. It coughed, then roared. Vicente released the handbrake and pulled away.

CHAPTER 36

THE STREETLIGHTS GREW SPARSE, the buildings more rickety, and desolate spaces stretched between dwellings. They were headed out of town. Palm trees leaned threateningly over the road in clumps, no longer planted in the neat patterns of urban avenues. Rachel steeled herself not to give up hope. Leaning forward, she could see the dark rise of higher ground silhouetted against the anthracite sky.

The car's headlights picked out the shadow of potholes on the crumbling road; Vicente steered round the worst of them. Then, after a couple of miles, he swung a hard right onto a dirt track, and they became unavoidable. With their hands still tied, the two of them were thrown to the gods and back on the bench seat. Rachel yowled as a steel spring ripped through the cracked leather and drove itself into her thigh. Ramón turned and grinned from his position in the front. Katie stared straight ahead as they bounced, seemingly immune to the chaos. Rachel knew that look. Katie was concentrating, like she did before a race. She focused on the finish, on the moment when everything was over and she had come out on top.

Suddenly, with a wrench to the wheel, Vicente pulled the

car off the road. He muttered something to Ramón, who got out and pulled at Rachel's door. She almost fell out as it swung open. A drowning panic rose within her.

'You. Get out.'

With a glance back at Katie, Rachel complied. She missed her footing and stumbled, falling to the ground at Ramón's feet. Katie shuffled across the seat to follow, but Ramón slammed the door and waved his pistol in her face.

'You stay there.'

Ramón was pulling at the front passenger door, pistol raised; he was getting back into the car. Rachel watched, her eyes wide. They were going to dump her here in the middle of nowhere, and take her baby away. She tried to scream, but the air emerged silent from her lungs.

Then Vicente got out from behind the steering wheel. He walked round the car, lifted a white piece of paper from his shirt pocket, and glanced at it. He pulled out his phone and dialled a number, his eyes shifting back and forth between keypad and paper. He held the phone to his ear for a few seconds.

'Nathaniel Virgo?' he said, eventually. His tone was flat, uninterested. 'Someone wants you to know that the stakes are . . . ' He hesitated, looking for a word. '. . . Sky-high, Mr Virgo. The stakes are sky-high.'

He paused for a moment, then looked over at her. 'Say something to your husband.' He held the phone up in the air.

Rachel gasped for breath. 'Nat.' It came out as a whimper. Not what she had intended at all. She wanted to pour out her heart, and all she had managed was a pathetic sob.

Vicente said nothing more. He turned away, and placed the phone, still open, on the roof of the car. Rachel could just make out the tinny shouts of a man's voice through the speaker. Was it Nat? Everything in her wanted to jump up, grab the phone, talk back to her husband's screaming, urgent voice. But she was paralysed, her eyes fixed again on Vicente.

He was reaching into a pocket with his left hand. He

pulled out a black metal tube nearly ten centimetres long. It was only when she saw him screwing it onto his pistol barrel that she realised what it was. He was half-turned away from her, so she could only see the corner of his eyes in the grim fire of the car's headlights. His face was heavy now, and darkness brooded behind the gaze fixed on the silenced gun. He sighed, the breath of regretful duty. He turned further round towards her. She saw the tense set of his shoulders. Sweat had made the white shirt cling to his chest. A breath of steam rose through the headlight beam.

She knew what was about to happen, but she could do nothing. In these moments, the instinct for survival should be automatic, unthinking as a drowning man's last gasps for air. But they weren't. She heard Katie screaming from inside the car, but couldn't pull her eyes off the raised gun barrel. In the corner of her vision, she could see the phone on the car roof. It glinted softly in the moonlight.

The screaming stopped. She heard a whimper and a cry, but couldn't tell whether this new sound came from her own lungs or from her daughter's.

A cicada chirped joyfully in the long grass, exulting in the scent, the open possibilities of another moonlit night.

Something in Vicente's face flinched as he moved his finger inside the trigger guard. Rachel dragged her eyes onto Katie's.

'It's going to be all right,' she mouthed. A mother's forlorn, desperate hope.

The gun discharged with a dull pop, like the crack of a twig broken underfoot. The cicada broke off its symphony for a moment, then took it up again, oblivious to Rachel Virgo's death.

CHAPTER 37

'HEY, KEEP IT DOWN in there!'

Nathaniel Virgo hardly heard the angered shouts or the banging on the wall from the adjoining room. He was silent now, sitting upright in the bed, still staring at his phone. He hadn't closed the drapes properly, and the room was lit by a weak, ghostly glow from the streetlights outside. With an effort of will, he lifted his eyes and fixed them on the framed picture of a poppy field on the far wall.

The red of the petals was wrong, too weak. The print had faded over the time it had been there; he instinctively knew that if he lifted the frame, moved it aside, there would be a slightly darker square of the pale green wallpaper, a shadow where the light had not reached for years.

The scene wouldn't play in his imagination. He heard Rachel say his name. Then the screams. He had never heard the noise before, but he knew they were Katie's screams. And then they abated, and he heard the sounds of a tropical night. There was a cicada in the background.

And then the gunshot.

How could he know anything for sure, when it all came through the wires of the telephone system? It was nothing but digital information, zeroes and ones travelling through optical fibres, beamed through the air, maybe bounced off a satellite. The shot he heard was a phantom, a recreation. There was no reality to it.

Like the poppies. They stood tall in a field, among grasses. But they were dead on the paper, a poor imitation of the truth, a cheap attempt to evoke the true dignity of the real thing.

The tears were hot on his cheeks now, and the poppies retreated from focus. He stared through them, and saw them only as petals prepared for scattering in a wild grief. Virgo let his head fall back, stared at the ceiling and let the air escaping his lungs measure the vast depths of the cavity within his chest.

CHAPTER 38

KATIE TRIED TO WIPE the tears away with her shoulder, but she was trembling too much to do the job properly. She could feel her hands shaking behind her back. This was shock: she knew that. She remembered the accident, remembered how the blunt disbelief filled her mind, refused entry to the anger, sent it coursing through every muscle and nerve.

She wanted them to pick up her mother's body, but she had been unable to speak. She wasn't even sure she had breathed again yet – her chest felt tight, constricted, like she had been squeezed into a tiny wooden box. And now they were driving away. She focused in on something, a goal. When this was over, she would come back and get her mother's body. She would make sure it wasn't left out here. That would be her goal now. That would be the point of getting through this.

She had done the impossible before. She had got up from her hospital bed and learned to walk again. She had gone back to the track and learned to run again. She had held a national track record for a while. She was a living testimony to the power of one step at a time. And then suddenly you were at your destination. You were Great Britain's junior sprint champion. Or you'd escaped your captors and come back to hold your mother's body in your arms. Everyone was always telling her she was no ordinary fifteen-year-old. And she would make this the time she proved them right.

Her eyes were clearing, and she could see the lights again. They were taking her back into town. Katie set her jaw hard, and tried not to let her body shake. She could control these muscles when she needed to run, and now, more than ever, she needed to be in control. Eventually, she let herself speak.

'Where are you taking me?'

The words came out cool and even. That was good.

Vicente was driving, but half-turned in his seat and leaned his head back to look at her. The moonlight shone on his face, giving his stretched-out skin a ghoulish glow.

'To Cardénas. To wait.'

He glanced back at the road, then turned to look at her again. 'It's important you do as I tell you, Katie Virgo. I have instructions to kill you if there is any problem. Like I killed your mother. Any problem at all.'

He faced front: the conversation was over. Katie stared at the dark, glittering sea that shone in the distance, and tried not to give in to the numb despair rising in her chest. *Like I killed your mother*. How would she get out of this? Somewhere over the water there was safety, but here, in paradise, she was lost. The locked doors and the guns rendered her powerless. There was nothing she could use to form a plan; she'd simply have to know her moment when it came. Keep all options open. Find out what you can. She steeled herself to speak again.

'Do you know why you were told to kidnap me? Do you know what this is about?'

'I know what I need to,' Vicente said.

'And what's that?'

'My bosses know someone who wants you to hand.'

That didn't make sense. Why would they want her? She was just a girl, just a teenager from far away.

But, as soon as she allowed herself to think it, she knew the answer. It was something to do with her dad. Her mother was dead because her father was in some kind of trouble. What kind, she couldn't imagine. Nothing like this had ever happened before; he had broken stories that sent people to jail, but he had never put his family in danger. He wouldn't. Would he? Katie's chest tightened so much she coughed an empty, painful heave that seemed to explode her lungs. She tried to catch a breath, but she was wheezing erratically. For a moment, she stared ahead, straight through the windscreen. Inside her head, she heard a voice. You're only fifteen, it said. You shouldn't have to go through anything like this. The voice made her want to break down in heaving sobs. But she didn't. She held her breath, took control. Her dad wouldn't knowingly do anything that might harm her. She would calm herself down, and she would find a way to get out of this.

'So,' she said. 'You killed my mother. You shot her in cold blood, and you don't know why? How do you live with that?'

Vicente turned to catch her eye. 'This is not your world, *señorita*. Did you look at the buildings in the town yesterday? They are full of bullet holes: Cuba wears her scars proudly – we don't cover them up. You are a child still, and you come here from a life of comfort and easy paths. Death and bullets are a way of life here, it has been so for decades now.' He looked back at the road. 'Welcome to the real Cuba, Katie Virgo. Smuggling and corruption and poverty and dirt and chickens and –'

Vicente screeched the car to a halt. Katie piled into the back of the bench seat in front, then looked up as a sore-ravaged mutt stared dolefully into the headlights.

'– and mangy dogs. Look at that. That's how America sees us. That's why we take pity on the wretched and have none for the rich.'

The dog moved out of the road, and Vicente slowly rolled the car forward again. Katie sat back in the seat.

'And that entitles you to kill people?'

'When it is necessary. My boss needs only one person. It was you or your mother. I chose you to live, and her to die.'

The words hit her like a truck. *I chose you to live*. That was it? Her mother was dead, and that was as much explanation as she got? He was right: this wasn't her world, and it was falling in on her, pounding her at every turn. But she had to survive. Her dad had to survive this too. She had to keep going. She could take the beating, for now, with the end in mind. Always the end in mind. She had discipline over her body, and her will. That was what made her so good. Believe in yourself, Katie Virgo.

'Who do you work for? What does your boss do?'

'He gives Cuban people a better life.'

'All Cuban people? Or has he just given *you* a better life?'

Was she pushing too hard? She could afford to push a little. They wanted her alive. For now.

'It ends up being for everybody. People buy things for their families here. It only takes one person in the family to be able to buy soap and medicine and schoolbooks, and everyone benefits.' Vicente turned in his seat. 'Who buys your schoolbooks?'

She said nothing. She was out of her depth with Vicente; he gave her no cracks, no handholds. She'd have to try the other route, the one she had seen her mother trying. It was easier, but much less appealing.

'What about you, Ramón? Do you have a family?'

He turned around. 'I'm young, free and single, baby.' His leery grin said it all: nasty. But predictable – she had to be grateful for that. He was no different from some of the older boys at school. When they got drunk, when the parties ran out of control, she saw the same looks. She found it astonishing, the power girls had over boys.

Vicente pulled off the main road and headed down a dark, narrow street lined with battered brick and concrete houses. The car juddered over the cobbles. A hundred metres up the street, Vicente pulled over to one side and cut the engine.

'We're here,' he said, turning in his seat. Katie was surprised to see how tired he looked.

'You can cry out all you want,' he said. 'In this street, everyone knows me. No one will come to help you.'

Ramón opened the door, gun in hand, and she got out. She stretched her arms upwards as far as the wire binding her hands would allow, curving her back and sticking out her chest. She glanced at Ramón to check he was watching.

'This way.' Vicente stepped over a small boy sleeping in the doorway of a house. He pushed the door open. 'Mind out for Miguel.'

Katie stood still in front of the child. 'Is he yours?'

Vicente halted and turned round to face her. 'His mother – my daughter – she died last year. We look after him now.' He narrowed his eyes. 'She died in her sleep. He was in her bed, beside her. And now he won't sleep in a bed any more.' He turned again. 'Come in and sit down.'

Katie stepped over Miguel and entered the room. The only light came from a dim, bare bulb suspended by a cord from the ceiling. The walls were plaster, unpainted, with a few pictures of the Virgin Mary hanging crookedly from rusty nails. A shelf on the far wall held a tackily ornate carriage clock. It said 11.15 and probably would do for ever. A dirty rug covered the central part of the concrete floor.

Vicente pointed to a cane-framed sofa under the shelf. 'Sit down there.'

She complied. 'What now?'

'Now, we wait some more. Do you want to sleep?'

She did. How could she want to sleep when she had just witnessed her mother's execution? For a moment, she hated herself, and everyone and everything. But then she let it go. She was suddenly too tired to feel anything. She had to get out of this, and there was no getting out from here. She needed to be as ready as possible when the time came. She ought to sleep.

'Yes.'

'Good. Sleep, then.'

The tiredness washed through her limbs as she relaxed. It was OK to sleep now. Even a few minutes would make a difference, prepare her for what was to come. As she slipped quickly out of the waking world, she opened her eyes for a last look. Miguel was staring at her from across the room, singing a Spanish lullaby in a hoarse whisper.

CHAPTER 39

THOMAS WHEELAN STRETCHED HIS arm out of the Escalade's window. He smiled and waved to Eleanor and Jennie as MacIntyre pulled away.

'You're happy about the details, Gabe?'

MacIntyre swung the vehicle round, and popped twice on the horn as he headed off the stone chips. Same routine, every morning. Even on Saturdays, when he took Jennie to her ballet class.

Was he happy about the details? His brother-in-law had run through it all again last night, after Ellie had gone to bed.

There was nothing in the details he was unhappy about: he was just generally unhappy. How many people were going to die for this? And would Red Spot be implicated – would there be anything in the software that linked back to him? But he had asked Wheelan all this a dozen times, and received the same reassurances on every occasion. Anyway, it was too late to pull out. It had been too late since the start, he realised. The minute he had taken up with Marinov and his entanglement software, it was already too late. So there was no sense letting Tom know how he really felt. He nodded.

'I guess so. You do the thing with the planes, I get out of there, you call in your people to swoop on the place. The

White House realises the extent of the threat and orders quantum security. We all live happily ever after. That it?'

'Pretty much.'

They were heading towards the Interstate now, and MacIntyre could feel his hackles rising at the creeping traffic. Why did traffic bug him so much? Was it the sense that his life could get halted, snarled up by vehicles outside of his control? There were people out there who had nothing to do with his life, and yet they could ruin his morning by sharing the same road. His progress was connected to them, tangled up with their lives, with their decisions about when they would leave the house, what route they would take that morning, how fast they would drive. He craved isolation from their influence.

'Do you really need me there, Tom?' MacIntyre said, glancing across. 'I mean, Marinov knows how to activate the entanglement software and I don't know anything about the quantum computer. He and Gierek put the thing together, after all. There's a thing I've got to do today.'

'You said you only needed the morning.' Wheelan looked over at him, held his eye for a moment. 'Truth is, Gabe, I'm just not sure about Marinov. I'd feel more comfortable with you backing me up.' Wheelan gave him a pat on the shoulder, just like Ellie's father used to do.

Like father, like son. That was a scary thought. He forced out a smile.

'OK,' he said. 'I'll be there.'

It was true; he only needed the morning. He just didn't like the exposure. He felt gratified at Wheelan's trust, at being first choice for a chaperone with Marinov. But to be there when the Homeland Security troops stormed in; that seemed risky. Even if Wheelan was their commander, it still felt like being caught in the wrong place at the wrong time. He had taken enough risks, surely?

'What have you got planned for this morning, anyway?' Wheelan asked. 'You got to do another set-up today?'

MacIntyre nodded. 'Something's coming up in East Asia. Once their markets are closed, I have to tap into our systems in the Jakarta grid again. We need a lift over there, and the conditions are perfect.'

Wheelan gave a whistle. He was drumming out a rhythm on the walnut dash. He seemed wired, ready to go. He was like that some days – just a little bit crazy. It was the pills, no doubt.

'You don't mind telling me this?' Wheelan asked.

MacIntyre shrugged. 'You know enough to indict me already. One more count isn't going to make any difference.' He looked across at his brother-in-law and grinned. 'Besides, you're family.'

The Interstate was groaning. The grin was still there on his face, and in a moment he would let it fall away without a trace. He hated the hold Wheelan had on him.

It was his own fault. MacIntyre couldn't remember how much information he had volunteered that Thanksgiving; he'd drunk too much to remember that night properly. They were in Florida, there was a barbecue; he could still smell the hot dogs. He had raised his eyes occasionally to check that the women were out of earshot. Ellie had caught his shifty eye and smiled her innocent's smile at him a couple of times.

He'd spilled his guts, confessed his guilty secret, and Wheelan had been enthralled. He saw the possibilities right away. No more threats to national security. No more 9/11. Tom had actually said that. Christ, that seemed cheap now, considering what they were going to do this afternoon. But at the time, when it counted, that had been enough. Wheelan knew that MacIntyre's brother had been in the first tower. Such a cheap shot.

But effective. He had handed over Marinov's number that evening, after another large tumbler of scotch. Four hours of thinking, and he had decided to do the right thing.

Once it had started, once Wheelan had the link with Marinov, everything was suddenly outside his control, and what seemed like the 'right thing' became less right every day.

That was the problem: the externalities. Marinov had good reason to keep the secret about the entanglement: to protect his operation. But what about the others? Gierek had broken cover. And that journalist – they still didn't know for sure that he was dead.

'You heard from Marinov today, Tom? Anything about the writer?'

Wheelan shook his head. 'Nothing. But I wouldn't worry: Marinov has a lid on it. If the guy is still alive, I'd give him a few hours, tops.'

What was he waiting for? It wasn't like Marinov to stand aside and let anyone live if it was inconvenient. Maybe the guy had something Marinov needed. What the hell could that be? Why in God's name did *no one* know what was on the disk? MacIntyre felt a jab of panic. He forced it away.

'This is my intersection. I'm heading out to the satellite, to get this stuff done. Can I drop you somewhere?' He looked across at Wheelan. 'What you got planned for the morning, anyway?'

'Just some stuff. I could tell you, but you know I'd have to kill you.'

Wheelan grinned at him.

MacIntyre came off the Interstate, then pulled over at the lights. Wheelan spied a cab and jumped out, whistling.

'See you this afternoon.' He slammed the passenger door shut, then climbed into the cab's rear seat.

MacIntyre watched it pull away.

I'd have to kill you. Wheelan smiled like it was all a game. Except it had always been clear that Wheelan's games were deadly serious. Thank God he was on America's side.

Cursing, MacIntyre pulled his Escalade back out into the streaming traffic.

CHAPTER 40

THE MORNING AIR WAS cold, and the sky a marble grey as Virgo stepped out of the hotel. It was still only eight o'clock, but he might as well walk around, clear his buzzing head. There was a cafe open across the street; his stomach was leaden, but he bought coffee and a bagel and walked down to the river. He had to fuel himself for the day, no matter how he felt. No matter what had happened to Rachel, he could still save Katie.

The flow was scarred by sculls cleaving the water, the rowers practising their careful, quiet slide through the current. He sat down on a bench, gripping hard at the coffee's warmth. The way the boats moved was extraordinary; so much effort, so many straining muscles, but the result was sleek and smooth, the velocity unchanging.

He was numb in the fog of a night's unrest. And yet things had to go perfectly today, for Katie's sake. It seemed ridiculous, too pedestrian, to be carrying on like this. But what else was he supposed to do?

A few geese honked around his feet. He pretended to throw crumbs along the bank; some birds shuffled away on a futile search, the rest stood their ground. It was impossible to know how Genovsky would react to his bluff. Would she go for it?

By nine o'clock, he couldn't wait any longer. He'd taken a map from the hotel's reception desk, but it only took a glance up and down the street to work out which way he should go: the sidewalk was filled with students heading to the day's first lectures. He fell in with them, listened to their easy chatter, and envied their optimism about the day.

The physics building wasn't hard to find. Its scale was impressive: the flat, featureless expanses of brown brick were broken only by large squares of shining glass, and it seemed tall and broad and imposing. Inside, though, it would feel like familiar territory.

They were all essentially the same, these places. Physics had a quiet disinterest in the outside world. It was a kind of nation-state; every departmental library held the same journals, every cramped office would contain a selection of books picked from the same small repertoire. There was a range of perhaps a hundred texts that you'd find inside every physics faculty, at least in Europe and America. And once you were inside, no one paid you the slightest bit of notice: if you wanted to wander the corridors, gaze at the names on doors, read the conference announcement posters pinned at random on the walls – another universal – you could do so for hours unhindered. Physics had no sense of danger, no sense of the suspicious stranger, no eye for a face. Or that was what he told himself. Something had to give you the courage to do ridiculous things.

Virgo pushed the doors open.

He stood in the spacious entry hall and let his eyes run over the display case crammed with faculty photographs. Some were in black and white, but most were colour. None were stylish, least of all Laszlo Gierek's. He was posed, shoulders drooping, in a tired beige sweater that sagged over his shoulders. His moustache was bulkier than when Virgo had seen him last. His eyes were brighter too, Virgo noticed, like something in the back of his mind was tempting him to grin.

Finding Gierek's lab wasn't hard. A peg-letter board next

to the photographs announced the location of all the faculty's offices; Gierek's was on the third floor, corridor C, room 29. A site plan on the opposite wall showed where to go. Virgo bounded up the stairs – the lift was shuttered and ancient, probably being used to shuttle liquid helium and nitrogen to and from the cooling plant he had noticed on his way in. He turned left on leaving the stairwell, then left again into corridor C. It was lit by fluorescent strips, and the walls, floors and ceilings were all painted in a faded off-white. Corridor C had all the atmosphere of a down-at-heel hospital.

Gierek's office was third on the right. With vain hope, Virgo pushed down on the dull steel handle. It resisted movement, and the mechanism issued a defiant metallic clunk. He pulled back from the door and scrutinised the notes pinned to the feltboard on its left. There were tutorial hours, a poster for an upcoming quantum information workshop at College Park, Maryland, and, scrawled in tiny letters on the back of a business card, a list of other places Gierek might be found. Labs 1A43, 1A45, 2B26. Virgo glanced up and down the corridor. There was no one around. He hesitated, and then thought better of trying to force the door. There would be easier, less conspicuous ways in.

The labs were all locked, as he suspected they would be. But each one had a list of four or five names pinned to the door. Gierek had a number of students, it seemed. Virgo picked the most exotic name from among them – Nickolas Tsankov. Eastern European? He rolled the name around his tongue, practising a pronunciation under his breath. As long as Facilities were of the usual kind – lazy and xenophobic – he would have the keys in minutes.

CHAPTER 41

FRANK DELANEY STOOD OUTSIDE the FBI's Boston field office and finished his cigarette. You couldn't smoke in government buildings these days. Or think for yourself. Jesus, what was he thinking, using his initiative like this? No one used their initiative in the Bureau any more – it was practically against regulations.

But it was worth it if it gave him back some peace. Nathaniel Virgo had bugged him for a couple of days now. The lie about the disk, the closed investigation. And then he came to Boston and gave a false address. A lot of questions there.

'Hey, Frank.' Lorraine passed him and entered the building. Like he'd seen her just yesterday. It had been, what? Five years?

'Hey, Lorraine.' He took a final drag, then squashed the butt into the sand. Time to go in.

Getting out had been better.

'Delaney. How you doing?'

Hal Morgan was giving him the concerned head-tilt from behind the huge, cluttered desk. Towers of paper rose up from coloured plastic trays sitting on each corner.

'Bullshit, Morgan. Like you ever cared.' Delaney allowed

his face to break into a smile, then moved into the Bureau chief's office and shook Morgan's hand. 'How's that paperless office coming along – any sign of it yet?'

Morgan motioned to the papers. 'It's coming any day now. Soon as I fill in the application forms here, Bureau'll have it delivered. Sit down, Delaney. How's things at Quantico?'

'Pretty quiet.'

'Quiet good or quiet like hell?'

Delaney shrugged. 'It's all hell, ain't it?'

'Can I get you some coffee?'

Delaney held up a hand. 'I'm good, thanks.' He hesitated, trying to find the right way to break out of the niceties.

'What we talked about on the phone...' he began. 'Nathaniel Virgo.'

Morgan eased back in his chair. 'I had a look at the file. Like you asked. Not much to go on. Wanted for questioning, that's it.'

'But the British are looking for him.'

'As I recall, we're independent now, Delaney.' Morgan's mouth twitched in a suppressed smile. 'Did no one tell you? There was some declaration. Back in 1776, I believe. We're very proud of it in Boston – it all kicked off round here. You should look it up in a history book. Pretty stirring stuff.'

Delaney ignored the sarcasm.

'So I'm asking a favour.'

'And I owe you a favour.' Morgan raised his eyebrows. 'Or I did. A friend of mine at the *Globe* just paid it back. Didn't you see the paper today? Your boy is front-page news.'

Morgan leaned forward again, then pointed to his secretary's office.

'See that phone there? That's the Frank Delaney hotline. Get some coffee, kick off your shoes, and take a seat in Rosemary's guest chair. Somebody, somewhere is bound to see your fella soon.'

CHAPTER 42

THE FACILITIES COUNTER WAS near the main entrance of the physics building, just beyond the wall of photographs. As Virgo approached, a fat, red-faced man with slicked-back silver hair looked up from the sports pages of the *Globe*. Virgo held his gaze and smiled.

'Hello, I am Nickolas Tsankov, one of Professor Gierek's students.'

The man looked up. He was wheezing heavily with every breath.

Virgo hammed up the accent. 'He is at . . . a conference in Japan, and has . . . asked me to fax him some papers from his office, for a . . . presentation he is giving this afternoon. I don't have his office . . . er . . . keys – he said you would lend them to me?'

The man grunted and heaved himself up from his chair. 'I can't give you the keys,' he said. He stood tall and inflated. 'It's against regulations. The professor'll have to call me or one of my colleagues himself if he wants something.' He succeeded in his effort to sound pompous and inconvenienced, and topped it off with a superior downward gaze.

Virgo took a breath and tried another tack. 'Are you Jerry? Professor Gierek said to ask for you. It is the middle of the . . . er . . . night in Japan. He said you would understand, and help him.'

Jerry glowed at the praise. He was wearing a name badge; it was almost too easy.

'Look, I can't give you the keys,' he said, deflating before Virgo's eyes. 'But I can sure as hell open up his office for you. That OK?'

Virgo nodded gratefully and headed quickly towards the lift. Jerry heaved along twenty paces behind him. As Virgo turned the corner and stood in front of the lift door, he noticed the alarm button. He glanced over his shoulder. Jerry was still out of sight. Virgo slapped the button and saw a red light appear above the shutters. He headed back round the corner and slammed into Jerry's stomach.

'The elevator's not . . . not . . . er . . . working, Mr Jerry,' he said. Was he overdoing it? 'Shall we take the stairs?'

Jerry hesitated and leaned to look round the corner. He saw the red light and grunted.

'It's the third floor, isn't it?' he said.

Jerry looked behind him, then at the stairs. He grunted again, and pulled a huge, rattling bunch of keys from his pocket. He flicked three of them round, and held the fourth between a massive forefinger and thumb. He handed the bunch to Virgo. 'This is the one you want,' he muttered. 'Be quick or I'll get my ass kicked.'

Virgo grabbed the keys and bounded up the stairs.

Closing the door behind him, Virgo took in the scene. There were piles of paper everywhere, most of them printouts from the web archive where researchers posted their papers before publication. Stacks of journals covered the desk. Running along the wall to his left, floor to ceiling, six rows of shelving heaved with texts on every conceivable area of physics. Many of them were in Polish.

Keys?

Where would Gierek keep his lab keys? Virgo knew time

was running against him. As soon as Jerry realised that his laziness could cost him his job, he would come looking. He only had a few minutes.

What he wanted to see wouldn't be in the office. It was in a lab somewhere, *wrapped up in a blanket in a cupboard*. He could still hear Gierek's voice.

But where were the keys?

He stepped into the room and pulled at the desk drawers. They were locked. He looked at the bunch of keys in his hand. None of them would fit these tiny locks. Beginning to panic, he tugged hard at a drawer handle. The force dragged the desk away from the wall, and a pile of journals slipped down onto a stack of papers on the floor, knocking them askew. Virgo looked around. There must be something here that he could use to lever the drawers open. There was a stainless-steel letter opener in a stationery holder on the windowsill. He grabbed it and set to work.

He was sweating in the institutional heat of the building and, after a few twists, the opener slipped from his hand. It gouged a track down the front of the desk drawer and clattered onto the floor. As he stooped down to pick it up, there was a sharp rap on the door. The handle turned.

'Are you still in there?'

Shit.

The door opened.

Jerry's eyes scanned the room, his gaze narrowing as he finally located Virgo, crouched under the desk, knife in hand.

'*Jeeezus*. What're you doin'?'

He took a step into the room, his bulky frame knocking the door aside. Virgo looked up as the door rebounded from its rubber stop. A bunch of keys, strung on a red and white striped cord, flew upwards, then clattered against the back of the office door.

On the door, looped over the coat hook. Blindingly bloody obvious.

'I dropped the papers behind the desk. I was just trying to

reach them.' Virgo gagged: he had also dropped the accent. He put the letter opener gently down onto the carpet. 'Got them... now, though,' he said, his vaguely Balkan roots miraculously restored. 'Shall we go?'

Jerry looked puzzled and said nothing. Virgo got up, one of the papers in hand, and threw Jerry his keys. 'Here you are. Thank you for your help. Professor Gierek was certainly right about you.'

He took the few steps to the door and patted Jerry on the shoulder, pushing him gently backwards. 'Can you show me where the fax machine is?'

Virgo opened the door and followed the huge frame out into the corridor. As Jerry fumbled to find the door key, Virgo slapped himself on the forehead.

This was getting like pantomime.

'Sorry, I dropped my phone in there,' he said. 'Just a minute.'

Jerry looked up as Virgo disappeared back inside Gierek's office and pushed the door half-closed. Deftly, he lifted the keys from the coat hook, and stuffed them into his trouser pocket. He emerged again, smiled at Jerry, and waved the paper in the air.

'Now,' he said, patting Jerry's shoulder again. 'Where's that fax machine?'

Jerry left him alone at the fax machine. After two minutes, Virgo sloped off and headed for the nearest of Gierek's labs. With a quick glance up and down the empty corridor, he slipped a key into the lock. It turned first time. Easy.

The lab was spartan and contained nothing interesting. There was a connecting door into a second lab, but this appeared to be a clean room for making circuit boards – or maybe optical disks.

The third lab, on the second floor, had to be the place. Virgo stepped out into the corridor, locked the door behind him and headed for the stairs. Two minutes later, his heart began to race. At last, the numbness was dissipating, and he was feeling something. It was the urgency of consequences. He had to find it. He couldn't think about Rachel, but he wasn't going to let Katie die. And he certainly wasn't going to leave her an orphan. He had to make this work.

The wooden benches and the shelves on all four walls were crammed with equipment. But what he was looking for wasn't on show.

A few cupboards ranged across the wall furthest from the door. Virgo glanced at his watch: it was 10.45. He didn't have much time to spare now. He turned and locked the door from the inside. Whatever it was, it had to be in there.

CHAPTER 43

KATIE VIRGO NURSED A vague memory of a cock crowing. Her shoulders ached and her neck was stiff. She had slept with her prosthetic on, and the stump of her left leg ached too, now. But she wasn't going to give the surprise away yet. She had a plan for that moment.

She opened her eyes. Ramón and Vicente were staring at her from low stools on the other side of the room. She experienced a rushing giddiness as her mind reloaded.

'What time is it?'

'About eleven,' Vicente said. 'You sleep like *el diablo*.'

She sat up. The room didn't look any better than it had in the half-light of the electric bulb. It was still dim, a faint light struggling through the dirty net curtains at the window. On the shelf, the clock still said 11.15.

A smell in the air wrenched at her stomach.

'Do you have any food?' She realised that her hands were now free.

'It's coming.' Vicente glanced at the door, then yelled, 'Miguel!'

A few moments later, the door opened, and the little boy came through carrying three plates. He held one out to her, and she took it.

'*Gracias.*'

Miguel studied her face for a moment, like he was trying to dredge up a memory. His eyes clouded, and he turned and gave the other plates to the two men, then sat down on the floor in front of Vicente.

Katie hardly chewed as she gulped down the food. It was a mound of rice and black beans with a little sausage sprinkled through it, but it tasted like gourmet cuisine. As she finished, she looked up and saw Vicente staring at her. He was stroking Miguel's hair, running his fingers through it fondly. The boy had cuddled up close to him.

Vicente pointed at her empty plate. 'We call it *moros y cristianos*. Moors and Christians. Because of the black and white. You want more? He pointed at his own plate, lying untouched on the dusty floor beside him. 'We might be here a while. You should eat while you can.'

He motioned for Miguel to give her his portion. She accepted it gratefully and bolted most of it down. She was ravenous, and it was good. It felt ridiculous to be accepting Vicente's hospitality like this; surely she should be throwing it back in his face? She was taking food from the hand that had killed her mother just a few hours ago.

Maybe it was human to put survival ahead of expressing her despair, her outraged anger. Her mum was dead. But she couldn't think about it all now. She wanted to be able to cry when she did, and she couldn't afford that yet. Despair could wait.

Miguel was back at Vicente's feet, leaning against his leg, having his head gently stroked. Vicente looked like a tender father with his son.

'What happened to Miguel's father?' she asked.

Vicente gave a half-smile. 'He's a lazy womaniser.' He turned to Ramón. 'Aren't you?'

Ramón didn't react.

Miguel's eyes bored into her. There was no way he understood their conversation; there was something else going on in his head. He started to sing softly again – the same soft melody he had sung the night before.

She lifted her eyes to Vicente. 'What is he singing?'

Vicente's eyes clouded, and his hand stopped still on the boy's hair. 'It's a lullaby,' he said. 'It says, "Go to sleep and wake up when the light comes again." His mother used to sing it to him. I think he is still waiting for the light to come for her.'

Miguel looked up at Katie again. After a couple of seconds, she forced herself to look away. What she had planned was going to be hard enough already.

CHAPTER 44

VIRGO STARED INTO THE cupboard.
This was it. This was what Radcliffe, Gierek – and maybe Rachel – had died for. His own life might depend on it. Katie's too. And it was just a grey box, about the size of a VCR, tucked under a dust sheet at the back of the bottom shelf of the corner unit.

Virgo's hands shook as he bent down and pulled it carefully out. It was strangely light. He placed it on the nearest bench, stepped back and looked at Gierek's machine. Maybe its phantom weight was due to the plastic casing. The machine was neatly built, but unmistakably self-made; the folds of the casing were less neat than those a factory would produce, and it was scratched around the screws. The rear of the box looked like a standard interface set-up: there was a power input, monitor output, some kind of modem or ethernet socket, and mouse and keyboard ports. Virgo crouched down to look in the cupboard again. As he knew they would be, the peripherals were all there: a flat-screen monitor, mouse and keyboard. Gierek was obviously a believer in minimal engineering; no futuristic interfaces for his creation.

What *was* this thing?

Virgo's breath came in quick, shallow bursts as he plugged in the leads. He hit the power switch and watched the screen anxiously.

Had Gierek bothered with passwords? He hadn't. It was ridiculous when you thought about it. But somehow not surprising. Virgo was no better, after all: he'd never turned on the security features of the wireless router in his spare room at home. Anyone could sit in a car outside and surf the internet at his expense. He hadn't even altered the administrator's password from its factory default setting; anyone with half a brain for computer technology could take over his home network without a thought. But there was always something more important to do – like actually use the damn thing to surf the internet or play online videogames from the comfort of his sofa.

He watched the operating system boot up, then open a blank dialogue box. A prompt appeared on the screen.

>**Load activator**

He put the disk in. The drive whirred into action. It worked.

>**Location:**

He shrugged, typed in B-O-S-T-O-N, then hit the return key. So far so good.

>**Facility:**

What the hell did that mean? He looked around, then back in the cupboard where he had found the machine. There were a few programming manuals. And a box of data disks: most were blanks, but there were two marked *Red Spot Virus Protection*. Nothing else.

Facility? He shrugged. R-E-D S-P-O-T. Return.

>**Accessing Red Spot in Boston. Please wait . . .**

Virgo stared at the screen. What the hell was this?

The screen went blank, then blue. Then the machine displayed a failure message that stopped Virgo's breath in his throat.

> **Unable to access Red Spot in Boston. No access to remote location. Unable to link to entangled data.**

Bloody hell.

Maybe it needed the other disk. Maybe it didn't work properly because he didn't know what to type in. Maybe this was just the prototype, and there were others. It didn't matter. Virgo knew enough now; Gierek had created a machine that appeared to use entanglement to offer remote access to data. It was too big. If this was what these deaths were all about, he was not going to be allowed to walk away from this. Whether or not Genovsky knew about the machine; whether or not it really did what it claimed. There was no question of it. He would be killed once he handed over the disk to Genovsky. No question.

He ran through the options in his head. There was only one sequence of moves where he didn't end up dead and Katie too. And even that depended on what Alexandra Genovsky knew. Gierek's machine was to be either his death sentence or his way out.

Virgo ejected the disk and slid it into his pocket. He looked at his watch. Time was still ticking forward. He disconnected the box from its cables, and wrapped it back up in its dust sheet. He wouldn't need the other stuff: the cables and the peripherals. But maybe some extra disks would come in handy. He picked up three of the blank disks. Taking a final look around the walls, he moved towards the door, slid back the lock, and turned the handle. He breezed out into the corridor, smiled at the two young men passing by, and pulled the door shut. He locked it, and stuffed the keys back into his trouser pocket. Two minutes later, with the box held casually under his arm, Virgo was walking back towards Kenmore Square. The numbness of the early morning seemed to have gone now. He simply felt disconnected, driven only by the dictates of the thing playing out in his head.

Then he saw the *Boston Globe* in the newsrack.

Virgo put down the box and fumbled for some change, then punched it into the box's coin slot. He stood, transfixed, and read the whole story. It wasn't the lead – he was down-page – but there was a picture. He stared out from the page like a serial killer. The photo had been taken from the *Herald*'s website and placed under the headline 'Fugitive lands at Logan'. *A British journalist wanted in connection with two murders flew into Boston last night . . . The FBI are appealing for anyone who has seen this man to get in touch directly . . . 'Do not approach him,' cautions Frank Delaney, assistant special agent in charge of the investigation . . . 'Virgo may be armed and he is certainly dangerous.'* The story ended with a contact number for Delaney.

Delaney. The interrogator in London.

A cold drizzle began to fall. Virgo tried to think but he couldn't bring his mind into focus. The chilled rain crept under the collar of his jacket. He folded the paper and put it under his arm, then picked up the box. He moved to cross the traffic, then pulled back. A paranoia crept over him: everyone would recognise him now, surely? Thank God they had only run such a small photo. He wondered whether the *Herald* had authorised its release. Charles would be playing along with the authorities, assuring them that Virgo was innocent, while doing as little as possible to help find him. He certainly wouldn't call Virgo now. Charles knew Virgo would call if there was some way Charles could help him.

Focus. He had to focus.

Well, at least he had the FBI's number if he needed it.

He looked at his watch again.

Back to the hotel. He still had time to get this right.

CHAPTER 45

ALEXANDRA GENOVSKY STOOD IN front of the bathroom mirror and glanced over the neat row of jars and bottles. They were arranged alphabetically on the chrome shelf above the sink, Chanel to Yves Saint Laurent. She despised herself for buying the eye cream – it was an expensive indulgence, even for her – but the commercial had somehow got to her, made her think she'd been neglecting her eyes. At least she had the money to do something about it: she remembered how her mother's face had sagged, the bags under her eyes growing by the week. There were no eye creams in Bulgaria back then; she couldn't remember her mother even wearing make-up. And now, here in America, her daughter had more make-up, lotions and creams than she knew what to do with. Over-compensation, they call it.

Not that her looks were anything special. She was OK – and there wasn't exactly much immediate competition for Vasil's attention. She had learned to make the most of her features; learned what worked, what got a reaction, what disarmed. And her eyes were her best feature. They trailed away at the corners: Cleopatra without the make-up, Vasil once said. But the scar was always there, pulling at his gaze.

MICHAEL BROOKS

She looked to her left. The cupboard on the powder-blue wall was stuffed with make-up bought in nervous, random forays. She wondered whether she should start putting some on now; the flight had left her looking sallow. But she was, as always, nervous to start. She seemed to put too much on. At least, it always seemed like too much. In powder rooms she saw other women putting on more, but when they finished, they always looked like they were wearing less. Was there some trick to making it disappear into the face? No one had ever told her how to do make-up. She sometimes thought about enrolling in a class. But her work made evening commitments too difficult. Every week she flicked through magazines, studying the models, trying to see how they did it. It was an addiction, a compulsion. But there were worse things to be stuck on.

They wore a lot of foundation, the models. But the lights worked for them, made them flawless. Boston light didn't work for her. She had never been flawless, even before the scar; as a child she had been prone to spots. Now they were gone, but the scar had taken over their role. There was always something. She leaned forward towards the mirror. Crow's feet. Last month's *Harper's* said they worsened with laughing and smiling, and with too little sleep. Smiling certainly wasn't the problem. She narrowed her eyes, set them hard like when she was concentrating, focusing on the now, the job that had to be done. The skin folded, creasing around the eyes. That was it, that was the problem. Her jaw stiffened too, the muscles contracting to accompany, intensify the stare. The face of a killer. The magazines didn't tell you how to deal with the lines that created. Or which cleanser might wash that dirt away.

Was there time for a bath? She liked the idea of languishing, stopping everything, just for a moment. The steam might help with the bruise on her cheek. Nothing in the magazines said anything about how to reduce bruising. Was it one of those things that only time could heal?

She wondered what Vasil would say. It was a faint green-yellow now. The scar ran behind it, through it, rose up above it. She ran a finger gently over the ribbon of raised tissue, from her eye socket down to the corner of her mouth, wincing slightly at the pressure. She did it again, pressing harder so that the skin blanched around the cherry red line. Vasil would say nothing at the sight of her discoloured cheek. He had given her worse. But not lately, not now that she was doing so well. She was glad to be useful at last; it made the gratitude easier to bear. Without Vasil's kindness, at best she would be sweeping out houses in Pravets, or maybe Sofia. She owed him everything: her training, her career, even her haircut. To be part of what he did, that was surely better than cleaning houses.

He didn't have to take her in, offer her a chance. But he was kind, and a town man, not small-minded like the villagers. A disfigured girl, a girl who couldn't keep what she saw to herself; who would want her in his house? But Vasil had offered to take her away from the shame, and her parents had eagerly consented. Or at least that's how it seemed to her. They were glad to be rid of her, glad to end the relentless rounds of gossip. There was something almost laughable about the villagers' whispered conversations: all they talked about – all there was to talk about – for three months was her opened face. The 'tell-tale cut', they called it.

Alexandra tried not to blame her mother. It wasn't really her fault – it was just a little white lie that had spun her world out of control. But she'd felt a paralysing, numbing shock as she stood there in the darkness of the wood, a quiet fourteen-year-old with big eyes, and realised that her mother told lies: that it wasn't wolves that made the woods dangerous at night. The world was a more complicated place than her parents had ever let her know.

When Milko ran yapping from the house in the moonlight she had decided to be brave. Her beloved pet was worth the risk of those ravenous jaws. She was almost a grown-up; she would not lie in her bed while wolves tore Milko limb from limb. She would not lie there and listen to his yowling and yelping.

She was almost upon the women before she heard their shovels cutting at the earth. Peeking through the trees, her teenage heart ripped in two, looking at the sad faces. There were twenty of them; broken women, standing at the back of a dirty truck, digging shallow graves for two of their companions, while the men smoked and watched and stroked their guns. She had stared at the scene for a full minute and then slipped away unnoticed.

The sound of shovelling still kept her awake at night. She suffered echoes of that scene, could feel the cold touch of moonlight, whenever she heard the peculiar scrape of steel on soft earth. The noise of the machines digging tunnels under Boston had tortured her for months.

The tell-tale cut. Everyone in Bulgaria knew what it meant, the slash from the eye to the mouth. Her parents wept, her mother hiding her face when she visited in the gloomy rooms of the convent. She remembered looking up from the bed, and seeing the wear on the back of her mother's hands, the skin just beginning to crack and sag away from the knuckles. And the sad, broken steps as she walked away. If only she had told little Alexandra the real reason you didn't go into the woods at night. All of the villagers knew about the traffickers, that their routes to the west took them through the woods. Everyone knew better than to stray in there at night.

The Sisters had been kind, especially on the night they found her, before they discovered the priest hanging in the church. Afterwards, they tried to keep his death from her, but she heard the rumours after a few days when her schoolfriends visited. Her dreams were haunted by a swinging body, blown by the draughts that seeped in under the door by the chancel; he swung back and forth, flashing across the figure on the cross.

Her friends soon told her what happened. They found out from eavesdropping on their parents' late-night conversations: surely, the adults whispered, even a fourteen-year-old girl knew better than to trust the priests? Everyone knew the Catholics were still afraid. The persecution was meant to be over, but the priests would still do whatever it took to keep the churches open. Their protection came at an unholy price: the priests told the trafficking gangs everything they heard from the confessionals.

She had long made peace with Father Anastas, and in her dreams she sometimes couldn't distinguish his face from that of Our Lord in his Suffering. It was twenty-two years since her last confession. She would have a lot to say, but eternity would be long enough.

There was no time for a bath now. She had to get to the office to wait for Virgo. He would come; he might even be there already. She wondered about his wife. Rachel Virgo looked OK in the photograph. They seemed happy, him kissing her as she smiled for the camera. Well, she was dead now. Simply because Alexandra Genovsky couldn't think of a reason to keep her alive. When Vasil called and asked if there was any reason to keep two hostages rather than one, she had no answer for him. There was a strange kind of beauty in this casual power over life and death. Virgo would be devastated. But he would be focused, at least. She needed that disk back, whatever it was. The disk she had pulled from Gierek's body was blank – or at least that's how it seemed. Now she had to get Radcliffe's disk. She needed to clear up all the loose ends before this afternoon. Vasil demanded it.

Alex owed Vasil everything; she knew it as well as he did. He had been her salvation, got her out of the village. He had seen her through the end of high school, paid for college, even helped her learn the more difficult programming languages. He had brought her to America when NASA called on his skills, and got her a job in the same building. Together they even helped get one of the shuttles into space; it still sent

MICHAEL BROOKS

a shiver down her back remembering the noise of the launch. People said it was like thunder, but it wasn't. It was like the Earth roaring to heaven.

    Virgo was nothing to her.

CHAPTER 46

THROUGH THE GAP IN the hedging, Virgo could just make out the number on the building across the road. 1629. He had spent the cab journey trying to subtly hide his face in case the driver recognised him. In the end, he had asked the driver to let him out some way down the road. It wasn't just paranoia; he was early. Besides, he wanted to feel in control of this. He was going to do this on his terms.

The traffic was loud and noxious, but the dull scent of vegetation and the salt tang of the ocean held up against the fumes. Behind him, he could hear the tinny percussion of halyards flicking against their masts in the harbour's gentle swell.

He shivered, and turned to survey the path surrounding the green that stretched to the ocean. Joggers, rollerbladers, dog-walkers, mothers pushing those huge buggies – everyone seemed to be moving towards the cafe glowing warmly at the entrance to the Long Wharf. Children were climbing on steel pyramids, or swinging on suspended tyres. Busy with its leisure time, Boston ignored him.

Genovsky's building was peppered with glass and arches. Rachel had taught him to recognise the traits of postmodern architecture, its columns and pretensions, and ostentatious rooflines. He glanced up and down the Avenue again, and beyond to the steel and glass towers; corporate America.

Rachel. The thought of her made his heart jump in his chest. He took a deep breath, then looked at his watch: 11.58. Fifty metres and four lanes of traffic held him back. He had what he needed; all he had to do was pull this thing off, and it would all be over.

Time to go.

There was a gap in the traffic, and he stepped out in front of a bus. Its horn blared a deep warning, and its flat front came at him like a battering ram. He ran, and made it to the median. The traffic here was hell – downtown Boston seemed to be nothing but smoke and fire, pouring asphalt and melting tar, digging and scraping like a scene from Dante. Another gap, another sprint, and he was there.

Genovsky's voice was tinny through the small speaker at the door.

'Nathaniel. At last,' she said when he announced himself. 'First floor.'

The white painted door shifted slightly as the lock released. The buzzer was still sounding when he slammed the door shut behind him.

He was standing in a wide, carpeted lobby. The walls were painted cream, and broken up by six Warhol prints. Under each one was an armchair covered in tan suede, and beside each chair stood a glass table. Fresh white lilies sat in crystal vases on the tabletops. A polished brass handrail disappeared up a flight of stairs that rose from the far right corner of the lobby. Genovsky paid a lot in rent.

Hesitant, he moved towards the stairs, then jumped back as a figure wearing a dark, well-cut suit appeared at the bottom step. The man didn't notice him; he skipped quickly past without a glance or a nod. Calm down. He could do this. Slowly, calmly, he went up the stairs.

The door from the stairwell opened into a cavernous space. The room was stuffed with antiques – even the wallpaper looked aged and distinguished. But nothing quite worked; it was unconvincing. He had done interviews in homes like this on occasion, where people had money but didn't quite know how to spend it. Like the city skyline, this place was striving for something, showing off, unable to exercise restraint in the face of unfettered resources.

He glanced around from the doorway, but could see no one. He was about to step further into the room when a lacquered door opened in the side wall.

Maybe it was the surroundings, but Alexandra Genovsky seemed taller and more poised than he remembered. She stared at him for a moment, but he couldn't decipher her expression. Best just stare right back. As she came into the room, he could see the bruising he had inflicted: it was more violet now, and the scar running down her cheek stood out as a dull red curve.

'Come and sit down,' she said. She indicated an area of plush sofas on her left.

He stood still. Genovsky eyed him with an amused curiosity.

'Come on, let's not play games this time. Sit down, Nathaniel.' Her tone was terse and reproachful.

He inclined his head slightly – it was meant to look reflective, like it was his own decision to move – then walked across the room and sat down on a luxuriously cushioned sofa. He sank into it, struggled upright again, and perched himself on the edge. Genovsky remained standing.

'Scotch?'

He shook his head.

Genovsky lifted two crystal tumblers from a silver tray, poured a slug of rich gold into each, and dropped in some ice.

She forced one on him. 'It's not poisoned,' she said. 'Have a drink, for God's sake.'

He took it, and sipped. The smooth burn was a curiously welcome sensation.

'I have your disk,' he said.

193

'That's good.' Genovsky sat down opposite him. 'Because, as you know, I have your daughter.' She smiled.

He didn't.

'Is Rachel dead?'

Genovsky didn't react at first. The smile was still on her lips, while her eyes bored into him. Did she care? Was she really that cold?

'Yes,' she said eventually. Something in her eyes shifted.

Virgo suppressed a shiver, and forced Katie's face into his mind. It pulled him back to the moment, away from Rachel. He felt guilty at the conscious abandonment of his wife. But he had to think of Katie.

He reached into his pocket and pulled out Radcliffe's disk. The plastic looked feeble, inconsequential in his hand. The case was scratched now, diffusing the iridescent shimmer of the disk inside. How could this be worth any life, let alone Rachel's? He pushed the tips of his index fingers against two of the sharp plastic corners, and watched the blood drain away, leaving his flesh a dirty yellow. He could feel Genovsky's eyes on him. Abruptly, he stood up again.

'Here's how this is going to work,' he said. He caught her eye, and held it. 'I went to Gierek's lab this morning. Some pretty fancy stuff there.'

Genovsky was watching him, her face impassive. He carried on anyway.

'I suppose you've seen Gierek's entanglement generator, but it was new to me. I think it was just a prototype, but it was surprisingly easy to use.'

Genovsky's face was frozen solid now.

Pure speculation. But the bluff might just work.

'I tried it out. I put your name and address and pretty much everything I know on a disk, and sent it to a friend at the FBI. I doubt you've got power over everyone there, Alex: I imagine that some people are beyond even Wheelan's control.'

Still nothing on her face. He took another sip of scotch.

'By the way, where does Thomas Wheelan fit into all this, Alex? Is he your boss, or Vasil's?'

For a moment, there was a flicker of something in her eyes, but then, immediately, she was simply returning his stare. She said nothing. He just had to keep going.

'The data is entangled and unreadable just at the moment, of course. You're certainly safe for about the next hour or so – not even the FBI can hack into this. But I set it up so that I need to renew the encryption every few hours. If I get out of here safely, and continue to be safe after Katie is landed, well, eventually I'll destroy the data permanently.' He paused. 'You and I are going to have to trust each other, Alex.'

Genovsky studied his face for a few moments.

'Trust,' she breathed, eventually. 'What do you know about trust?'

She sat down, and fingered the scar on her cheek. 'I trusted someone once and got my face cut open. I never forgot the lesson.'

Virgo was transfixed by the finger running along her scar. He saw her wince, almost imperceptibly – it was something in her eyes – every time the fingertip slid across the bruise.

'They made the priest stick the blade through the skin next to my eye. His hands were shaking and I felt every tremor as the metal tore a little more, pushed in a little bit further. Then they made him slide the knife down to my mouth.' She mimicked the slide with her finger.

Genovsky's tranquil expression caught hold of him.

'I was fourteen,' she said. 'That was when I learned about the consequences of trust.' She looked up. 'How old is your daughter?'

Virgo didn't answer. This woman didn't care how old his daughter was. The beatific smile faded from her face. Her finger still played along the scar. He tore his eyes away from it.

'Here you go. You've got what you wanted.'

He threw the disk to her. Genovsky caught it deftly, strode over to a desk in front of the window, yanked irritably at a drawer and pulled out a silver-grey laptop computer. She opened it up, released the disk tray and put Radcliffe's disk in, then closed it up. After thirty seconds, she looked up.

'It's blank,' she said. There was no attempt to hide the threat in her voice.

'It's the formatting. It's to do with the entanglement.' Virgo narrowed his eyes and maintained the cold bravado. 'Where's the disk you took from Gierek's dead body, Alexandra? What was on that? Put the two together. Think about what he had achieved.'

Careful. Not too much. She was studying him again, but she said nothing.

'You've got your disk. You've got everything. Now I want my daughter flown home. We don't want to have the authorities involved, do we? I bet Wheelan wouldn't want anything stirred up that he might not be able to control.'

She turned to face him, still betraying no reaction to the name. An icy silence hung in the air. Genovsky was staring into his face. Was his plan about to unravel? A cold threat simmered in her gaze, and the scar and violent bruising made her even more intimidating. Eventually she spoke, but her eyes were still studying him.

'OK,' she said. 'I'll make the arrangements. You're free to go.'

'How will I know Katie is safe?'

Genovsky smiled coldly. 'I'm sure she'll call you when she's home.' She turned to leave the room, then paused and turned back.

'Tell me something,' she said. There was an unpleasant edge to her voice, and the curve of her lip betrayed a sly smile. 'How do you know I won't have you killed next week?'

He stood still, and held Genovsky's gaze. 'Because that would decrypt the information I sent to the FBI. I'm not going to tell you when I plan to finally destroy that information. And because I have also sent a note to my lawyer, to be opened on the event of my death or Katie's, detailing everything I know about you and your project.'

He held Genovsky's gaze for a few seconds. Eventually, she looked down at the floor, then back up at him. She still seemed amused, though the chill had returned to her gaze. He couldn't tell if she believed his bullshit.

'Goodbye, Nathaniel Virgo.' She walked across the room and opened the door she had come in by. A moment later, he was alone in the room.

You're free to go. He stood, dazed, where Genovsky had left him. What was he going to do now? The chemical comedown of anticlimax flowed through his bloodstream.

And what about Gierek's prototype – or whatever it was? What the bloody hell was an entanglement generator? Whatever it was, it was sitting in the wardrobe of his room at the hotel. He couldn't take it home. He couldn't hand it to the FBI – he didn't want anything to do with them until Katie was at least safe, and could corroborate his story. Was he just going to leave it in the room and walk away?

He didn't have to decide that right now.

He pulled open the door to Genovsky's office and descended the stairs, feeling as disconnected as he had done on the ascent. He was ambling, a foot hovering over each step before it fell. At the bottom, he pulled the door open, and a blast of cold air hit him full in the face. Ahead of him across the street, beyond the laurel hedge and the swathe of grass, the boats rocked back and forth. Their masts and halyards were still clinking together, but the noise seemed tuneful now, like a childish percussion.

He breathed deeply. The rain had stopped. Things were looking better. Genovsky had let him go.

His foot paused mid-step.

But why? She, or the people she worked for, had been ruthless at every turn. Radcliffe, Gierek, Rachel . . . why, after all of this, would Genovsky let *him* walk away? Did she believe him about the disks and the FBI? Was she worried that Wheelan would be exposed? Was he even right about Wheelan?

He would just have to hope so. But it wasn't his problem. It couldn't be. Even if this involved the Secretary for Homeland Security, even if America was besieged by a thousand hijacked planes, it was Katie who mattered. Katie was the only story here. She was his only responsibility.

The people passing along the footpath below were hunched against the bitter wind. A cloud swept across the sky over the sea. He felt the chill now, too: the elation, even the comedown was dissipating fast. He buttoned up his jacket and stuffed his numb hands into its pockets. His fingers felt the absence of Radcliffe's disk.

Briskly, he skittered down the steps onto the sidewalk and moved out to the edge of the street. He had to get back to the hotel. He had to be ready the moment Katie landed. He had to talk to her before she even got through immigration. A passing cab pulled over at his anxious wave, and he climbed in.

CHAPTER 47

GENOVSKY WALKED QUICKLY, KNOWING she'd be late for Vasil if she didn't hurry. They were meant to be meeting for a quick lunch at Les Zygomates. She didn't want to phone him; she'd simply have to turn up flustered. If she was first there, that would give her time to cool down; if he beat her to it, then she would at least look like she had hurried.

It was an act of will not to take a cab; South Street wasn't far enough away to bother getting involved with the grinding traffic, but Genovsky hated walking under the gleaming skyscrapers of the financial district. If she looked up, the reflections in the glass disoriented her; it felt as if the buildings were falling. She looked down at the pavement, or at the people coming towards her, souls occluded by suits.

Like Gabriel MacIntyre. She hadn't met him yet – that would come later today. But from what Vasil said, his suit mattered more to him than his soul. He had jumped at the entanglement software, no reservations. She hadn't been in on the early stages of the sale. Something strange had gone on between Vasil and Laszlo in the weeks before. There had been a new tension between them, an increased intensity in Laszlo's servitude. That was when she had first felt excluded, like she was a hired hand, not a partner, in Vasil's enterprises. She became so upset she had even dared to ask him what was going on. He said nothing, of course. Vasil was properly focused, single-minded even, when a project was coming to fruition. If it didn't concern her, he wouldn't include her. It was only fair.

And he did tell her eventually. Vasil and Laszlo seemed to emerge from that period happier than she had ever known them. She had actually heard Vasil laugh at one point. Laszlo just looked dazed and relieved, like a man released from death row. And MacIntyre was suddenly the centre of their world.

He paid a lot of money, too: they were almost at what they needed. Or what Vasil needed; it had never been about money for her. She had nothing when he took her in, and she needed nothing more now. Everything she did – the clothes, the presentation, the programming, the co-ordination, the killing – was for him. It was what she owed him. She glanced at her reflection in the office windows. She was looking good today. Black Chanel, the trouser suit he liked.

The skyscrapers eventually gave way to brick and arches; the galleries and lofts, the old warehouses of the leather district, were more trustworthy. She liked it here, among the artists with their strange tattoos.

As she passed the restaurant window, she glanced in. Through the smoked glass, she could see Vasil, his long silver hair scraped back into a ponytail. He was sitting at their usual table, examining the back of his left hand. She felt a shot of nerves – she never knew how he would be. Sometimes he was happy to wait, to indulge her failings. And sometimes he didn't have the time or the patience.

She ran up the steps and pushed the door open, clothing herself with a look of hurried apology. To her relief, he gave her a thin smile. She sat down opposite him. He was wearing a black suit, and the multicoloured tie she'd bought him for St Lazarus's day. It was a mess of orange, green, pink, yellow and blue; it had reminded her of the costumes she'd worn in the village processions. The blue was the colour of the Bulgarian sky in spring.

'He arrived at the last moment, but it's all in hand,' she said. 'I have the disk.'

'All in hand, or all done?'

She hesitated. The restaurant was busy and loud with conversation and laughter, people from the financial houses entertaining each other on bottomless expense accounts. There was so much money in this city. People said it had a soul, a heart, but she'd never seen it. Genovsky preferred the honesty of the cities in the south, where greed was open, worn on the sleeve. Here, they pretended it was all about something else, about Harvard and MIT, about knowledge and learning and improvement. But people were people, whatever business they were in. It was always about money.

'All done.' She didn't want to lie to him, but she knew how he could be. Loose ends upset him. And this one wasn't really loose. She had both the disks now: between them, they would be able to figure out what was going on with the entanglement.

'All done. We can put his daughter on the plane. He won't take any risks. Once today is over, we can get rid of him.'

'Why wait? Why didn't you kill him once you had the disk?'

She looked from side to side. Vasil had leaned forward to whisper, but his voice was still too loud. She didn't know enough about what Virgo said, about the entanglement generator, to tell Vasil the truth. Not yet. She realised she was staring at the black and white check of the floor, and quickly raised her head to meet his gaze.

'I didn't want to worry about a body. Not here. Not today.' Here was a chance to change the subject. 'Is everything ready?'

Vasil leaned back in his chair. 'It's all ready.' He smiled, and she felt a thrill.

201

They looked over the menu in silence. After a couple of minutes, Vasil leaned forward again, and ran a finger over her cheek. 'He gave you quite a pounding.'

She flinched and pulled away. 'I've had worse.'

'Still, I can't help but feel we owe him something.' Vasil pulled a phone from his jacket pocket. 'And it won't hurt to keep the stakes high a little longer.' He looked down at the phone and frowned, then held it up. 'No signal in here. I'm going outside. If Artur comes, I'll have grilled pears, then the catfish.'

She watched him through the window. When he ended one call, he dialled another number, and his face became hard. He seemed to be in an argument – something changed in his face when he was angry, but she could never see quite what it was. The second call only lasted half a minute.

When he returned, she waited for him to say something, but he seemed lost in thought.

'You haven't told me about the . . . the threat,' she said eventually. 'Where are the planes coming from?'

'Lots of places.' Vasil smiled, almost imperceptibly. 'Including Cuba.'

It took her a moment to work out what he meant. She didn't know why it upset her: she had been happy to kill Virgo, after all. She still would be. And his wife was nothing to her. But his daughter – that felt different; fifteen was so young to lose your life. She should know.

'There's no screwing this up, Alexandra. This deal is . . . it could make everything worthwhile. All those years . . . Even that –' He reached out and touched her scar again. 'Have you done all the checks? The feeds are in place?'

'Everything is in place. Wheelan's had the Oval Office link set up for days. The only difficulty has been in keeping up with the Pentagon's key changes. Someone has to spot that the transmissions are encrypted again. But Wheelan says the quantum computer has got the transition time down to thirteen seconds now. That's thirteen seconds we lose every fifty-seven minutes. This thing's really powerful, Vasil.' She looked up at him, searching for a hint of a smile, an acknowledgement of all they had achieved together. There had been almost no difficulties, only the problem with Paul Radcliffe. And they had dealt with that now, wiped it away. She was sure Vasil must be pleased at how things had turned out.

He looked at her, seemingly amused, for a moment. Then he turned away, looking for a waiter. No sign of one anywhere. He turned back.

'So he – Virgo – will do nothing while his daughter is on the plane?'

She wondered if she should have killed Virgo already. For his daughter's sake. No, she had done the right thing. She was right to check out his story. There would be plenty of time to dispose of him later.

'No. He won't do anything,' she said. And she couldn't help what was going to happen to his daughter. She looked at her watch. It was too late to change anything now.

Vasil was watching her. The amused smile was back. 'It's better this way. Now we just have a teenage girl to deal with. Do you remember how easy it is to keep teenage girls in check, Alex?' His smile broadened. 'You were no trouble, were you?'

Genovsky stared back at Vasil, through him, into the past. He was right to be so callous. They had a job to do.

But it did seem different now. Now that they were ripping apart the life of a young girl, she felt something shift. Somehow, it weakened her, and she couldn't allow that to happen. She forced herself back into the room.

'We should order,' she said. 'Where are all the waiters today?'

CHAPTER 48

IT WAS A SOUND Katie had only ever heard in black and white movies: the tinny ring of an old telephone bell. It seemed to take Vicente by surprise; he jumped to his feet and scurried out of the room to answer the call. Miguel followed him out, leaving her alone with Ramón. He grinned at her, and pointed the gun at her head. But he also seemed to be on edge, not quite sure how he was meant to behave now. Edgy didn't seem like such a good state for him to be in: it was time for her to start talking.

'Ramón, where did you learn English?'

He looked at her, suspicious. 'From the radio. And from working in hotels. Tourists teach you many things.' He raised his eyebrows. 'I taught the tourist ladies many things too.'

The leery grin returned. He really was a stomach-turner, like the worst of the boys she knew. She feigned an embarrassed giggle. It almost hurt.

'You speak very well. I –'

Vicente burst back into the room. 'Time to go,' he said. 'Now.'

She felt immediately sick. The last time Vicente got a call he marched them out to her mother's execution. It was all starting up again. Something inside her had got used to the calm of sitting, captive, in this dirty room. Her left leg was hurting badly now – she'd had the prosthetic on for way too long. But she still wasn't going to betray its presence. Not quite yet. With a skill born of desire not to stand out, Katie forced her body forward and stood up, her weight resting entirely, but imperceptibly, on her right leg.

Miguel appeared at the door and watched as Vicente bound her hands viciously tight behind her back again. Was that something that would stick with him forever? It was nothing compared with the scar she was planning to inflict on him.

Vicente pushed her out into the brightness of the day, and opened the car door. He had transformed again: the man who'd gently stroked Miguel's head was gone. Where did he go? How did Vicente crush that side of him down so far? And how did it ever come back?

She looked up and down the street; it was empty save an old woman walking slowly away from them along the cobbles, her back bent over and her frame leaning heavily on a crooked stick.

Vicente shoved her into the back seat of the car and the jellied springs sagged underneath her. Through the dirty window, Katie could see Miguel watching from the doorway. He continued to stare at her – they stared, wide-eyed, at each other – as the car pulled away.

'Where are you taking me?' Katie said. Her voice came out flat, lifeless.

Ramón turned and leered; he was back on form. 'You want me to take you?' He raised his eyebrows and laughed. Vicente turned his head and scowled at him.

'Varadero,' he said. 'The airport.'

They were out of town within minutes, driving along a flat, smooth highway. Though Katie caught a glimpse of the sea only occasionally, she could tell they were sweeping along the coastline. The landscape was lush, the verdant hills behind the road rising into the perfect sky.

Vicente was driving fast, overtaking everything in their way. She was losing the ability to think. Her mother's last whimper filled her mind. She had to pull herself together, she had to find the right moment. The monotony of the road gave no opportunity for surprise – her only hope would be at their destination.

Roadside fruit sellers punctuated the route, sheltering in the shade of palm trees. Katie felt an increasing isolation. She had no status, no rights, nothing she could draw from. It was her against them. The road signs, with their black silhouette of a plane at take-off, gave her a pitiless countdown. Twenty kilometres, then sixteen, then ten, then five. There was no way she could do anything now. Not until the car stopped. And there was no reason for them to stop until they arrived.

If they were just going to put her on a plane, wouldn't she be a liability? She could tell the aircrew what had happened to her. Why would they let her get on a plane – would it all be over by the time she landed? If all this had been about her dad, did that mean he was dead now? Was that it? Surely that made a difference. If he was dead, and these people were untraceable, they would let her go – she was of no use. The thought made her stomach heave and lift, equal and opposite reactions.

What if he was alive? What if he had negotiated her freedom, and this was how it was to be? She had to know more.

'Are you going to put me on a plane to London?' She spoke loudly to overcome the noise of rubber on asphalt. There seemed to be a hole in the floor of the car somewhere; exhaust fumes were rising into her nostrils.

Vicente glanced back at her. 'We are going to put you on a plane. That's all you need to know.'

'And then I'm free?'

'When you land, then you are free.'

'And if I tell the people on the plane I was kidnapped and that you killed my mother?'

'They will land the plane at its destination, and they will

tell you to go to the local police. They will contact the Cuban authorities, who will find nothing – not even the body.' He paused. 'Oh, and our colleagues will kill your father.' He said it casually – an afterthought. Katie tried not to hear it. It wasn't true; she was leverage, not the reason he would live or die. But at least this meant her father was alive. Maybe he really had negotiated her safe return. She needed more information.

'Are you coming on the plane?'

Another pause. 'No.'

Ramón laughed. 'Vicente does not like planes.'

Vicente leaned across and cuffed him around the head. Why would they put her on a plane alone? None of this made sense. She couldn't trust them: she had to take control. She could get out of this, and she would.

Ramón was still laughing. Ramón was the weak link. Vicente was cool and could even be kind, but when he had to shoot people dead, he did it. Ramón was a moron. And she could handle morons. She watched the road ahead, and prayed.

CHAPTER 49

THEY WERE THERE. KATIE'S heart pounded in her chest as Vicente pulled into the airport car park and drew to a halt between two huge coaches. Ahead, through the windscreen, she could see the low tiled roof of the terminal. It looked more like a village than an airport; the site was dotted with palm trees and low buildings with red-tiled roofs.

Vicente opened the car door, took a knife from his pocket and cut her hands free from the cable. As the stiff copper wire fell onto the seat, Katie saw the crystal sparkle of the newly cut metal. The angle was right. If she could just pull back a little more of the plastic insulation, it would do the job.

'If you do as we say, you will be fine,' Vicente said.

'And if I don't?'

He fixed his gaze on her eyes. 'You know I will shoot you dead if I have to.'

Katie allowed herself to collapse back on the seat while holding his gaze.

'It won't make a difference to me,' Vicente continued. 'Whatever happens, I will walk away from this. It's really up to you.'

She smiled in grim acceptance. The wire was in her pocket. As Vicente walked ahead of her towards the building, she let her finger touch it, slide back and forth over the edge. It was razor sharp. Her thumbnail caught the plastic, and pulled at it, peeled at it. She began to hang back, just a step or two, so that Ramón was close enough to touch her. She knew he would. At first just a hand on her back. But just before they left the shelter of the coaches she felt his hand slide downwards. Despite the instinctive shiver she didn't allow herself to withdraw from his grasp. She was fifteen and beautiful, and she would use that to her advantage. She concentrated on walking without a trace of a limp, setting her face into a smile, then looking over her shoulder from time to time to catch his eye. His face was shiny from sweat, a drip running down the side of his forehead. His grin bared teeth stained by tobacco. He disgusted her. But she would have to live with that.

Fans whirred in the ceiling inside the terminal. Katie felt otherwordly, as if she was floating through the crowds of smiling tourists. A party had just arrived, and their tour organiser was anxiously waving them through towards the coach park. She yearned to turn and run and join them, but that wouldn't be enough. She had to have her captors taken out, or taken captive. She prayed again, this time for police.

Vicente led them straight past the row of check-in desks, towards the departures gate. Ramón kept close, still touching her whenever he could. Across the concourse, she could see two armed police in blue uniforms. Vicente paused in front of a closed door. It said *Prohibido La Entrada*. No Entry. Time was running out. Once through that door, she would be on a hidden path.

'I need to go to the toilet.' Katie pointed across the concourse. 'Before I get on the plane. I really need to go. It's just there.' Then she pointed at Ramón. 'He can come with me. To make sure I behave.'

For the first time, she saw doubt in Vicente's eyes; he seemed genuinely unsure of himself. He looked at Ramón, then back at Katie.

'OK,' he said. 'Quickly.' He muttered something to Ramón, who touched his belt to reassure Vicente he was armed. Ramón pushed Katie gently in the direction of the toilets. She glanced back at Vicente. He was staying by the door, looking left then right, up and down the concourse. Waiting for someone.

Katie's heart thumped in her chest. She could hear Ramón's breathing behind her as she led him into the cubicle. It was just large enough for the two of them. His hands were on her as she shut the door, pulling at her blouse. His breathing was loud and deep. She could feel a hardness as he pressed his crotch against her, and a grunt sounded in his gullet. Her stomach turned as she kissed his neck, and her hands shook as she reached down into her pocket. He was pulling at her skirt. She pushed his hands away, gave him a coy look, then started to pull the skirt up.

She knew how he'd react. Everything in him would stop when she revealed her prosthetic. He would be confused for a second or more, not knowing how to react. Just like all the other boys.

It gave her the time and space she needed.

With a slash of copper wire, Katie Virgo cut Ramón's throat.

She thought the blood would cover her, but she spun him away in his shock, and it pulsed onto the wall of the cubicle as his knees crumpled. Ramón was gasping and gurgling, and Katie could hardly bear to breathe as she watched him. She waited for the sound to stop before she opened the door.

Vicente saw her come out of the toilet alone, and moved towards her. She began to run. She was limping now; no one could run properly on a standard prosthetic, and the lining had rubbed away at her stump. But she timed it perfectly; there could be no doubting that Vicente was chasing her. She put her hands to her head and screamed as she ran. 'Help me. *Ayuda. Là.*' As she reached the two policemen, she turned and pointed. '*Socorro!* Help!' Before Vicente could stop and lose himself among the crowds, two 9 mm pistols were aimed at his head.

Katie hardly heard the screams of the tourists. She saw the area clear, and felt a surge of triumph overwhelm her. The scene was stationary: the policemen crouched in aim, and Vicente standing in front of them, hands raised. All she could hear was the rush and whoosh of blood as it raced around in her head.

She had done it. She was free.

CHAPTER 50

THE HALL WAS READY. The sight of it thrilled Genovsky: that they had come as far as this seemed impossible. The huge array of electronics racks facing them, the antennae and dishes on the roof, the wall-mounted display screens and speakers hanging from the ceiling gantry; she had organised every bit of this day, and it would be flawless. Her eyes stopped on the small silver box, only the size of a large suitcase, standing on a tall black steel bench beside the platform. It was all for this. This, their greatest achievement.

When she'd first seen the quantum computer, when Laszlo had handed it over, she had run her fingers over the corners of its grey casing and knew immediately that it needed something grander. It had to be polished and beautiful. She couldn't understand why Laszlo would have made its final covering so ugly. He had spent decades working on it. And when he had finally done it – achieved the impossible – he dressed it like a cheap PC. It had looked like the things they produced back home: the glorious squalor of the Pravets computer, the product of a grinding communist state where vision was to be subverted for the people, ploughed into the fields, shared and diluted, rendered useless.

Vasil had shown breathtaking vision; he began to pull all

this together so many years ago. He saw where things were going: the conjunction of smuggling – the drugs and guns and people – and the science of secrets. She felt privileged to be part of it: one of those sent out to work in the land of opportunity, where vision and daring were rewarded. Laszlo never showed the same gratitude; he never got over betraying his friends for the chance to carry on his research. He lived in fear, and died of shame.

They competed, fear and shame. Right up to the end, he was terrified of what they might do to him. And he was ashamed he had used his genius on their behalf. Fear was a truer guide. Fear kept him alive. Shame, the shame that led him to bring Paul Radcliffe in on his secret, that was what had killed Laszlo in the end.

She knew the better way: gratitude and debt. And love. She was almost sure she loved Vasil. Not love in the glossy magazine sense, not that husband and wife kind of interdependence; she did not deceive herself into thinking that Vasil depended on her. He could live without her, she knew that. But she orbited him, lived in his gravity. It was just how things were; you came into someone's path and they were so much bigger than you couldn't escape their pull. And so you orbited, and you gazed inwards and you knew you'd never escape. You did what you could, everything you could, made them glad that you and no other soul were their satellite. It was simpler, stronger like that. Equal, mutual need was destructive. If two identical stars orbited each other, they spiralled in. They ended up destroying each other, and nothing survived. Like Nathaniel Virgo was spiralling in on his dead wife right now. It was no one's fault; not his, not hers. But that didn't stop everything collapsing in on itself to an assured mutual destruction.

She and Vasil would walk away from this, their fortunes assured, to a new life where there were no more projects: just the two of them, secure and blissful. Vasil had bought her a spinning globe, told her to pick a country. She wanted to go to Australia. She had always wanted to go to Australia: her parents' encyclopaedia back home had pictures of the strangest animals. She used to look at it in the early mornings, before school; she fell in love with the kangaroos, their tiny infants peeking out from the pouch. That looked like the right way to grow up.

She thought fleetingly of Virgo's daughter.

'Alexandra.' She looked up. Vasil was smiling at her, but it was his working smile, the one that required instant obedience. 'Are you ready?'

She was ready. Vasil was putting a lot of faith in her, letting her handle so much tonight. And she would not disappoint him: whatever was going on with Virgo and the entanglement generator, she wouldn't let Vasil down. This would be his crown, his mark of ascendancy complete. Years ago, in his house in Pravets, he had told her he would do great things, things that would make him richer than anyone in that stinking town, richer than the thugs that trafficked frightened women through moonlit nights, beating them to death if they tried to escape their fate. And here he was, here *they* were, in the vanguard of a revolution.

She walked across to the front of the hall. A few technicians were fussing around the casing, checking connections, then glancing at their laptop screens to register the outputs. There was no input yet, that would come later. For now, the machine rested in its potential, its drives and data buffers sitting happily in superposition. Strings of atoms – set in nothing more complex than a peculiar plastic, Laszlo had said – in their billions, each one in two different quantum states at once: simultaneously binary 0 and binary 1. And when the data came, it would push them one way or the other. Then the final coup de grâce: the laser pulse that swept through the molecules at the speed of light, its energy first entangling their strange hybrid states to run a billion calculations at once, then falling away to collapse the quantum states into the binary code for the final result. The key. The key to the White House communications codes. And to their new life away together.

Wherever that would be – Vasil had said he didn't like the idea of Australia. She would let him decide.

CHAPTER 51

KATIE STOOD STILL, HER heart beating out of her chest. It was over.

A tall, wiry man in a brown suit walked calmly into the scene. He was holding a gun in his left hand, and the policemen lowered their weapons in deference to his. Secret police? Everything was under control. The man caught hold of Vicente's shirt, and beckoned to Katie.

'Please,' he said. His smile told her he wasn't fazed by anything. 'This way.'

He moved towards the door where Vicente had stopped. He opened it and, keeping his gun trained on Vicente, courteously stepped aside to allow Katie through.

She found herself standing in a cavernous hall that was criss-crossed by an intestinal mess of conveyor belts carrying tagged luggage. The cases and bags were flowing out into the light, out to waiting trolleys. Then they were going away from this place. She felt tension relieve in her shoulders at the thought. *She* was going away from this place. She heard the door close behind her, and turned round.

The man in the brown suit was aiming his pistol at her chest.

'You were very careless there, Vicente,' he said, quietly. He reached into his jacket and pulled out a sheaf of papers. Without taking his eyes off Katie, he handed them over his shoulder. 'Take these. There's been a change of plan. You're going with her. The plane is ready.'

Vicente took the papers. Katie stared at the gun, transfixed. She had done everything possible to win her freedom. How could she still be in this nightmare? She couldn't move, couldn't think, could hardly even breathe. She was crushed, defeated.

She forced her chest to expand, to take in air. It was a setback, but she wasn't defeated. Not yet. She would exhale in a moment, and she would be cool again. She would begin to calculate, to plan her next escape.

She exhaled.

'Why would I get on this plane?' she said.

She would not be beaten down by this. She had just killed a man. Now, there were no limits.

'Because your father's life depends on it.'

He knew it was the one claim that would make her hesitate, and she hated him for it. She believed this man in a way she hadn't Vincente. She had already tried to get away once – this time they would make sure there wasn't another chance. And if her dad's life was really at stake, she wouldn't take it anyway. Thousands of miles apart, they were in this together.

'How do I know that?'

'Because he's already in America trying to save you. Do you have his phone number? We could call him right now.'

Vicente reached into his chest pocket. 'I have it.' He handed over a crumpled piece of paper.

'Good. Then let's call him.' The man punched the numbers into his phone, and put it to his ear. A few seconds passed. Katie wanted to wake up. More than anything, she wanted this to be just a nightmare. Just a bad dream. The man's voice seemed distant, like it was carried to her on a melancholy wind.

'Nathaniel Virgo? My name is – well, let's just say Rafael.

I have your daughter here. Would you like to speak to her?' He held out the phone.

Katie used all the strength she had to keep standing, and took the phone with a quivering hand.

'Dad?'

'Katie?' Just the sound of his voice was enough to break her. She couldn't speak.

'Katie? Love? Are you OK? What have they done to you?'

'They . . . they killed Mum.' She mustn't cry. 'They shot Mum. Right in front of me.'

She was losing the fight, whimpering softly into the mouthpiece. She was a teenager again. 'What's going on, Dad? Why are they doing this? Are you OK? They told me you're in danger.'

She yelped as Rafael tore the phone from her grip.

'Mr Virgo, your daughter will be put on a plane in a few minutes.'

Katie tried to retain some control of herself. She had to listen to anything he said, for something she could use.

'Let's just say she will end up somewhere on the east coast.' Rafael looked at her and unleashed a grim smile. 'If you do all you are asked, she may just be fine. If you don't, you will certainly never see her again. I would suggest that you comply with all that my colleagues are requesting of you.'

He snapped the phone shut and stepped forward so that his face was just a few inches from hers. He smelled of tobacco and coffee.

'Now. Here's the situation. You know he's relying on you, and you are relying on him. I would suggest you don't cause any more trouble.'

CHAPTER 52

NATHANIEL VIRGO STARED BACK at the poppies hanging, lifeless, on the wall. He couldn't bring Katie's face to mind. His own daughter's smile, the flash of her eyes – it all eluded him. He wanted to remember that she was real, that the voice he heard was really hers. But all that came was a head, a face, framed by splayed hair and dirty asphalt. It should have been Katie's face, but it was Rachel's.

His mind was playing tricks. He knew the scene; he had just finished calling the ambulance, and he was talking to Rachel, telling her that there had been an accident. That Katie had been hurt. Rachel kept saying she didn't believe it. Just hung there on the other end of the phone not knowing whether it was true. While he gazed down at his daughter's blank expression and screamed at everyone else to get back.

He felt the adrenaline of the moment again, the outrage that made him want to chase the car, made him think he could catch it, that this would be one of those times where people report superhuman strength, miraculous speed.

But then the moment was gone, and all he had felt was weakness. He'd stared into Katie's face and felt hollow; the rage had sublimated, become fear and pain and sorrow. Here she was, the beauty that he had helped bring into the world,

MICHAEL BROOKS

lying in gravel and blood. It was the blood that had first led his eyes to the twisted, inhuman leg. His vision followed the trickling stream as it traversed the tiny rapids of the asphalt's grit and ran down to pool in the gutter. It created a shallow puddle around the smashed-up bone and ripped muscle, the torn skin and the twisted sneaker. Katie's foot was stuck out at an impossible angle from her perfect ankle.

Her hair slide lay in the gutter, next to the foot: plain, brown, plastic and broken. He had picked it out of the congealing blood simply because it was something he could do. He knew instinctively he couldn't pick up his daughter, despite the deepest cravings within him. He had to wait for the ambulance. He could see how her limbs would hang, droop and twist away from her torso, and he feared a crunch, a grind of gristle, as sinew ripped further from bone under her near-dead weight.

But now the hair matted against the road belonged to Rachel. He saw her in the same place, another victim of his work, his drive, his faults.

It was true. Of course it was true. He had destroyed his wife, just like he had nearly destroyed his daughter. He did not deserve any pity here in his desolation. He deserved only to be held here, imprisoned in this hell, his heart stopped.

Like his heart had stopped when he saw Katie wave and smile and step across at the crossing's insistent, beeping call. She had glanced up, seen the green, walking figure illuminated, followed all the rules her daddy had carefully taught her before she had even started school. Katie Virgo knew how to cross a road. For all the good it did her.

What good were rules when some junkie's shredded mind forgot every rule he'd ever been taught?

They caught him from the witnesses' accounts. He was nineteen. A middle-class boy, back from university for the weekend, rushing out to meet his friends. His terror and remorse were only appropriate, Virgo felt, as he watched him – despised him – from the gallery. The boy's teeth chattered in the courtroom when he spoke, like he was some cartoon coward. He admitted he was high at the time. Flying, he said.

And somehow Katie forgave him.

She just got over it, rolled with it, while he wanted to die.

He had lived with the blue lights flashing through his dreams for a while. His nights were full of blue and white, and the red and yellow of the McDonald's restaurant across the road, the place they were supposed to meet. Sometimes, he still saw the scene when he passed one.

In the end, the dreams had faded. It was Katie who'd healed him. He watched her come back to life, struggle through her physical therapy, grin and grimace as she tried each new prosthetic. She was born again on every one. His little girl was still a track star. She had even gone back into the school's climbing gym and learned how to rise again, how to resume the battle against gravity with her three good limbs. She was stronger, more tenacious than she had ever been. Katie would never be beaten by anything. Sometimes, he could hardly see her for the tears in his eyes.

Rachel had told him it wasn't his fault so many times that he had even started to believe it. Journalists chased leads every day, she said; every day someone rang up their daughter and said they were going to be twenty minutes late. Who was to know that the split second at the end of that twenty minutes – that particular twenty minutes in all of the universe's eternity – would change a life? Who was to know when the car that jumps the lights would arrive? We were all a split second away from it, every day of our fragile lives.

Virgo looked away from the poppies and turned to the window. Out there, somehow, he would find his deliverance. He would be Katie's salvation, and he would have his revenge for the outrage of her mother's death. The baseness of that instinct simultaneously impressed and astonished him. This fight was real. And he would win it.

CHAPTER 53

'FOLLOW ME.' RAFAEL LED Katie and Vicente to the edge of the luggage hall and through a small door. They emerged into the light, with the flat expanse of the airport's tarmac and runways stretching out in front of them. He was heading towards a large jet whining in the space between two parking bays. Engineers on a wheeled gantry were working on something halfway down the fuselage. As they got close, Rafael shouted something to the engineers, and they packed away their tools.

A flight of steps led up to the plane's front door; Rafael halted at the bottom step and told them to wait. He moved quickly up into the plane.

Katie turned to look at Vicente. He was staring at her.

'Ramón?' he said. 'What happened to Ramón?'

She looked down. There were flecks of blood on her blouse. She didn't want to say it out loud. She said nothing, just looked defiantly back at the man who murdered her mother. He accepted her silence and looked away.

Rafael appeared at the doorway, and beckoned them up the steps. Vicente pushed her in the back with the barrel of his gun. She turned and stung him with her eyes. Sometime in the last few moments, Vicente had started to look out of control, frightened. She remembered what Ramón had said: Vicente doesn't like planes. She despised him now, wanted to spit at him, but she wouldn't do that. She wouldn't come down to that level, where she was no better than them. She felt the nudge of metal in her back again. What was she going to do? What *could* she do? Vicente was going to be able to bring a gun onboard and there was nothing she could do about it.

A Cuban stewardess sat them in two seats in first class. She was insistent that Katie be next to the window, with Vicente at the aisle. Rafael watched them sit, then raised a palm at Vicente, who waved back. He tried to smile, but the muscles in his face were too tight to relax into a grin.

'The quieter the better,' Rafael said, smiling. 'Enjoy the flight.'

And then he was gone.

The engines began to whine louder, then higher. The plane started to move.

The captain's voice resounded in the cabin's loudspeakers.

'Ladies and gentlemen, we do apologise for the delay to your flight to Montreal this afternoon. We are assured there will be no further delays, and have just received clearance for departure.'

Montreal? Canada? It would do.

The captain repeated the message in Spanish. Katie tensed as they reached the runway. She could feel the brakes holding the plane back as the engines roared ever louder. Vicente was praying, his face ashen, and she felt a strange pity for him.

The din heightened as the captain released the brakes. Vicente prayed faster and louder.

Twenty seconds later, they were in the air.

CHAPTER 54

VIRGO PULLED THE PHONE from his pocket and switched it off. It was his connection to Katie, but it was better not to be traceable just yet. And she wouldn't be able to call him from the plane anyway, that much was clear. He stared at the blank screen. When she had landed and was free, she would call. It would be her first thought, for sure. What was the flight time from Cuba into the US? He would take the risk and switch the phone back on in a few hours. Once Katie called him, and had got herself safely into police hands, he'd head to Logan. He'd be able to call Imogen then too; maybe her National Security Agency contact, this David character, would be able to smooth their passage out of the United States. Virgo was in no doubt that he'd be picked up by the FBI minutes after he bought a ticket, but that would be OK if Katie was safe and if someone high up in the US agencies could vouch for him. It would work out, he told himself. They would fly him back to London under guard, and he was confident that he'd be able to supply them with enough information to get Alexandra Genovsky taken out of the picture. Maybe Wheelan too. If he could point them to the people who killed Radcliffe and Gierek, then he would surely be cleared of everything. They might even have time to stop the hijacks. Even if the conspiracy did go to the top, there was no reason to hold back.

Once Katie was safe.

Should he eat something? He was hungry, but he wanted to try to get some sleep, prepare for whatever was to come. He would eat when he woke, if there was time. Sleep? He was in denial. But he might as well go along with it. He set the alarm on his watch to wake him up at six o'clock, and lay down on the bed. He put his hands behind his head and closed his eyes. All he could see was Rachel. He couldn't even see Katie any more, couldn't bring her face to the front of his mind.

With a start, he jerked upright. Had he dreamed it?

Tap tap tap.

It was no dream. Someone was at the door.

He sat motionless on the bed.

OK, think.

The FBI? If it was the FBI, they were being surprisingly polite – the tapping was almost apologetic. It didn't want to be heard. But it was also insistent: three taps just about every ten seconds. He had listened to it four times so far and still couldn't think who might be trying to get his attention. Genovsky? His heart raced faster. No. Quiet and subtle wasn't her style. As the next taps started, he moved silently over to the door. It might just be next door wanting to know if cable was working.

'Who is it?'

There was a pause, then a whisper.

'Nathaniel, let me in. It's Daniel Born.'

CHAPTER 55

VIRGO STOOD WITH HIS back to the closed door, and stared. A flurry of questions raced through his mind. Eventually, he decided on the most pressing one.

'What the hell are you doing here?'

Born was wearing a sapphire-blue shirt with a button-down collar. Parallel creases ran down on either side of the chest, relics of the folds that fitted it into a sales box. He wore it with its tails flapping loose, pushed out at the front by his belly. He'd shaved. He'd even washed his hair recently: as he stroked some strands out of his face, Virgo could see it was soft, not straggling.

Born looked around the room, then pointed to the desk chair. 'Can I sit down?'

Virgo nodded, and Born eased himself into the plastic swivel chair. Virgo went to sit on the edge of the bed. Even before he reached it, he realised there was a more important question.

'How did you find me?'

'I followed you from Alexandra Genovsky's place,' Born said. He was grinning, but nervously, like a child climbing onto a rollercoaster.

'What were you doing there? And what happened at your

cottage? Why did you let Genovsky get away?'

Born held up his hands to parry the questions. 'I ran, Nathaniel. I'm sorry. After you left I just ran from the house. I couldn't think in there, and she was coming round, and . . . I couldn't hit her, and . . . I knew she wouldn't let me get away if she could stop me. So I just ran.' His face lightened. 'I'm so glad to see you. Alive, I mean.'

Virgo struggled to read Born's face. It was almost blank, like the face of a harmless simpleton.

'But she was tied up,' he said.

'I suppose she got herself free after I left. She could have reached a kitchen knife, or something.'

Virgo stared at him for a moment. This all seemed unlikely. Worse than unlikely.

'So why are you here? And how did you know where to find Genovsky?'

Born seemed not to notice the edge in his tone, and offered another uneasy smile.

'I told you, she offered me a job once. She told me how to find her.' He paused, then his words came out with more measure, more sobriety. 'I knew she would come after me. I'm here to save my skin. To get rid of her before she gets rid of me. She's covering up a leak and she's going to wipe away all trace.'

'And how are you going to get rid of her, exactly?'

'I haven't figured that out yet.' Born leaned back in the chair. 'So, is it over for you now? Have you got yourself – and your wife – out of this tangled web?'

Virgo stared into Born's eyes. What was he doing here now? Why had he come all the way to the US?

'What do you know about Genovsky?'

Born paused. 'Look, I don't blame you for being suspicious.' He seemed to relax into his chair at the invitation to talk. He ran a hand through his hair. 'She's got some huge project going on in a warehouse north of the city.' He sat forward, his expression and tone suggesting conspiracy. 'If it's to do with the quantum computer, I hate to think what. There are armed guards, and some huge, blacked-out trucks moving in and out of the place. I was out there watching earlier. I think it must be some kind of trial for the system.' Born raised an eyebrow. 'Did she say anything to you about it?'

Virgo shook his head. He couldn't stop staring at Born. What had happened to the lazy recluse he met in Oxford? He had turned into someone who was strangely proactive.

'Did you find out whether the disks were entangled together?' Born asked.

There was an unmistakable enthusiasm in Born's voice. Had Born crossed the Atlantic because he wanted to trace a quantum breakthrough? Was he that obsessed? Was it still all about the work? Virgo felt a wave of exhaustion wash over him. He didn't care about what was going on now. Genovsky could be breaking the laws of physics or masterminding the ultimate evil; he just wanted the world to leave him alone. With Katie.

'I didn't ask her anything,' he said.

Born looked disappointed, and stared into the wall. 'I'd love to know how Laszlo did it,' he said

Virgo forced himself to think. The facts: Born was here, he didn't know why, and he had to take control of the situation. He had to engage in this again, if only to make sure Born didn't mess things up. But how? Could he deceive Born too? Born would require a slightly different kind of lie.

'I found something in Gierek's lab,' Virgo said. 'Something interesting.'

Born's eyes widened. 'Really? What?'

Virgo went to the closet, and pulled out the box.

'This was hidden in a cupboard.'

Born shot him an admiring look. 'What does it do?'

Keeping one hand firmly on the casing, Virgo reached for his jacket and pulled out one of the blank disks he had found in Gierek's lab. 'I used it to entangle this with another disk,' he lied. 'It's the most incredible thing. This disk and its partner can sense each other when they're in completely separate drives. You keep one disk in here, the other in any other drive. It's extraordinary.'

Born looked around. 'So where's its partner?'

'It's headed for the Boston FBI.'

Born looked surprised. 'Why? What's on it?'

'Genovsky's name, address, and present occupation.'

'And when were you planning to activate the disk?'

'Once Katie is safely under police guard.'

Born said nothing.

'They're flying her out of Cuba. As soon as she gets to a police guard, I'm going to put Alexandra Genovsky behind bars.'

Still Born said nothing. He was looking down at the mottled brown carpet, deep in thought. Like a doctor who doesn't know how to break bad news.

'What?' Virgo asked after a few seconds' silence. 'What's the matter?'

Born took a deep breath, and looked up.

'I'm not sure your daughter's going to make it to a police guard,' he said. Born's tone was hesitant but deliberately matter-of-fact: I don't want to tell you this, and you don't want to hear it. But this is how it is.

'What makes you say that?'

Born held out his hands, defending his line. 'I told you I'm not sure,' he said. 'But just after you left, I followed Genovsky to a restaurant downtown. After lunch she came out with a man – tall, with long grey hair in a ponytail. They were going separate ways, but at the last minute he shouted something to Genovsky. He told her not to worry about the girl, that she would be one of hundreds. He said nobody would make the connection.' He looked up. 'Genovsky looked a bit scared or maybe just annoyed, or something. Like he was slighting her. She didn't say anything. She just walked off.'

No. Born must be mistaken. Or lying. They were both tangled up in lies and half-truths. *Was* Born lying?

'I spoke to Katie,' Virgo said. 'She was getting on a plane. The guy putting her on the plane said everything would be OK if I just sat tight.'

Born arched an eyebrow again. 'Who's the guy? Maybe he doesn't get to decide?'

Yeah, maybe.

'I'm sorry, Nathaniel.' Born's voice was soft and unsure, like he had never had to show kindness before. It seemed genuine. Maybe that part was. After a couple of moments, Born lifted his gaze.

'Did you ever find out what happened to Gupta?' he said. He seemed to have his enthusiasm back. 'That's why I'm here. I think they're wiping out the opposition. The best quantum cryptography people. The only ones who can keep data secret if there's a quantum computer. And if they've got a quantum computer, they're not going to let anyone live who knows about it.' He paused. 'I'm right in the frame: Genovsky knows what I know. I came over to stop her before she kills me. That's still my plan. And now, I think, it has to be yours.'

Slowly, thoughtfully, Virgo shook his head.

'No,' he said, with a tone of defiant resolution. 'My plan has to be to get Katie safely off that plane.'

Born pursed his lips, and looked up. 'OK,' he said. 'Your plan first. Then mine.'

A silence hung in the air between them. After a couple of seconds, Born broke it.

'I can get us in,' he said. 'Into the warehouse, I mean. I found a hole in the side of the building. I think it must have been overlooked – it's some kind of goods exit, and there's a half door inset into it. The lock's broken.'

'How did you get that far? I thought you said there were armed guards?'

Born smiled. 'I think this set-up has been put together in a hurry. There's security at the front, but the perimeter patrol's lazy. I dived under the fence – there's several places where the ground has been dug out under the wire. Must be . . . I don't know, raccoons or something.' His eyes scanned Virgo's frame. 'If I can get my fat belly through, you can certainly make it.'

'And then what? We walk in and ask Genovsky to halt her dastardly deeds? Where's our bargaining power?'

Born raised an arm and pointed to the bed. 'Right there,' he said. Virgo turned his head and looked down at Gierek's machine.

Born had no idea what it really did. Neither did he. But he knew what Genovsky believed. That was enough.

'OK,' Virgo said. 'We should go.'

He bundled the machine back into the blanket, tucked it under his arm once more and followed Born out of the door. They walked side by side down the corridor to the elevator lobby.

Kenmore Square was looking more miserable than ever. It was already getting dark, and a cold rain began to fall as they emerged onto the sidewalk. People were shuffling hurriedly along the street, newspapers covering their heads as if they knew this was only the start of things. Virgo could see his breath condense against the red neon signs of the diner across the street. He thought of Rachel, and Katie, and shivered. Born pointed down the street, away from the square.

'My car's down here.'

CHAPTER 56

OH GOD, NOT TODAY. Thomas Wheelan pulled over, leaned his head against the steering wheel and tried to fight the nausea. Should he get out, get some air? At least with the rain and the late afternoon dark nobody would see him throwing up on the side of the road.

This had happened before, just occasionally, but today was not a good day for it. Could he call Eleanor, ask her if there was anything different about these pills? Not today. He would have to get through.

He chugged a couple more down. Maybe they were low-dose. Eleanor couldn't always control the supply, he knew that. She relied on her maid. What was he doing, a future president, relying on his sister's maid? When today was over, when everything in his future was clear, he would check into the clinic. He had friends at church who would swear they were on vacation with him for those few weeks. That was the beauty of the United Methodists: they understood the power of addiction. They were always ready to help.

Wheelan lifted his head and grimaced. The fog in his mind was clearing now. He wasn't going to throw up. The pills were a low-dose benzodiazepine; that must be it. Ellie wasn't to know; he would just have to take more of them today than usual. He opened the door and got out of the car, then grabbed at the black-painted metal of the door: standing up made his head spin. It was a cruel twist, that he was in this state after all that had happened to Joshua. But better that he knew how it felt to be so powerless. When in power – and clean – he would never forget. He would be a stronger leader for it, more empathetic, more understanding of America's problems than any president in history.

The rain soaked his hair, cleared his head. Wheelan watched the cars rush past. These people, the souls passing him by, were everything that today was about. It was going to be tough, but it was the right thing to do. By the end of the day, at the cost of just a few hundred lives, America was going to be on the right track again. No regrets.

Not even about Gabriel MacIntyre. It wasn't that Wheelan was comfortable with the plan. Eleanor was a good sister, and he would never do anything to hurt her. Or little Jennie. When all this was over, he'd make sure that they were taken care of.

But Gabe was out of his depth. Always had been, ever since he started dating Ellie. What was it their father had said? You can take the boy out of Arkansas . . . And Gabe's own father had just talked about 'them black folks'. Right up until the day he died, he had hated Gabe for marrying into a 'nigger' family. For years, all the years the old man was in the care home dying his slow, spiteful death, Ellie would cry over the kitchen table while Gabe went to sit at his bedside.

It was a shame about Gabe. You had to hand it to him: he had stood up to two fathers to marry his sweetheart. But there had to be a scapegoat, and it's not like he hadn't already strayed from the straight and narrow. He had become greedy, lost sight of that bigger picture. There was no room for regret: this was vital work. Wheelan knew he would have no trouble standing tall in a courtroom. Not that his case would ever make it to the judicial system. He had been too careful for that.

MICHAEL BROOKS

The rain started coming down harder, sharper, like wet steel spikes. The pills were kicking in now. It was time to go.

The thing at the burger joint still bugged him. Marinov hadn't said anything about needing another meeting with Gabe, and his people were too late to get anywhere near the conversation. If there was something amiss, he wanted to be in on the move to put it right. He had plugged plenty of holes at this stage in an operation. He used to do it himself, back when he wore a uniform to work. Suits were OK, but there was nothing like a uniform to focus the mind on a job that needed doing.

That was the trouble with seniority: he missed the action. You got good at something – anything – and they put you in a job where you took responsibility for people who couldn't cut it. They doubled your salary, put you in a suit, and employed someone else to do your old job half as well. Government: the maintenance of mediocrity. Still, he could change that. And then there would be no more waste. He might have failed his own family, but he would stop the waste from ruining others.

Wheelan shook the rain from his hair and lowered himself back into the car. At least he could trust Marinov. That was the beauty of a single-minded, profit-seeking entrepreneurial partner. Marinov wasn't interested in Washington politics: he just wanted the money. But all he had so far was Wheelan's deposit – $18 million; nothing compared with his full asking price. He had waited seventeen months so far, and in a couple of days there would be a miracle: money would be tumbling out of the Washington sky. And as long as there were no leaks or catches, Thomas Wheelan's stock would be rising as fast as the black budget cash was falling on Marinov's head. He would check in at the ranch, kick the pills, and hit the ground running, heading straight up Pennsylvania Avenue.

CHAPTER 57

'NICE,' VIRGO SAID, CASTING an eye over the tan leather interior. The Lexus smelled new and luxurious.

The rain was hurling itself from the sky, obscuring the view through the windscreen and drumming insistently on the roof.

'It's just a rental.'

A conversational cul de sac. Virgo tried not to think about Rachel. And failed. His fingers ranged over the blanket-covered box of electronics on his lap. What was this about? Why had Rachel died?

At Heathrow, Genovsky had said Rachel would be sent home. She'd lied. But lying wasn't the surprise. The surprise was that *he* had walked away from her office. Why would she try to murder everyone who knew about a couple of missing computer disks but then just let him go?

They were on the Mass Pike, heading east towards the Expressway. As the roadway dipped into a tunnel under Massachusetts Avenue, the drumming of the rain halted. In the sudden quiet, he heard Born singing quietly along to a song on the radio, some soft soul number.

Born shot a glance at him. 'You know this song?'

Virgo shook his head.

'Ray Parker Junior. 1980. Arista records.' Born paused. 'Great song.' He smiled. 'I got laid to this record once.'

Was this guy for real? He listened to a few lines as Born carried on singing.

'*Inside you and inside your mind*? She fell for that?'

'Hey, in 1980 I was pretty cool. What were you, eight? Nine?'

'Older. Fourteen.'

'Yeah? Well I was nineteen, an undergraduate whiz-kid at Oxford, and well on the way to a glamorous career in research. I did OK with women.' They were coming up to the Expressway. Born hesitated, then switched lanes: I-93 North. 'Are you telling me physics didn't ever get you laid?'

'Didn't Ray Parker Junior do the *Ghostbusters* theme?'

Born laughed. 'OK, so he wasn't cool for long. Anyway, he was past his best by then.' He glanced across again. 'Come on – you never went to a party and told girls you were unlocking the secrets of the universe?'

Virgo stared through the windscreen. What had happened to Born? He seemed too positive, too excited.

'That line must have worn thin long before I got to use it,' Virgo said.

They lapsed into silence, and listened to the rain and the radio. The flashing lights of a plane appeared below the cloud, coming into Logan.

The city was darkening fast, and the streetlights blurred with the smears and drops on the car windows. The heavy traffic was a mess of washed-out tail lights. Eventually, Born broke the silence. 'Do you know why I agreed to do that interview with you?'

Virgo shifted in his seat. 'Because you were so pissed off at the university?'

'No. Well, yes. But mainly it was that article you did for *Playboy*. I meant to ask you about it, but never did. How did you get an article on physics into *Playboy*?'

Despite himself, Virgo laughed. 'It was the Polish edition. It's not like I was partying with Hugh Hefner.'

'No, but still . . .'

'Anyway, how did you get to see that?'

'Laszlo. Laszlo Gierek sent it to me. He thought it was hilarious.'

'He reads – read – *Playboy*?'

'I don't know if he *read* it, exactly, if you know what I mean. He had it sent from Warsaw. Reminded him of the old days back home, I suppose. Anyway, he thought I'd be interested to see physics in among the porn. And then you emailed me a couple of days later.'

'It was syndicated.'

'What?'

'*Playboy* bought the story from the *Herald*, translated it, and bunged it in. Did you see my picture on the contributors page?'

Born shook his head and laughed again. 'So you've had your picture in *Playboy*? That's fantastic. That, surely, must have got you laid?'

'I was already married by then.'

Born's smile evaporated. 'Of course.'

They fell silent again. They passed Exit 26: Storrow Drive and the Museum of Science.

'I nearly got married once.' Born said it softly, wistfully.

Virgo let it hang for a moment. 'What happened?'

'I chose physics. I just spent more and more time working, got obsessive – it was when I thought I was about to crack the quantum computer. You know, work out how to build one. In the end, she just walked away.'

'I saw the room. Upstairs in your house.' Virgo threw the phrase out as if it was a question.

Born grimaced. 'I could never bring myself to clear it out.'

'Are you still in touch?' Virgo already knew the answer.

'No.' Born's jaw tightened.

237

They drove on in silence for a couple of minutes before Born spoke again.

'She was a bookbinder. She liked pretty things, old things, stuff you could rub your fingers over, feel textures and smell. She chose that house – the cottage. I'd live in a gasworks, but she had to be absorbed by the things around her. They had to fill her senses.' His voice had faded further, melting into the insistent patter of the rain. 'I was too far away. She didn't stay long enough to redecorate, even. We bought the cottage because it had so much potential. Like me, she always said.'

Virgo hadn't been listening. 'I thought you cracked the quantum computer in one night? That's what everyone says.' Even before he'd finished speaking, he regretted the words; it was insensitive.

Born seemed not to notice. 'Yeah, I heard that too,' he snorted. 'I think it was the press office made that up, just before they decided to fleece me for everything.' He shifted his weight in the seat. 'You know, it didn't bother me that the machine was all my work and they were claiming rights over it. But I was really fucked up at the time, taking all kinds of pills. Becca had just walked out, and the university knew I was on a knife edge. I couldn't leave the house I was so messed up. Some kind of aggravated agoraphobia, the doctor said. And they kept on summoning me to meetings about this machine that had cost me my future. I just lost it and told them they couldn't have it. Told my lawyer to stop them at all costs.'

He leaned forward, into the steering wheel, stretching out his back.

'Becca was the love of my life. Stupid to let some machine get in the way of that.' He glanced across again. 'But you've got to understand what it's like to work on something like the quantum computer. I knew Becca was the one. But then there was the machine. You know, even now, if I had the chance to choose again I'm not sure what I'd do.'

They were heading out of the city, crossing Bunker Hill

Bridge in the rain. The streetlights were further apart, and the landscape ahead was as dismal and grey as the sky above them. The traffic had thinned to a trickle now; they were leaving the city behind. It made him nervous. Why weren't they just going to the FBI, the police? If Born knew where the operation was, surely they could get the authorities to close it down?

He couldn't take the risk: who knew what Wheelan had set in motion? Virgo was wanted in connection with two murders. But maybe Wheelan didn't even know about him. Most likely, Genovsky had said everything was in order: that she had the disk. Everybody likes to look competent in front of their boss. And it wasn't worth him risking an appearance on Wheelan's radar when he didn't know what it would do to Katie's chances. Someone had wanted him to walk away from all this – that was what Rachel's death was all about. And it wasn't Genovsky, he was pretty sure of that. Most likely, it was Wheelan. No, he had to keep his head down.

Wheelan. He was assuming it now, like there was a proven link. Like it wasn't just his hunch, a wild stab in the dark. He needed to know more, but how? Did Born know anything? Virgo felt a buzzing in the back of his head, like he was missing something. Something to do with Born. And Rachel. Something that wasn't quite right.

'So, who is Genovsky?' Virgo said. He tried to keep his tone casual, as if they were discussing someone they'd bumped into in the street. 'Who does she work for?'

'I don't know much. When she made me that offer I told you about, she said it was a job where I could work how I liked – alone, with a hand-picked team, or whatever. I would have all the money I needed for equipment. The only catch was that it wouldn't be public domain: it was private enterprise and I couldn't publish. But she wouldn't say what the enterprise was – we never got that far. Like I said, Laszlo told me to walk away.'

Virgo turned in his seat. 'So you never wondered about it? You never gave it another moment's thought?'

Born glanced over at Virgo and shrugged. 'I did check her out a bit. I dug into her history. She was a NASA administrator a while back. But that's not how she started: they brought her over from Bulgaria as a high-level programmer – *hey, shit*.'

A huge truck rumbled past them, horn blaring. Its spray drowned the Lexus, and Born fought with the wipers to find a faster setting. '*My God*, this country is scary. The size of that thing . . .' He shuffled his weight in the seat.

'What was I saying? Oh, yeah. Did you know the Bulgarians had the world's best programmers? Stalin made them responsible for developing computing for the entire Soviet bloc. In the long run, he did them a big favour – they had to do it on a shoestring budget and they got very good at innovative thinking. It's like the Russians with theoretical physics: it seems like it's in the blood, but really it's just the product of harsh expectations.' Born paused and glanced in his rearview mirror, then over again at Virgo. 'People are capable of anything, given the right threat.'

'So Genovsky was a good programmer. What else?'

'Not much. She was obviously good at handling people – that's how you get pushed into NASA's admin staff. I never found out why she left. I suppose she got a better offer.'

'So what makes you so scared? What makes you think she won't just forget about you?'

'If a Bulgarian with unfettered cash and an interest in quantum physics calls me, it's not going to be because they're striving for world peace. Remember Georgi Markov and the ricin-tipped umbrella? Bulgarian secret service.' Born glanced towards him, flicked a grin, then set his eyes back on the road. 'And when Laszlo said what he did back then . . . I'm seeing horse's heads, if you know what I mean. I walked away once, and then you brought it all back again and pulled me into this. I don't think these people leave you alone. Once your name comes up, that's it. Come on, *come on*.' He was trying to shift lanes. 'When the same woman then connects my name with a plot to break her cover, I'm not going to wait around for her to find me: better to get on the front foot, get in first. Laszlo told me that when you get in with Genovsky, there's no getting out. He said it's like an abusive marriage.' Born glanced across again. 'What would you do?'

Virgo shrugged. What could he say?

That thing, that missing link, was still bugging him, tugging at his attention. What *was* it?

They drove on in silence. With a few indecisive mutterings, Born took an exit: Everett/Hendersonville. The gloomy rise of heavy industry piled into the blue-grey of the darkening sky ahead.

CHAPTER 58

THOMAS WHEELAN ROLLED HIS car through the gates. He was OK now; on double dosage, but OK. This was it. The feeds were in place, the tapes ready to roll and there was a lockdown over this sector: he had done his bit. If Marinov had done his, if the software in the planes worked like it did in the test, this would all be over in a few hours. He parked facing away from the entrance. It still felt odd to be driving himself around, but taxis weren't an option at this stage: the thing was best contained. He needed a couple of secret service people to lead the security team and hang with him for protocol, but he had leverage on both of them. They'd do as they were told without question and without reporting back.

Marinov had chosen the codeword for the door. Copenhagen. Wheelan smirked as he muttered it to the guard. Marinov could be funny when you got past the murderous stare. Copenhagen. Birthplace of the quantum theory. That was for Gabe, he figured.

The two men were already waiting in the main hall. Two of the security detail were standing close to the machine, AK-47s slung casually over their shoulders. He hoped his men had chosen their team and their equipment well. When it came down to the wire, this had to look good, like an independent job carried out by well-equipped mercenaries. If there were any bullets fired, they had to be the right kind of bullets, from the right kind of gun. There would be an inquiry, and there would be analysis. And, if all went according to his meticulous plan, no one would even question his story.

Wheelan stepped forward. The woman ahead must be Alexandra Genovsky. She was hanging around the door, checking her watch. She looked nervous. Beautiful, but highly strung. High maintenance, probably. Maybe that was what drove Marinov to such a high price.

That and the high-tech set-up. Wheelan looked around. He couldn't help but be impressed: he had said that it should all look credible, like the operation was being run by professionals. But though he'd supplied the guards, he hadn't quite expected everything else to look so – well, so James Bond.

Not that it wasn't worth paying for a convincing display. Today's charade would change everything for the security services. Starting today, they would be on a path to win every war. Terror, cyber-crime – he smirked, that one was ironic – drugs: everything would cave under the power of what they would create now. In a sense, Joshua wouldn't have died in vain. It wouldn't be a waste if this succeeded. He had failed as a father, and as a husband. He was alone now. But he could still do some good.

He shook hands with his brother-in-law first.

'How are you, Gabe?'

The man looked a wreck. Wheelan hoped he could hold it together for as long as they needed him. 'Everything OK?'

MacIntyre nodded, but without conviction.

Marinov's handshake was strong and swift.

'Everything is ready,' he said. He shot a glance across the room. 'Everything is OK, yes, Alex?'

She nodded.

'Let's begin.'

CHAPTER 59

THEY HAD BEEN DRIVING for forty-five minutes when Born slowed the Lexus to a crawl. The headlights lit up a pair of twisted and broken iron gates, and a tall crane standing sentry over them. The car rolled silently through the gap between the gates, and headed down a muddy track pitted with shallow pools of rainwater. As the track wound through its twists and turns, the headlights streaked over jagged piles of rusted steel: cars, trucks and the occasional naked chassis. Ahead of them was a dark line of trees. It looked like a place things went to die.

'Classy neighbourhood,' Virgo murmured.

Born shook his head. 'This isn't it. We're going down the hill behind the trees.'

As they rolled towards the dense foliage, Born cut the engine and the lights. He let the car's momentum ebb away, then put the transmission into park.

'I'm not taking this in,' Virgo said, holding up the box.

Born hesitated. 'The entanglement generator? We should.'

Virgo shook his head. 'We'll come back for it if we need it.'

Born seemed unsure for a moment, then shrugged. 'OK. We'll put it in the boot.'

Born opened his door. 'Watch your step. It's nasty underfoot.'

Virgo climbed out of the car, his right foot splashing noisily in a shallow puddle. He made his way towards the sole light in view: the one in the Lexus's open boot. He placed the box carefully inside, and Born closed the boot. The dark was total now. For twenty seconds Virgo stood still, unable to see anything in the darkness. Slowly, shapes began to materialise. Another rusting crane towered perilously above him, its boom reaching out into the dark, a bridge to nowhere. At the trees, twenty paces ahead, he could just make out Born's crouching shadow. He was beckoning, urging him forward. Virgo could just about distinguish the darker blotches of the puddles in the mud, and stepped cautiously towards Born.

'It's down there,' Born whispered, pointing past a wire chain-link fence. The ground fell away beyond, and the orange glow of sodium lamps rose up from the dip. Virgo wrapped his jacket tighter around him and wiped the rain from his face.

'Come on,' Born hissed. He moved forward and Virgo followed, shivering. The fence was old and sagging between its posts. Born gripped some links near the ground and yanked them up. Crouching down, Virgo slipped easily underneath, then turned and held it up for Born to follow.

Below them, the bleak landscape of an industrial park stretched over the valley. There were several small buildings dotted around the expanse of concrete, but one vast hangar, the closest building to their vantage point on the slope, dominated the unit. The north-east corner of its roof was spiked with an array of antennae and satellite dishes. He could see no sign of life, but there were a dozen vehicles parked to one side of the main building. Beyond that, tall perimeter fencing ran across the far edge of the concrete. The access gate was out of sight, possibly hidden behind the furthest, smallest hangar.

Born reached out a hand to grab Virgo's sleeve, then

started down the slope. They moved quickly, propelled by gravity, but the thick undergrowth gripped their feet. The damp seeped through Virgo's trouser legs as he reached the ground. Ahead of them, the blue corrugated-steel cladding of the largest hangar filled their view. Born moved to his right, skirting the building until he reached its south-west corner. He gripped the steel and leaned so that his eyes were just beyond the building's edge, his left leg rising as a counterbalance. After a couple of seconds, he pulled back.

'Our entrance is just round this corner,' he whispered, pushing his dripping hair behind his ears. It's a roller hatch. We're going to run to it, I'll pull it up, and you dive through. OK? Once we're in, I'm not sure which way to go – I never went further than that chamber. But I've got a pretty good idea where the action is. So stick close to me and don't make any noise. We don't exactly look like we're invited guests.'

Virgo wiped the rain from his hair and face. His feet felt cold and wet inside his boots, and his trousers clung to his legs. But he had been colder and wetter. 'OK,' he nodded. Born turned and peered round the corner again, then looked back.

'Now.'

They crouched and scuttled the thirty yards to the roller hatch. It was a metre off the ground and two metres square. Born lifted it with little effort, and Virgo climbed in.

He found himself sitting on a conveyor belt inside a large, white-panelled room. There were a few dozen packing boxes strewn across the floor, but otherwise it was empty. As Born followed him through, he moved along the belt, then stepped down onto the floor. He felt a rush of adrenaline flood through him, delivering a sense of dizzy elation.

They were in.

CHAPTER 60

KATIE WAS STRUGGLING TO stay awake. The memory of her mother, and of what she had done to Ramón – and, worse, Miguel – continued to play in her mind. But it wasn't enough to stop her from falling asleep. Should she just give in? Was there anything she could do now?

Nothing but sit and get through this. For her father's sake. How could she be in this position, where his life depended on her? It was all wrong. When she'd had her accident, he took care of her, he stroked her head as she lay there. She was his little girl. How could she save him?

And she didn't know enough to take both their lives in her hands. It was no use asking Vicente: it was obvious that he now knew nothing more than she did about what was going on. She wondered whether he had even been on a plane before. He'd been terrified by the take-off. He was quiet now, but he'd talked unceasingly about his family – not seeming to care whether or not she was listening – for the first hour of the flight. It was odd that he hadn't mentioned Ramón after that first question. She wasn't going to bring it up; she could hardly bear the thought of what she'd been driven to do. Her mind flashed to her friends, to Gemma, to the things they talked about. They'd sworn to tell each other everything, to keep no secret from each other. How could she ever tell Gemma what she'd done today?

Katie closed her eyes to keep the tears from forming. Miguel was singing inside her head. She had made him an orphan. She had killed a little boy's father and turned him into an orphan.

She couldn't think like that. She had no choice. At school, they would all talk occasionally about what they would do if some man tried to abduct them, or rape them. They were all agreed: you did everything you could to get away, everything you had to. Whatever it took. Miguel's father had kidnapped her, would have happily raped her. She couldn't hold herself to blame for anything.

She could get up and ask to speak to the pilot. The cabin crew wouldn't allow it whether they were in on this or not. And, for all his apparent docility, Vicente was still armed. Katie looked around the cabin, wondering if there was some kind of sky marshal on board. If so, he or she would be back in economy. She had no chance of spotting a marshal anyway: that was the point. In a few hours, she would be landing in Montreal. And, one way or another, it would all be over.

CHAPTER 61

VIRGO LOOKED AT HIS watch. Born was listening intently at the door. What was he waiting for – cocktail hour? Eventually, he squeezed carefully down on the handle, cautiously pulling it open, and poked his head into the corridor outside. With a nod, he summoned Virgo to follow him out of the packing room. For a moment, Born paused, assessing the layout left and right. He chose right.

He looked almost comical, jogging his bulk through the narrow corridors. They moved quickly, the thin ocean-blue carpet deadening the sound of their footfalls. At the first turn, Born halted with a raised palm, and peered round the corner. Virgo pulled up behind. The hand waved him on again – Virgo couldn't help smirking; Born really was hamming it up, military-style – and they turned the corner. This corridor's walls were painted a pale green, and they passed a number of closed white doors leading off from either side. Halfway down, another corridor led off to the left. Born paused at the junction, then took the turn.

He took them through several more turns, but the corridors were all empty. Virgo was disoriented, but he felt sure they were heading to the centre of the building. Suddenly, at a crossroads, Born pulled to a halt, causing Virgo to bundle into him. Born looked at his watch, then took the right turn into yet another long, narrow corridor. Its walls were painted in an industrial orange. There were three doors along its length, all on the right hand side.

How long were they going to keep this up?

Then: click.

He knew what was wrong.

Born hadn't reacted when Virgo had mentioned Katie back in the hotel room. He knew about her. He already knew.

And now Born was delivering Virgo – and Gierek's machine – to Genovsky. He was tying up her loose ends.

Everything in Virgo fell into silent concentration. There was no decision to make: he knew enough now. Now he had to sidestep the clumsy trap.

He flicked his left foot into Born's ankle. As Born stumbled, Virgo crashed the back of his fist into his right cheek, knocking him against the orange wall. Born was off his guard, and another blow to the head knocked him out. Virgo opened the nearest door. It was a small room with three chairs. And, more important, no people. Grabbing Born's ankles, struggling against the dead weight, Virgo dragged him into the room and shut the door.

His mind raced back over the path they'd taken through the building. It was a blur, but if he could head back towards the south-west, he would surely find that green corridor again. He crouched over Born's prostrate body, and rifled quickly through his pockets. The key to the Lexus was in the inside pocket of his jacket. With it, Virgo found a handgun.

He looked it over for a moment. He had never fired a gun. But then he had never knocked anyone out before yesterday, and now he'd done it twice: this was proving to be a prime moment for new experiences. He got up, put the Lexus key in his pocket and stuffed the gun into the back of his waistband. He pulled his jacket back down over the bulge and moved towards the door. Time to find Genovsky.

He reached for the door handle, but something grabbed at

his ankle, and he wheeled round. Born had started to come round already. He was up on one elbow, his right eye darkening and caked blood on his chin.

'Give Katie a chance,' Born croaked.

Virgo hesitated, then pulled out the gun. He held it by the barrel, like a cosh, over Born's head. 'What do you know about Katie? Tell me what's going on,' he hissed.

'Genovsky told me to find out what I could about Gierek's machine and bring you in with it,' Born replied. His voice was still slightly slurred. 'She didn't kill you yet because she's worried about the entanglement generator: she thinks it will decode what's on the disks.'

All the stories about Gierek's box of tricks really had worked.

'So you're working for Genovsky now? At the house – she talked you into it?'

Born lifted himself upright. 'I told you. The quantum computer is my life's work – the only great thing I have ever done.' Born motioned out of the door. 'It's there, Nathaniel, down the hallway, ready and waiting. Would *you* walk away?' His voice was almost pleading.

That was the trouble with obsession. It clouded judgement. Born had already lost most of his life to the quantum computer, and now everything that remained of his integrity was falling over the edge.

'So you learned nothing from what happened with Becca?'

'The machine is all I have left now.'

'What about all that stuff about physics, finding the meaning of existence? The university exploiting you? Genovsky the criminal, the gangster –'

Born raised his eyebrows in response. His eyes were still cloudy, like he had downed a drink too many. 'They're all gangsters, Nathaniel. It's just that some of them operate within the law.'

Such calm treachery. Virgo brought the butt of the gun closer to Born's head.

'And what about the plane? Were you lying about Katie too?'

Born seemed unmoved by the display of aggression. 'No. She's on a plane headed for the US. Genovsky called and told me about it when I was coming over to you. She told me they'd be taking over Katie's plane, and that I should use that if I needed an extra reason to get you here with the entanglement generator.'

Virgo started to feel the approach of panic – his stomach was plummeting, and his breathing had become laboured and shallow. There was no time for panic now. He took a deep breath.

'So what's going on in here?' he said.

'They're using the quantum computer to listen in on encrypted communications between the Pentagon and the White House. I don't know what they're going to do to the plane, exactly. Divert it for a bit, I guess. Give themselves something to listen to.'

Then he saw a glimmer of hope. They couldn't arrange a hijack on Katie's plane just like that. Could they?

Born must know something else. Virgo grabbed Born's shirt.

'Tell me more, Born. How come you're on Genovsky's team now?'

'She needed a new Gierek. That's why she didn't kill me.' Born looked genuinely scared. 'She had a knife strapped to her ankle – she cut herself free as soon as she came around. I agreed to work for her if she didn't kill me.'

Bastard.

'I'll bet it wasn't a tough sell, was it?' Virgo hissed. 'Back in Oxford, you had a gleam in your eye even then. You took the disk from her car, didn't you? When we couldn't find it on her, you went out of your way to get it, then told me it wasn't there.'

Born looked down at the floor. 'I had a look at it. It seemed blank, like the other one. Why would Laszlo be carrying a blank disk? It's something to do with the entanglement.'

Virgo looked to the door.

'How long before they find us here?'

Born looked up again and shrugged. Virgo moved towards the door.

'Don't, Nathaniel.' Virgo paused, a hand hovering over the handle, and turned to look at Born. His eyes were pleading; he seemed genuinely concerned. 'You can't just blunder in there. If this goes smoothly, if there's no trouble and no leaks, there's a chance Katie will walk off the plane. If it doesn't, she'll be dead. Either in the air, or before she's past the airport boundaries.'

Katie will walk off the plane? Born's naivety was almost touching.

'And me?'

'You?' Born squared his gaze on Virgo. 'You're dead already.'

Blunt. But realistic.

Virgo breathed deeply. 'So what do we do?'

Born eyed him with curiosity. He seemed suspicious that Virgo had given up so readily.

'Come with me,' he said. 'Let me show you what's going on.'

Born stood up slowly, wobbled a little, then led him out of the door. They walked quickly towards the end of the corridor, then stopped at a set of double doors and peered through their narrow strips of wire-reinforced glazing. It took Virgo a dozen heartbeats to take in the scene.

CHAPTER 62

THE HALL WAS ENORMOUS. Most of it was given over to the trappings of an operations room; half of the far wall was covered with a huge display divided into various component squares. Two small displays on the right were blank, except for labels at the top of each screen. One read 'Pentagon'; the other 'Oval Office'. An enormous map of North America filled the biggest area. It was speckled with flashing white aeroplane-shaped silhouettes.

At the front, six armed guards in black uniforms stood, ten metres apart. A dozen technicians shuffled around briskly behind them, moving between banks of monitors and control consoles. In front of the consoles, a huge black metal box stood on a silver trolley. It was the size of two large coffins, one stacked on the other, and was covered in connectors and strung with cables that led to the three racks of electronics sharing the trolley's platform. And next to it, on a black platform, was a small – insignificantly small – shiny silver box. Somehow, he knew: that was it. Genovsky's quantum computer.

She was standing by its side, speaking with three men. Her face was glowing under the lights that hung from the false ceiling.

'I've got to get her over here,' Born said. With a glance at

Virgo, he pulled one door half-open and stood in the doorway.

'Who's she talking to?' Virgo asked from behind the other door.

And then he saw him. The man on the TV. Thomas Wheelan.

Born replied without turning his head. 'One of them is Gabriel MacIntyre,' he said. 'Which is interesting.'

'Who?'

'Red Spot Industries. Don't you read the papers? He's the man that brought it to global domination.'

Red Spot. Like the disks in Gierek's lab.

'What about the others?'

'The one with the ponytail is Genovsky's boss, Vasil Marinov. The other – the black guy – I don't know. But he looks familiar. Maybe –'

His voice tailed off. Genovsky had spotted him.

She forced out a smile, then said something to the men in front of her. Instinctively, Virgo pulled back behind the door. He didn't want to be seen. He could hear Genovsky's heels clacking on the floor as she moved towards them. She was in a hurry.

'Did you get it?' She sounded stressed.

'I got it,' Born replied. 'It's in the car outside.'

'Good. Where's Virgo?'

It seemed the ideal moment to step forward. It wasn't: Genovsky pushed Born back through the door, which slammed into his face.

'Ow. *Fuck*.'

Great entrance.

Genovsky was standing right in front of his face. He resisted the desire to wipe a hand over his nose to see if it was bleeding. She stared at him for a moment. Beads of perspiration hung on her brow. She glanced back into the hall; as her head snapped back round, she noticed Born's black eye.

'What happened to you?'

Born said nothing, but turned and led them back along the corridor, and into an office. There were four upholstered chairs in the room, two desks and a filing cabinet. The walls were painted cream, but there were nail-holes and stains where pictures had once hung.

'Nice place,' Virgo said. 'Who's your decorator?'

Genovsky looked him over for a moment before she spoke. 'What are you doing, Virgo? You sent my name to the FBI. You want to use entanglement against me? Did Born tell you about the entanglement in the flight control software? What are you doing to your daughter?'

She turned and walked back towards the door. She was agitated. She was vulnerable here, he knew it. She wouldn't want a body now. She wouldn't want to be explaining herself to the boss at this stage of the operation. He could afford to push it. As she reached the door, she turned back to face him.

'You know how many people I have killed to keep this' – she waved in the direction of the main hall – 'under wraps?' She was still sweating, and a silver string of saliva was caught between her parted lips. 'Believe me, Nathaniel, you will soon be one of very, very many.' Her voice softened slightly. 'If you won't help me, I can't help you.'

'How can I help you, Genovsky?'

This woman couldn't keep still. She stepped back towards him, and came right up close. She was wearing little make-up, and he could see the contours of the scar as they rose and fell in the bruised cheek. It was strangely elegant; there was something about it that highlighted her cheekbones. He pulled his eyes away from following its course.

'I need that machine. And I need to know what it does.'

'In exchange for what?'

'I'll do what I can for your daughter.'

Time to push it.

'Like you can do anything. Aren't you playing a bit part here? That's the Secretary for Homeland Security in there. What makes you think you can help?'

She hesitated, and he saw it. 'I am operating the entanglement. With the planes. If I turn it off, everything goes back to normal. She will survive.'

Bingo. And Genovsky really did believe it. But he needed more.

'Entanglement? How does that work?'

She didn't bite. 'I need the machine, Nathaniel.'

He had run out of rope – he could see it in her face, even before she spoke. He could figure the details out later. When he had got out of this.

She looked at her watch. 'Let's get the machine.'

Virgo moved towards the door. 'I'll need Born's help carrying it in.'

Genovsky laughed. And then she turned to Born. 'You have a gun, don't you?' she asked.

Born shrugged apologetically. Genovsky frowned then pulled a gun from her shoulder holster. She handed it to Born. 'I'll be back in two seconds,' she said. 'If he moves, shoot him.'

She slipped out of the room. Virgo looked around, then at Born. He could probably make it; Born wouldn't fire the gun, he was almost certain of that. But then he might not make it out of the building that way. Where had Genovsky gone?

Too late. She was back. And she had company.

'This is Daniel Born,' she said to the security guard standing by her side. The guard had a blond buzz-cut, and the kind of jaw that right angles were invented for. His arms were folded over a machine gun that hung from a strap over the bulging globe of his shoulder.

'Daniel Born is going to prove something to me. He is going to take this man outside to his car, and then shoot him. You are going to make sure that happens, then you are going to help Born carry a piece of electronics back in here. You put it in here, you come and find me. OK?'

Born was staring at Genovsky. She looked at her watch again. She was up against the clock. Virgo knew the feeling.

There was a knock, then the door opened and a squat man stepped into the room and beckoned to Genovsky. 'Mr Marinov is looking for you,' he said.

Genovsky hesitated, then nodded to the guard. 'I'll be in the hall.'

She looked at them for a moment, and swept quickly out of the room.

There was nothing to be gained from hanging around now.

'OK,' Virgo said, pointing politely towards the door. 'Shall we?'

CHAPTER 63

IT WAS THE SHEER number of planes on the display that overwhelmed Gabriel MacIntyre. He stood, impotent, leaning against the railing that supported the racks of equipment, and stared at the shiny silver box. Then up at the display again.

Every one of those flashing dots had Red Spot software in the navigation systems. He had been proud and excited to win those contracts – the airlines always checked code thoroughly; the contracts were a testimony to the company's strength.

Trust Marinov to know they didn't check the upgrades nearly so thoroughly. It had been easy to upload his entanglement patches to the systems. They now had remote control, like with the power companies. But remote control over a competitor's pricing systems was one thing – remote control over a plane's navigation system was plain terrifying. You shouldn't mess with things like that. Thank God for the entanglement. Flipping a bit on a plane as it came in over the Atlantic was heinous, but at least no one would know how it had happened. He would have to learn to live with the responsibility, but at least he wouldn't have to live in jail.

He shifted his feet and looked round the room. Where had

that Genovsky woman gone? Marinov was over there, chatting with Tom like they were out on a golf course somewhere, discussing the best way out of the rough on the sixteenth. Occasionally, they looked up at the screen, but most of the time they were engaged in animated conversation.

He couldn't see Genovsky anywhere. What was the deal with her, anyway? When they met, she took his hand in her grip like she'd been told to grind it into dust. She had eyes that would freeze your soul, but when she talked about the entanglements, they lit up like it was her school science project. She seemed to want to pal up with him just because he knew about the quantum computer. Like she'd had this secret for years and finally found someone she could tell, someone who might understand.

And yet she was the hired killer. *Jesus*. How fucked up was all this? Why did he have to be here? What could he add to this set-up? If it was so terrifyingly powerful, why couldn't the government just go ahead and pay for it? Why were they here going through all this? There must be a way to work it out, for Marinov to get his payback, his development money. It didn't make sense to set up the fake sting. If Tom Wheelan wanted to make America stronger and safer, get the money to put together a quantum cryptography network, why didn't he just take the goddamn quantum computer into the Oval Office, plug it in and show it off? Why the elaborate routine? Was he missing something?

'You ready, Gabe?'

It was Tom, striding towards him, smiling his fake smile. MacIntyre pulled himself back into the room, crushing all the unresolved questions back down inside him.

'Ready for what? What's gonna happen now?'

He could see a nervous glint in Tom's eye. It was matched by the way he was fiddling with something in the pocket of his suit pants. Pills, MacIntyre guessed. The look was something to do with the pills. It was the same look he'd seen last night before dinner, before his wife gave Tom the new stash.

MacIntyre felt happier when he saw this weakness; it gave him hope, it let him off the hook. We're not human, we're just biochemistry. We're just slaves to the molecules. We're being manipulated by atomic forces.

'We're about to take control of the first plane.'

Tom's words fell into the back of MacIntyre's mind while the front struggled not to fall into despair at the tragedy of his existence.

'It's time to start the show, Gabe.'

The show? Seriously? This was so out of control.

They were being manipulated by atomic forces. And somewhere up in the heavens, a plane was about to find out how they felt.

Jesus. How did he get into this? What had gone so horribly wrong – *so fucking goddamn horrifically wrong* – that he was involved with a gang of grown men using quantum theory to hijack a plane?

It was all so absurd, so pathetically absurd, that he just stood there grinning. He was actually grinning. And Tom was grinning right back at him.

Jesus.

CHAPTER 64

VIRGO, BORN AND BUZZ-CUT marched up the corridor in single file. When he turned his head, Virgo could see Born pointing the gun limply at his back. He could feel the cold steel of the gun tucked into his waistband. And behind Born, out of sight, he could hear the steady rhythm of Buzz-cut's heavy boots. He would have to time this perfectly. Virgo set an eager pace: five minutes later, they were scrambling up the steep bank. By the time they had crawled under the fence and arrived back at the Lexus, Born was struggling for breath.

Virgo put his hands behind his back. 'Here we go, then.'

Buzz-cut looked on, amused, his arms still folded over the gun. A professional smirk played on his lips. He was watching amateur hour.

Born's hands were shaking. Virgo's hands were reaching into his waistband. This would be tricky. What did he know about safety catches?

But it was dark. That would give him an extra quarter-second. Then the smirk would be gone. How long before Born cracked? This was clearly killing him. Suddenly, he was facing the reality of what he'd got into. The rain had stopped, and the moon shone clear from the gunmetal sky. Born stood silent, his head hung low. His hands were shaking more wildly now.

There wasn't time for this.

'Daniel?'

Born looked up. In the moonlight, Virgo saw a childlike face. His eyes were wide and rimmed with tears. He was just about to break.

As Born lowered the gun and turned apologetically towards the guard, Virgo took a leap, spinning around the car. The gun was out and raised before he landed. He pumped the trigger. The first shot hit Buzz-cut's shoulder and knocked him to the ground. Virgo had to stand tall to get the second shot over the car's bonnet and into the forehead.

Born stood, frozen to the spot.

'Tell me about Katie's plane, Daniel.'

Two seconds passed before Born answered. He looked like a frightened child. 'They're using entanglement like a remote control. They've taken over the navigation system.'

'How the hell would they do that? You'd have to have something on board that was quantum-controlled.'

'That's what Gierek achieved. A quantum interface for electronics and software. Genovsky said Red Spot have been using it for months now to manipulate competitors' prices.'

There was no time to argue this. Born's face was earnest enough.

'How do you turn it off?'

'Genovsky has the control, like she said. It's a key-operated over-ride.'

This, at least, was believable.

'And who are these people?'

'Organised crime.' Born shrugged nonchalantly, like he had thrown in his lot with the local church knitting group.

'With quantum computers?'

'Genovsky does the high-tech stuff – they even have a blue-sky sector. It's like IBM with Uzis. And no need for lawyers.'

Born was quite something – he had stopped even noticing

the body at his feet. Like he just flipped into extreme autism at the opportune moment: no empathy. Which made him pretty much useless for now.

Think.

'OK,' Virgo said eventually. 'Time to get the machine.' He tossed Born the keys.

Like an automaton, Born went round to the back of the car. Virgo followed. One crack with the butt of the gun, and Born crumpled into the mud.

Virgo dragged Born's limp form to the side of the Lexus, and then further into the dark, towards the trees. The keys were still clenched in Born's fist. Virgo pulled them from his grip and moved back to the car. He closed the boot, and jumped into the driver's seat.

Wait.

It would be unpleasant, but maybe worth it. Just in case. He got out of the Lexus, and went over to the guard's body. The sizing was all wrong, and there was a bullet hole in the left shoulder. But this was no time for sartorial unease.

Stripping the corpse was difficult; the dead weight made it a cumbersome task. Virgo propped up the torso and removed the jacket, resisting the temptation to rip the shirt off, and worked methodically through the buttons. He let the torso thump back down onto the gravel, removed the boots, then unzipped the trousers.

Virgo gathered the clothes and threw them onto the back seat. He dragged the stripped body to the trees and laid it next to Born. A treat for when he came round.

Virgo climbed back into the driver's seat and started the engine. He slapped the car into reverse. The wheels spun on the wet mud; he took a deep breath, trying to let the adrenaline abate, and then let his right foot press more gently. The Lexus moved smoothly backwards.

Two minutes later, a half-mile from the junkyard entrance, he pulled over to the side of the road, and reached for his phone.

CHAPTER 65

FRANK DELANEY, SPECIAL AGENT in charge of a non-existent investigation, was taking a leak. The telephone receiver had sat idly on its cradle all day. No one had seen Virgo. Or at least no one who wanted to report it. Morgan had left for the day. Rosemary was there, though. Delaney suspected Morgan didn't want to leave him alone in the empty office, didn't trust him that far.

Morgan said Delaney could hang around the Boston field office for a day or so without causing too much trouble. But any longer and people would start asking questions. No one minded his presence – he was welcome to visit. But everyone knew he'd asked to get out and taken the first post he was offered at Quantico. Everyone assumed he'd lost his edge.

Was that what this was about? Did he have something to prove now that Nancy was long buried? Was he ready to come back?

He hadn't yet worked out what to do if someone did spot Nathaniel Virgo. Morgan had promised him a team and some back-up, even a helicopter if he needed it. But Morgan was smart, repaying the favour at minimal risk. Once this was over, the code of honour would be satisfied and he'd be free of obligation.

It was too late to go back on his testimony now. And that wouldn't bring Nancy back anyway. He had cleared Morgan, made the gesture that said he called it right. Maybe he did, maybe he didn't. But Nancy was dead, and it would be a dust-crawling son of a bitch who wanted to make Morgan pay for that. Everyone knew the blame lay higher up. Right at the top. Ever since Homeland Security took over the Bureau, everything had turned to shit.

Delaney zipped his fly, and moved across the grey floor to wash his hands. If someone saw Virgo, he would stop at nothing to bring him in and find out what was going on. Virgo was into something, that was for sure. There were bodies, there was the lie about the disk, and there was someone up high who didn't want anything investigated. How high? That he didn't yet know. Maybe it was the right level for a little retribution. Maybe it was higher. Either way, here was his chance to do something. To pay the bastards back for screwing Nancy over.

The dryer was deafening, and still roaring behind him as he came out the door and headed back up the stairs. He took them two at a time, bouncing at the thought of getting back into something. He still had the fire in his chest.

'Frank.'

Rosemary was stood at the door to her office.

'There's a caller for you. Says he's Nathaniel Virgo.'

CHAPTER 66

A FULL MINUTE PASSED IN the darkness. Maybe they were setting up a call trace, getting out the recording equipment. Did they still do that? Probably not – this was the digital age, they probably had caller ID.

At last, a deep voice resounded over the line.

'This is Frank Delaney. What can I do for you, Virgo? You about ready to come in?'

Delaney's voice sounded deep and trustworthy. A man you could rely on. God, he hoped so.

'I didn't kill those people. I need you to come and get me. And you need to bring support. The people who killed those men are assembled in a warehouse about half a mile from where I'm sitting now. They are hijacking planes. My daughter is on one of them. Delaney, this goes to the top of Homeland Security.'

Did he need to say more? Would Delaney go for it? Why wouldn't he?

And why wasn't he saying anything?

He felt a strange temptation to spill his guts; Delaney had a way with silence.

'I can explain everything, but you have to get down here soon.' Still no response. Virgo lost it. 'Delaney, did you hear me?' He was shouting into the phone. 'They're tapping into the White House's communications. This goes all the way up. My daughter's on one of the planes. They've already killed my wife. You've got to come here and help me.' He paused, waiting for a response, some word of reassurance. None came.

'Hello?'

'I'm here, Virgo. Where can we find you?'

Virgo hesitated. He didn't know where he was. Brilliant. He really didn't have a clue.

'A junkyard north of the city. Somewhere north of Everett? Overlooking an industrial complex. That's where they are – in the complex.' He felt ridiculous. 'You can trace me by my mobile signal. Can't you triangulate from the transmission masts, and pin me down within a few feet? You're the detective, for Christ's sake.'

There was a pause. 'Already onto it. Stay there.'

The line went dead.

CHAPTER 67

HE HAD NO INTENTION of staying there; Delaney sounded trustworthy, but who didn't when their livelihood depended on it? Virgo had sounded trustworthy to Born only a few minutes ago, before he clubbed Born over the head. And Born had sounded trustworthy to him back at the hotel. Well, almost – he was glad he'd had the sense to lead him in the same lie he told Genovsky, just in case. So no, he wasn't going to stay there and wait for the FBI to make up their mind. But he could give them another few minutes of phone signal for their tracers. He had another call to make.

The buzz repeated five times so far. He knew Imogen's answerphone kicked in at nine rings. What time was it in the UK? What would she be doing?

Seven rings. Eight. And – finally – she picked up.

'Imogen? It's Nat.'

There was a pause before she spoke.

'It's the middle of the night, Nat. What the hell . . .'

'Imogen, I need your help. I need you to call your contact at the NSA. I'm deep into something.'

He had to take a breath. It was all too unreal, but talking to Imogen like this, that made it too real. His mind was melting. He had to hold it together. For Katie's sake.

'Imogen, I'm in Boston. Rachel's been killed. Katie's on a hijacked plane and – you're not going to believe this – the head of Homeland Security, Thomas Wheelan, is in on this. I don't know what they're doing – it's all happening out of a warehouse north of Boston. It's something to do with the quantum computing people I met at Baltimore. One of them got killed, and I followed it up. That's all I know. It's all gone to hell, Imogen, and I'll take any help I can get.'

Breathe.

Imogen was silent. Too much information?

'Imogen?'

'You're serious, aren't you?'

Virgo interrupted her. 'I'm very serious. Katie's plane is likely to be shot down in the next hour or so. There's a guy from Red Spot – a Gabriel MacIntyre – involved too.'

'What do you need to know?'

'Anything. Something. I've told you pretty much all I know. If you can find out how you'd fly a plane by remote control, that might be useful. But I've not got much to go on. There's an Alexandra Genovsky, Wheelan, and Gabriel MacIntyre of Red Spot Industries. But put quantum stuff and Homeland Security together and you've got the guts of that report you got hold of. Maybe Wheelan was setting something up when your guy at NSA leaked his stuff. Maybe he can help. But this has to be quiet, Imogen. If I contact the authorities, Katie's dead for sure; Wheelan would be the first to know. And I'm already wanted for double murder.' He paused. 'It's been a hell of a day.'

His attempt at humour fell flat into the mouthpiece. Rachel was dead. He'd said it out loud to someone who knew her. Everything felt different now.

'Nat,' Imogen said. Then she fell silent again for a moment.

'Nat, I'm sorry. God . . .'

She didn't know what to say. Of course she didn't know what to say.

'Can you help me, Imogen?'

Silence.

'Imogen?'

'OK. Yes.' She sounded decisive. 'I'll call you back when I have something.'

Virgo closed the connection, then turned off his phone. Would the FBI have been able to listen in on that call? How the hell would he know? It wouldn't hurt him if they had. They would surely be amazed that Imogen had taken it all so calmly. Thank God for Imogen.

He turned the key in the ignition. His breathing was shallow, and his mind was racing through the next moves. Had he worked it out properly? Could he second-guess Delaney? Could he trust him?

He rolled the Lexus round in a lazy U-turn, and drove back towards the junkyard. A hundred yards in front of the gate, Virgo turned the car around again, and reversed into the darkness of a narrow side lane. He backed up thirty metres until his side window looked out on a long dark path. At the end of this path, in the moonlight, the chain-link fence stretched out across the face of the junkyard. He opened the door of the Lexus and walked up to the fence. From this angle Virgo could see the lone, decaying sentry tower of the crane that rose into the sky just beyond the entrance. Another path ran to his left, towards the gates.

Perfect.

He went back to the car and waited, trying to ignore the threatening silence of the neighbourhood. The closest housing must be a mile away. Nothing but derelict buildings and high fences. A bat flitted across the moon. Somewhere in the distance a cat screeched. He half-expected Stephen King to tap on the window. How did he get to be four thousand miles from home, hiding out in a stolen car surrounded by darkness?

The quiet rumble of engines heralded their approach. A colonnade of dark vehicles, some trucks, but mostly 4WDs, rolled past, their lights dimmed. The cavalry. They had obviously found nothing in the spot where the triangulation had sent them. Now, they were hunting blind, in the dark. They were bound to head into the junkyard he'd mentioned. They would seal it off and look over the warehouse. And, when they were in position, he would tell them just where the action was going on. And it would all be over.

He could barely breathe.

There had been no more trucks for a couple of minutes. They would have secured the perimeter of the junkyard and be combing through the rusting carcasses by now. He could see it, in his mind's eye: black jackets, gold lettering, rifles and night sights. Would they find Born? Or would he have crawled back to Genovksy? What about the stripped guard?

His stomach plunged. He'd forgotten that he killed a man today.

Virgo forced himself to step out of the Lexus. Even in this constricting alley, he felt exposed. At least he had got used to the dark. He pulled the gun from his waistband.

The moonlight was almost bright enough to see by. *Click.* That was the safety catch. *Click.* On. *Click.* Off. He enveloped the grip in both hands. The gun felt strangely heavy as he lifted it in front of him. Did he have to carry a gun? Was this stupid? Would they shoot him when they saw it?

No, it would buy him the respect he needed. The bargaining space. Delaney's ear.

He walked forward in the shadow of the wall rising to his left. Ahead he could see two roving spotlights. One caught the crane tower at the front gate, then swung onto the boom. Would the agents be freaked by the ghostly shapes caught in the lights? They would certainly be jumpy. He lowered the gun.

Up at the fence now, just fifty metres from the gate. Three tall 4WDs, unmarked, ranged across it. There was another vehicle just twenty metres ahead of him, parked where the high wall to his left stopped and the path he was walking began to fan out at the junkyard entrance.

It would do. He moved up to it, and looked through the rear windscreen. It was empty.

This was crazy. He had interviewed a lot of people in his time, but negotiating with the FBI? That was something else. They would shoot at the sound of his voice – he was wanted for double murder and he was carrying a gun.

They'd be justified in shooting him; no one would blame them. Agents' lives were at risk. What if Wheelan had put out a shoot-to-kill on him? *Jesus.* It really didn't pay to take on the guy at the top.

He was crazed, shouting, waving a gun. We had no choice. He could hear it now.

Virgo acted before he could play any more of the aftermath out in his head.

'Delaney!' His shout slumped into the wet earth.

'Delaney!' It was too late to back out now. He gave it everything.

'De-laaa-neeey.' He sounded crazed.

He was crazed.

Virgo had never felt like this. The tension in his body seemed to stop time and light up the night. His heightened senses were crippling. The scene before him played out like it was lit by the staccato fire of a strobe light. The echoing clicks of safety catches disengaging threatened to burst his eardrums. He felt like a fly: he could see every movement, every shifting shadow as the agents turned on their heels, desperate to locate him. Slow motion – stop motion – as the searchlights on the vehicles scanned around, across, over his hiding place behind the windscreen.

'I've got a gun. I want to talk to Delaney.'

'I'm here, Nathaniel.'

That was – bizarrely – disappointing. The deep voice boomed across the night without the aid of a loudhailer.

Every time he had seen something like this at the movies, there was a loudhailer.

What to say?

'It's Delaney. Talk to me, Nathaniel. No one's gonna hurt you.'

Yeah, right. Through the windscreen, Virgo could see him. Fit and broad and confident. And trained in negotiation. He would know how to reach an agreement without the use of violence.

'They have my daughter, Katie, on a plane coming in from Cuba,' Virgo shouted. 'It's being hijacked.' He paused. 'They killed my wife. I didn't kill Radcliffe. You know who I am by now. I'm a journalist. Nothing more.'

No response. Worth a shot. 'Wheelan knows. Ask Thomas Wheelan about this.'

'Nathaniel, step out from behind the vehicle. Put down the weapon. We don't want to hurt you, Nathaniel. You carry a weapon, you place yourself at a greater risk.'

He knew that.

'You have to help me free Katie. You have to help me. You . . .'

He stopped himself – he was ranting.

He was crazed. We had no choice.

He tried to calm his breathing. One, two. One, two. In, out.

'We will help you, Nathaniel. Listen, we want to help you. Step out from behind the vehicle and put down the weapon.'

One, two. One, two. In, out. He pursed his lips as he panted. It had begun to rain again, just a drizzle. Virgo wiped his face dry. He saw Delaney's face lift to the sky. There was a throbbing in the air.

A helicopter. OK. Good. They were taking him seriously.

'I'm coming out.' Virgo reached out and placed the gun on top of the vehicle. The black metal glinted in the searchlights, the beads of rainwater throwing prismatic colours off the surface. He stepped out, hands in the air.

'That's it, Nathaniel, nice 'n' easy.'

ENTANGLEMENT

Delaney walked towards him. His gait rolled, like his legs were carrying too much muscle.

'Stay calm, Nathaniel.'

The helicopter throb was growing louder. It was deafening. The strobe lighting came back, and the scene retreated from Virgo's vision. Delaney was moving towards him down a long, dark tunnel, his voice echoing off the black walls.

'That's it, stay calm. It's gonna be OK. There's no hijack – we'll sort everything out downtown. It's all over now. All over.'

Virgo was thankful that his senses had moved into slow-motion: it gave him the edge. The time to process Delaney's words when all hell was falling from the sky.

From their position on the ground, they could all see the helicopter dipping down from the darkness, lit from below by roving floodlights. But Virgo was the first to react – to recoil as it floated too close to the unlit tower of the rusting crane. The swinging lights must have blinded the pilot at the wrong moment. He yanked too late on the joystick. The first sound of rotor on rusting steel was something from the movies – the ring of clashing swords – but the noise immediately became a thud and a screech and a metallic clatter of shredding, chattering steel. And as the helicopter's body swung sharply into the crane, Virgo was already on his toes and turning.

No hijack.

He had the edge when the agents fell to the ground to escape the plunging tail rotor.

Downtown.

Enough edge to grab the gun from the roof and crouch.

All over.

He ran back into the darkness. With the impending firestorm, no one was even looking at him.

Delaney was a liar. Like Genovsky. Like Born.

You're dead already, Nathaniel.

No. It was not all over. Not yet.

The helicopter's fuel tank ignited. As he ran, he felt the heat of the fireball rage on his back. He heard shouts and screams, but he didn't dare look behind.

Virgo's boots held his ankles upright as he skidded round the corner. Ahead of him the open door of the Lexus gaped, welcoming him to its luxury. He had the ignition key in his right hand, the gun in his left. His heart banged in his chest.

Don't look back.

It didn't matter who was chasing him; how close they were. All that mattered was getting the key into the ignition.

He dived into the seat. The key went in first time. He yanked on the door as he pulled away, thrown back into his seat as his foot floored the accelerator pedal.

No lights. Not yet. He could make out the end of the alley-way; it glowed orange with fire, like the sky above.

As he emerged onto the road, he threw all his weight into the steering wheel. He braked at the same time, and the car swung sharply round. He hit the accelerator again. In the rear-view mirror, the orange sky quickly grew dim over an empty road. The helicopter had taken out half the FBI's fleet of vehicles, trapping the other half inside the junkyard.

Ahead of him lay an open road. And a dead end: now he had added FBI agents to the body count, his plans were looking pretty washed up.

They were meant to save the day. That was the whole idea, whichever way things worked out. Once Genovsky had believed the stuff about Gierek's magic box, once he had bought Katie some time, the FBI were the cavalry riding in against a blazing sunset. That really wasn't going to happen now.

It was over.

He drove towards the docks. The heavy sky crushed him; he felt its pressure on his skin, it squeezed the air from his lungs and hung on his limbs. It was all he could do to keep driving.

He was at the harbourfront now, dawdling through a

deserted lot, headed for the ocean. He didn't know whether he should stop at the sea wall. If he never surfaced again, would Genovsky bring Katie safely to the ground? He couldn't remember the plan. Nothing was real any more, nothing but the piteous, ineffectual corner he was crumpled into.

Ahead of him, through the dark, he began to see flashing lights in the atmosphere, flights climbing and falling at the airport, souls coming and going, sharing the air with his only daughter. Maybe his wife, too; somewhere beyond sight, Rachel was in transit between two worlds. Everything in his life had melted in chaos.

He pulled up short of the wall. He didn't even have it in him to drive into the ocean. He cut the engine and the lights, and watched the flashes ascending and descending in the darkness.

Except they weren't ascending now.

Nothing had taken off for a few minutes. He waited, his eyes focused at the blackness across the water. After ten minutes, he knew it from the creeping chill in his guts. But after twenty minutes without a take-off, it was a sure thing. Everything that could fly was being brought to earth. Or kept there. Something had happened to a plane somewhere, and he was pretty sure he knew what.

This was no time to sit watching the night sky fall empty. He fired up the car again and swung it round. He hadn't come up with a plan yet. But that's what final journeys were for.

CHAPTER 68

'EVERYTHING ON THE GROUND *is staying there, Mr President.*'

'What can you tell me about this plane? Are you telling me that hundreds of people died just because of a technical fault?'

'Sir, there was no squawk. We had no voice transmission from the cockpit. We can only assume a hijack. But we simply don't know anything for sure yet. Troops are already recovering the debris.'

Gabriel MacIntyre felt a bead of sweat drip down his spine. They had done it. They were listening to the decrypted feed from the White House Situation Room. The thought made him nauseous.

'You look a little peaky, Gabe.' Thomas Wheelan's eyes burned into him.

He was a lot worse than peaky. But to say anything, or not? What the hell. He had a right to be heard – he had gone along with this plan because he was an equal partner. No, a vital partner: if it wasn't for him, they couldn't have got the software onto the planes. And he had certainly shouldered an equal share of the risk.

So why the hell had they changed the plan without him?

'We were going to call it off just before it went critical,' he said. The words came out quavering, but there was nothing he could do about that. 'It was meant to scare and then disappear. You've just triggered a federal investigation.'

'And I've already prepared its conclusions and recommendations, Gabe.'

Wheelan's face was deadly serious. 'Hundreds of lives were lost when US fighter jets were forced to shoot down three planes. But it would have been much, much worse had the Department for Homeland Security not been using its intelligence sources to nail down the situation so quickly.'

Marinov stepped up. 'And it's now clear that the US government has no choice but to fast-track a better path to complete surveillance,' he added.

Marinov said it just like a broadcaster, like he was playing a role. Had he and Tom been practising this? Like it was some kind of sick cabaret?

Marinov's lips carried the slightest trace of mockery as he continued. 'With quantum technology, these attacks on our nation could have been avoided. And, thanks to Thomas Wheelan's work, we now have that technology within our grasp. A thousand lives were lost tonight. But hundreds of thousands more will be saved. The war on terror is, to all intents and purposes, over.'

Marinov paused. For applause? MacIntyre was struck dumb.

Wait up. Three planes?

'Did you just say three?'

Every one of the targets on the map was carrying Red Spot software – that's how they picked them. One link back to the company was bad enough. But three?

'Relax, Gabe. The entanglement is untraceable, remember? Want to pick the next one?'

He couldn't respond. He had just heard the one word he

didn't want coming over the loudspeaker. Someone – the Chief of Staff? – just said it.

Software.

'... there is one possibility, other than a physical hijacking, sir. There is software in the flight-control system that allows remote access.'

'We can fly planes from the ground?'

'Some planes, Mr President. Via the transponder that emits the "hijacked" signal. It's possible that there was no squawk because the transponder was compromised.'

'You're telling me someone else was flying the plane?'

'It's just a possibility, sir. The software is still active in some US-built aircraft. Certain other nations have stripped it from their control systems.'

'Jesus, Bob. Get me a list of all the vulnerable planes in the air. Right now. And where is Wheelan?'

MacIntyre's jaw locked. Christ. They were going to take the flight-control software apart. How untraceable could the entanglement be? There would be some code there – surely it was traceable, whatever Marinov said. He wished he knew less economic theory and a lot more about the stuff his company actually sold.

'Gabe? Hello? You wanna pick the next one or not?'

'Allow me.' Marinov stepped forward. 'There's a flight out of Cuba, headed for Montreal. We can fly it in towards Boston. It's getting towards the right position to give us a spectacular little threat.'

Wheelan shrugged. 'OK.'

'Alex,' Marinov called. The woman looked up from the control console. 'The Cuba flight is next.'

She stared at Marinov, then nodded, and turned her back to them. MacIntyre saw her begin to hit some keys. He felt a surge of panic. Boston was surely a bad idea. He had offices here. Not to mention family.

'Wait.'

He watched Genovsky halt her tapping and turned around. She looked at Marinov.

Wheelan gave him a pitying look. 'Gabe, it won't get anywhere near,' he said. 'You really are a worrier.'

MacIntyre breathed deeply.

'You said I could choose.' Christ, he sounded like Jennie and her friends arguing over which doll got to ride in the front of Barbie's beach buggy. Still, might as well hold him to something. Way to go, iron man.

'Fly something into Los Angeles.' He forced out a smile. 'I have competitors on the west coast who could do with a little wake-up call.'

Wheelan glanced at Marinov. 'That OK with you? We'll do the Cuban flight after.'

Marinov shrugged, then turned to the woman. 'The United flight from Houston into LAX, then.' He smiled at her. 'For old times' sake.'

She spun on her chair and fired it up.

CHAPTER 69

VIRGO KNEW HE WAS safe enough for the moment; no one would know the car. None of the agents – those who had survived the fireball – would have seen anything of it. He had that on his side, at least.

He was driving back the way he came, towards the junkyard, still without a plan. It occurred to him that hundreds, maybe thousands of people were sitting on these planes, and he only cared about one fifteen-year-old girl. Should he make a call to the police, get them to the warehouse, and just hope Katie got out alive? Would that be the right thing to do? What it was to be a human being. What it was to have the burden of free will.

He had to eat. His stomach was knotted with hunger, and he was starting to get dizzy: his body needed food.

There. That was the great thing about America: you were never more than half a block from a burger joint. The next one up was a McDonald's. His stomach knotted further at the golden arches. He hadn't been in one in two years now.

The red flash of a plane's lights passed overhead. He couldn't mess around. Big Mac, Coke, and a plan. For Katie's sake.

He ate quickly, letting his mind blank out for a few

minutes. The sweet smell of the burger filled the car. When it was gone, he wished he'd ordered two. The fats and the sugar quickly began their work, and the dizziness faded. He began to think again, assessing his options . . .

Well, that didn't take long.

The FBI would be putting everything into finding him. What did they have to go on? Not much; he was in a pretty good position. As long as they hadn't seen the car, and as long as he managed not to get pulled over by any traffic police, he would be OK. Still, it didn't feel good to be wanted. On two continents. With his picture in the newspaper. Did these things go away once you'd cleared your name, or did they drag around your ankles for ever? As things stood, he certainly didn't want this on his résumé. And that was why he had to go back. He had no choice. Virgo turned and threw his trash into the back seat.

Of course.

The uniform. Would the FBI have found the dead guard? Maybe. But maybe not. The fireball would have pulled them back.

It took him a couple of minutes of wriggling to drag the clothes on. He tugged at the jacket, and glanced sideways at the shoulder. The clothes were so oversized that the bullet-hole fell at a different place on the shirt and the jacket. It was hardly noticeable. In the dark of the car, at least.

What else did he have? The box. Gierek's machine.

He popped the boot open, got out of the car, and picked it up. It was too light. Not that he had any idea how light it should be, but it was no heavier than a VCR. He got back in the car, then dropped the box gently down on the front passenger seat.

What was this thing?

He stared at it for a moment, willing his mind to penetrate the plastic casing and learn Gierek's secret. Entanglement. Einstein's spooky action at a distance. He didn't believe it. He didn't want to believe it, either, but that wasn't the point. The

MICHAEL BROOKS

secret of instantaneous wireless communication, faster than the speed of light. Inside this flimsy plastic box?

Something sparked across his mind.

Bulgarian programmers. Internet security software. Flimsy plastic.

It was too obvious, surely?

There was no sense hanging around, but he might as well have a look. He had the plastic case off in a couple of minutes. And the contents confirmed his suspicions. Clever Laszlo Gierek. Whatever was going on at the warehouse, it wasn't what Born was thinking.

Virgo put the case back on the box and shifted the car into gear. Here, at last, was something he could use.

CHAPTER 70

IT TOOK TEN MINUTES before anyone noticed.

'We have another one, sir. Flight 436 into LAX unresponsive and deviated from flight plan. It's descending, sir.'

'Where's it headed?'

'Present course has it hitting downtown Los Angeles.'

'Oh, Christ. Do we have a shadow?'

'Twin fighter escort scrambled. They will engage the aircraft in five minutes.'

'And where will the debris land?'

'If we take it out immediately we establish contact, it will hit mostly farmland and scrub. That's according to our best calculations.'

'And if we wait?'

'We could triple the casualties. Unless we hear from the aircraft we have to act straightaway, sir.'

'Where's the list I asked for? Is this one of the vulnerable planes?'

'Yes, sir, it is. The full list is on its way.'

MacIntyre listened to the President breathe a deep sigh. What had they done? He wished he could sigh: he could hardly breathe.

He looked around. Marinov was sitting down now, staring at the huge map on the screen. The woman had moved to the back of the hall. Tom was pacing, and smiling.

He was smiling.

The minutes crawled by in silence.

'We have contact, sir.'

'Can the pilots see anything? There's still nothing from the plane?'

'Nothing, Mr President. The pilots report passengers waving frantically. They can't say any more than that. They can't really see anything, Mr President. But there are still no comms from the plane, and the course has not deviated at all – there's no question of the target destination. We are moving into the high casualty zone in thirty seconds, sir. We need the command now.'

'Three hundred and twenty-four people not high casualty enough for you, Bob? That's the number I'm about to blow out of the sky.'

'Sir?'

'Do I have any choice?'

A pause.

'Destroy the target. You have my order.'

'Yes, sir.'

MacIntyre retched. Twenty heartbeats later, the flashing blip – the plane, the lives *he* had chosen – disappeared from the map screen.

'Looks like we lost contact,' Tom said. 'Two down, two to go.'

Two to go?

'You said we'd take out three, max.'

His brother-in-law smiled. 'Well, let's see how time goes, shall we? What are you worried about, Gabe? Getting caught? I thought you'd be way past that by now. After all these months of profiteering, you still don't believe in the power of entanglement?'

He turned to Marinov. 'Shall we do the Cuban plane now?'

MacIntyre still felt sick. Nothing else. Just sick.

CHAPTER 71

FIFTY-FIVE MINUTES AFTER running from the FBI, Virgo was rolling the Lexus towards the gates of the warehouse complex. This time, he was going in the front door. This time, there would be no creeping about.

The razor wire glinted in the moonlight. Virgo parked to one side of the entrance, got out and slammed the door loudly. He opened the passenger side door and pulled Gierek's box of tricks up off the seat. He walked up to the closed gate, and rapped on the rain-drenched steel with his fist. A curtain of glittering drops fell to the ground in front of him. A large dark-skinned man, wearing the same uniform as Virgo, came out of a hut on the south side of the gate.

'Can I help you?' he growled.

'I'm from the other site,' Virgo said. He held the box aloft. 'Genovsky wants this. Tell her Nathaniel Virgo is here with the delivery.'

The guard looked Virgo up and down, then turned on his heels and went back to the hut. A minute later, he returned, and opened the gate. 'Someone'll be here to get you in a minute or so,' he muttered. 'Come and wait inside. It's gonna pour again in a second.' Virgo looked up at the mottled sky and followed the guard to the hut.

Inside the prefab cabin, sixteen monitors, stacked in two rows of eight, displayed random, monotonous views. Most were of empty corridors; the only monitor containing any action was fed from the main hall. The camera was positioned in one of the front corners. Virgo could just make out Alex Genovsky standing at the back of the hall, arms folded. There wasn't enough resolution to read her expression, but her body language screamed impatience: she would be glad when this was all over.

Amen to that.

Someone knocked on the door. Virgo looked up and through the window. He couldn't see anyone, but he saw the rain had indeed started up again. The guard grunted loudly that it was open. The door swung back to reveal the squat figure of Daniel Born standing under an umbrella.

'I got asked to pass on a message to Genovsky,' Born shouted against the clatter of rain. 'I decided to respond to it myself.'

He looked Virgo up and down, but made no comment on the uniform. Virgo couldn't tell if he was smiling or screwing his face against the windswept spray. 'Are you coming back in?'

Virgo nodded. Once he was out, Born offered Virgo a share of his umbrella.

'Thanks,' he said. 'I'm sorry about the clubbing. Really.'

Born rubbed the back of his head. 'I didn't think I'd see you again,' he said. 'What made you come back?'

'I had a revelation.'

They walked in silence for thirty seconds, Virgo's mind chugging through the branching consequences of his game plan. The rain drummed against the umbrella, a rhythmic pulse. To tempt Born straightaway, or to hold back?

No harm in throwing out a teaser.

'Do you want the good news or the bad?'

Born turned his head to look at him, but said nothing.

'The bad news is you've joined the wrong side,' Virgo said.

He paused for effect before he plunged in. 'The good news is I can get you out.'

Born looked confused. 'What do you mean?'

Virgo tapped on the plastic. 'The answer's in this box. But if I'm to get you out, I need you to keep it from Genovsky. Just for a while.'

He sensed Born's pace slacken.

'Don't make a scene, Daniel. Believe me, you of all people don't want Genovsky to know about this.' He strode a little faster. Born was skipping to keep up now. 'Just follow my instructions and I'll get us both out of this.'

No response. What was Born thinking?

'I'm curious, Daniel,' Virgo announced as they sauntered past the guards at the entrance to the main hangar. 'If you can walk in and out of here like this, why did you bring me in through the back?'

'If we pulled up at the front gates, you'd have jumped from the car.'

'You had a gun – you could have forced me in.'

'I'm a physicist, Nathaniel, I've never fired a gun in my life. I thought that would have been obvious to you by now. Anyway, I figured my plan was better. I scouted out the site, found the gap in the fence at the back. I was quite proud of myself.'

They were in a corridor flanked by ochre walls. This time, though, everything in the building gave the impression of a shaky impermanence; that it could all be pulled apart in moments. He didn't know how long Katie had. He had to move things along.

'How did you gain Genovsky's trust so quickly?'

Born shrugged. 'Like I said, she needed someone who knew quantum stuff.' He turned to his right into an orange-painted corridor. At the far end was a set of double doors. Virgo suffered a stab of recognition. They were almost there.

'So you have access?'

'If I explain what I'm doing, yes.'

'And Genovsky's key for the remote control? For the plane, I mean.'

'You mean *planes*,' Born said. He stopped walking and stared Virgo full in the face. 'They've already taken two down – your daughter's is up next.'

Virgo could see Born shaking. Under the bravado, the man knew he was in over his head. Virgo tried not to think about Katie. It was Born he had to concentrate on now. This had to work, and panic wouldn't help him.

'Can you get the key?' he said.

'No, I don't have access to that. She carries it on her.'

It was time to lay out the cards.

'Does the term Faraday cage mean anything to you?'

Born stared at him blankly for a moment, then shrugged. 'Of course. It's a metal casing that doesn't allow electromagnetic signals in or out.'

'Imagine you wanted to build something that had to emit and receive signals – would you encase it in metal?'

Born looked puzzled. 'Of course not.'

'Look at the entanglement box, Daniel. What's it made of?'

Born looked, then touched.

'Plastic.'

He mumbled the word, like it was the worst news he had ever heard.

'Why would Gierek encase his ground-breaking entanglement hardware in plastic, Daniel? Could it be that a metal case would be a problem?'

Born had stopped walking. No wonder; for him, it was all over now. Gierek had been mimicking entanglement with wireless broadband. Dressed it up to look like something more impressive – but made sure the wi-fi signal could still get out. That simple. Gierek knew people too well. He knew they believed what they wanted to.

'You looked inside?' Born asked. His voice was flat.

Virgo halted, then nodded. 'But I didn't need to. Not if I'd thought about it.'

They were standing a dozen paces from the doors that led into the main hall. Born was staring into the wall. Virgo felt a strange kind of guilt, like he should have protected Born from the truth. The clock was ticking. How much time did you give a man to grieve over shattered dreams?

None.

'Daniel, you're a scientist, not a gangster. You're better than all this.'

No response.

'I have to get that key, Daniel,' Virgo said. 'Will you help?'

The loudspeaker in the hall boomed into life.

'We're getting reports of a third plane, Mr President. This one's up out of Cuba. It's turning from the recorded flight plan. Fighters have been scrambled. Three minutes to contact.'

Born looked into Virgo's eyes, then nodded towards the hall. 'And so it's a cheap trick in there too, isn't it? This is all for nothing.'

Virgo nodded. There were no words.

CHAPTER 72

'JESUS MOTHERFUCKING CHRIST, FRANK.'
Delaney stared at Morgan, but said nothing. What could he say? Two of Morgan's men were dead. Morgan had let him go out into the field with a team who should have been safe at home with their families by now. Why had he called out the chopper? They had gone out to arrest one man, a journalist. Not a fucking mafia outfit. How did it get to this? Delaney felt a mild shock, but mostly he just felt numb. Maybe he wasn't up to all this. Maybe the Bureau's shrink was right.

No. There had been an accident. It wasn't his fault.

'Aren't you going to say anything?'

Morgan was pulling at his hair. Literally pulling his fucking hair out. His face was flushed red, the blood vessels inflamed on his cheeks.

What was there to say?

'Stay here, Delaney.' Morgan picked up his jacket. 'If you value your life, don't move from that spot. Both our careers are over tonight, but if you move from this office, your life will also be over. Before dawn. I promise you that.'

He moved to the door, then paused.

'You're just a washed-up asshole who ran out of balls.'

Spittle flecked out from his lashing tongue. 'End of story. If you had balls, you would have shopped me, not held me to a promise. I tried to give you a break tonight, but you screwed that up, like always. Screwed it up for both of us. It's not about Nancy any more, it's about you, Frank. You just haven't got what it takes. Now, if you'll excuse me, I have to go and explain what the fuck you've been up to. *Jesus*.'

He clattered down the stairs.

Delaney sank into a chair.

It was an accident. Nothing more.

Or was Morgan right? Was he a washed-up asshole?

Screw him. Morgan was the one who got Nancy killed. When it came down to it, the buck stopped with him. And yet he was still running this outfit. Where was the sense in that?

Thomas Wheelan. Why had Virgo shouted something about Thomas Wheelan?

Morgan's computer pinged. A new message. He hadn't logged out, then. Delaney got up from the chair and stuck his head out the door. There was no one around. He pulled back inside, nudged the door closed, and headed round behind Morgan's desk. The computer was live, and he clicked the message open.

A multiple hijack situation. All planes grounded. All field offices were on full alert.

They have my daughter on a plane coming in from Cuba. It's being hijacked.

Virgo was right. *Jesus.*

But was he right about Wheelan?

CHAPTER 73

SHE COULD SEE THAT Vasil was pleased. Of course he was. This would be a very lucrative day's work.

Katie Virgo's plane was minutes from catastrophe, but Genovsky was managing not to feel anything. She felt a twinge of sadness that Nathaniel Virgo was dead. It wasn't regret: it was the same sadness as when she shot Laszlo. But what choice did she have? Laszlo had decided it for her with his actions. The sadness came from understanding that his potential would never be properly realised. It was like abandoning a promising student halfway through their tuition.

She would get over it. And at least Virgo's death had an upside: Born had pulled the trigger. He had made the transition. He'd understood the cost involved in this kind of science. It was hard, and dirty. This wasn't some abstract idea-testing, tinkering around with things that no one would ever care about. This was real, it had real consequences – life and death consequences – and it was rewarded with progress far beyond anything you could achieve within government or university labs.

She had got used to killing people far quicker than she thought possible. Vasil had needed to force her, goad her, the first few times, but then it started to take, she started to see the point, that it was often the best option for everyone involved. Most of the people she killed had made choices that led them across her path. They knew the risks, and death was often a better option than a lifetime of watching their backs.

Born was an exciting recruit. She had always known he would be. It was disappointing that he hadn't risen to her challenge the first time round, but there was still time for him to flower. It was important that she surround herself with good people. She had to assemble something that would impress Vasil, something they could leave running – with all the right securities in place, of course – when they left.

Vasil had chosen South America, not Australia. Paraguay, at least for a while, he had said. Then, one day, it would all stop. They would go back to Bulgaria. He hadn't promised, but she felt it would happen. They could live a beautiful life there. They would grow old together. Maybe they would even have children, and she could dress them up for the festivals.

Someone was tapping her on the shoulder.

'Ms Genovsky.'

It was Daniel Born. He was carrying the box. This was all working out.

'I need you out here for a moment,' he said.

He tapped the box. She turned and looked at the men. They had hardly noticed the intrusion: the broadcast from the White House was too compelling. The President sounded like a defeated man.

'I want a patch through to the F-16s this time. If I'm going to kill a few hundred more people, I want to do it with my eyes open.'

'Yes, Mr President.'

'We have to nail this down, Bob. In the last hour, I will have thrown a thousand families into mourning. This has got to stop.'

Wheelan looked around and smiled at Vasil. Neither of them seemed to see her there.

She could go. Just for a minute.

CHAPTER 74

KATIE CRANED HER NECK to see if it was still there. Just moments ago she had caught it in her peripheral vision, a shadow of grey against the black sky, a tall tail fin sweeping upwards. A fighter jet was flying alongside the cockpit of their plane, as close as the pilot dared. But, in the darkness, it was unlikely he could see enough to make contact. There it was again. After a couple of seconds, it peeled away, and disappeared.

She felt a curious calm. Perhaps it was everything she'd been through already. Perhaps there was a limit to the amount of stress one person could experience inside a few hours; perhaps she had run out of the ability to care. Katie could hear the captain appealing for quiet behind her in the economy cabin; even though he was speaking Spanish, there was no mistaking the tone: he was apologising. The controls had been disabled. All communications channels were unresponsive.

Some of the passengers at the front of the economy cabin had evidently heard the announcement he'd just finished in first class, and started shouting across him as he began.

He broke into English. 'Please, as yet, there is no cause for alarm.' He was pleading, straining to make himself heard above the rising clamour. 'We are still flying perfectly normally.'

He didn't mention the shift in their heading. She had felt it; surely everyone else did too?

'Please, I would ask that everybody remain in their seats, with their seatbelts fastened. We are investigating the situation and will keep you informed the minute we know anything more.'

He began to speak in Spanish again, evidently repeating the message. The cabin crew moved up and down the aisles, checking belts were fastened, doing their best to keep the panic out of their faces. It was more than the passengers could manage. Most of them had the wide eyes of terrified children. Vicente had sunk low in the seat next to her, and was whimpering a rhythmic prayer. He had done a lot of this since he got on board. She hoped he was praying for forgiveness.

She couldn't feel like that; she couldn't just sink into despair. She was better than that. And this wasn't all over yet. She felt a fragile peace descend. She could only sit now, and assume they would survive this. If it all depended on her, she would make sure they survived.

The stewardess, the one who had talked to Rafael in Varedero, was giving her strange looks. Katie couldn't decipher them: were they an instruction to maintain the silence, or some accusation of blame? She'd seen enough Hollywood films to know what the fighter plane was for. If this were a film, though, her dad would be onboard with her; teenage girls didn't die like this, alone and defeated. She looked through the window. She hadn't seen the fighter plane again, but she guessed it was dancing in their slipstream, waiting for the command. The thought brought the panic back to the surface, and her heartbeat quickened. She breathed deep, summoned all her strength. Somewhere down there in the blackness, her dad was working to save her. And he would succeed.

MICHAEL BROOKS

It would be all right. She had no one but herself to tell. So she told herself again. It would be all right.

CHAPTER 75

VIRGO BREATHED DEEPLY, EXHALING through pouted lips. His heartbeat was rising quickly again. He prepared his mind, just as his body was preparing itself.

Standing there, just behind where the door would open, he was invincible. He could crack the back of her skull before she even saw him. He would do it too. If he killed Genovsky, it would only be for Katie's sake, not for revenge. To save Katie. Genovsky had started this. And this was how she had forced him to finish it.

He looked down at his shaking hands. He was human; so was Alexandra Genovsky. But this was about survival. She had shown no mercy, no sign that she believed there was any other way than one of them killing the other in pursuit of the prize. Whatever that was.

How in control was Genovsky? Was she just letting it unfold, did she care what happened to his daughter, what had already happened to his wife? How much had she told her bosses? Could she call the shots at all? He'd felt something when talking to her on the plane, like there was some kind of humanity there. Maybe that was just her skill, her manipulations? But he couldn't help feeling that, whatever her mannerisms, whatever language she used – spoken and unspoken – there was something honest there still. Her eyes had betrayed something that had never quite given in, never quite accepted her circumstances as the final outcome. He shook his head, recognising the hazard of concern. There was no reason for her to care about Rachel. It was the quantum computer, the sale, that mattered to Genovsky.

That was her only point of weakness. And that was untouchable. You don't have a choice, he told himself. Just like she said. Sometimes, you don't have a choice.

He had lost track of time. His watch was useless: the absolute time was irrelevant now. There would be a command soon that would destroy his world, spoken by the most powerful man on the planet. All time was now measured relative to that command. And he didn't know when it would come.

His breath was coming so heavily that it forced his chest against the confines of his jacket. And something was digging into him with each inhalation.

His phone.

Imogen.

He reached into the chest pocket of the jacket and switched the phone on. He wanted to be traced now, and he needed to know if Imogen had found something. Anything. As the phone came to life, the display told him he had a strong signal. And no messages. Nothing.

He was still on his own.

Where were they? What if Born had decided not to help? What if he had simply handed over the box, and whispered to a guard – told him where Virgo was holed up?

Had he read Born properly?

He had. The door opened, and he heard Born speak.

'It's just in here, Ms Genovsky. After you.'

CHAPTER 76

THE NOISE SURPRISED VIRGO. As he smashed the gun into the back of Genovsky's skull, there was a splintering, an unmistakable high overtone, like the strain of porcelain chipped. Then he was surprised that he could register surprise in the short time it took Genovsky to crumple to the floor. She stared up, her eyes blank. Virgo looked away, towards Born. He stood open-mouthed, eyes wide, in the doorway.

'I think you've killed her.'

Virgo breathed again. 'Shut the door.'

He knelt down, and felt for a pulse. He hadn't killed her. He went through her pockets. There had to be a key. Born said there was one.

He looked up. 'Help me turn her over.'

They pulled her onto her back. There were five pockets in all. In the trousers, two front, one back. In the jacket, one over each breast. But no key.

No way out.

Fuck.

She had left him with nothing. This woman had stormed into his life, shot it to hell, brought him halfway around the world, had his wife killed and put his daughter into a deathtrap. And she had given him nothing in return. How was that fair? How was any of this fair?

He stood up and kicked Genovsky's body with everything he had. The smouldering anger burst into flames inside him and he couldn't hold back. He was no better than her, really. Victimised by circumstance, he responded with an act of senseless violence.

Fuck. Despite himself, he kicked her again, even as Born tried to pull him back. Genovsky's body shuddered, absorbing the blow. But this time he heard something: a metallic rattle, a shiver of steel. He stooped quickly down again, put a hand on one shoulder and shook the torso. The sound came again, metal sliding over metal. It was from under Genovsky's neck. Virgo pulled her shirt open, shredding the delicate silk. A button flew past his face. There was a metal chain around Genovsky's neck, its flimsy links dulled by the passage of time. It looped down to the floor, disappearing between her shoulder blades. One hard yank and it would break away. Virgo started to pull, but her blank face, with its bruised cheek and gently curving scar, broke his resolve. He lifted her head, and pulled the chain through her dark hair. She had auburn highlights.

Virgo held the chain in front of his face. It had a small steel key. Next to the key, grey and tarnished except where, in tiny slivers, the key had scratched it into a crystalline shine, hung a St Christopher medal. He looked up at Born. 'Is this it?'

Born didn't have time to respond. A knock yanked their attention to the doorway.

'Ms Genovsky?'

It was one of the guards.

'Mr Marinov and Mr Wheelan want you back now. The President is about to issue the order.'

Born responded with an authority that took Virgo by surprise. 'We'll be out in just a second,' he called.

He looked at Virgo, then stepped forward and took the chain.

Something in Born's eyes made Virgo let go. Something had changed. Born gripped the St Christopher medal between finger and thumb and held it in front of his face. He changed his focus and looked through it, fixing an intense stare on Virgo. Then, without a word, he stepped out of the room.

CHAPTER 77

KATIE HAD FELT THE plane change its heading again. They were descending now. For a fleeting moment, she thought the captain must have regained control. But he had emerged again from the cockpit, pale and thin-lipped, and was discussing something with the cabin crew in agitated whispers. The fighter plane had come back into view for a moment, too, but that was gone again now.

This wasn't how it was meant to be. There was no catastrophic lurching, no spinning, nothing to indicate the plane was in trouble. The cabin was oddly quiet, the silence of resignation punctuated only by the occasional scream or whimper of a passenger overcome by a moment of panic.

Katie didn't know what she felt. If she stopped and thought about it, allowed herself to think about it, she simply felt responsible. For the first time in her life, she felt the weight of responsibility for people she didn't even know. Somehow, for some reason she couldn't fathom, she was connected to this. All these people were sharing a plane with her, and she was taking them to their death.

She looked at Vicente. He was staring at the seat in front now, his dark eyes blank.

'Do you know what's going on?' she said.

He offered no response. Katie made to get up, out of her seat. He reacted, reaching into his waistband for the gun. But she knew he wouldn't do anything. She had no idea whether his work was driven by some revolutionary bent or the pursuit of wealth. Maybe he just wanted an equal share. But he seemed broken now, and without purpose.

'We are going to die, Vicente,' she said. 'All these people are going to die if the plane's controls aren't restored. If we don't crash, we'll be shot down.' She pointed at the window. 'There's a fighter plane out there. No one's going to let this plane get anywhere near a city.' She paused. He just kept staring ahead, into space. 'If there's anything you can tell me, tell me now. Think of Miguel. Don't you want to go back and see Miguel?'

He turned and looked at her, but said nothing.

Vicente didn't know anything. She knew that. But if she was responsible, so was he. No one was ever responsible alone.

'I'm going to speak to the pilot,' she said. 'I have to tell him what I know.'

When he spoke, his voice was quiet and distant. 'You are right. We are going to die,' he said. His eyes returned to the seat in front.

Katie looked at him for a moment, then pulled at her prosthetic. She had loosened it off, let it breathe, and putting it back in place was the last thing she wanted to do. Why not just sit there like everyone else, and let what would happen happen?

That wasn't how she worked. She was a fighter. That's what had got her back on the track; that was what would get her out of this. Somehow, she would get herself – and everybody – out of this.

She rose out of her seat. Vicente put a hand on her arm.

'You can't do anything,' he said. 'The pilot can't do anything. It's all out of our hands now. It's in the hands of God.' His grip was strong, but Katie tore her arm free. Vicente sat upright and pulled out his pistol. But he didn't lift it from his lap.

'I can do what I can,' she said. 'God or no God.' She felt a mild surprise that the gun held no terror for her.

Katie nodded towards the pilot. He was standing at the front of the cabin, staring over the heads of his passengers. 'He is going to die thinking he should have done something to save the plane. At least I can make him understand that it's not his fault.'

She looked back at Vicente. 'I'm doing this for you, too. To give you the chance to decide not to stop me. To realise that you respect these people's lives more than you respect your cause, whatever it is. You have to understand something, Vicente. If a life is worth anything, it's worth dying for. So go ahead and shoot me if you want.'

Katie got up and walked towards the front of the plane, but before she'd walked more than a few paces, the pilot had disappeared back into the cockpit. She felt the plane lurch into a steep descent. Was that the pilot? Or was that something – someone – else? She hesitated and her gaze dropped to the floor. There was nothing she could do now. Katie looked up as a stewardess placed a hand on her arm.

'You need to get back to your seat,' she said.

Katie nodded and turned back towards Vicente. This was out of her hands now.

CHAPTER 78

GABRIEL MACINTYRE KNEW THIS feeling, and he knew he had to fight it. His throat was tight, his mouth arid, and he couldn't relax his back. The crackling tones from the loudspeakers made him flinch. If he could just let it go, round out his shoulder blades so he could breathe... This was not the time to have a panic attack.

The disembodied voices mocked him.

'We have less than two minutes, Mr President.'

'I'm fully aware of the time. We are not going to do this before we have to. Lieutenant Horowitz, do you have visual contact with the crew?'

'I do, sir. But I have received no indication the pilot is able to alter his present heading.'

'What about you, Lieutenant Hill?'

'Same situation, sir. We've tried everything we can think of, Mr President. We're awaiting your order.'

MacIntyre could hardly swallow the mineral water he'd reached for. How the hell did Tom think they would get away with this now? The plan was to get the President's voice on tape, capture some decrypted communications. They'd done that now. The plane was just a device, that's what Tom had said. It was never meant to go this far. And where were his troops? Surely they were meant to be here by now? At this rate, they were all going to jail. If they were lucky.

Ellie would never forgive him. He knew her well enough to know that she wouldn't stop loving him, but she could surely never forgive this. He had screwed up, big time. He had worked so hard for everything they had. But it had gone too far.

When did he start to feel he had to earn her love, that he could lose it, that it couldn't come for free? She had loved him before he was anyone; he knew that from way back, when they were at college. She used to tell him when they were lying on the campus lawns outside the frat house. She still told him now, before she fell asleep at night. But he didn't accept it like he used to. When had he started replacing acceptance with effort?

Whenever it was, that path had led them here, and it was going to pull them apart. He was guilty as sin. He had put Tom in touch with Marinov, he'd made sure the entanglement software was installed in the planes. Gabriel MacIntyre was right bang in the centre of it. The FAA, the airlines, the manufacturers – they all kept records, and when people died, everything went to hell. When you could talk about a rectifiable software fault, a coding error, another patch on the patch, no one made a fuss for more than a day. Everybody needed this stuff. The fact that they were prepared to put up with such badly written software made that perfectly clear. But when something went wrong on this scale, there was no recovery.

Where was the strike force? They were meant to be here by now. This was all meant to be wrapped up. He hoped the machine in front of him was worth it. It was powerful, at least: Tom was right about that. Jesus Christ, he was sitting here, drinking mineral water and listening in on decrypted White House communications. He was listening to the

President and a fighter pilot talk about the imminent death of another 300 people.

Tom and Marinov had moved across the hall. They had their backs to him, and were discussing something in whispers. He was glad to be excluded. The less he knew the better. When it came to court – and he knew now that it would – it was better that he was in the dark on some things. They didn't look worried. Not one bit. And neither did anyone else. There were half a dozen guards dotted about the place now, and maybe ten or twelve technicians tinkering with the equipment, but everyone seemed ridiculously calm. Was no one listening to this stuff?

The level of security was laughable, really. That must be the great thing about a senior position in Homeland Security – who were you going to worry about? Tom could keep all the other agencies in the dark, and no one would suspect anything except a non-specific, non-disclosable threat to national security. It was a walk in the park.

The woman, Genovsky, had been gone a while now. He looked back at the main entrance. The guy who had called her out, the guy with the box, was just coming through into the hall. Genovsky had introduced them, but he hadn't taken any notice. What was his name? Something Born. Talk about your archetypal science geek: wild hair, jutting-out belly, the works. It made you pull in your gut just looking at him.

'One minute, sir.'

Marinov and Tom were headed back towards him. Whatever they had been talking about, they looked smug. Maybe this would be OK. Maybe they were about to pull the plug. They certainly had everything they came for. He tried not to catch their eyes; best just to look calmly away.

Born was heading towards the front. He hesitated. He didn't seem to know what he was looking for. A couple of the technicians gave him funny looks.

Then MacIntyre heard the clatter of running feet behind him. He turned, then turned back.

Holy shit.

What was Born doing?

'Stop. Stop or I'll shoot.'

Tom had drawn a gun and was sprinting down the hall, shouting with urgent abandon.

Born stopped, his hand on the console. Tom pulled up fifteen paces from him, gun levelled.

'Stop right there,' he said. His voice was hard like granite. MacIntyre could see his brother-in-law's eyes. They were popping wide, like he was being strangled by the Invisible Man. Wouldn't want to be Born right now, he thought.

Tom was flicking the barrel of the gun upwards. 'Get your hands up in the air,' he spat. MacIntyre had never seen Tom like this. His brother-in-law's eyes narrowed, just for a moment.

'Who the fuck are you?'

Wouldn't want it to be me, MacIntyre thought again.

CHAPTER 79

IT WAS DARK OUTSIDE now, and the lights of Center Plaza twinkled as rain splattered against the windows. Delaney leaned across to see if anyone out in the main office was taking any notice of him. The office was a wasteland. There was nothing going on out there; everyone was in the field, at the airports.

OK, so Virgo knew about the hijackings. Or he knew about one, at least. What Delaney couldn't figure out was, why? Was there a link to the quantum computer? Unlikely. Whatever the truth, the authorities would crucify Virgo when they got him. But it would be after the hijack stuff was over; no one except Delaney knew the two were linked.

And, maybe, Thomas Wheelan.

What was he supposed to do with that information? He had received a direct order to stay put, stay out of everything. But wouldn't it be beautiful for a washed-up FBI agent to nail Thomas Wheelan? Wouldn't that be poetic after everything Homeland Security had done to the Bureau?

What was it Virgo had said? His daughter was on a plane coming out of Cuba. What was her name? Katie. Katie Virgo.

Absent-mindedly, he opened a browser window on Morgan's computer and opened a search engine.

Katie Virgo.

There were a million hits. Mostly astrology sites.

Katie Virgo London.

That narrowed it down. There were still thousands of hits. A catering business, a graphic designer in North London... He scrolled down the list. Jesus, there was everything here – a woman offering Reiki massage, a violinist with the London Symphony Orchestra. A fifteen-year-old amputee who broke a British junior paralympic sprint record last year.

It sounded like a freak show. Delaney couldn't help himself. He double-clicked and opened the page.

It was from the *Richmond Observer*, some two-bit South London newspaper. The screen took a couple of seconds to load.

As the page flashed up, Delaney's elbow slipped off the desk. It was him.

Nathaniel Virgo.

He was standing on an athletics track, smiling for the camera, his arm round a young girl with a prosthetic leg. Delaney stared at the prosthetic for a full ten seconds. What was it, a titanium spring or something? It looked like you could jump over the moon with that thing.

Katie Virgo, in vest and shorts, was grinning like a chimp. She had her arm round her father on one side, and round an attractive woman on the other. The caption said that was Rachel Virgo, Katie's mother.

Now deceased.

Christ. What did you do with stuff like this? They looked so happy. The kid was a champion athlete. The cheesy smiles said it all: at that moment, those were the proudest parents on the planet. Delaney couldn't take his eyes off the screen. Wasn't this everything everybody should have? A wife, a husband, a daughter who made you so proud it felt like the top of your head would flip off.

Virgo had it all this time last year. Now, there was damn near none of it left.

Something flashed in the corner of the screen. Delaney dragged his eyes onto the message feed. Another hijack, a plane heading towards downtown Boston. He felt a moment of alarm, but they would shoot it down long before it crossed the city's air perimeter. He was safe. All the passengers would die, but he would survive. Again. Cruel chance. That's all there was.

Something in the message caught his eye. He scanned it again and felt his heart stop for a moment.

The plane was coming out of Cuba.

Morgan had access to the passenger manifest; he had to admit this new computer system wasn't all bad. Hurriedly, Delaney scanned the list.

Katie Virgo wasn't on it. But she was on board. He knew it.

His eyes flicked back to the cheesy, grinning shot. It was probably just an annoying evening job to the photographer, just another assignment that meant a late dinner and no TV. But Delaney felt it turn him around.

There was something worth saving here. And someone worth nailing. But how?

CHAPTER 80

VIRGO HEARD WHEELAN'S SHOUT. The hall was just a short sprint away: dressed in the guard's uniform, no one would see his face if he played it right. He drew the pistol as he ran. He had to stop running before he hit the doors; no matter what was going on inside, he couldn't afford to be noticed.

He pushed at the door and slunk into the hall, dropped into a crouch. Seven guns. There were seven guns pointing at Born. His made eight. There was nothing he could do now. Born had his back to them, his right hand on the key inserted in a console at the front. Had he turned it yet?

'Thirty seconds, Mr President.'

He hadn't.

'Take your hand off the instruments.'

Virgo darted his eyes across the room. Thomas Wheelan had a gun trained on Born. His voice was steady, unruffled, and he had a strange smirk on his face, like he was hoping Born would do something stupid. In the silence, Virgo could hear a tiny, repeated beeping fill the room. It came from the equipment behind Born and sounded like a heart monitor, regular, reliable, understated. *Beep, beep, beep.* The miracle of life just carrying on as normal.

Virgo felt his stomach tighten. He had done this, made this happen. He had wilfully crushed Born's dream. He had calculated the maximum impact, manipulated things until Born felt like risking it all. No wonder he'd decided to go this far. What about Genovsky? What would she do when faced with the truth? If she was still alive, that was.

The beep was still there. Coming from the shiny silver box, another of Gierek's machines. *Beep, beep, beep.* Slowly, Born swung round, keeping his right hand on the key. The look on his face said it all: a manic, determined set to his jaw; grim, thin lips with the blood pinched out of them by the grip of his teeth. It was the look of a man who had finished with it all. A man about to die.

Born locked his gaze onto Virgo. The two men stared at each other for a moment. Virgo wanted to read something into the look, but all he saw was emptiness. Born turned the key. It was a tiny movement, almost nothing. The work of a few strands of muscle fibre, a slight displacement of the carpal bones.

The noise of a single shot cracked off the walls. The bullet entered the side of Born's head, throwing him back against the console. He slid towards the ground.

Wheelan was a dead shot; no one else needed to fire. Daniel Born, the man who invented the quantum computer, was dead.

The beeping had stopped.

A wave of shock hit Virgo, almost knocked him over. He had brought death on yet another soul. In the back of his mind, he could remember the scene in Born's kitchen, the decision he'd made not to run but to save him. Now, with a little insight, a little cunning and a few well-chosen words, he had sent him to his death. Saving him once, twice, a thousand times, didn't count now. Born was dead and Virgo felt the weight of it.

Silence hung in the air. Ten, maybe twenty seconds passed. No one moved.

'The pilot reports control restored, Mr President. We are bringing the plane to the ground. Landing at Logan in ten minutes. Runway cleared and ready, agency forces already in position.'

'I have to go and make some phone calls, Bob. I want to know everything about this incident. Everything. And nothing else leaves the ground tonight. Send someone to my office the minute you have anything.'

Virgo fought the euphoria. But that was it. That was what he had wanted to achieve. Born had made his own decisions. And Born had redeemed himself in the end; he'd driven Born to turn from one path and take another, to save Katie. He hadn't driven him to his death. That was Born's choice.

He could feel his calf muscles begin to burn in the crouch. What were the other guards doing? Following their lead, he slowly stood up, then lowered and put away his gun.

What now? Keep still. Blend in. Then get out. No one knew him. Katie was OK. They were bringing her plane into Logan – there wasn't time to alter that now. Now he had to get out. Now he had to go and throw his arms around her.

Wheelan still had the gun in his hand and the smirk on his face. He walked up to Born's body and kicked it away from the console.

'The Cuba plane is immaterial,' he said. 'We have all we need now.'

MacIntyre deflated: his relief was visible, even from across the room. But he hadn't heard what Virgo had heard. The words signalled closure; the tone said anything but. Something new was about to begin.

Marinov was watching from across the hall. His eyes were almost sparkling with fascination. Virgo felt it, too. Something was about to happen between Wheelan and MacIntyre, something Wheelan had been looking forward to for a long time.

The silence was loaded now.

Which made it a really bad time for Virgo's phone to ring.

CHAPTER 81

IT WAS STILL RAINING, the lights outside were still twinkling, and Frank Delaney was still staring at the picture on the screen.

What was he going to do? What could he do – what could any one person do, faced with the cruelty of the unfolding world?

Part of him wanted to do nothing. He wanted to go back to Quantico Creek and paint birds and reeds and brackish water. But now he knew that wasn't what Nancy would want. Nancy was dead. That whole entanglement thing, that notion that she and he were still connected, it was just wishful thinking. Escapism. If Nancy was sending him a message it was here, loud and clear, in Katie Virgo's broad, beautiful grin. Life was for the living. He wanted to think Nancy still painted through him, but Nancy was dead and gone. There were all kinds of reasons for that. He had messed up, Morgan had made a bad call. Maybe Nancy had slipped in her instincts, too. But whatever the explanation, she was gone. Even something as strange and hokey as quantum entanglement didn't change that.

And Katie Virgo was still alive. Delaney dragged his eyes back onto the message feed.

The update came through like a sign from heaven. The plane's controls were restored and it would be coming into Logan. It'd be landing in minutes, and all local agents would be engaged in offloading and interrogating the passengers. Delaney shifted his weight, made to get up from the chair, then sat down again.

He had a choice to make. He could sit here, mesmerised by the screen, watching the reports coming in. Or he could do something.

He could get to Katie, preserve her testimony, follow the trail right back to Wheelan. But he wasn't going to call anyone. Not this time. This time, it would be his op. And it would be beautiful. The Secretary for Homeland Security was about to see what one of his agents could do.

CHAPTER 82

VIRGO HELD STILL. IT seemed like his phone had been ringing forever. Maybe no one here would know it was his – on the trains in London, on the commute up from Richmond, no one could ever pinpoint whose phone was ringing. Everyone dived into their bags or pockets, like the whole world shared a single ringtone. Maybe he would get away with it.

Who was calling? Katie? Imogen? The FBI? They would surely have traced his signal by now. He forced his mind back into the hall. No one was moving. The lights were still flashing on the displays at the front, and the silver box still stood resplendent on its dais. Born's body was lying in a pool of darkening blood.

Whatever happened now, at least Katie was safe. The plane would be grounded, inspected, the passengers interrogated. But not killed. Not shot out of the sky, or flown into a city skyscraper.

Marinov and Wheelan were both staring at him. So much for the power of positive thinking.

He could run, but what would that achieve now? His hand itched for his gun, but that, too, would be a pointless move.

Finally, it stopped ringing. *Thank God.*

Wheelan broke his stare and looked at his watch. 'It's going to be time to wrap this up very soon, Vasil.' He looked over at MacIntyre.

'Gabe,' Wheelan said. His voice was flat, disconnected. MacIntyre stared at him, eyes wide. 'It's over, Gabe.'

Wheelan raised his gun. Virgo felt panic rise within him. He should stop this execution. But there was nothing he could do.

Wheelan squeezed the trigger. MacIntyre fell over backwards. Dead, just like that.

Virgo fought to stay still, not to react.

My God.

Wheelan seemed nonplussed by the act of slaughter. He turned to Marinov. 'Where's the woman?' he said.

Marinov looked around, then back at Wheelan. He was about to say something, but the door behind Virgo opened, and Genovsky entered on cue. She passed right by him. He could see that the hair on the back of her head was matted with blood. Virgo hadn't noticed the injury he'd inflicted; he'd been too busy assaulting her for the key. Her blouse was ruffled and torn, and her trousers sat slightly askew on her hips. Her hair was falling over her face. She looked dazed, still.

'What the hell happened to you?' Marinov's voice was hard-edged, wary.

Genovsky walked further into the hall and looked over at Born's body. Then MacIntyre's. She was stood ten metres away from him now, and Virgo could see her eyes were cloudy.

'He took the key,' she said. Her voice was little more than a whisper. 'Is it over?'

She looked back at Marinov. He was pointing a gun at her face. His eyes were blank, yet terrifying.

'I gave you that key, Alexandra. I gave you control of part of this operation – and you let me down. First Gierek, then

Virgo, now this. You have become a liability.'

What to do? Virgo felt a ridiculous sense of responsibility, like he owed it to Genovsky to intervene. Was this vestigial chivalry – an evolutionary reaction to a damsel in distress? It was hardly that complicated. He'd put Born into the firing line, and now he had done the same to Genovsky. It was guilt.

Wheelan saved him the decision. 'Put the gun down, Vasil.' He sounded like he was enjoying himself now. 'It's fine. And with MacIntyre's unfortunate death, we'll need her testimony.'

Testimony. That wasn't a word you expected to hear from the lips of a man who had just cut short hundreds of lives. Genovsky, dazed as she was, obviously had the same thought.

'Testimony?' she said, turning to Wheelan.

'About the entanglement.' Wheelan walked towards her, smiling. 'About Red Spot. And the quantum computer. You're going to be the Department of Homeland Security's star witness.'

Genovsky looked over at Marinov. There was an insistent pleading in her gaze; Virgo felt its pull on his emotions and his breathing shallowed for a moment. Marinov's face remained stone-hard.

Wheelan was still smiling, but now with a freezing stare.

'He sold you to me, Alexandra.' He paused. 'For the good of this country you adopted. But we might be able to get you out in ten to fifteen. As long as things are straightforward.'

Genovsky continued to stare at Marinov, like Wheelan didn't exist. Like his words would be wiped away if Marinov just smiled at her.

Virgo could hardly look at her. The things men did.

Still Genovsky stood there, motionless. Her expression only changed when a precise, clipped double beep fractured the silence in the hall. She turned towards the source of the sound, and her eyes widened in recognition.

'Nathaniel.'

She smiled. Somehow, absurdly, she brought a smile up out of her broken heart.

'Nathaniel Virgo,' she said. 'Did someone just send you a message?'

CHAPTER 83

'ALWAYS-ON'. THAT'S WHAT they called it. Modern communications technology was certainly a wonderful thing – in the right place at the right time. There were times Virgo had been in corporate press conferences when a call had given him a welcome excuse to leave. Even a text message during a difficult interview could provide the resourceful journalist with a neat means of changing tack. But here, blending in, hoping not to be noticed, a text message was not what Virgo wanted.

Genovsky looked like she was in suspended animation, staring past him, working through the branches of her game. Marinov had just sold her out. Would delivering Virgo buy her back?

She obviously thought it was worth a try.

She turned to Marinov. 'This is Nathaniel Virgo.'

That was it. Her face was almost blank as she said it, emotionless. That could be the concussion, of course. He let his hand move to his chest pocket. If all was lost, he at least wanted to know what the message said. Slowly, coolly, he reached into the pocket. They raised their guns. He pulled out the phone. They stared at him. He flipped it open.

It was from Imogen.

It said: *Get out of there. Now.*
He looked around. Thanks, Imogen. Fat chance.

CHAPTER 84

HER MIND STILL FOGGY, Alexandra Genovsky struggled to understand what Wheelan could have meant. She stared at Vasil, the man who had saved her, given her a new life. He'd heard about her shame, come to her house and told her parents he needed a housemaid. They'd been through so much together since then, and now they'd achieved everything he'd been working for. No. Wheelan was bluffing. When this was over, she and Vasil would start the rest of their lives together.

Vasil moved slowly across the hall towards Virgo. First, he took the phone and glanced at the screen. Then he put a gun to Virgo's head.

'Who's that from?' Vasil's voice was calm and confident. She'd always admired his strength.

'No one you know,' Virgo said.

Virgo impressed her, too, somehow. He was about to die, but he kept his dignity.

Vasil pressed a couple of buttons on the phone. 'Imogen?'

He closed it with a snap, and dropped it into the breast pocket of his jacket. 'I'll be getting to know Imogen very soon.'

'You're really not her type,' Virgo said. 'She dates the

good guys.' He smiled, but Genovsky could see it wasn't there in his eyes. He was scared. And so he should be.

'Hey, but then what do I know?' Virgo added. 'I thought Alex here was your type, and you're about to sell her out.'

Vasil looked over at her. His eyes were intent, serious.

Virgo called out to her. 'Have you worked it out yet, Alex? MacIntyre's dead. So it'll be you. Your final act of loyalty to Vasil Marinov: testifying to the power of the quantum computer and then spending the next thirty years of your life in jail.'

Virgo was bluffing, she could tell. He was trying to talk his way out of this. She didn't want to look at Vasil. But she had to glance.

He was staring back at her, and she couldn't read his face. She never had been able to. If he loved her, he showed it with his body, with the occasional kind word, by what he did.

Virgo's voice cut through her thoughts. 'The thing is, Alex, Gierek wasn't the genius you thought. Neither is Marinov. In fact, he's nothing more than a hacker, a cheapskate. Alex, there is no quantum com–' A sharp crack cut him off in mid-sentence. Vasil had slapped the gun across Virgo's jaw.

But too late. She didn't need him to finish the sentence.

There is no quantum computer. Of course. Why did they need a quantum computer when they had Wheelan and the feeds from the Situation Room? She almost wanted to laugh. She had wanted to believe that Vasil had done it. But he didn't need to. It's true what they said: love is blind.

CHAPTER 85

KATIE VIRGO STOOD AMONG the passengers on the runway apron. They were huddled together like frightened sheep, forty metres from the plane. She could see Vicente, his gaze fixed on the terminal building. His lips were moving. It was unlikely his god would get him home now, however hard he prayed. A dozen FBI agents kept them in place, encircling them, hands on black rifles. The flashing orange of the vehicle lights created a pulsing, sinister glow on the guards' faces, but that wouldn't stop her.

Agents moved in among them and began pulling some of the passengers out and leading them away. Once she was taken, that would be it: questioning, holding. Nathaniel Virgo would not be their problem. She had to get out of there.

She had her prosthetic fixed back on. The respite when she'd loosened it on the plane had helped; she could wear it for a little while longer now. For as long as it took. She moved to the back of the crowd, towards the plane.

There was no darkness anywhere: the portable lights reflected off the white fuselage, throwing a ghostly pallor over the crowd. There were no shadows to run into.

How had it come to this?

The guards would be on her soon: they seemed to be removing people at random. They had probably taken fifty passengers away in the past five minutes. She had to decide, and quickly. She faced the plane. There was a chance she could slip through the cordon unnoticed, and find a shadow behind one of the plane's enormous tyres. If she created some kind of a distraction, then ran, crouching, under the plane . . .

A hand fell on her shoulder.

'Katie Virgo?'

She spun round. Fight or flight? The man was showing her a badge, but she didn't listen to the name. He was big, although she could probably land a punch, then run. But where?

His eyes stopped her plan in its tracks. He looked more worried than she was. He looked behind him, then leaned in and spoke in a whisper.

'Katie, I know about your father.'

Katie heard herself breathe again, a deep rush of air leaving her lungs. She studied the man's face. It was a stupid thing, when people said someone had an honest face. What did that mean? But there it was in front of her: an honest face.

'Let's go, then,' she said.

The eyes stole a glance down at her leg. He knew.

But he didn't say anything; he just pushed gently at her back, guiding her along with the growing flood of passengers being led towards the terminal. She looked back, over her shoulder. In the distance, receding now, she saw Vicente being led away. They took him alone, not as part of a group like the non-Hispanic passengers. He didn't stand a chance.

Inside the terminal, the stream of bodies headed through a door marked *No Entry*. Airports were really starting to piss her off.

The man leaned forward and whispered in her ear. 'Start walking tall, like you own the place, like you're with me. We're breaking away now.'

As they turned a corner, he pulled her out of the stream. They stood still for a moment, watching the crowd pass. He lifted a hand to his black earpiece.

'OK, we're coming.'

He turned to face her. 'We're needed back at the main entrance.' His voice was over-loud, but she forgave the hammy delivery. The main entrance sounded good to her.

Maybe she didn't look like an FBI agent, but she could sure as hell hold herself like one. They hurried confidently back through the terminal. The agent flashed his badge a couple of times, but no one challenged them. It was that easy. As they came out through the entrance, a huge black truck flashed its hazard lights and its door locks clunked.

'Get in the back. And keep down.'

Katie opened the rear door and collapsed onto the bench seat. She heard the engine roar into life, then they pulled away, the acceleration throwing her against the backrest.

CHAPTER 86

EVERYONE SAID THAT THE communists bred the most inventive problem solvers. NASA employed Bulgarians because they were the best programmers. Even when she had only been working as an administrator, the researchers she managed told her to join their team. It was as if American schools taught that there was something in the water over there, something that made Eastern Europe raise dangerously clever sons and daughters. No wonder the Cold War lasted so long.

Well, here she was, living proof that Bulgarians could be stupid, too. *There is no quantum computer.* Alexandra Genovsky almost wanted to laugh.

How long had it been since Gierek gave up on the quantum computer and offered a neat deception as a substitute?

She should have seen it. How did Vasil see it, when she didn't? Simple: he was one of the clever ones. He had spent years developing communications programs for NASA. And he'd obviously put his experience to work.

How did she not see it? Was she just too enthralled by the science to see how unnecessary it all was? There was just no need for entanglement to control remote systems. Suddenly, in the past few years, the internet was everywhere, connected to everything. The entire air-traffic control system of the United States, power companies across the globe – everyone's systems were connected, via off-the-shelf software and the internet's optical fibres, to almost every computer on the planet. If anyone could get their software installed inside the firewall, they had an open door. And when you were the world's leading supplier of firewall and anti-virus software, like MacIntyre's company, how hard was that? All Vasil had to supply was the communications coding. The rest was simple hacking.

She couldn't help feeling a sense of shame that she had fallen for it all, just like MacIntyre had. She'd thought she was better than that. It turned out she wasn't: she had killed for Vasil, she had recruited for him, cleaned up when there was a mess. But that was all she was good for. If she'd had half his brains, she'd have known. Even Virgo had duped her – she knew now that story about the entanglement sent to the FBI was all a lie.

Virgo was on the floor. She could see blood pouring from his bottom lip, but Vasil wanted to do more damage.

'Get up.'

Vasil was pulling Virgo to his feet. Virgo looked strangely calm. Someone in his position had no reason to be calm. Vasil leaned close to his face.

'What do you know about the quantum computer?'

Virgo smiled, like he had been asked that before.

'I know that it's an expensive white elephant. Why spend billions of dollars when you can just corrupt, blackmail and manipulate the right people? You've got living proof right here.'

He pointed to Wheelan. 'Let me guess. He feels America is vulnerable without quantum cryptography. Wouldn't hurt his argument if he could show that someone had broken White House encryption. And what better way than to pretend someone has a quantum computer already?'

Genovsky looked over towards Wheelan. The corner of

his mouth was turned up in an almost imperceptible smirk. Virgo was right on target. He was good – better than she was. She had wanted to believe they had achieved all this.

Vasil turned to Wheelan. 'How long?'

Wheelan checked his watch. 'A few more minutes. We should wait. Better that they hear some gunshots on their way in.' He looked at Virgo.

'In a few hours from now, plenty of people will take the evidence and conclude there is – or was – a quantum computer. What makes you so sure they're wrong?'

Virgo didn't answer. He changed the subject.

'Why did you kill Gabriel MacIntyre?' he said. 'He would have been the perfect witness for you – credulous and credible.'

'Because he was surplus to requirements. And we need one silent scapegoat.'

Genovsky didn't want to hear what was coming next. She already knew what Virgo was going to say. He stared at her.

'He *was* surplus to requirements,' Virgo agreed. He turned towards her and stared. 'He isn't any more. Is he, Alexandra?'

He kept his eyes on her as he spoke to Wheelan. 'Now that Alexandra knows about the fake, her testimony is not going to be very convincing at all.'

'You're right, of course.' Wheelan looked like he was thinking. Just for a moment. And then, with a smile, he seemed to make up his mind.

'Vasil.'

That was all Wheelan said. He said it with a flick of his head towards her. That was it.

Genovsky watched Vasil swing his arm away from Virgo, rotate it towards her. His face looked troubled but resolute, like a mariner sailing into a storm. It was the same look she had seen on Vasil's face the night the priest was forced to cut her. She had never told Vasil she saw him there, almost out of sight, behind the rows of other men. When he came to her

MICHAEL BROOKS

house, she had pretended not to recognise him. It didn't matter that he had been there, giving silent assent to her punishment. He had rescued her, that was enough. She had forgiven him. Now he was pointing a gun at her. Just for a moment, colourful parades flashed through her mind, visions of a Bulgarian summer, she and Vasil watching the celebrations. The village children were wearing flowers in their hair. She locked her gaze onto Vasil's face, searching for the bond between them. Vasil hesitated, and she thought she heard children singing.

Then his finger squeezed the trigger. The explosion from the muzzle drowned out the melody, and sent her into an echoing blackness.

CHAPTER 87

THEY WERE CLEAR OF the airport's commotion now, racing across the bridge towards the lights of the city.

'That was almost too easy,' Katie said, sitting up. 'What did you say your name was?'

'Delaney. Frank Delaney. I'm with the FBI.'

'Where are we going, Frank Delaney?' Katie asked.

He hesitated before answering. 'Away from here. Somewhere safe.'

That was all he had planned, to get her away, safe from Wheelan and his people. That would be his contribution.

'And where's my father?'

More hesitation. 'I'm not sure.'

Her face loomed large in his rear-view mirror. 'What do you mean, you're not sure? Where is he? What's going on?'

What to say? That he, Frank Delaney, had made a bad call, let Virgo down, and thrown him further into danger? Or that he had disappeared after escaping the FBI? That he had no idea where Virgo was? Delaney said nothing, but he could tell from her eyes that wasn't going to be enough for Katie Virgo.

'You said you knew about my father.' She was hauling herself into the front, one hand on the passenger seat, one hand on his. She vaulted through like a gymnast, her left leg trailing slightly, but still making the move.

'What do you know?' she said, settling into the seat beside him and fixing him with a bold stare.

'He's involved with something – some people – who were hijacking the planes.'

'And where is he now?'

'I don't know.'

'Well, where are these people?'

Jesus. And he thought he was going to be a hero for getting her away from the airport.

He looked across. She was still staring at him.

'Where are they?'

'He said they were in a warehouse just north of the city.'

'How far away?'

'Ten minutes from here.'

'So that's where we're heading.'

It wasn't a question.

Delaney swung the truck across two lanes. She was right – why stop now? This would be his retribution. And his rehabilitation. He would leave her in the truck, out of harm's way, and go and sort out this mess.

'That's where we're heading,' he said.

Finally, she stopped looking at him, and glanced at the road ahead.

'That's where he'll be,' she said. 'In the middle of everything. I guarantee it.'

Delaney stepped up the pressure on the accelerator and set his jaw. The streetlights flicked past, lighting up his way. This felt like destiny now. In this moment, with this kid sitting here beside him, he felt like he had a purpose again.

CHAPTER 88

THOMAS WHEELAN COULD HEAR nothing but the hiss and crackle of the machines. The lights on the consoles behind Born's prostrate body were still flashing, but the Situation Room had long fallen silent. They were out of there now; there was only static. Wheelan looked at his watch again. A few minutes and his people would be here.

This would all be wrapped up in a few hours, then there'd be the inquiry, then the plaudits and praise for his operation, and then he could slip away to Vermont, to the clinic. A few weeks and he would be clean. Maybe Eleanor could go with him, now that she had no husband to look after. She'd need a vacation, once the funeral was over.

The journalist was staring straight down the barrel of Marinov's gun. They could get rid of him now, but there was no hurry. It would be more convincing to have his time of death coincide with the cavalry's rush into the building. They could wait. This would be Virgo's death-row experience. Another innocent man dead. At least, for once, it was a white man.

No, Eleanor wouldn't come with him to rehab, of course; she still had little Jennie to look after. He felt a twinge of regret at his niece's loss. No one should lose their daddy at that age. But it was for the greater good; she would grow up in a better world because of that loss. He would make sure of that. Gabriel MacIntyre's death would be of more use than his life.

It was a shame there were no surviving witnesses to the power of the quantum computer. It would have to be just his word that stood up for the idea. It wasn't a disaster; he'd simply have to play it right. And he could do that, no problem. He would get a quantum cryptography network out of it, and they would begin to take the drugs trade apart. And he would win the next race for the White House. America had no choice when there was a God-fearing, tough-talking national hero on offer.

Wheelan checked his watch again. He would kill Virgo as the troops stormed the building. He would do it himself; Virgo's would be his last murder. No one would describe killing Vasil Marinov as murder.

CHAPTER 89

AS THEY SPED THROUGH the dark, Katie tried not to think about her mother. Without immediate danger, the scenes of the past day were rushing in on her, assailing her mind. She saw the body lying there in the grass. She wondered whether anyone had found it yet. She would make sure they went back to get it. She would stay focused now, hold it together, find her dad. Then, when all this was over, they would grieve together.

She turned to Delaney. 'So, you have a team in place?'

He glanced back at her with a shifty look. 'I'm on my own,' he said. He hesitated, then got his answer in before she asked. 'Long story.'

She left it at that.

'How did you find me? How did you know what I looked like?'

'I googled you. The Bureau's computer system is a crock of shi–' he pulled out, pretty much too late. 'It's pretty lame, but at least we have internet access. There's a picture of you on your local paper's website. On an athletics track. You're quite the achiever.'

She knew the picture. She saw it again in her mind, and the focus zoomed in on her mother. She ran her fingers through her hair. Anything but that thought.

'But how did you know the plane was coming in here, to Boston? We were meant to go to Montreal.'

'Two planes get blown out of the sky in one night, everyone's watching the next one. The wires were full of it. Once your change of heading was posted, it wasn't hard to figure out where they'd bring you down. Anyway, I think someone wanted you brought into Boston if you got out of this alive.'

Her stomach took a leap. 'Two planes got shot down? Is that what all that stuff at the airport was about?'

Delaney looked across, a grim frown on his face.

'I don't know what's going on, but your old man's gotten himself into something very nasty here.'

She didn't know what to say. How many people were on those planes? Was this all about her dad? Or was he an innocent bystander in all this? If it was limited, if there was a fence around it, just her and her mum and dad, she could maybe have coped. But hundreds of people she had never met, and their families and their friends were all pulled into this, too. A tear rolled down her cheek. She wiped it away, trying to stop the madness, the despair reeling through her mind. This was spilling so wide. If all these people's lives were thrown into destruction and heartbreak because of them, then . . . then what? What could she do? What could anyone do? Lie down and die?

No. She wouldn't do that. She could fight. She couldn't do anything for the people whose lives had been shattered in the past few hours. But she could make sure she didn't let the chaos rip any more of her own world apart.

After a couple of minutes of silence, Delaney looked across again. 'I haven't asked you if you're OK. You've had a hell of a ride.'

Katie shrugged.

'I'm OK.'

CHAPTER 90

WITH A SUDDEN JERK, Delaney pulled the truck off the road and brought it to a halt. There was nothing but dark woods ahead.

'If I'm right, the complex is just past the trees. I don't know what the reception'll be like. I'll just have to wait and see.'

'We,' Katie said. She stared at him defiantly. '*We'll* have to wait and see. I'm coming too.'

'No,' Delaney said. 'You're staying here. Where it's safe.'

'Try and make me.'

She saw Delaney hesitate. His gaze shifted to her leg.

'Can you do this?'

'I can do anything,' she said. The words came out cold, determined. She was ready. She reminded herself that she had handled things, done things, in the past twelve hours that she would never have dreamed were within her abilities. But that was the beauty of necessity. Nothing seemed impossible, distasteful, immoral even. Survival was everything.

'We're going to have to be quiet,' Delaney said, opening his door. She forgave the patronising tone. Forgiveness, too, was easier when it helped get an essential job done. She jumped out and the undergrowth crackled beneath her feet. Delaney shot her a warning glance. Fair enough. She'd keep the noise down.

They moved quickly. The sky had cleared, and the moon shone bright through the trees. She was surprised how agile Delaney seemed; she was struggling to keep up with him, and while she tripped and fell a couple of times, he never lost his footing. Suddenly, he pulled her up sharp and pressed her down into a crouch. They had reached the end of the trees. A hundred metres of grassy scrub stretched ahead of them, and then there was a tall chain-link fence. She looked across at Delaney; she could climb it, no problem. But him? He didn't look so agile.

If she had to leave him behind, so be it.

'What do you know about the inside of that building?' she said.

He looked at her, blank-faced. 'Nothing.'

'OK. Stay here.' She stood up and coiled for a sprint. Delaney grabbed her arm.

'What are you doing?'

'I'm going in.'

'Without me? Unarmed?'

'What have you got?'

Without letting go of her, Delaney pulled a shining black handgun from a holster on his chest, then reached into his jacket. He had a knife too, an eight-inch hunting blade. She took the knife.

'Can you handle that fence?' Katie said.

'Climb it, you mean?'

She nodded.

'You want to climb a twenty-foot fence in the moonlight?' Delaney looked at her, incredulous. 'With your leg?'

His grip tightened around her bicep. 'Listen, Katie. You're a hell of a girl, but you're no use to your father shot dead on the fence. I'm no action hero, but I know what I'm doing. I've got cutters. We'll be under in five seconds. Now, keep low and stay with me.' He pulled her out from the trees.

It was the longest hundred-metre sprint of her life.

CHAPTER 91

SHE HAD TO ADMIT it: Delaney was right. It took him three seconds to cut a hole in the fence. She crouched and dragged herself through first, then held it up for him to follow. They were at the side of what seemed to be the main building. On the roof, she could see satellite dishes and aerials. Now they had to find a way in.

There was no door on this side, and the front entrance was out of the question. They hadn't seen any guards yet, but they'd be there, at the front, if anywhere.

She let her fingers run over the steel cladding. If there wasn't a door, there wasn't a door. The rivets would give her enough purchase to climb onto the roof; perhaps there was a way in from above?

Delaney was moving down to the back of the building. He paused at the corner, his gun held straight out in front of his face, then swung quickly round. He pulled back, and beckoned for her to follow. She ran to him.

'Anything?' She whispered, almost mouthed the words. Delaney shook his head.

It was time to go upwards. Alone. She pointed to herself, then to the roof. He looked at her, puzzled.

'I can do it,' she whispered.

MICHAEL BROOKS

She could do it. Her prosthetic was no good for climbing, but she had three other limbs. They were strong, and she was light. It might give her the edge; they wouldn't be watching the roof. The steel bit into her fingertips. These were terrible holds. But her muscles were good enough. She winced at the stretch, the pain of forcing her weight onto a single joint of a single finger. But she had known worse pain. It would be gone in a moment. After every moment of pain came a moment of relief, and each time she was nearer the roof.

A piece of cladding shifted under her weight; the millimetre of movement was enough for her toe to slip off its rivet. The ground was ten metres down now, and she was hanging on by her calluses. The moon went behind a cloud, and the shadows of the rivet heads above her disappeared. Now, she was climbing blind. She shut her eyes.

Concentrate.

Four more reaches, four more agonising pulls against gravity, and she allowed herself to look again. The lip of the roof was just beyond her fingertips. She was there. One last toehold, and she could grasp at the protruding roof sheets.

She looked down. The shadowy head of a rivet stuck out from the steel. She sank her right foot onto it, then pushed. It was moss, not a rivet. It gave way without even a scrap of resistance, and she began to fall.

The cartoons she and her friends sometimes watched on lazy Saturday mornings were right. Something about falling gave you an extra moment of realisation, time to think. It also gave you an extra reach. As she hung by one arm from a piece of plastic roof sheeting, Katie was grateful for that.

Below her, Delaney was nowhere to be seen. The tendons in her arms were screaming in the dark and her head was filled with the sound of rushing blood. But that didn't stop her from hearing the trucks.

They sounded distant. It was nothing more than a rumour of a rumble, like a resonance between the tyres on the road and the vibrations of the building held in her fingertips. But she knew that they were coming this way.

Contracting her bicep enough to give her free hand a hold was going to be painful. She wasn't heavy, but this was just physics. They had studied this in class last year, and for once she'd been paying attention. The laws of levers meant that her arms were going to have to strain to the limit.

In her head, she counted to three, then moved.

It hurt, burned like hell. But now she had two hands on the roof. More leverage, a risky torsion in the wrist, and she could get her elbows up there too. On three, again. Seconds later, she was up, stepping carefully along the edge of the roof. Katie could see the lights now – the trucks were maybe a couple of kilometres away. She knelt down to examine the roof panels. Flat-head screws held them in place; Delaney's knife would make short work of lifting a panel to get her in. How far inside had he got? She hadn't heard a gunshot yet – maybe that was a good sign.

It was raining again, and her hair slapped and stuck on her face as she worked. The second screw put a notch in Delaney's blade, but the rest turned easily. The panels overlapped, but there was no sense trying to get two free. She'd lever up this one and get in before the rain made her clothes too heavy. She slipped in, dragging her prosthetic behind her, without making a sound. So far, so good.

It took a moment to filter out the drumming rain. The gantry seemed secure enough; she crawled gingerly away from the outer wall. There was some give, but her instincts had been right: there was no indication it would buckle under her weight. She just had to be careful not to move too fast: slow and steady.

The rain was getting harder and louder. She heard engines now, not rumbles. And she could hear conversation. It may have been from further ahead; it may have been from below her feet.

There was only one way to find out.

MICHAEL BROOKS

The knife slid into the ceiling tile without a sound. She hooked it up, pulled it free and squinted through the gap. And then she saw him.

He looked terrible. There was blood all over her dad's face, and he was pale and bruised. But he was unflinching, his eyes focused on the face behind the gun. They were ten metres away maybe. She looked up again, across the gantry. The struts got very thin towards the centre of the ceiling – too thin. She would need to get up onto the central girder that ran above them. How much time did she have? There was no way of telling.

CHAPTER 92

NATHANIEL VIRGO STARED AT the pistol barrel.
Get out of there. What did Imogen's message mean? Things were going to get worse? Or things were going to get wrapped up, so don't get caught in the crossfire? Well, thanks for the warning, Imogen, but it was academic now. Staring a 9 mm pistol in the face, Virgo knew that getting out of there was a distant dream.

He had done what he set out to do. Katie's plane had landed, and she would be in some FBI holding pattern now until someone could corroborate her story. Delaney, maybe? Once the hijacks had started, surely Delaney would have realised he hadn't been making it all up. The luxury of another phone call would be good right now. Just to check Katie was home and dry.

But he had saved her. She may never know, but he'd done it. In the end, that was what mattered.

Saving himself was going to prove a little harder. He hadn't expected Marinov to shoot Genovsky so quickly. No goodbye, not even a hint of regret on the man's face. It seemed to Virgo that *he* felt more regret, more guilt about Genovsky's death, than Marinov.

Those weird eyes were narrowed and cold now, intent on

the next shot. Him. But Wheelan would be the one to call it – he clearly had the masterplan. Yes, getting out of this was really going to take some doing.

'So all this is for a quantum cryptography network?' Virgo forced his eyes to flash at Wheelan, but the gravity of the gun barrel quickly pulled them back.

Wheelan walked over to stand beside Marinov. 'You make it sound like a bad thing.' He looked like a man without a care. 'We can do it – there just isn't the political will. Tomorrow, there will be.'

'Surely, there's a better way than shooting planes full of people out of the sky?'

'You know of one?'

'I think it's called democracy. People elect a government to make difficult decisions. Like whether there's a credible threat to justify the expense of a dedicated quantum cryptography network.'

Pompous, but provocative.

Wheelan eyed Virgo reproachfully, his head on one side. Like he'd just asked a stupid question at a press conference. 'You don't think the fact that we have been listening in on the White House shows there *is* a credible threat? Gabriel MacIntyre knew I was right. For the first time in his life, he made a decent choice.'

'You make it sound like you're all heroes. But you're not going to do badly from this, are you? You'll be the man, after all. The guy whose operation exposed the quantum computing threat. Competing for the top job with someone?' He thought back to where this had all started, Imogen's NSA buddy, the leaked report. What was the name? That was it. Time for the long shot. 'David, for example?'

Wheelan's face went blank. Not the desired effect. There was no way to go but forward.

'Well, let's hope David doesn't find Marinov. It'd be a disaster if it all started to unravel. What with him being the only weak link left.'

He saw Marinov's finger squeeze on the trigger. Then it relaxed. 'David?' he said, his eyes flicking to Wheelan.

There wasn't anything more. That's all he knew: David, something in the NSA. That's all she'd ever said. Virgo felt a tremble through the floor. Time to speed things up. Time for an ad lib.

'David doesn't think much of the advanced projects, does he, Thomas?' Wheelan's face didn't flicker. 'He doesn't like the ridiculous stuff: entanglement generators and the like.' He was warming up now. 'It's like he sees right through them – he knows that buying an agent is easier than buying a quantum computer. You don't crack codes, you find a crack in the wall.'

Surely, they had all felt the floor shake just then? Something was coming their way. He took a little leap of faith.

'Didn't Wheelan tell you about David, Marinov? He's the one who's been standing in the way of your money. He's been opposing the development of a quantum computer.'

There was something in Marinov's eyes now: a little light. He turned his head to Wheelan for a moment.

Wheelan didn't flinch. 'I don't know what or who he's talking about.'

'I'm talking about a friend of a friend who works for the NSA,' Virgo said. He was so out of his depth, he felt like laughing. But maybe it didn't matter; Marinov was looking uneasy. Maybe that was all he needed.

The trucks were just outside.

Wheelan inclined his head again and smiled. 'Can you hear that, Mr Virgo? Personnel carriers. I hear the sound of an evening drawing to a close.' He drew a gun, then shouted to the guards around the room. 'Remember your orders: no resistance. You so much as scratch my people, I will shut down your mercenary asses for good.' He turned to Marinov. 'Let's clear this up now.'

CHAPTER 93

KATIE HEARD WHEELAN'S SHOUT. She also heard truck engines cutting out. Where was Delaney?
She was on the central lintel, in the middle of the ceiling. It was a four-foot jump to the next lintel, and if she missed she would crash through the ceiling and break her back right in front of her dad. Right before those people killed him. That was not her plan.

She swung her arms back and forth for momentum. And then she jumped.

It wasn't perfect, but it was a landing. She scrambled up onto the cold steel, hoping her judgement was right. The guy with the gun should be straight down from here.

She hooked the toes of her right leg – her only toes – into the frame of the lintel. Hanging from one leg would send her slightly askew. But if she locked her ankle, the grip would hold. Time to let go.

Slowly, her abs let her torso downwards. For the first time in her life, Katie was glad of the rigorous sit-ups routine her coach put her through. Reaching back, she pulled the knife out of her belt, then stuck the point into the tile. It lifted, clean and silent. The view was perfect. There was a bald spot on the guy's crown, pulled clear by the tension of the band holding that ridiculous silver ponytail. She weighed the knife carefully in her hand, then gripped the handle between thumb and forefinger and let gravity point the blade towards the centre of the earth. She squinted down the shaft.

The lights reflected off the steel, its shimmer mixing into the silver of the hair. The aim was perfect. It would hit the bald spot. She hesitated, stopped breathing, wondered whether she should really do this. And then she saw the thumb pull back on the safety catch. Who said going to the movies didn't teach you anything? At least she knew when a gun was about to be fired. From somewhere outside the room, she could hear the sound of running steps.

'It's time, Marinov.'

She couldn't see where the voice was coming from. Not from the guy with the gun and the ponytail. She didn't know anything about him, the man she was about to kill. But she guessed his name was Marinov.

CHAPTER 94

WHEN PHYSICISTS TRY TO understand how the human body holds itself upright, they think of it like a pencil held point-down on the tip of someone's finger. It doesn't stay upright naturally; it needs constant re-adjustment, feedback from the brain's motor functions that compensate for any slight imbalance. Nathaniel Virgo knew this because he had once written an article about it, centred around a researcher who spent his days pushing people over in order to study how they stay upright. The article came back to him in the split second he spent watching Vasil Marinov's failing motor functions struggle to do their job.

Marinov remained upright, his face blank, for half a second before his body dropped. The knife was already buried deep in the skull before Virgo saw it. There certainly wasn't time for any reaction to register on Marinov's face.

Virgo had seen something fall from the ceiling; his next thought was that Wheelan was looking the other way, watching the door, as he delivered the command for Marinov to shoot. So Virgo dived for Marinov's gun, thought he could catch it before it clattered against the floor.

He couldn't.

Wheelan spun round at the noise. But Virgo had the gun.

Now they were in stand-off, and the guards had raised their weapons. It was six against one. But he had Wheelan at the end of his barrel, and the guards didn't have a clue what to do.

Virgo prayed no one would think about the knife sticking out from Marinov's skull. Somebody up there, up above the ceiling, was on his side. God? Delaney? Delaney was the least unlikely.

'Give it up, Wheelan,' Virgo said. Bluff of the worst kind. Why would Wheelan give it up? This wasn't going to work.

A deep voice ripped across the hall.

'*Everybody drop.*'

Wheelan didn't look round, he just broadened his smile at the shout. He flapped a hand to the guards, motioning them downwards. The guards looked at each other for a moment, then shrugged and let their weapons fall. They had their orders. Wheelan's people were here. All six guards in the room lowered themselves to the floor.

But that was because they didn't know the voice. Even Wheelan didn't know the voice. Not like Virgo knew the voice.

Virgo set his expression hard, and stared into Wheelan's grinning face.

'Over here,' he shouted. 'What took you so long, Delaney?'

Wheelan dropped his grin. And his gun.

CHAPTER 95

DELANEY LOOKED AROUND AT the guards. 'You people need to run. The plan is aborted. Get out of here.'

They did just as Delaney said. Now, that was impressive.

'That goes for us, too, Virgo.' Delaney looked over his shoulder, then back at Wheelan. 'Whoever the new arrivals are, they're on their way. Do we shoot the Secretary for Homeland Security, leave him or take him?'

Did they have to go? What if this was Imogen's guy coming through for them? Surely, everything would be cleared up?

And what if it wasn't?

They had to go.

It made no sense to shoot Wheelan. Not if Virgo was trying to clear his name. But leave him here? Not an option.

'We have to take him.'

'OK,' Delaney said. 'But we have to find Katie first.'

Whoa.

'Katie?'

'She's here somewhere. She climbed up on the roof.'

He hadn't seen that coming. It was Katie. Katie had saved his life. His fifteen-year-old daughter had dropped a knife into Marinov's skull to save her father's life. After everything that had happened to her in the past twenty-four hours, she was still right here with him.

He looked up at the missing ceiling tile.

'Katie?'

'Dad.'

She swung down. He ran over to where she was hanging, and caught her as she dropped. He didn't say anything; neither did she. It was all in the lock of the arms, the joined physical presence. It was the hug of the century.

Delaney broke them up. 'Touching family moment, but really, we have to go. You,' he said, jerking the gun barrel into Wheelan's cheekbone. 'You are going to run like you're a college track star.' He turned to Katie. 'Like this young lady.'

'This way,' Virgo said. He glanced down at Katie's prosthetic.

'It's fine, Dad,' she said. 'Really.'

For once, he believed her. He turned and led them towards the back of the hall. He could already hear the dull clamour of striding boots coming their way. He charged into a fire door, and it flung wide. As he led them out, he heard machine-gun rounds clatter into the night air.

CHAPTER 96

VIRGO'S EYES TOOK A few seconds to get used to the night. Even with the light spilling out from the open door, and the white lamps mounted on the hangar roof, the dark seemed to envelop him. Fifty metres across the concrete, he could make out the red and white barrier at the gates. But that was fifty metres straight, and he knew they couldn't afford the exposure.

He moved through the shadows towards the perimeter fence, but Katie held him back.

'No, this way,' she whispered. 'Delaney cut the fence.'

He allowed her to take the lead; she sounded like she knew what she was doing. Delaney could handle Wheelan. Or not. If he shot him dead, it wouldn't be Virgo's problem.

Katie pulled at the wire. It came up, and he rolled under as she held it. Delaney and Wheelan came next, disappearing into the darkness. He helped Katie through last. Something in him said he should be protecting her, letting her go first. But she was beyond that now. She didn't need his protection. She had saved his life; she was *his* protection.

'This way,' she said.

The gunfire was louder now; outside the hangar, coming

closer. They were surely out of time. He tried to look back, but Katie pulled at him as she ran.

'Delaney's truck is just here, through these trees.'

Maybe they could make it.

They drew level with Delaney and Wheelan. Delaney reached into a pocket and handed Katie some keys.

'Dad, come on. It's not far.'

She moved into overdrive. She had speed he'd never seen. How did she run so fast on a normal prosthetic? This was as fast as he had ever moved. His lungs burned, and his legs were starting to cramp. They were among the trees now, and the ground was soft and treacherous. The gunfire was almost deafening. He looked back: somewhere behind him, Delaney and Wheelan were wheezing through the darkness, punctuating the fire with heavy draws of breath. He looked ahead again: something glinted in the moonlight.

Delaney's truck.

'Start it up, Katie,' he called. 'I'll get them into the back.'

He dropped back. Delaney and Wheelan were struggling towards the truck. They were taking too long, but there was nothing he could do. He looked back at the truck. Why hadn't Katie started the engine? He could see a silhouette, something moving in the front, but there was no sound. He accelerated towards the truck again, leaving Delaney and Wheelan behind him, and pulled open the back door.

A voice cut through the darkness.

'Well, you must be Nathaniel.'

A tall, blond man jumped down from the front passenger seat. He had a walkie-talkie in one hand. And a big cheesy grin plastered over his face.

Suddenly, Virgo heard it. Silence. The gunfire had stopped; an eerie quiet, like at the end of a fireworks display.

'It's over, Nathaniel,' the man said. 'Nearly 700 people have been killed for this phantasm, but it's over now.' He raised his eyebrows. 'I presume it's a phantasm – the quantum computer?'

He stepped forward and extended a hand. 'David Hoch. Imogen told me you needed some help. Thank you for alerting us to all this. That was a good call on the remote flight-control systems. I checked the access codes to the ground radar stations that talk to the planes. There was some neat sidestepping, but Homeland Security's fingerprints were all over it. At NSA we've always wondered if the back door into those systems was really such a good idea. Now, we have an answer.'

For a moment, Virgo just stared, unable to speak. Then, slowly, in a trance, he shook Hoch's hand. Behind him, he could hear Delaney and Wheelan arrive, fighting for breath.

Wheelan stepped slowly forward, Delaney's gun in his back. 'Who are you?' he asked Hoch. Hoch eyed Wheelan carefully. 'Mr Secretary. We've sparred through intermediaries, but we've never met. I'm David Hoch.'

Hoch looked up at Delaney. 'Do you have cuffs?'

Delaney nodded. 'Yessir.'

'Then cuff the man. And don't set them too loose.'

Style. That was the only thought in Virgo's mind. Here was a man with bags of it. He looked around. Soldiers in plain black uniform had surrounded the truck. The good guys.

Hoch called towards the truck. 'Miss Virgo, get out of the car, please.' He turned back. 'You're going to need one hell of a debriefing, Nathaniel,' he said.

CHAPTER 97

HOCH LED THEM BACK to the road, where two sleek black Lincolns were pulled up in convoy. He opened the rear door of the second one and ushered them in.

Katie sunk into him, under his arm. That was it. There was only the two of them now. The realisation hit him like a blow to the diaphragm, and he caught his breath. Rachel was gone. The love of his life, his college sweetheart, the one who knew all his secrets. Gone.

What he had left of her was here, under the tightening grip of his left arm. Katie: beautiful, precious, amazing. But. But . . .

He jabbed at the guilt brooding in his brain. He felt ungrateful, like the precious gift of his daughter should be enough. But it wasn't. He wanted Katie and Rachel. Both, not just one. A piece of the whole was missing.

He leaned his face down and kissed Katie's hair.

'What happens now?' she said.

He didn't know. Did it matter? 'I'm sure we'll find out.'

A tear ran down Virgo's cheek as the engine fired up.

They rode in silence, and Virgo eventually gave up the fight to stay awake. He drifted in and out of sleep, and then –

suddenly, it seemed – the Lincoln's engine cut, and the doors opened.

'Katie, sweetheart.' She was asleep. He nudged her gently awake, and she stirred.

He got out; she followed. They were in the car park of some government building. He had no idea where he was; even when awake he'd been unable to read the road signs through the Lincoln's darkened windows. He took Katie's hand and followed the driver across the car park and through a bright red fire door. A narrow corridor stretched ahead. It was entirely bland: white walls, grey non-slip flooring, no markings. A few white-painted doors led off it, but the driver gently guided them straight towards the half-glazed door that faced them at the far end.

Virgo felt a vague unease. It couldn't possibly all be over now. He gripped Katie's hand tighter as he pushed at the door. She had said nothing since she woke up in the Lincoln. She'd probably been hoping it was all a dream.

He saw little through the reinforced glass before he opened the door. The corridor curved round to the left; ahead of him, a steel staircase stretched up out of sight. They followed the curve of the corridor until it opened out into a huge space. The air was hot and close, obviously cycled and recycled through the cooling fans of the dozens of computers that stretched in neat rows into the distance. Overhead, he could hear the air-conditioning strain.

Ahead of him, Virgo was mildly surprised to see Hoch was already in the building. He was chatting with someone. Hoch stepped forward as Virgo entered.

'Nathaniel, have you met Akshay?' He gestured towards the man beside him. 'This is Akshay Gupta. From Cambridge?'

It took Virgo a moment to realise what the name meant to him. *Gupta is being dealt with.*

'Akshay, this is Nathaniel Virgo.'

Gupta looked puzzled for a moment, then his face lit up.

'Nathaniel Virgo,' he said, striding across the room and offering a hand. 'Thank God you've made it here.'

Virgo's hand swallowed Gupta's. He couldn't bring himself to let go. And he couldn't think of anything to say. Gupta seemed to hail from a previous existence; even though he didn't know the man, he felt an affinity with him. Somehow, since they had been threatened together, there was a bond, a link. Waves of deep emotion, long held back by momentum, crashed inside him and ricocheted up his gullet. He glanced at Katie. The intensity abated for a moment, and he seized the chance to push the stress back down, to regain control.

'Katie, this is Akshay Gupta. He develops quantum cryptography.' It occurred to him that she probably had little conception of what that was. She'd find out soon enough. 'Akshay Gupta; my daughter, Katie.'

They shook hands.

'I understand you've had a terrible time, Miss Virgo,' Gupta said. 'I am very sorry for your loss.' He looked concerned for her; Katie managed a brief smile in acknowledgement, but said nothing.

'I thought you were dead, Akshay.' Virgo blurted it out, but he was past caring. Suddenly, he had to sort everything out in his whirling head. 'I thought Genovsky's people had . . .' He tried to make the statement sound nonchalant.

Gupta extended his grin. 'Kumar said you came looking for me. I got called away. My bosses –'

Hoch cut in. 'I'm sure you two are keen to catch up, but we still have some work to do.'

Suddenly, a thousand thoughts crowded into Virgo's mind. 'Where's Delaney? He saved my life. And Wheelan? What happened to him? Are you going to –'

Hoch held up a hand. 'Calm down, Nathaniel. Please, come with me. You too, Katie.' He beckoned for Gupta to follow.

What was Gupta doing here, at the centre of some NSA operation?

Hoch led them to a room off the main hall, and waited for them all to go in before he followed and shut the door.

It was some kind of lounge, informally laid out with easy chairs and low tables. To one side, a table was laden with fruit, pastries and an array of bottles and glasses.

'Please, sit down. Have a drink – you've earned it,' Hoch said.

They each moved to a chair. Virgo sat with an arm around Katie. Hoch went to the table and picked up a huge bottle of scotch and four glasses. He poured three scotches slowly, then a tumbler of water, and handed them round.

Katie gripped the water, took a sip, then broke the silence in the room.

'Will you get my mother's body?'

Virgo squeezed her tighter.

Hoch looked blank for a moment, then his face crumpled into a concerned frown.

'I'm sorry – God, what you've been through. Yes, we will. Can you tell us where it is?'

She nodded. 'There's a man in FBI custody – Vicente. He was on the plane. He –' She stopped herself.

'He what?' Hoch leaned towards her.

'He knows where she is.'

Virgo turned his head to look at Katie, but said nothing. He suddenly realised how little he knew about what she had been through.

Hoch leaned forward. 'I'll get right on it,' he said.

Virgo felt Katie crumple slightly under his arm. A burst of anger hit him.

'David, can you tell us what's going to happen now?' He turned to Gupta. 'And you – where did you disappear to?'

Gupta looked up at Hoch for permission to speak. He put his glass down on the table. 'I got a call summoning me to Cheltenham – to Government Communications Headquarters,' he said. 'They fund my work. And one of the terms is unconditional obedience.'

'They knew something was going on?'

Gupta's face was blank. 'I don't know what they knew.'

'So why are you here?'

'Because you are. I was flown over to assist with tracking you down.'

Virgo closed his eyes for a moment. How had all this happened?

A silence hung in the room.

'So what now?' he said eventually.

'You can relax,' Hoch said. 'We're going to fly you home.'

'Just like that?'

'Not quite – we need to talk. But the threat is over. You're going to be OK.'

He felt Katie's body shift. OK? Apart from the hole ripped through their lives.

'But you're aware what I know? That a senior government figure is responsible for all those planes getting shot down?'

'Any number of people know it. Think of all the mercenary guards in the hall. We didn't catch all of them, we're fairly sure of that. If we don't make it public, there'll be undeniable rumours on the internet in a few days anyway.'

'So the whole thing is going to come out?'

'Your involvement doesn't have to.'

That would be good.

Hoch hesitated. 'But the UK intelligence services will know,' he said. 'There'll be a file on you.' He looked at Katie. 'On you both.'

'Will you cover up my mother's death?' Katie asked, her voice quiet.

'I would imagine it will go on the record as one of Cuba's few violent crimes against tourists, I'm afraid.' Hoch looked into Katie's eyes. 'I am sorry,' he said. 'No one should have to go through what you've been through.'

She didn't reply.

Eventually, Hoch moved his gaze away. He looked at Gupta, then at Virgo.

'I don't think my troopers left much of value in that hangar, you know. Was there anything worth keeping?'

How should he know? He shrugged. 'Not that I brought in. My contribution was to bring a wireless internet router that Gierek had fitted inside a plastic computer casing. Not exactly irreplaceable.' Virgo hesitated. The entanglement was a sham, but the activator disk did contain quantum-scale bits. At least, that's what Andy had said. Was that as far as Gierek got? Had he given up? Or had he stalled Marinov? Maybe Gierek had been buying time. Maybe the whole hacking scenario was Marinov's way of sidestepping Gierek's brick wall. He would never know now. There were just too many bodies to make sense of everything.

And he wasn't going to be involved any more.

'You know, the irony is Wheelan is going to get his way now,' Hoch said. 'I always stood against investing too much in the quantum stuff, and every time he heard about the NSA attitude, he always went further and further. I leaked the document to Imogen because I wanted the extent of his bullshit to be known. He commissioned a report to give to the President. For the President's eyes only. Wheelan wanted to blind him with science, convince him there was a threat and a solution.' Hoch paused. 'In the end, I suppose the leak just forced his hand.'

All heads in the room turned as a large figure appeared in the doorway. Hoch rose from his seat.

'Ah, Delaney,' he said. 'You'd better come in and say your goodbyes.'

CHAPTER 98

AN ARMED ESCORT WAITED at the door as Frank Delaney made his way into the room. Katie was the first to her feet.

'Thank you, Agent Delaney,' she said. She stretched up to kiss him on the cheek.

'You've nothing to thank me for, Katie Virgo,' he said. 'I'm the one who should be grateful. It's a rare thing to meet someone with so much fire in their belly.'

Katie smiled. There was a sadness to her smile, though, like she feared the fire might have gone out now.

Delaney softened his voice. 'I'm sorry about your mother,' he said. 'I hope you get to say a proper goodbye.'

His eyes shifted to Virgo. He extended a hand. 'I'm sure these people will sort out everything you need, Nathaniel,' he said. 'And I'm sorry –'

Virgo cut him off. 'Please, don't apologise. There was nothing you could have done any differently.'

Delaney nodded at Hoch, then took a last look at Katie before leaving the room.

'What will happen to him?' Katie asked as the door closed behind Delaney.

'He'll be debriefed, like everyone,' Hoch said.

Katie took in the response without speaking.

'Is he in trouble?' Virgo asked.

Hoch's mouth formed into a conspiratorial smile. 'We're all in trouble,' he said.

Something exploded in Virgo's head. He rose to his feet. 'And so you should be. Your leak – Imogen's story – started all this,' he said. He took a breath, looked at the door, wanted to walk. 'My wife is dead.' He could barely control his voice. He looked down at where Katie was sitting, staring at Hoch. 'All those people died because you wanted to expose Wheelan's simple-minded thinking about security?'

'Calm down, Nathaniel. Come on, sit down.' Hoch waved a hand towards the seat. 'We knew nothing about the planes. I'm just trying to explain. Gierek knew about Wheelan's belief in the power of quantum technology: Marinov was obviously exploiting it. And Gierek knew how far-fetched some of the claims were – after all, he'd been involved in creating the hype when they began fleecing MacIntyre. I think Gierek got worried it was all going to come out. Or maybe he couldn't stomach Wheelan's stunt with the planes. Either way, I think he was going to let Radcliffe know what was going on. That's where it started – not with the leak.'

'You knew about MacIntyre?'

'We were closing in on him. We just didn't have the proof we needed.' Hoch smiled. 'If you have any Red Spot stock, I'd sell it now,' he said.

Virgo didn't smile back.

'Look, Nathaniel, I'm truly sorry you all got caught up in this. But you have to know that we didn't orchestrate any of it. Rachel died because Thomas Wheelan had her killed. And he will be brought to justice.'

Virgo took a few breaths, then sat. He turned towards Katie. She looked exhausted.

'So, what happens now?' he said.

'We have no choice now. Wheelan made that clear.'

'You're going to build a quantum computer?' Virgo stared

at Hoch, incredulous. 'But it's a sham, you can't possibly think –'

Hoch shook his head. 'No, believe me, that is not going to happen. But we *are* going to implement a quantum cryptography network. That's another reason Akshay is still here. No one thought it possible that someone could eavesdrop on the Situation Room's communications. Wheelan proved that assumption wrong. We need to plug that hole.'

'And quantum cryptography is the answer?'

Hoch paused, and leaned forward again. 'Do you know how the government ensures that no one listens in on its communications?'

Virgo shrugged.

'They created something called SIPRNet. It's known as high-security communications fibre, but really it's just ordinary optical fibre set inside hollow steel tubes that are welded together. The reason it's considered secure is that the pipes and welds are all checked at regular intervals, to make sure no one has tapped into the fibres to listen in. It's top-quality welding, of course, but does that sound like a high-tech security solution to you?'

Virgo frowned. 'You're not serious – that's not how it is?'

Hoch's face said he was deadly serious. 'That's exactly how it is. And can you imagine just how embarrassed the NSA will feel about this? We are responsible for secure communications, and we are high-tech freaks. We don't want steel pipes welded by beer-bellied knucklehead contractors. What do we want, Akshay?'

Gupta had picked up his glass again. 'Quantum cryptography,' he said.

'Damn right.' Hoch paused. 'You can't tap into quantum cryptography unnoticed – it's perfectly secure. Do you see where this is leading, Nathaniel? Wheelan was senior enough to know the weak points of the system and intercept the codes. Hell, *I* could do the same, if I had a mind to. We have to make sure that's not an option.'

Virgo held up a hand. 'With all due respect, we aren't really that concerned about US security at the moment,' he said. 'What happens to us now?'

Hoch smiled in a grim self-admonition. 'You're right. I'm sorry.' He leaned back in the chair. 'Let's get you out of here. Come with me.' He stood up. 'Akshay, will you excuse us for a few minutes?'

They were getting out. Virgo couldn't quite take it in. They were actually going home. He gripped Katie's hand as Hoch led them out of the room.

They followed him further into the complex, past the rows of computers and into a short corridor that branched off from the main hall. He halted at the last doorway. A framed imprint of a hand was fixed to the doorframe at shoulder height. Hoch pressed his palm into the mould, and Virgo heard the faint click of a lock released.

The office was spartan, with a desk, a chair and a low black leather sofa.

'Welcome to my world,' Hoch said, motioning for them to sit down. 'For today, anyway. I just got here yesterday and I'll be out again tomorrow.' He moved to the desk and picked up a sheaf of papers.

'I need you to sign some things before I can let you go. They're just non-disclosure agreements, but they bind you to silence regarding the affairs of the last few days. I hope you can understand the need for that.'

'Does that mean I can't tell Rachel's parents what happened to her?' Virgo asked.

'It does. And it means you can't write about any of this, either.'

The irony. He'd moved to the quiet beat and found the story of his career. And he was about to sign it away. But what choice did he have?

He looked across: Katie was staring at Hoch, her eyes concealing a furiously calculating mind.

'Is it binding on minors?' she said.

God, he was proud of her.

'It is. If you don't sign it, I have powers to hold you both. Another irony: Wheelan got those powers signed into law last month.'

Hoch put the papers back down on the desk. 'I'm sorry, but there's too much at stake. I'm dealing with the aftermath of mass murder by a high-ranking government official. I represent the families of everyone who died. I can't let any of this get out through official channels – at least not until Wheelan is brought properly to justice.' He shrugged. 'I need control of this, Katie. A lot of people died today at the hands of the state.'

Katie sucked in her cheeks, then let them go again.

'What do you think, Dad?'

What did he think? He took a couple of deep breaths.

'I think we have to sign, sweetheart. We need to leave this in the past.'

Easy for him to say – he hadn't just watched his mother die. He searched her eyes. Could she get past this?

She broke her gaze away from his.

'OK,' she said. 'I'll sign.'

Hoch nodded, and handed them the papers and two pens. 'They're marked with crosses where you need to sign.'

So that's what it felt like. Signing the US version of the Official Secrets Act was like renting a car: you had no idea what you were really doing, no idea what you were liable for. But at least it got you on the road. Virgo felt his spirits lift a little.

Hoch took the papers back. 'I've already sent out word that you were involved as an innocent party. There'll be a clean-up – you might find your house is a bit messed up. And you'll have an exit interview with the security services in the UK – they'll want to talk to you before they close their file.' He paused, then looked at Virgo. 'They'll only close it; they won't burn it. And, as I said, obviously you won't ever be writing anything about this. In fact, your editor and any other staff involved will also be required to sign confidentiality agreements.'

Virgo said nothing in reply. It was all done.

The phone chirped. Hoch picked up the receiver.

'Yes?' Hoch glanced up at them. 'OK, we'll be there in a couple of minutes.' He hung up.

'Your plane tickets and your permits to travel are ready. There's a car waiting to take you to the airport. Coming?'

He led them back through the building, out to the car park.

Within minutes, they were in another sleek Lincoln. Or maybe the same one – maybe government cars all looked the same. Hoch leaned through the rolled-down window.

'I'll make sure you're both debriefed by the right section, so you don't have to worry about what you can and can't say. Otherwise, I'm sure you realise what the restrictions are going to be. Goodbye, Katie. Goodbye, Nathaniel.' He stepped back, and the car pulled away.

They were free.

CHAPTER 99

THOMAS WHEELAN SAT IN the holding cell, listening to the quiet echo of his lawyer's receding footsteps. The troopers had taken his pills away. He was beginning to shake. He tried to bring his mind to heel, let his thoughts unfold slowly. Sober contemplation, Reverend Lowden called it.

Let justice roll on like rivers, and righteousness like a mighty stream.

He had achieved a lot. Not everything, but a lot. And there was a chance he would survive this. Edward said he'd been counsel in similar cases; things often weren't as dark as you'd expect for someone in his position. His was a difficult job that required difficult decisions. No one could expect him to make the right decisions – whatever *right* meant – all the time. And the White House would be keen to keep as much of a lid on the whole episode as possible. There were a few hundred bodies, but political careers had survived worse than that, Edward said. A lot worse, in point of fact. And the pills might be a mitigating factor.

But the presidency was out.

Wheelan knew that anyway. He'd known it from the moment he found out David Hoch was involved. You didn't get fingered by someone that high up in the NSA and still get to run for president.

Still, Hoch's involvement meant a lot. It meant that the details of this operation had come to the notice of senior decision makers. Even if there was no quantum computer, it was clear that communications security had to be better. The hints to the Los Alamos people had gone some way towards preparing the ground, but Hoch would definitely have to do something now.

And everyone would benefit. If US government agencies started using quantum security, the criminals would have to work so much harder to launder money, to get drugs into the country, to feed people with the recreational chemicals that were sending this country down the toilet. Whatever the verdict, Thomas Wheelan had served his country well. Between his father and his son, he could hold his head up high.

And in the end, that was what mattered.

Edward would get him the pills he needed. One step at a time, sweet Jesus; Reverend Lowden sang that every morning. Reverend Lowden knew what it was to be in recovery. He would help. And then Thomas Wheelan would return to politics – maybe he would run for Congress – and go on to make this country a safer place for every citizen. One step at a time.

CHAPTER 100

VIRGO STOOD, DOOR KEY in hand, Katie by his side, looking at the house. The front window had been repaired.

He put the key in the lock, turned it, and pushed open the door.

'Bloody hell.'

The house was in chaos. It had been rifled, turned upside down without care for the contents. He and Katie moved through the tumult of the downstairs rooms together, touching nothing, saying nothing, just looking. Old photos were lying on the floor, spilled from their packets. The kitchen cupboards had been emptied, and plates lay smashed on the slate tiles. Upstairs told the same story. In Katie's bedroom, her TV was lying on its side, the screen cracked. The soft toys on her bed, relics of her infant school days, had been slashed open, their stuffing pulled out. Somebody had been through this place in a frenzy.

Maybe it was Genovsky. Maybe it was the police or the intelligence services looking for clues to explain Gierek's death.

Genovsky, Gierek. MacIntyre, Born.

Virgo wondered how long their ghosts would be with him.

MICHAEL BROOKS

On the flight home it almost seemed they had gone; he and Katie had slept for most of the way, and they arrived feeling almost relaxed. An intelligence officer met them off the plane, and led them somewhere into the bowels of the airport, where he plied them with coffee and questions. But he only seemed interested in establishing their state of mind, ensuring that they would be amenable to an interview at a later date. They were driven home in a black Mercedes.

To this.

He and Katie stood, side by side, surveying the wreckage of their home. A thought flitted across his mind: Rachel would hate to see this mess; best clear it up straight away. Then it hit him, like a blow to the stomach. Rachel would never see this mess. Or any mess. This was home to just two people now. His hand found Katie's, and they went back downstairs.

Katie cleared the debris off the sofa, and they sat down. They stared at the chaos in a troubled silence. He put his arm around her, and she came closer and rested her head on his chest. He leaned down and kissed her soft hair. They were facing a mountain. But they would face it together.

A NOTE FROM THE AUTHOR

TWO HOURS AGO, AS I write this, I walked out of a meeting at the Bank of England in Threadneedle Street, in the heart of the city of London. The Bank is responsible for maintaining financial stability in the UK; 32 per cent of the UK's gross domestic product relies on the finance sector, the highest percentage of all the industrialised nations. The country really can't afford for anyone to lose confidence in the ability of the banks to keep their money – and their secrets – safe.

No one in the city will talk about how much money they lose through fraud on every trading day: that's a figure the banks would rather not divulge. What they do say – did say at this meeting – is that they now have to react to the threat of a quantum computer.

It was back in 1994 that a researcher called Peter Shor came up with the skeleton of a computer program that could break every code on the planet. Almost every code we use is based on the assumption that finding the factors of really large numbers is very, very difficult. But it may not be. No one has ever proved that factorisation on this scale is difficult. Mathematicians know that there could be a kid on the next block who works out how to do it tomorrow. And if that kid was smart enough to place a call to the right people, he or she would soon be very rich indeed.

Shor's algorithm showed that a machine using quantum technology, where the data is stored on individual atoms rather than pieces of silicon, could do the factoring. And the National Security Agency, the centre of US spying technology, jumped on the finding. That same year, it began to pour vast amounts of money into the construction of a quantum computer. That construction might be a work in progress for a while yet.

Or it might not. Something interesting happened ten years on from Shor's breakthrough: the cash injections began to level off. That might be because the NSA has quietly employed the kid down the block who worked out how to factor large numbers; maybe it now knows how to break into every encryption on the planet, and no longer needs a quantum computer. Or it may be that after a decade of tightly focused research, the world's best quantum computer was still laughably primitive; perhaps the NSA simply considers a useful quantum computer unattainable.

Or perhaps it now has one.

Whatever the truth about the quantum computer, its existence and its likely capabilities, one thing is emerging as an inevitable truth. The only data that is protected from this machine's prying eyes, the only data that is guaranteed to be safe for the next fifty years, is data that has been encoded via quantum cryptography, which uses the laws of physics to hide information in photons of light. The meeting I attended at the Bank of England was a first attempt to get the banks to talk to quantum cryptography researchers; the two cultures are coming together to find the best way to bring the strange nature of the quantum world to bear on the economies of nations.

There is much that is uncertain about the future; our energy sources, the stability of sovereign states, the numbers of next week's lottery. But the quantum revolution, where we put the awesome powers of atoms and photons to work, is a certainty. In fact, it's already here.